BABY BAILINO

BY DINA SANTORELLI

Praise for *Baby Bailino*

"Highly recommended! Dina captures an amazing story and writes it incredibly well."

—Brandon Webb, *New York Times* best-selling author

"Dina Santorelli writes a terrific thriller. *Baby Bailino* will grip you to the end—and long after."

—Andrew Gross, *New York Times* best-selling author of *The One Man*

"Dina Santorelli has done it again—delivering a taut thriller with believable, flesh and blood characters and a story that stays with you."

—Anne Canadeo, best-selling author of the Black Sheep Mysteries

"I couldn't put it down. And that's the truth."

—Dan Ribacoff, polygraph examiner and author of
I Spy: How to Be Your Own Private Investigator

"Just when I thought I had the characters figured out, along came another twist and turn in this action-packed thriller full of heart and soul."

—Kathleen M. Rodgers,
author of the award-winning novel *Johnnie Come Lately*

"Was on the edge of my seat! Dina pulled me right through the book with her captivating storytelling and characters. If you liked *Baby Grand*, you're going to love *Baby Balino*!"

—Eric Davis, former Navy SEAL and author of
*Raising Men: Lessons Navy SEALs Learned from
Their Training and Taught to Their Sons*

"*Baby Bailino*, the fast-paced and gripping sequel to *Baby Grand*, is a must for readers addicted to suspense. Dina Santorelli is a natural storyteller, and *Baby Bailino* is action-packed, richly plotted, and loaded with characters you won't soon forget!

—K.L. Murphy, author of The Detective Cancini Mystery Series

Praise for Dina Santorelli's *Baby Grand*

Best-selling organized crime thriller on Amazon Kindle
Top-rated mystery/thriller on Amazon Kindle
Honorable mention, genre fiction, 21st *Writer's Digest*
    Self-Published Book Awards

"A perfect thriller from Dina Santorelli—heart-stomping, emotion-packed and utterly surprising. Readers will be gripped by the tightly woven story and richly layered characters. A terrific read!"
                    —Ellen Meister, author of *Dorothy Parker Drank Here*

"What an enjoyable read! It pulled me in at the beginning and didn't let go until the last page. Very difficult to put down! I'm already looking forward to the author's next book."
                    —Joseph Mugnai, publisher, *Family* magazine

"A superb debut for Dina Santorelli. A well-crafted novel that's also a page-turner. *Baby Grand*'s a winner; you won't want to put it down."
        —Julia Markus, critically acclaimed biographer and winner of the
                    Houghton Mifflin Literary Award for her novel *Uncle*

"Dina Santorelli has the gift of a natural storyteller, and *Baby Grand* sweeps along at a frantic pace, plunging the reader into a tale with wonderfully real characters you care about. It's very human, very exciting, and absolutely engrossing."
                            —Chris Nickson, author of the
                    Richard Nottingham series of historical mysteries

"Dina Santorelli has a natural talent for weaving together characters and scenes, creating a plot that grips tighter with every page. If you value your sleep, do not read before bed!"
                    —Torre DeRoche, author of *Love with a Chance of Drowning*

Books by Dina Santorelli

Fiction
Baby Grand
Baby Bailino

Nonfiction
Daft Punk: A Trip Inside the Pyramid

Nonfiction (Collaborator/Contributor)
Good Girls Don't Get Fat: How Weight Obsession Is Messing Up
Our Girls and How We Can Help Them Thrive Despite It
Bully: An Action Plan for Teachers, Parents, and Communities
to Combat the Bullying Crisis
I, Spy: How to Be Your Own Private Investigator
Raising Men: Lessons Navy Seals Learned from
Their Training and Taught to Their Sons

dinasantorelli.com
elunamedia.com

Cover design by Natanya Wheeler
Interior designed by Wooly Head Design
Production management by Stonesong Digital

For daydream believers everywhere

BABY BAILINO

BY DINA SANTORELLI

1

B aby Faith stuck her chubby fingers into the bowl of fruit and shoved a fat, ripe strawberry into her mouth. Her lips, which formed a natural pucker, closed over it, her new teeth clamping down to release the sweet juice, which dribbled down her face and onto the coloring book.

"Careful, sweetie," said Jamie, who was watching her from the living room sofa. "Don't forget to use your napkin."

The little girl reached for the paper napkin on the coffee table and gave her mouth an obligatory wipe before dropping it onto the floor and plunging her hand back into the bowl. This time, she came up with a slice of banana. She stuck that into her mouth, too, and grabbed a broken blue crayon with her sticky fingers, drawing a series of lopsided circles around a connect-the-dots image of a princess.

Jamie flipped through the magazine on her lap without really reading it. She felt warm, but had already opened all the windows in the room, the curtains flapping in the light breeze. The shadow of a man passed across them, his image silhouetted by the beige linen, and Jamie tightened her grip on the magazine. Even after a year in her new place, she still wasn't used to the steady foot traffic that traveled across the windows of the first-floor apartment in Queens, a far cry from the relative calm of the suburbs. She heard a familiar set of keys jingle, and the doorknob of her front door turned.

"Edward . . . doorbell," she called, closing the magazine.

"Right, sorry," her brother said, closing the door and stepping back out.

Jamie had given her brother the key to her apartment for emergencies only, and although he had been trying to give her some space for the past two years, Edward was set in his ways. She got up from the couch as the doorbell rang.

"Who is it?" she said.

"Very funny," Edward said as Jamie swung the apartment door open.

"See? That wasn't so difficult," she said.

Edward entered the living room and placed several plastic bags of groceries on the floor. "*There's* my girl!" he said, spotting Faith near the coffee table. He swooped down to pick her up.

At the sight of Edward, Faith lifted her hands into the air, and he spun her above his head like a propeller.

"You are getting so big!" Edward said.

"Careful, she's got a mouthful of fruit." Jamie picked up several of the grocery bags.

"Fruit, shmoot." Edward tossed Faith into the air. "C'mon, give your Uncle Eddie a big fat, mushy kiss right here." He pointed to his face, and Faith plastered her wide open mouth onto Edward's cheek like a suction cup.

"Take it easy, Uncle Eddie. You're going to reinjure your shoulder."

"Shoulder's fine. Good as new."

"Yeah, sure it is."

Edward had been back to the orthopedist three times in the past six weeks, according to Trish, but Jamie knew he wasn't about to tell her that, probably because he didn't want her to worry.

"There were no agents outside," Edward said, trying to hide his concern. "They left already?"

"There's no reason for them to be here. They need to go help some other damsel in distress," Jamie said with a forced smile. She had to admit, she had grown accustomed to the FBI agents protecting her and Faith for the past two years, but today was to be a new day, and she was ready to get on with her life, alone with her daughter. She carried the bags into the kitchen, placed them on the table, and began pulling out the grocery items.

"What are you feeding this girl, James?" Faith was sitting on Edward's shoulders as he walked into the kitchen, a big, red circle stamped onto his cheek, courtesy of Faith's fruity kiss. "I think she gained ten pounds from last week."

"Looks like I'll be feeding her cereal," Jamie said, eyeing the six boxes of Cheerios Edward had bought.

"Hey, I had a coupon for those. Couldn't pass them up."

Edward placed Faith into her high chair at the kitchen table, and the little girl scrambled for the security strap, which she quickly pushed behind her back.

"Wait a minute, little one," Edward said. "We have to strap you in."

"She doesn't like being strapped in," Jamie said. "You'll have to—"

"Well, sometimes we gotta do what keeps us safe." Edward reached behind Faith's body to pull the strap forward, and the little girl slapped his hand.

"Noooooo," Edward said sternly, pointing his finger at her. "No hitting." He shot Jamie a look as Faith began to cry.

"Edward, don't give me that look. All babies do that. It doesn't mean anything."

Faith, her face all blotchy, raised her hands into the air so that Jamie could pick her up. Jamie reached for a pop-up book that was lying on the kitchen table and placed it on the high chair tray. The little girl immediately stopped crying and opened to the first thick laminated page, unaware that Jamie had reached behind her for the seat strap and buckled her in.

"See? Problem solved," Jamie said.

"More like problem averted." Edward crossed his arms. "We have to teach her not to do that, you know. She's not always going to get her way."

"C'mon, Edward, you're making a big deal out of nothing.

How would you feel if you were being strapped in and held against your . . ." She caught herself. "I'm sorry."

Edward shook his head. "Don't be."

"I mean—"

"James, really, it's all right. It's behind us."

Jamie blocked the image of Edward hogtied and gagged in the back of the Ford Flex from her mind and returned to unpacking the groceries. She pulled five cans of soup from the third plastic bag. "Another coupon?" she asked with a smirk.

"I like soup," Edward said.

"Wait, does that mean you're . . ." Jamie furrowed her brow. "Edward, honestly, you don't have to."

"I'm staying."

"But you—"

"I already told Trish," he said adamantly. "I'm staying with you and Faith just for a few days. Till I know everything is okay. And that's it." He jammed the plastic grocery bags into one another, placed them in the recycling bin, and left the kitchen in a huff.

Faith lifted her eyes from her book to watch Edward go. Her splotchy face was regaining its cheery color. The little girl smiled, her upper and lower eyelids meeting sharply at the corners and making the gaze of her dark brown eyes intensify. Jamie felt a familiar pang in her chest; she smiled back at her daughter, although it took every ounce of strength for her not to turn away. Faith looked more and more like *him* every day.

Edward returned with the rest of the groceries and placed them where he knew they belonged in her cupboard. "Now, I'm the one who's sorry," he said, closing the last cabinet.

Jamie put her arm around him. "Aren't we a sorry pair?" she said. "Don't worry about it."

The telephone rang, startling them, and Edward reached for the phone.

"Don't answer it," Jamie said.

"Why not?" Edward looked at the Caller ID. "Private number."

"It's the press. I'm sure of it. They've been calling all morning."

"How did they get this number?"

Jamie shrugged. She had changed her number three times in the past six months, and the media managed to figure it out every time.

Edward put the phone back in its cradle. "What time is it happening?" he asked.

"Agent Wilcox said they were transferring him sometime this afternoon."

"Wilcox should have left somebody here, until it's done," Edward said.

"Edward, the transfer's taking place up north, *miles and miles* from here—a four-hour drive." Jamie reached for a bowl, sprinkled a handful of Cheerios into it, and placed it on Faith's high chair tray, but the little girl pushed it away and rubbed her eyes. "He can't be in two places at once."

"I think you're being naive. We know what that guy is capable of, and how many people are loyal to him."

"Wilcox said there is nothing to worry about, that—"

"And you believe him? That there's nothing to worry about?"

Jamie didn't answer.

"I didn't think so."

Edward turned on the small television set on the kitchen counter. The screen warmed to *Dora the Explorer*, which attracted Faith's sleepy eyes until Edward changed the channel to CNN. Faith yelled in protest and threw her book onto the floor.

"Hey," Edward said. "No throwing."

Faith cried again and reached for Jamie.

"Edward, do me a favor and put this on in the living room," Jamie said, trying to ignore the large banner headline that filled the television screen: *Bailino Transfer Imminent*. "I'm going to put Faith down for her nap. She's tired, and I don't want the TV to wake her up."

"Don't baby her, James." Edward turned off the set. "We have to treat her like we would any other child."

"She *is* any other child," Jamie said with a frown.

"You know what I mean." Edward leaned down to kiss the top of Faith's head. "See you later, Faithy," he said, but the little girl leaned away from him. "You see that?" he asked Jamie.

"She's mad because you yelled at her." Jamie unbuckled the high chair strap.

Edward crossed his arms. "Holding grudges at fifteen months old?"

"Is it any surprise?" Jamie lifted Faith from the high chair. "You know who she takes after."

Edward's eyes opened wide.

"*You*, dummy. I meant you. *Geez* . . ." Jamie said and hurried into the small bedroom beside the kitchen.

The smell of baby powder settled over her as she sat on the wooden rocking chair in the corner of the small bedroom and rubbed Faith's back. She could feel her daughter getting ready for another cry, so she started to sing:

> *"Mid pleasures and palaces though we may roam . . .*
> *"Be it ever so humble, there's no place like home . . ."*

The little girl quieted, but fidgeted, trying to find the right position.

> *"A charm from the skies seems to hallow us there . . .*
> *"Which seek thro' the world, is ne'er met elsewhere . . .*
> *"Home. Home. Sweet, sweet home."*

The old song had been a favorite of Jamie's mother, and it had quickly become a favorite of Faith's. The little girl assumed her usual position, placing her head in the crook of Jamie's neck, and without fail, Jamie's mind flashed back two years to when tiny Charlotte Grand held the very same position atop Jamie's chest, her chubby arms clasped around her neck, the two of them sitting in a closet turned into a makeshift nursery far, far away from home.

Jamie cradled the back of Faith's head and sighed. Those four days with Charlotte—followed by the media frenzy upon the little girl's safe return to her father, New York Governor Phillip Grand—seemed to follow Jamie everywhere, like a shadow. The "check up" calls from Special Agent Wilcox and the FBI. The paparazzi. The whispers and the stares. The nightmares that danced under her eyelids when she tried to sleep at night. The way Edward scrutinized every move Faith made as if they were some clue that would uncover a hidden truth.

Faith's breathing became even, but Jamie kept rocking, her mind fixated as it often was on the darkness of that log cabin bedroom, on the strength of his body, the caress of his hand. She tried to change her focus to something happy, and Reynaldo's face appeared in her mind's eye, as it often did. Jamie could still see him standing there in that dirty garage, his paperwork spread out across the counter, looking at her and Charlotte when they burst through his door as if he had just seen a ghost. She could still feel his floppy thick hair in her grasp and the security of his arms. Kind, gentle Reynaldo, who had helped her when she and Charlotte needed him most, no questions asked. Kind, gentle Reynaldo, who couldn't understand, as much as he tried, why Jamie desperately wanted to have this child, despite everything. Despite *him*.

Over the past two years, friends and family members had suggested Jamie read up on research that dealt with the acceptance and legitimacy of a child of rape, but Jamie had felt nothing but love and a fierce protectiveness for her baby, who was now sleeping peacefully in her arms, from the moment she found out she was pregnant. Reynaldo may have loved Jamie, and she him, but if he could not accept Faith, it could have never worked between them. It was nearly impossible for Jamie to block out the circumstances surrounding Faith's conception when she was reminded of them every time she looked into her daughter's eyes; she didn't want to be reminded of them when she looked into Reynaldo's eyes, too.

Edward appeared at the doorway to the bedroom. "He's on his way," he whispered. "The news 'copters are following the van on the highway. Finally, it's almost over."

Jamie gave her brother a small smile as he left the room. She wanted nothing more than to believe that this was the end of all that ugliness, yet as she watched her daughter sleep, she couldn't shake the feeling that it never would. She crossed her ankles, feeling for the semiautomatic gun that she kept in a holster at the side of her calf, a present she had bought for herself, despite Edward's reluctance. She thought of her NRA firearms training certificate and manuals that were tucked away neatly in her nightstand drawer, replacing her old yoga CDs, which had been moved to the trash. These days, safety came in the form of a pistol, not a pose. Until two years ago, she had never thought much about the Second Amendment or of herself as a gun person. Until two years ago, she never had a reason to, but if Bailino or anyone else found a way to come after her or her daughter now or anytime in the future, she would know how to handle herself. She would be ready. And, this time, she would be shooting to kill.

2

Don Bailino sat at the back of the prison transfer van, his handcuffed wrists resting on his lap. Outside, two helicopters—one law enforcement, one media—hovered at ten and two o'clock, while four state police and federal vehicles served as an escort while the van sped along the highway. All along the route, people had lined up wherever they could—atop overpasses, inside high-rises, across long stretches of fields—to get a glimpse into Bailino's bulletproof window, their smartphone cameras in hand. Inside the van, six armed prison guards and two federal marshals sat in front of him, their eyes darting from the van windows to all three exits, which had been sealed and padlocked. It was no secret that, from time to time, prisoners escaped custody during one of these transports—often because someone missed a crucial safety step—but this time, the authorities were taking no chances.

The transfer from the federal medical detention center in Boston, where Bailino had spent the last year and a half convalescing after a six-month stint at Albany Memorial, to the Stanton Correctional Facility near Albany was set to take just under three hours. The route had been carefully plotted with highway entrances and exits cordoned off—traffic diversions that, in several hours, were sure to snarl the evening rush hour in four states. It was as if the President of the United States himself were in town.

Bailino closed his eyes. The sun had finally broken through the gray sky, and it was the first time he'd felt sunlight on his face in nearly two years. He took a deep breath and waited for the resulting chest pain stemming from the gunshot wounds, but over the past twenty-four months that pain had become barely perceptible. It was amazing, Bailino thought, how the heart could heal.

It was the chubby guard's turn to check Bailino's restraints, which were inspected every half hour. The guard stood, pulling up on his belt, which was no match for his hefty gut, and he strutted down the van's center aisle looking like a bloated peacock. Bailino lifted his handcuffed wrists into the air, as was the routine, and was surprised when the guard spoke to him.

"You're being such a good boy," the guard said with a smile. "I thought you were supposed to be some kind of badass."

Bailino returned his hands to his lap and glanced at the guard's name badge—*Bernie Brooks*. Bernie stumbled his way back to his post as the van veered off the smooth asphalt onto a bumpy off-ramp that yielded to a two-lane country road. A small blue sign denoted the nearest gas stations and restaurants; below it, a small white sign read: *Prison Area: Do Not Pick Up Hitchhikers*.

"Almost home," Bernie called. He traded satisfied looks with the other guards.

Bailino was familiar with this stretch of road. He had built the corporate headquarters of his company not too far from there, and his home was only about another ten miles west. He hadn't stepped foot in either for two years, and in all likelihood he never would again.

That morning, his lawyer had met with him one last time to iron out the last details of his plea agreement.

"Life in prison, no eligibility for parole," his lawyer had said. "Frankly, you should consider yourself lucky."

By pleading guilty to all charges, Bailino had managed to dodge the death penalty. Law enforcement agencies throughout the state— and the country—had been outraged, particularly after the gruesome murder of one of their own, Detective Sergeant Mark Nurberg, at Bailino's hands. Police officers were hungry for an ugly trial that ended only with one result: Bailino dead. After he took a deal, they had rallied, demanding that Governor Grand step in and push for the death penalty, as he had with Gino Cataldi and other cold-blooded killers. Although the restitution of the death penalty had been a cornerstone of Grand's campaign for governor—and would be, as pundits had been predicting, of his impending run for the United States presidency—the governor had been uncharacteristically quiet on the matter of United States versus Don Bailino.

"And Joey?" Bailino had asked his lawyer.

"Full immunity, contingent upon your full confession," his lawyer had said. "All assets have been moved to the accounts as you have designated."

"And?"

"And the details of the plea bargain are being held tightly under wraps. Just as you requested and agreed to. Nobody will know the terms."

"Good," Bailino had said.

As far as Bailino could tell, the Cataldi crime family still didn't know Joey was Bailino's biological child, unless ToniAnne or Joey had told them otherwise, and he hoped to keep it that way. With Joey safely tucked away at MIT in Cambridge, Bailino had intended to spend the rest of his years at Stanton, dodging shivs and food poisoning, and he would have been content with that, but the birth of Faith Carter had changed everything.

The Stanton Correctional Facility emerged in the distance, its gray brick exterior a familiar sight to Bailino, who had visited the prison regularly since the 1980s when Gino had first been remanded there. It wasn't until this moment that Bailino even wondered what had happened to the body of the old mob boss after they put him to death by lethal injection two years ago. He assumed Gino had been buried with the rest of the Cataldi family in Queens, inside an ostentatious tomb visited by huddles of little old Italian ladies in black, but for all he knew the bastard was floating somewhere in the Atlantic Ocean.

The transport convoy came to a stop outside the prison gates, and the guards inside the van all stood as if on command and readied their weapons. A crowd that had been sitting near the entrance gates stood and began to taunt the van as the bright lights of the news cameras flooded the bright afternoon with even more light. Bailino could feel Bernie eyeing him, but he continued to stare outside.

The prison's automatic gate opened, and Bailino's vehicle drove through, while the others remained outside the electric fence that was topped with vine-like barbed wire. The van maneuvered toward a main building not far from a watchtower, where several armed guards paced, surveying a prison yard where inmates dressed in orange federally issued jumpsuits ogled at the transport through a chain-link fence, eager to see the infamous new resident who would be joining their ranks. The van swerved to the right of the main entrance, backed toward a narrow alleyway, and came to a stop. The guards remained standing until there was a series of clanks and the back door to the van opened, revealing another handful of armed guards.

"All right, Bailino. On your feet," Bernie said.

The guard nearest Bailino pulled him up and nudged him forward with the barrel of his gun. Bailino took one last look around the van before stepping down onto the pavement and into the sunlight.

Despite the circumstances, it felt good to be outside again, and Bailino tilted his head north and gazed at a cluster of trees lining the low mountains in the distance, where his Upackk factory was located.

"Let's go," Bernie called. "We ain't got all day."

As the guards moved in formation and established a tight circle around Bailino, reporters lobbed questions, while prison inmates yelled assorted obscenities and wisecracks. Bernie led the small group of guards toward the building like a schoolteacher escorting his pupils back to school following a field trip.

"Here we are, Bailino," Bernie said as he opened a side door to the prison. "Home, sweet home." Inside, rows of armed guards flanked the narrow hallway like a receiving line.

Bailino stepped onto the prison's cracked tiled floor, greeted by the familiar smell of ammonia. He smirked. He wouldn't be spending enough time at Stanton to call it home, that was for sure, and as soon as he was out—which would be soon—he made a mental note to find Bernie Brooks and kill him first.

3

Governor Phillip Grand watched Bailino enter the gray building on the flat-screen television in his Executive Mansion office. He had a full-day's agenda planned and hadn't expected to catch any of the live coverage of the prison transfer—a transport that was expected to gain more viewership than O. J. Simpson's infamous white Bronco ride. However, like the millions of others watching the journey unfold on their digital screens, he wanted to see what had become of the man who had abducted his daughter two years ago, committed multiple murders, including a respected police detective, been shot by his abductee, with whom he fathered a child, and somehow lived to tell the tale.

As the cameras zoomed in, Phillip expected to see a far less formidable Bailino, a man whose body had undergone a long healing and recovery process from the two gunshots that Jamie had fired and the resulting collapsed lung and other maladies, but the man on the television screen was far from frail. The hair was grayer, if only around the temples, but the months of hospital confinement seemed to restore, rather than strip, Bailino's health and stamina. He appeared fighting fit.

Phillip turned off the set and leaned back in his swivel chair. He didn't know why he had expected anything less from his long-ago army buddy. He knew what Bailino was capable of—an inner strength that seemed to stem from, as much as it defied, his rough-

and-tumble upbringing on the streets of Brooklyn. Every day, for two years, Phillip had been waiting with trepidation for the phone call that would tell him the news: that Bailino had somehow escaped from the prison hospital, leaving a bloody trail of injured physicians and nurses, or how he had disappeared without a trace, but the day had never come. All week long, with Bailino's prison transfer looming, the news networks had been reporting the unlikelihood of his escape, interviewing organized crime historians and retired prison guards and wardens. Still, Phillip couldn't shake that nagging feeling that Bailino would find a way to get out. Some wild animals couldn't be caged.

A sharp breeze shifted the black heavy drapes as well as the plastic flap of the half-eaten bag of Oreo cookies on Phillip's mahogany desk. He pulled the drapes back, letting in what little sunlight there was—a large cloud had passed overhead. Normally, the view from Phillip's private office was quite remarkable with its unobstructed vista of the Hudson River and the lush hills and valleys surrounding it, but today it appeared dreary and lifeless. Or maybe that was just his mood.

Phillip turned toward his desk and bumped into the glass display case that held the antique pistol his father had given him two Christmas Eves ago. That thing was a monstrosity, and Phillip would just as soon keep it in the closet along with the antique bullets his father had slipped to him after dinner that day—"just in case," he had said, as if the Redcoats were going to storm the Executive Mansion during midnight mass. Phillip wasn't sure whether the pistol was meant to be a gift or a punishment. His parents hadn't approved of being kept in the dark about Charlotte's abduction, and Phillip guessed he couldn't blame them. It was Katherine's idea to mount the pistol in a display case—"just imagine your father's head at the end of the barrel," she had said—so it looked like Phillip was stuck with it.

He gathered some paperwork and opened his office door, startled to see one of Wilcox's FBI agents, whom he had forgotten had been standing there. With Bailino's transport scheduled for that day, Wilcox had dispatched additional manpower to provide an extra layer of security for the governor and his family.

"Governor," the fresh-faced FBI agent said with a nod.

"The transport's complete," Phillip said. "I don't think you guys need to hang around here anymore."

"Not until I receive authorization, sir," the agent said.

"Very well." Phillip gave the young agent a slap on the back. "Thank you for your service."

Down the hallway, tiny footsteps came running up the stairs as Charlotte barreled toward her father, her blond curls bouncing around her happy face.

"Daddy, Daddy!" Charlotte jumped into Phillip's arms. "Look what I made you!"

"What is it, Charlie?" Phillip asked, lifting her up and taking an object made of bendy clay that had not yet hardened from his daughter's hand.

Rosalia appeared huffing and puffing at the top of the landing. "I so sorry, Governor Phillip," she said. She put her hand on her chest, her fingers resting on the ruffled white lace of her dress to steady her breathing. "It's getting harder and harder to keep up with that one."

"Don't worry about it, Rosalia. I'll take her." Phillip examined the item in his hand. "Ah, now what is this?"

"Can you guess?" Charlotte asked, her bright blue eyes wide with excitement. "Can you guess, Daddy? Huh, huh?"

"Well, let me think. . . ." He glanced at Rosalia who made a gesture with her hands. He recognized it as the American Sign Language sign for watering can.

"It's a flowerpot, of course," Phillip said.

"Daddy, you're so smart!" Charlotte wrapped her arms around her father's neck and squeezed until Phillip gave her a raspberry on her neck and she giggled.

"Okay, cookie, let's go show Mommy what you made. We'll have to plant some seeds inside it right away."

"Let's plant pumpkin seeds, Daddy. Ro Ro loves pumpkin pie, right, Ro Ro?" she called to Rosalia.

"Yes, *Carlota*," Rosalia said, cupping Charlotte's face as the governor passed by with her. "I will make a nice pumpkin pie for Thanksgiving with the pumpkins you grow."

Downstairs, Katherine was in the kitchen huddled over two laptops, a steaming cup of coffee between them.

"Well?" Katherine asked when he and Charlotte entered.

"Mommy, Mommy, look!" Charlotte jumped down from her father's grasp and reached for the flowerpot in Phillip's hands.

"Not now, Charlotte," Katherine said, her eyes darting between screens. "Mommy's working."

"He was just transferred." Phillip mussed Charlotte's hair so that her moppy curls flipped from side to side. "To Stanton. Were you watching it?"

Katherine motioned to the series of tabs she had opened on her screens. "I was doing everything not to watch it."

"Yeah, well, so was I, and then, like everyone else, I couldn't stay away."

Charlotte climbed onto Katherine's lap and stuck the flowerpot in her line of sight. "What is it, Mommy? Can you guess? Can you?"

"Well, I really can't if you're shoving it in front of me like that."

Charlotte pulled the clay pot back so that it was dangling precariously over one of Katherine's laptops.

"Actually, let me take a closer look at it." Katherine pulled it toward her and studied it.

"No hints, Daddy." Charlotte pointed a stern finger in Phillip's direction. "Let Mommy do this by herself." She sounded exactly like her mother every time Phillip tried to help Charlotte accomplish a task.

Still, Phillip tried to make eye contact with Katherine. The relationship between Charlotte and Katherine seemed to grow stronger after Charlotte's abduction, Katherine trying harder to be an attentive parent, but he worried that something as simple as a wrong guess might set them back—both of the Grand women were so very proud.

"It's a flowerpot," Katherine said simply, without any assistance. "Ask Rosalia to go with you and get some dirt and you can fill it up."

Charlotte was overjoyed. "My Mommy and Daddy are the smartest people ever!" she yelled and went running up the stairs calling for Rosalia.

Phillip watched her go. He still felt a small pang of worry every time Charlotte left the room.

"Well, that's a relief," Katherine said.

"What is?" he asked, fearful that she meant Charlotte being gone.

"Bailino, Phillip. Being in prison. What did you think I meant?"

"Never mind." Phillip wrapped his arms around her. "About Bailino . . ."

"Phillip, enough. Let's not let this person interfere in our lives any more than he already has, which leads me to . . . You still haven't looked at any of these applicants." She pushed a stack of resumes in his direction. "There's only so much I can do, you know."

The executive branch of the state of New York had been operating without a press secretary for the past five months, which meant Katherine had been picking up the slack. Since Maddox, the Grands' trusted friend and colleague, had double-crossed them and collaborated with Bailino in the abduction of Charlotte, Phillip and Katherine had been even more cautious about the staff they hired, from chauffeurs and maids to office interns. Their circle of trust had grown so small that they had been operating on a skeleton crew ever since the incident.

"I know. I will," he said, running his hand through his gray hair. "You know, I was thinking maybe . . ."

"She won't do it, Phillip. Face it. You're going to have to get over it."

Phillip had asked Jamie Carter if she might consider taking the position when her brother Edward had been in the hospital and she had been staying at the Executive Mansion. Her work as a freelance writer and marketer made her suitable for the job, and he probably trusted Jamie more than anyone else he knew other than his mother, Katherine, and Rosalia, but Jamie had declined. He couldn't blame her. She probably wanted to be anywhere other than in and around Albany.

Phillip ended up hiring a former local newsman who had impeccable references—he had worked with some of the senior legislators in the state senate—but Phillip couldn't shake the feeling that something was off about the guy, and he fired him after only three months. Since then it had been a series of revolving men and women. Nobody seemed to stick.

"Don't forget the meeting with Clark of the Republican National Committee this morning." Katherine sounded almost giddy. "Remember, you need to express serious interest in the presidency, while making your reelection plans clear."

Phillip's second term had been eventful, filled with legislation that he had been proud of, but all of that had been overshadowed by Charlotte's abduction and eventual return, from which Phillip had emerged as either a sympathetic father figure or a veritable hero, depending upon the published account of the events to which constituents subscribed. None of those accounts had been completely accurate, of course—unauthorized books never are—and no one knew, not the FBI and not even Katherine, how much Phillip had known about Don Bailino's involvement in the kidnapping and how it had practically paralyzed him. *Some hero*, he thought. Still, political experts had predicted that Phillip would be easily handed a third term as governor of New York in the fall, leaving state democrats scrambling to find anyone willing to oppose him and take the loss.

And with the national Republican Party eager to reclaim the White House, whisperings of Phillip's potential run for president had already begun—hence, the meeting with Clark. Polling indicated that Phillip had a whopping 90 percent approval rating, highest of any elected official currently serving in public office, including the president. Apparently, nearly everyone in the country was in love with Phillip Grand, except Phillip Grand.

"Katherine," he said, "maybe now isn't the best time . . ."

"Like hell it's not." Katherine stood up and put the empty cup of coffee into the sink. "We've been waiting for this for a long time, Phillip. Let's not get cold feet now. In fact," she closed one of her laptops, "now's the perfect time. With Bailino's incarceration, people are talking about it again. You're trending on Twitter. You should use that."

"Use a felon to run for president of the United States?"

"You know what I mean."

He did, but he didn't like it. The abduction of his daughter had been the worst thing to ever to happen to him; turning it into a professional plus point filled him with disgust. So far, neither he nor Katherine ever spoke of the incident publicly, and, as far as he was concerned, he never wanted to.

A series of red circles lit up the baby monitor, which was perched on the kitchen counter. An irritated wail emanated from its speaker. Normally, Phillip Jr. woke up in a pleasant mood. Phillip decided that this mood change in his son, who hadn't even been born when those dreaded events had taken place, indicated that he didn't like Katherine's plan much either.

"Philly's up," he said.

"Rosalia!" Katherine called as she sat back down at her seat. "The baby!"

Phillip rested his hands on Katherine's shoulders and whispered into her ear. "Why don't you get him?"

"Me? But I'm in the middle of—"

Phillip planted a quick kiss on her lips.

"Oh, all right." She got up from her chair and headed toward the stairway. "I just don't see why we're bothering to pay for a nanny if you want me to do everything myself."

"Oh, please, not everything. Don't be a drama queen."

"Why not? I'm everything else around here," Katherine said with a flourish before disappearing up the stairs. He heard her yell, "Never mind, Rosalia. I've got it. *Again*."

Phillip opened the pantry door, quickly stuck his hand inside, and pulled out a chocolate chip cookie from an already opened box he had stashed in the corner. He stuffed the cookie into his mouth, checking to make sure Katherine hadn't caught him, but was startled to see Special Agent Wilcox standing at the entrance to the kitchen. Wilcox had become a familiar sight around the Executive Mansion for the past two years—Charlotte referred to him as "Willy"—but Phillip hadn't expected to see him today.

"Agent Wilcox, what a pleasant surprise. Come in."

"Sir, I'm just letting you know we were informed that the inmate has been transferred and incarcerated." Wilcox refrained from referring to Bailino by name, if he could help it.

"Yes, I saw it on the news."

"I'll be pulling my men shortly. Just wanted you to know."

"You didn't have to come all the way here for that, but, as always, I appreciate it," Phillip said. Wilcox had been looking out for the Grands, as well as Jamie and Edward Carter, ever since Bailino had first been hospitalized. He used his personal time to check in from time to time, particularly when Jamie had gone into labor and was in the hospital. He was a good man, and Phillip had put him on his mental list of candidates for a possible cabinet post should Phillip be elected president. "Thank you for everything."

"My pleasure, Governor."

Wilcox joined the rest of his team in the mansion's main lobby and exited as Katherine returned with Little Phillip in her arms.

"How's my big boy?" Phillip asked, extending his arms.

"He was full of poop, if you must know," Katherine said, handing the child off like he were a baton. She wrinkled her nose.

"Why do you think I sent *you* up there?" Phillip winked as he took his son.

"Very funny." Katherine returned to her laptop. "Have you thought about what you're going to say today? To Clark?"

"I thought that was *your* job."

"Yes," she pushed the stack of applications toward him again. "It is. *For now.* I jotted down some bullet points, but you should really prepare, Phillip. This is a conservative group."

"I'm a conservative guy." He nuzzled the little boy, who giggled.

"*Right, Philly? I'm a conservative guy.*" Philly clapped his hands on Phillip's nose.

"Not to them. You may as well be Bill De Blasio. They're going to want to know why you didn't push for the death penalty on Bailino. You'll have to know what to say."

"I *do* know what to say." Phillip placed his son into his high chair. "The guy pled guilty, Katherine. Protocol is to show leniency. It's pretty much what Bailino agreed to. Full disclosure for life imprisonment. No death penalty."

"Sure, but that didn't mean you couldn't make a stink."

"You mean, you think I should have pushed?"

"Why not? It benefits you, politically. Plus, you know as well as I do that this guy is a threat while he is alive."

Phillip sighed. He knew Katherine was right. Pushing for the death penalty would have been vintage Phillip Grand, and had he pushed hard enough, he knew he could have made a solid case for lethal injection, sending Bailino to death row. However, he hadn't, and he wasn't sure why. Bailino was dangerous—that was a fact—but long, long ago, they had been close. Bailino had saved his life more than once in the military. Was it possible that there was a small part of Phillip that felt, despite all that had happened, that he had a duty to now save his?

Katherine closed her laptop. "Listen, I don't want to fight."

"Neither do I." He reached out and stuck his finger inside the waistband of Katherine's charcoal skirt and tugged. "Truce?"

"Truce," she said with a nod.

"So, what should we do then?" Phillip pulled his wife toward him.

Katherine put her arms around her husband's neck. "I know," she said.

"What?" He blew softly into her ear.

She reached down for the printouts and stuck them in Phillip's hand. "Study your bullet points," she said.

"You always say the sweetest things," Phillip said, taking the paperwork from Katherine as Philly banged on his high chair tray.

"Trust me, if we play our cards right," Katherine said, "there will be plenty of time for that other stuff. *Mr. President.*"

4

The wobbly wheels of the small oxygen cart squeaked as Paolo Cataldi pulled it into the living room. He shooed the dog out of his armchair and carefully turned around and sat, his body conforming to the familiar folds of the fabric.

"Mary!" he barked, yanking the oxygen cart around his feet and to the right of his chair.

"What?" Mary yelled from the bedroom.

"Can you make me a bologna sandwich?"

"Now? We just had lunch."

"No, tomorrow," Paolo hollered. He scratched at the wax inside his ear.

Mary shuffled into the room, tidying up as she moved along—a fluffed pillow here, a swipe of dust there. In her heyday, Mary had been a statuesque woman of five-foot-nine, but in recent years she had developed a noticeable hump on her upper back. Although the condition was most likely the result of a lifetime of insufficient calcium and exercise, plus the smoking, which didn't help, Mary liked to say it was due to her having to stoop for more than fifty years in order to appear shorter than Paolo, who was only five-foot-seven. In other words, the hump was Paolo's fault. As was everything else.

"You want me to turn the TV on?" she asked as she was passing the set.

"No, I want it quiet." He leaned his head back against the worn fabric and closed his eyes, hoping she'd get the hint, the hiss of the oxygen tank slicing the air.

"Suit yourself." Mary disappeared into the kitchen.

He peeked through one eye to see if the coast was clear before reaching underneath his chair cushion for the small box of chewing tobacco he kept hidden there. It was pushed too far down, and his clawing at it only made it go down further.

"Goddamn it," he said with a huff as Mary returned with his quickly prepared sandwich, the bologna sticking out like a tongue from the bread. If she had spent more than five seconds making it, Paolo would have been surprised. She placed the paper plate of food on the small circular table next to Paolo's armchair.

Paolo eyed the sandwich. "What's with the toothpicks?"

"I thought I'd be fancy."

"You're a regular Martha Stewart." Paolo reached down, his hands fumbling with the plate.

"A thank-you might be nice," Mary said.

"Yeah, it would be."

Mary bent down, accentuating her hump even more, and switched on the laptop computer perched on the rolltop desk in the corner of the room.

"What are you doing?" Paolo asked. "I told you I want it quiet."

"I won't bother you," she said.

"You're bothering me already."

Mary sighed and returned to the kitchen as the laptop screen came to life.

Paolo's hands trembled as he set the plate onto his lap. His Parkinson's acted up whenever he tried to perform a simple task such as eating or brushing his teeth. He wrapped one of his knobby hands around a half of sandwich and with the other tried to remove the toothpick, but he couldn't grasp it.

"Goddamn, fancy . . ." he muttered before he was able to pull the small slice of wood out and drop it on the plate. He brought the sandwich to his mouth and managed to take a bite, but the trembling caused the mustard to smear under his nose and onto his breathing tubes.

"Son of a bitch. Where's my napkin?" he thundered.

"Hold your horses." Mary came out of the kitchen holding a tall glass of iced tea, which she placed on a coaster to the side of her laptop, and rested a napkin sheet that had been ripped in half on the table next to Paolo.

"What? We can't afford a whole napkin?" Paolo said.

"Waste not, want not." Mary reached for Paolo's breathing tubes. "You want me to wipe that for you?"

Paolo swatted her hand away. "No, thanks. I got it."

"Suit yourself," she said. She sat down at her computer and began clicking.

"Do you need to make all that racket?" Paolo asked.

"I'm just making up an email for my peeps. No racket."

"Your *what*?"

Paolo yanked the oxygen tube out of his nose and from behind his ears and wrapped it around the arm of his chair. He was about to take another bite of his sandwich when the phone on the table next to him sprang to life, startling him so much that he dropped the sandwich onto the floor.

"For Chrissake," Paolo muttered, throwing the other half of the sandwich and the paper plate onto the floor as well.

"Well, you're in a mood," Mary said. She got up from the computer and reached down to pick up the sandwich.

"Forget about that and just get the fucking phone, will you?"

Unfazed, Mary picked up the handset. "Hello? . . ." she said. "Yes, he's here."

"Who is it?" Paolo asked. "I might not be here."

"It's Marco."

"I'm here. Give me the damn thing." Paolo stuck out his hand impatiently. "And do me a favor and make yourself scarce for a few minutes."

"What am I supposed to do?" Mary pointed at the computer. "My—"

"Your *peeps* can wait," he said. "Go dust off some old Easter palm or something."

Mary sighed heavily this time and left the room.

"Hello? Hello?" Paolo shouted into the air space in front of the telephone receiver. His hand was shaking so much that he couldn't place it anywhere near his ear. "You're going to have to talk louder. My wife is sending me to an early death."

"Can you hear me now?" screamed a tinny voice from the headset.

"Yeah, yeah, I got you. Perfect. Everything ready?"

"Yeah, the bastard will be in for a real surprise in a few hours," Marco said, before adding, "Excuse my language, Aunt Mary!"

"Don't worry, that old bat isn't here."

"I heard that!" Mary screamed from the kitchen.

"Remember, we're stretching this out for that poor fuck," Paolo said into the air in front of the phone. "We have lots of time. Bailino ain't going anywhere. Let's make it count."

The FBI had been guarding Bailino night and day at that hospital for nearly two years, and Paolo had had no access to him. Now that Bailino was out from under the protection of the Feds, Paolo wanted answers, including the whereabouts of his godson, Leo, who seemed to disappear. The last record there was of Leo Cataldi was his videotaped appearance at Stanton to visit his father on death row on April 4, 2012. Apparently, no one had seen or heard from him since, including Joey who was the only one—other than Bailino—who was left to tell the story of the events in the log cabin two years ago. Conveniently, everyone else was dead, and that Jamie Carter person didn't seem to know where he was either, at least that's what she had told the Feds. She and that damn kid had had federal protection, too. Paolo thought of his taxpayer money paying for the protection of Bailino and his brat, and his hand holding the telephone receiver shook violently.

However, he finally had Bailino in a place where he could reach him. In federal prison.

"I want information, Marco," Paolo said, careful not to say anything incriminating on the telephone. "I've waited too long."

"I know, Uncle Paolo," Marco said. "I won't let you down."

Mary walked into the room carrying a vacuum cleaner and dropped it at Paolo's feet. He glared at her, but she ignored him.

"Don't hang up after you talk with your Uncle Paolo," Mary called in the direction of the phone as she unwound the cord from the vacuum. She picked up the paper plate that Paolo had thrown onto the carpet and placed the sandwich pieces on it. "I want to talk to my sister."

"Okay, Aunt Mary," Marco yelled.

"Don't forget your toothpicks, fancy pants," Paolo said, pointing them out on the carpeting.

"Very funny," Mary said. She picked them up and left the room.

"Marco," Paolo asked, "is the meeting set up for next week?"

"Yes, Uncle Paolo."

"Good, good." A few of the old coots were still around, and they needed to hash out the Bailino issue. The families may not have had the manpower or the muscle they once had, but they still had the wherewithal. And with Gino gone, it was time for Paolo, at age seventy-three, to get his time in the sun. "Keep me posted on any developments."

Mary came into the room with a bottle of furniture polish, and Paolo handed her the phone.

"Fran, you there?" she yelled into the receiver.

"You gotta do that now?" Paolo asked, motioning to the furniture polish. "I'm eating here."

Mary covered the telephone receiver with her hand. "Eating what?"

"The bologna sandwich you're going to make me, without toothpicks this time, so I don't impale myself. Besides, I don't know why you're cleaning. No one comes here anyway."

"And whose fault is *that*?" Mary uncovered the phone. "Yeah, Fran, I'm here," she said and wandered into the kitchen.

Paolo settled into his chair and snapped the breathing tubes back into his nose. He dug his hand down with all his might into the seat cushion, the confinement of the space alleviating some of his trembling, and managed to get his fingers around the container of chewing tobacco, which he pulled out and hid behind his back—a little treat for after his sandwich.

He thought of Bailino being processed into Stanton, and a smile crossed his face. Goddamn Bailino sang like a canary the minute he came to, gave his brother Gino up to cop a plea, but after all these years he was finally going to get what was coming to him. One way or another. Paolo would see to it.

5

"Geez, *hermano*, go outside or something."

Reynaldo was lying face down on the couch. He had taken the day off on the advice of his brother, Pedro, to keep from having to hear customers at the garage chat about the transfer of Don Bailino to Stanton. Just when Reynaldo's nightmares had suddenly subsided, the transfer brought them roaring back again. In his most recent one, Don Bailino was standing over Reynaldo as he tried to breathe, but couldn't catch his breath, and he woke up gasping for air. And if Reynaldo was feeling this way, he could only imagine what Jamie was going through.

"Call her," Pedro said, handing him the phone.

"I can't." Reynaldo dropped the phone onto the floor. He felt like a tree whose roots were wrapped around the sofa.

"Just do it, Rey."

Reynaldo lifted his head and searched the room for an excuse to avoid calling Jamie. He eyed the pair of gardening gloves and bucket of tools that were lying by the front door next to his muddy pair of galoshes. "I don't have time. I need to garden," he said. He had taken up the hobby not long after Jamie broke it off with him, after trying tae kwon do. He had read somewhere that gardening was supposed to relax him, but, after two seasons, he could never seem to get anything to grow.

"Gardening is no replacement for a girl, *hermano*."

Reynaldo buried his head under a decorative pillow. "What will I say?"

"Say you are a big dumb-head and that you are sorry, and that you're just checking on her to make sure she's okay. Girls like that shit."

"It's too late for that."

"It's never too late, *hermano*." Pedro opened a drawer of the dining room cabinet, rummaged around, and then opened another. He poked around the knickknacks and behind their mother's old formal china dinnerware.

"What are you looking for?" Reynaldo asked.

"Money," Pedro said. "I know your hiding places."

"Cut it out." Reynaldo threw the pillow at him and sat up on the couch. He reached into his pocket and pulled out a small wad of cash. "How much do you need?"

"How much do you have?" Pedro asked, sitting next to him.

"Pedro, I'm not in the mood."

"What else is new?" Pedro reached in to grab some money, but Reynaldo yanked his hand away.

"I have an idea." Pedro eased Reynaldo's hand back and plucked a twenty from the roll of bills. "I'll take this for the pizza. You take the rest and go shopping. Buy yourself some new cologne, something Jamie will like."

"It's not that easy."

"It *is* that easy." Pedro picked up the phone that was lying on the floor. "Here."

Reynaldo tossed the phone onto the loveseat. "Did you say *pizza*?"

"Yeah, for the party."

"What party?"

"The one me and Ricardo are having here tonight."

"*Here*? Why not at your place?"

"Our house is a mess, Rey. We can't go there. Aunt Ro doesn't clean as good as she used to."

"Aunt Ro shouldn't be cleaning your apartment at all, *hermano*." Reynaldo gave him a playful punch in the arm.

"No? Then who is supposed to clean it?

"Pedro. . . ."

"It was Ricardo's idea to have it here. He said that you wouldn't mind."

Ricardo always said Reynaldo wouldn't mind, and each and every time Reynaldo *did* mind. "Wouldn't mind what?"

Pedro hesitated.

"If you want me to—"

"Yesterday, some *señoritas* came to the garage looking for you."

"Yeah, and?"

"They were from out of town and wanted to meet the great Reynaldo, the hero."

"I'm not a hero."

"The guy who helped capture the crazy Don Bailino?! Of course, you are!"

"I didn't—"

"Rey, you really gotta work on your publicity. You're missing out on a whole lotta *hooha*."

"I don't understand what this has to do with—"

"Well, you weren't there, at the garage, you were at the bank . . ."

"*And?*"

"Well . . . and Ricardo accidentally said that he was you, that *he* was Reynaldo."

"'Accidentally' . . ."

"Well," Pedro said, "both names *do* begin with the letter *R*. I don't know what Mama was thinking . . ."

"Funny how Ricardo doesn't get mixed up when the bill collectors come into the garage."

"And," Pedro continued, "the *señioritas* said they would stop by the garage this morning to set up a time—"

"Which is why you told me to stay home this morning." Reynaldo sat up on the couch. "It's all starting to make sense."

"You catch on quick, Rey." Pedro gazed at his reflection in the glass of the china closet. He fixed his hair. "In Ricardo's defense, the girls are awfully cute. Plus, your name is on the mailbox, so it will look good—you can even leave some of your mail around, maybe Ricardo will sign some junk mail that the girls can take home as souvenirs." Pedro smiled, happy with himself. "Anyway, you're changing the subject, Rey. Call her. You know you want to."

"I can't." Reynaldo wanted nothing more than to talk to Jamie again, but he was too ashamed. He had reacted badly when Jamie told him about the baby. It was selfish. And stupid. She would never forgive him. "So what time is this party?"

Pedro stuck the twenty-dollar bill into the front pocket of his jeans. "I hate to be the one to have to tell you this, Rey, but I don't think you're invited."

"You realize that this is *my* house, Pedro."

"I do realize that, yes."

"And that these girls think they are coming to see *me*."

"I know. Pity."

Reynaldo shook his head and got up from the couch. He grabbed his car keys from the kitchen counter and his leather jacket from the coatrack. "Do me a favor and don't make a mess. I expect the place to look like it does now."

"No *problema*, big brother." Pedro opened the door, ushering Reynado outside. "Oh, and if you see Aunt Ro, remind her that we prefer the raspberry scent in the bathroom, not the apple cinnamon."

"Pedro, I—"

"Don't come back before eleven, Rey. And, remember, knock first." Pedro shut the door.

Reynaldo stood alone on the porch of his home, his size-thirteen feet obscuring the *Welcome* on the worn mat outside his front door. The sun was setting, and a chill swept through the front yard, gently rocking the porch swing. He once imagined a truckload of children on that swing. He thought again of Jamie and hoped that she was okay.

His Ford Escort sat in the driveway like a tired old friend. Even though Pedro and Ricardo had repaired the car so that there was no visible damage from the crash two years ago, there still seemed to be scars that only Reynaldo could see. He got into the driver's seat, put his hands on the steering wheel, and glanced into the rearview mirror. Across the street, his neighbor was watering her garden, the sun reflecting off the metal gate, and for just a moment he thought he could see the headlights of Don Bailino's Ford Flex barreling down on him. He shook the image off, started the engine, and backed out of the driveway. As he headed north toward his Aunt Ro, his home got smaller and smaller in his rearview mirror until it disappeared. Yet, he had a feeling that no matter how hard he tried, his nightmares never would.

6

Bailino was escorted down a long hallway, his federally issued uniform folded neatly across his arms, still handcuffed at the wrist. On top of the clothing were his toiletries—deodorant, soap, and toothpaste. His medical paperwork had arrived at Stanton hours before he did—he had been cleared for general population—so he was able to bypass the usual round of evaluations. He was simply photographed, fingerprinted, palm-printed, assigned a prisoner identification number, for which an ID card had been prepared, and sent on his way, with the added bonus of shackles around his ankles. The whole intake process took no longer than twenty minutes.

He had had no personal belongings to submit—no photographs, cards, or even money—having come from the prison hospital. His gold cross, which had hung from his neck ever since he was an infant, a big, ornate thing that must have seemed ridiculous on a baby, had been taken off when he had arrived at Albany Memorial. Although it was returned to him after surgery, he gave it to Joey before his transfer to the prison hospital in Boston since the prison system prohibits the wearing of visible religious medals and most other jewelry. He missed the feel of the cold against his chest.

Bernie had been relieved, as had all of his day-crew cohorts, and a new set of guards had been assigned to Bailino, a trio of bright-eyed and bushy-tailed fellows who looked like they were ready to give him some fresh hell.

The leader of this little pack was a beefy gym-rat-type with a head of buzzed white hair that contrasted the narrow jet-black goatee that ran from the middle of his bottom lip to the end of his chin. He had a habit of cracking his neck by tilting his head to the left, which, even after only ten minutes, was getting on Bailino's nerves. His nametag read *Phil "Whitey" Whitestone*.

Phil and the gang led Bailino down a series of corridors, each new section of building separated by a thick metallic door through which they had to be buzzed, a harsh *beep* trumpeting their arrival every twenty yards or so.

"This way, newbie," Phil said after the fourth buzzer and led Bailino into a narrow corridor that opened up to a bi-level lobby-like section of the prison featuring double rows of prison cells. The inmates—notified by buzzer of each impending arrival—poked hands, noses, and mirrors through their cell bars in order to gawk at the incoming party.

Bailino looked straight ahead as the guards led him along the top-left row of cells and stopped at an empty unit at the far end. One of the guards waved his hand toward an office located within an alcove on an upper level, and there was another annoying beep—this one with a lower register—and the gate to the cell opened. Bailino gave a quick glance at his neighbor in the cell to the left—a scrawny old man, whose clothing appeared three sizes too big and who gazed at him with sad, sullen eyes—before stepping forward, but he was blocked by the arm of Phil.

"Uh-uh," Phil said. "Not so fast." One of the guards took Bailino's clothing and tossed it onto the cot in the cell. "This way first."

The guards had the cell gate closed and ushered Bailino around a few corners and through a long passageway that was musty and dank. As they rounded another bend, they came upon a guard seated at a desk before a wall of ceramic white. Eyeing Bailino, the guard nodded to their group and set off another buzzer, which opened a door behind him. Bailino then felt a not-so-gentle push forward and found himself in a large shower stall—a row of nozzles, resembling coat hooks, lined both the left and right walls. At the end of the large cavernous space were six inmates, cloaked in orange, staring back at him.

"Have fun, boys," Phil said with a smile before sealing the door shut, leaving Bailino with no one around him for the first time all day.

The men on the other side of the room were dark-skinned and full of ink. Three of them had their shirt sleeves rolled up to their elbows, and one had his hair back in a long ponytail that he had fashioned into a braid. Another was a bit lighter, a grizzled middle-aged guy with jet black hair with gray around the temples. Bailino glanced around the large room. There were two high-barred windows on the far side that seemed to be getting the last of the direct sunlight, which meant, Bailino assumed, they were facing west. On the right and left sides, a chain of vents about a square foot in size were covered with metal grates. Other than that, it was all metal piping and ceramic. The showers were the only rooms at Stanton without security cameras.

One of the inmates on the other side moved toward the center of the room—careful, labored steps—and the remaining five followed suit. Bailino did the same until he was only seven or eight feet from the leader of the group. The guy facing Bailino had a tattoo of a tear just below his left eye, and Bailino smirked.

"Juan Alvarez." Bailino stuck out his right hand, curling his left shackled wrist behind it. "I remember you when you were *this big*. How long has it been?"

"Long time, *amigo*," Alvarez said. He took a step forward and shook Bailino's hand.

"Been treating you okay in here?"

"I get by." Alvarez glanced at the entrance. "We don't have much time."

"You got it?" Bailino asked.

Alvarez gestured to the guy on his right, who came forward and handed Bailino a folded piece of tape. Bailino shoved it into his mouth.

"You sure you want to do this? It may be safer for you in here than it is out there."

"I know," Bailino said. "But I gotta go."

"You may have some time," Alvarez said. "I hear they don't plan on doing it right away. Want you to suffer some. Want to know about Leo." Alvarez tilted his head, as if he wanted to know about Leo, too.

"I figured as much," Bailino said. "You know, your mother came to see me at the hospital. Early on."

Alvarez's eye, the one with the tear tattoo, twitched imperceptibly, and his square jaw softened. "How did she look?"

"She looked good, said the medication was helping with the pain."

"I don't get to see her much. Always in solitary," Alvarez said. "Thank you for what you did for her. I don't know what she woulda done if you hadn't hired her at Upackk. Obamacare ain't gonna pay for that shit."

"Don't worry about it."

Alvarez rolled the sleeves of his orange shirt up to his elbow, like the inmates. "Ready?" he asked, and the other inmates straightened.

Bailino got down on his knees. "Go ahead."

Alvarez cleared his throat. "Welcome to Stanton, old timer!" he shouted in the direction of the wall separating them from the guards. With that, the six men leaped toward Bailino and beat the shit out of him.

7

amie stared at the nightlight in the corner of her bedroom. A short in the wall was causing it to blink ever so slightly, and she watched the series of flashes as if looking for a pattern, a message from the unknown telling her that everything was going to be all right.

Now that Bailino was locked away in prison, presumably forever, she was supposed to finally put everything behind her, get on with her life, and plan for the future, both hers and her daughter's. And she was ready to, but as the day turned into night, a sense of dread had come over her, and she had begun to feel more fearful than ever. She felt for the gun on her calf. With the FBI agents gone, she had decided to sleep with it, but she had a feeling she wouldn't get any sleep at all. She got out of bed and twisted the nightlight off, felt her way back, and pulled the covers over her head, letting the darkness settle over her like an extra blanket.

There was a knock on her bedroom door. "Is everything all right?" Edward asked.

Edward must have heard her moving around. "Everything is fine," Jamie lied.

She heard him tiptoe away. Outside her bedroom window, the colorful backsides of the three-story houses lined up like a rainbow, their fire escapes zigzagging down their facades like snakes. The isolation of Bailino's log cabin had turned Jamie off to wide open spaces, and she decided to trade in the grassy front lawns and fenced-in backyards of Massapequa for a small apartment in a two-family home in Glendale, Queens, a neighborhood cramped with people and not far from a busy supermarket, diner, and city park.

Of course, Edward had balked. With Jamie living in his basement apartment, Edward felt he could keep her and Faith safe, but Jamie knew the move was good for him, too. The two of them needed to learn to let go.

Jamie's phone beeped, signaling that she had received a text. She reached over to the night table where her phone was charging. She swiped the screen and was surprised to see a familiar name:

Reynaldo: Jamie, hi. How are you? I just wanted to say that I was thinking about you today. The news is stirring all this stuff up, and it's hard to escape. I mean . . . You know what I mean. Are you OK? You don't have to text back if you don't want to. Sorry this is coming to you so late—were you asleep? I've wanted to send it all day and finally worked up the nerve. It will probably be morning when you read this. If you read it at all. Maybe you'll delete it. Maybe you're busy. I'm sorry. I'm babbling. Don't worry if you can't write back. I know you have a lot on your mind. I guess that's it. Good night. Please kiss Baby Faith for me. I think about her too. Signed, Reynaldo. P.S. I feel terrible for the way things ended. And hope you don't hate me. I am an idiot. P.P.S. Aunt Ro says hi.

Jamie unplugged her phone and placed it on her pillow next to her head. She reread the text. For a second time, Don Bailino had brought Jamie and Reynaldo together, two people who probably never would have met otherwise. It was a reminder that sometimes in darkness, there is light. She closed her eyes and smiled. Her first real smile of the day.

8

The *bong* of the doorbell reverberated in the dark bedroom.

"For Pete's sake," Mary said, turning on the light. "Who the hell can that be?"

Paolo slowly turned over onto his back, the rigidity of his bones making the task take longer than it should. He glanced at the clock on his night stand. It was 10:15.

Mary flipped the blankets back and stood up, using her hands to make sure all the rollers in her hair were still there. She stood in front of the window. Her curvy silhouette was more rounded at her hips than it had once been, but Paolo had to admit, hump notwithstanding, she was still a good-looking woman.

Mary reached for her robe, which was hanging on one of the bed posts. The doorbell bonged again.

"Ain't you gonna get that?" Paolo asked.

"What do you think I'm doing? I gotta put my robe on first. I can't just go down there with my boobs flopping around."

"Why not? You flop them around here all the time."

"Yeah, well, that's because it's just you." Mary slipped on the robe, cinched it at the waist, and shuffled over to the closet.

"Now what?" Paolo asked.

"I need my slippers."

"Why don't you get your purse and raincoat, too?" Paolo growled.

Mary waved a dismissive hand and left the bedroom.

Paolo reached to turn on the light. Mary had attached a thick cord to the switch on the lamp so that he would be better able to grasp it. After a two-minute struggle, there was finally a click and light spilled into the bedroom, giving the old blue wallpaper a greenish tint. He heard shuffling, and Mary returned.

"It's Marco," she said. "Should I have him come up here?"

"If he wants to talk to me tonight, you will. Otherwise, by the time I get myself downstairs it will be next Thursday." Paolo tried to sit himself up in bed.

"Oh, let me help you."

"I can do it," Paolo huffed, but accepted Mary's help anyway. "Oh, and—"

"Yeah, I know, make myself scarce." Mary adjusted Paolo's breathing tubes in his nose. "Am I poking you?"

"I'll give you a poke," Paolo said with a nudge. "Send the kid in."

As Mary left, Marco Celli popped in his head, a lopsided smile on his face. The kid looked so much younger than his fifty years, probably because he didn't have a worry in the world. He still lived at home, with his parents, and didn't have to be concerned about paying for food, gas, electricity, or any of the thousands of channels he had on cable television, which is probably why Paolo still considered him a kid. He wasn't the brightest pencil in the pencil case—not that it mattered. Fran's brother had gotten him a job with the New York Port Authority after he dropped out of college for the third time, and after twenty years of twiddling his thumbs on the taxpayers' dime, Marco was now retired, living large on a New York City pension, which was spent on who knows what, since his utilities were already paid for, and was probably doing twenty times better than half of the little shits who terrorized him in public school.

It wasn't until Marco stepped all the way in that Paolo noticed the kid had put on a ton of weight, probably from all that *not working*. And he had a full head of hair, too—what a goddamn waste. Still, he was a good kid who was eager to make Paolo happy. And Paolo needed him.

"Jesus, kid. You reek. Did you rob a cologne store?"

"Hi, Uncle Paolo." He bent down and kissed Paolo on both sides of the face. "I hope I wasn't interrupting anything."

"Nah, what are you talking about? I was expecting you. Is it done?"

Marco peeked through the bedroom door, presumably to make sure his Aunt Mary wasn't there. "Yes."

Paolo chuckled. "Lemmee see."

Marco dug into his pocket and pulled out a cell phone. He swiped it a few times and showed Paolo a photo of Don Bailino in an orange jumpsuit curled up on a ceramic-tiled floor, bruises to his face, his ankles shackled.

Paolo howled with laughter. "How do you like that, *you fuck*?" he barked at the phone.

"Uncle Paolo . . ."

"Where did you get the phone, kid?"

"Disposable. Target had them on sale, but—"

"Good. Paid in cash?"

"Yeah, but—"

"Even better. Let me see the photo again . . ."

Marco held the phone up closer to Paolo's face, and Paolo gazed at it with satisfaction.

"Okay, kid," Paolo said, "what's with all the buts?"

"We didn't get any information from Bailino. They asked about Leo, but he said we should go fuck ourselves," Marco said glumly.

"That's what I was hoping for." Paolo gave Marco's cheeks a light slap with his shaky palm.

"Wait, I don't understand . . ."

"Never mind," Paolo said. "Early tomorrow morning, I want you to reach out to someone. Open the drawer. I need you to write something down. I got a paper and pencil in there."

"Tomorrow morning? How early?" Marco opened the drawer and pulled out a notepad and pencil.

Paolo sighed. "You can do without your beauty sleep for one night, kid," he said and relayed the name and phone number. "You need to send a text to that number and then get rid of that phone."

"What should the text say, Uncle Paolo?"

Paolo's eyes narrowed and his thin lips curled into a smile. "Three words: *Burn it down*."

9

The news media gathered on the grounds of the Executive Mansion, fanning out across the long red-brick driveway as far back as the black iron rails of the perimeter fence. Phillip viewed them from his office bathroom. It had been a long time since he had allowed so many press people inside the gates. He reached for his necktie hanging from the corner of a shelf, twisted it into place, and looked into the mirror.

"They're really buzzing around out there, aren't they?" Katherine called, with more excitement than he'd heard from her years. She poked her head into the bathroom. "It's as if they know something," she said with a devilish smile.

"You think?" he asked, fiddling with his tie.

"That you met with Clark yesterday about a possible run for president?" She pushed his hands away and knotted his tie. "It's only what every political reporter has been speculating about for months." Katherine's cell phone buzzed, and she looked at the Caller ID. "Ugh, it's that Jim Olsen again from *The New York Times*. Remember that puff piece they ran on you last fall?"

"Yeah."

"Well, that apparently means that I owe him one, and he's been bothering me for scoops ever since."

"You know the game, Katherine. What does he want to know?"

"He wants an exclusive on your announcement, I'm sure, as if every reporter in the country isn't already here and talking about it."

"They do look especially excited, don't they?" Phillip peeked outside the window again. The reporters were chitchatting animatedly as if they were about to watch a parade. "I didn't think I was all that exciting, frankly."

"People want change, Phillip." She grabbed his hand and pulled him out of the bathroom. "The current administration is winding down. There's rampant speculation about who will make the list on both sides, who can carry their respective party to victory. And, if you ask me, you're at the top of that list. Now, let me look at you." She put her hand to her chin and studied him, head to toe. "Yes, the blue suit was a good choice. Warm, but not too cuddly. Likeable, but serious. Good for holding babies and vetoing bills. Very presidential."

Phillip rarely felt like a grown-up, let alone presidential, but he enjoyed his wife's enthusiasm. "I'll be as presidential I can, while being as coy as I can. Will that make you happy?"

"Very. Let me grab my phone. I think I left it on your desk," Katherine said when there was a knock at the office door.

When Phillip opened it, the strange face caught him off-guard, but he remembered that, with the bigger media presence, Wilcox had left a few agents behind. Phillip was glad. He needed the extra manpower to keep the bag-check and metal detector lines from spilling out onto Eagle Street.

Phillip nodded a greeting. "Yes, what is it, ah . . .?"

"Brandon, sir."

"Yes, Brandon, are they ready for me?" Phillip gave his tie one last quick pat.

"I've been advised to tell you to turn on your television, sir."

"Television?"

"Phillip . . ." Katherine was looking at her phone. Her face appeared ashen.

"What is it?" Phillip asked. He picked up the remote control on his desk and turned on the television. As the screen warmed, an aerial view from a CNN helicopter showed a billowing fire, flames deep red and yellow shooting into the sky from the roof of a large warehouse. A line of fire trucks circled the facility, which was collapsing panel by panel under the intense heat despite the arches of hose water trying to combat the blaze.

"Jesus, what building is that?" Phillip asked.

Katherine nodded to Brandon, who closed the door to the office. She put her hand on her husband's shoulder. "It's Upackk," she said.

"What?" Phillip stared at the screen.

A leading distributor of shipping, industrial, and packing materials, Upackk operated seven warehouses across the country— including this one located in Albany—and had almost single-handedly revolutionized the loose-filled packing and cushioning business. The company employed hundreds of people within a fifty-mile radius and had been Bailino's pride and joy. Phillip moved closer to the screen. Tiny pieces of shredded paper—perhaps remnants of Bailino's award-winning packing materials—filled the air, along with the ash and smoke, coating the ground with what looked like black confetti.

"Was anyone hurt?" he asked. He tried to listen to the commentary, but the CNN anchor was talking on the phone to an apparent eyewitness who had virtually nothing concrete to say.

"I don't know. I don't think so." Katherine read her smartphone screen. "They're reporting that the fire started early this morning. Quote . . . *Witnesses reported seeing the company of Don Bailino go up in flames just after eight o'clock* . . . Unquote."

Technically, Phillip knew that Upackk was no longer Bailino's company. Bailino had cleverly passed ownership to eighteen-year-old Joey Santelli, descendant of the notorious Cataldi crime family, whom he had mentored over the years, and managed to keep the company running despite his legal troubles. Officially, Joey was CEO, but while he was away at college the company was being run by a guy named George, who had been promoted from Albany warehouse supervisor to vice president and handled the day-to-day operations. Phillip knew that George had also been an FBI mole for years. The FBI long suspected Upackk was a front of some kind, but nothing had ever been proven—even with a guy on the inside.

Still, despite its questionable legal dealings, the company was beloved locally. It offered jobs and stability in a volatile economy, not to mention onsite childcare and laundry services, and its workers were grateful. It never ceased to amaze Phillip what people would excuse in order to put food on the table or money in their pockets. Even with the company's founder deemed a felon, it had been business as usual for Upackk for two years. Until today.

CNN kept switching its views of the fire, the voices of the commentators changing. "What's going on?" Phillip asked. "What building is that? That doesn't look like New York."

"It's not." Katherine stood closer to the TV. "That's Upackk's Texas facility." She pointed to the bottom of the screen, which read, *West Dallas, Texas.*

"Texas? Jesus, how many warehouses are burning?"

Katherine consulted her smartphone and took a breath. "All of them."

"All seven? What the hell is going on?" Phillip said when a chill went through him. If these fires were what he thought they were, there hadn't been this level of mob activity in years. He looked outside again at the throng of reporters. Their excitement suddenly took on a different meaning.

Katherine joined him at the office window. Her phone buzzed, and she showed him the screen. It read: *Olsen from the Times.* She silenced the call. "You'll have to postpone the press briefing," she said.

"Postpone?"

"Phillip, you can't have people remembering that Phillip Grand first spoke about a possible candidacy for president as the capital of New York was burning to the ground."

The land line rang, and Katherine picked it up. "Katherine Grand . . ." She listened. "Uh-huh . . . uh-huh . . . I'll be right there," she said before hanging up. "That was the comptroller's office. You need to meet with the board of fire commissioners."

Another knock at the door startled them.

"Come in," Phillip said.

The door opened, and across the threshold, Rosalia was holding Phillip Jr. in her arms and Charlotte by the hand. Both children were dressed in their Sunday best—Philly in a navy blue suit to match his father's and Charlotte in a red, white, and blue spring dress. Philly's hair had been gelled and combed to the side, while Charlotte's springy curls were bouncing freely atop her head.

"Daddy," she exclaimed with a twirl. "Look at me!"

"Daddy's busy right now, Charlotte," Katherine said, joining Rosalia and the kids in the hallway.

"You look beautiful, Charlie," Phillip said. He approached them, but Katherine held up her hand.

"You"—she pointed at him—"get to work. That's an order." She turned her attention to the nanny. "Rosalia, it's a false alarm. It looks like there will not be a media briefing today."

"No?" Rosalia asked, confused.

"But, Mommy, I'm wearing my special flag pin." Charlotte pointed to the collar of her dress.

"I'm sorry, dear," Katherine said, "but we're going to have to reschedule."

Confused, Charlotte looked at Rosalia.

"Mommy says we smile at the TV cameras another day," Rosalia translated.

"Don't worry, Charlie," Phillip said, "you'll get to show off your pretty dress soon and—"

"You're dawdling, Phillip," Katherine said. "You need to get on the phone with the board."

Phillip frowned. "But what exactly—"

"Gee, if only we had a press secretary," Katherine said, grabbing Charlotte's hand and closing the door to Phillip's office.

Phillip returned to his desk, nearly bumping into that damn antique pistol display again, and opened a Word document, but he couldn't focus. His thoughts turned to Jamie Carter, as they always did when there was a media matter. He knew he needed a press secretary, probably now more than ever, but as Bailino's company burned on the screen behind him, the last thing he wanted to do was drag her back into this mess—unless, he feared, she already had been.

10

Bailino stared at the dirty ceiling, the vision in his right eye blurred from the swelling that came at the hands of Alvarez and his gang. The guards had carried Bailino to the infirmary, where he stayed long enough for some quack to throw a Band-Aid on a cut on his nose before shuffling him off to his new home—a six-by-eight cell.

The solitude suited Bailino just fine. Isolation was usually something he sought by choice. It gave him time to think, and over the past two years, that's pretty much all he had done, using the bed rest, the stillness, to think deeply and meditate, to will his body to heal, cell by cell. Over time, his keen senses had become even keener. He had learned to distinguish footfalls and speech patterns—he could tell which nurse was on duty simply by the way she pushed the mobile aneroid sphygmomanometer across the hospital floor. He could tell what the cafeteria was serving for lunch long before he received the daily menu and knew how hard it was raining by the smudge of the cardiologist's mascara.

Every now and again, he thought of Jamie Carter. He could still envision her sleeping face on his pillow, the way she held Charlotte Grand in her arms. He remembered her determination when she shot him in the chest, the rage he had felt, and also the love.

"Hey, Bailino."

From the corner of his eye, Bailino saw one of the guards—a

black guy with a beer belly they called Hop—stop at his cell. All morning, as the news of the Upackk fires spread throughout the prison, the guards had paraded by, one by one, to offer their condolences, which consisted of throwing lit matches through Bailino's bars and citing lines from films such as *The Towering Inferno* and Stephen King's *The Firestarter*. Some of them were laughing so hard that they had to be reprimanded by the warden. He imagined it was Hop's turn for a little fun.

"Sorry to hear about your company, man," the guard said instead. "That's some serious shit. Looks like somebody's real mad at you. Damn, my sister's baby daddy worked at Upackk. You know that?"

Bailino lay motionless, his eyes on the ceiling.

"First job he'd been able to keep." Hop said. "My sister had a hard enough time getting child support from that fool because he was always so damn lit. Guy finally cleans up his act, and this happens. Go figure. You think he'll qualify for unemployment?"

Bailino didn't answer, nor did he think Hop expected him to.

"Anyway, it seemed like a nice building you had there. Musta taken a lot of years to do that—and all by yourself."

Hop shuffled away and began to whistle a melancholy tune before stopping to reprimand an inmate a few cell blocks down for clogging the toilet with one of his shoes.

Bailino turned his body gently to face the wall and pressed his bruised cheeks to the cool concrete. As instructed, Alvarez and his men had concentrated the punches on Bailino's face and arms, where his skin was exposed and the bruises visible, staying away from his vital organs and particularly his chest, where Bailino had had his surgeries. He ran his finger inside his T-shirt to feel for the surgical scars, a habit of his, before reaching under his tongue and pulling out the piece of tape Alvarez's man had given him. He unfolded it and read the hastily scribbled penmanship: *415.*

There had been three escape attempts at Stanton in the past thirty years, none of them successful. The first guy tried to scale the fence in the recreation yard, and he ended up impaling himself and spending weeks in the infirmary. The second guy took a guard hostage and made it all the way to the prison library before another guard took him out, although he managed to slice the throat of the guard he was holding and kill him before he died.

The third attempt had been made by none other than Gino Cataldi, who decided, years before death row, that he wanted to go out in a blaze of glory. He got his hand on a piece and planned to shoot his way through the prison gates or die trying. He did neither. The piece jammed, and the extent of Gino's damage had been only to delay the lunch hour of a handful of prison guards.

Gino's next plan had been the opposite: to sneak out. He had Bailino look into all aspects of Stanton's history—blueprints, photographs, newspaper articles, anything he could get his hands on. Stanton was originally built in the 1800s, which was considered the heyday of the New York prison system. Rumor had it that the prison was built atop a labyrinth of underground passageways that once served as a way for the prison help to go to and from work, leaving their horses, and eventually their cars, far enough from the prison so that the convicts couldn't get at them. Bailino could never confirm this and decided that had been some kind of legend, stories that inmates told one another to give each other hope or to whip up a sense of mystery as their days ran into one another. As far as Bailino could tell, there was only one way out of Stanton: through the front door.

Bailino slowly got up from the cot and planted his feet on the floor. He felt good, considering. He walked toward the cell bars; a guard, about ten yards away, was whistling the theme to the *Lone Ranger* and heading in his direction. Bailino placed the piece of tape on the floor near the bars. Prison worked a lot like the outside—proper documentation was required to get anything done, validating the procedure and keeping everyone on task and on the same page so there would be no mistakes. He quickly walked to the back of his cell just as the shadow of the guard appeared.

"Hey, Bailino," the guard said, "did you hear the one about the mobster who spent twenty years building a company only to have it burn to the ground?" He had one of those staccato machine-gun laughs and proceeded to shoot up this section of the cellblock with it. "Don't worry, fella. You'll be able to make another factory when you get out of here. Oh, wait . . ." And he laughed again.

Bailino glanced at the guard's nametag with his good eye: *Adam Jensen*. He had a line of pockmarks along his cheeks that brought to mind Leo Cataldi.

"You eyeballing me, fella?" Jensen asked.

Bailino turned back around and cooled his other cheek on the cell wall until he heard the guard grunt and trundle away—*shuffle, tap, pause, shuffle, tap, pause*—down the corridor. When it was quiet again, Bailino returned to his cot. He lay down, pulled the threadbare blanket up to his chest, and turned so that he could see with his good eye the spot where he had placed the piece of tape. It was gone.

11

J amie pushed Faith in the swing, the air flowing through her wispy dark brown bangs, which blew away from her face with every arc forward. The park was crowded today. The dribble of basketballs mixed with the sounds of the light traffic along Central Avenue, and children scurried around, their mothers shouting after them in a variety of languages with sippy cups and Ziploc bags of snacks. The noise comforted Jamie like a protective netting, making her feel shielded and anonymous. She was glad that she had decided to take a walk while Edward ran some errands.

"What a beautiful little girl you have there," said a mother who plopped a toddler boy into the swing beside Faith's.

"Thank you," Jamie said with a smile.

Faith was one of those children who blossomed in the sunlight. She had simple needs and often wanted nothing more than to stretch her legs and run. When Faith cried as an infant, Jamie found that if she carried her to a window that the daylight alone would calm her, Faith's eyes drawn to the sky, the clouds, and the trees. As a little girl, Jamie had been more of what they now call an *indoor child*, studious and shy. It was only lately that she, herself, was learning to appreciate the outdoors.

A gray Escalade with tinted windows came screeching down Central Avenue, drawing the attention of the moms and dads, who instinctively grabbed for their children. Jamie's heart thumped, as it often did with sudden noises, and she stopped the swing with her hand. She had become wary of large SUVs. The car pulled into a parking spot and jerked to a halt.

When no one emerged, Jamie felt for the gun on her calf with her other leg, as had become her habit, stuck her hands under Faith's armpits, and pulled her from the swing. Faith cried in protest and straightened her legs, and one of her sneakers got caught in the leg holes. Jamie tried to wrench it out when the driver's side door of the Escalade opened and out walked Bob.

Jamie hadn't seen Bob in about a year, since she moved to Queens, but she could recognize him anywhere. Whatever the setting, he had an air of detachment that made him look as if he were walking in front of a green screen background. Dressed in clothing that probably cost more money than she paid in a month's rent, he exuded an air of superiority that she was more than familiar with. When he lifted his designer sunglasses from the bridge of his nose to take in his surroundings, he pressed out his chest, as if he were showing off muscles that he didn't have. Bob beeped his car alarm and headed right for Jamie.

"I thought I saw you in here," he called to her. "I just stopped by your place."

"What happened to the PT Cruiser?" Jamie asked, placing Faith back into the swing and giving her a push. The little girl watched Bob suspiciously, her dark brown eyes in sharp focus.

"Nah, I traded it in. Wanted something new." He checked out the mom pushing the little boy next to them. "A little cramped around here, isn't it? This must be what Ellis Island looked like."

"I like it."

Bob nodded, but Jamie could tell he didn't approve. There were too many strange faces, too much noise, too many distractions. Jamie knew that if Bob were in a public place, he much rather preferred to have all eyes on him.

"She got so big." Bob motioned clumsily toward Faith. He had always been awkward around kids. When Edward's children were little, they had a tendency to climb all over Bob during holiday get-togethers, like a cat who manages to find the one person with a cat allergy. Bob would make every excuse to leave. "How's Edward?"

"He's fine."

"He must be logging some serious miles with you so far away."

"He's getting used to it," Jamie said, waiting for the real reason Bob was there. He never paid her a social visit. Even when they were married. "So what can I do for you, Bob?"

Bob scratched at his five o'clock shadow, a signal that Jamie knew meant he wanted something. "This whole Bailino thing is drudging this stuff up again."

"Yeah, I know. Hopefully, yesterday was the end of it," she said, but from the look on Bob's face, Jamie could tell that he hoped it wasn't.

"My publisher called me yesterday," he said.

Bob said the word *publisher* as if it were laced with gold.

"She said the sales of the book have been through the roof this week," he said. "And with the paperbacks about to—"

"The answer is no, Bob." Jamie stopped swinging Faith, whose eyelids had begun to droop.

"James, you haven't even heard what I'm about to say. This could help Faith."

Jamie gently pulled Faith from the swing, making sure her sneakers didn't get stuck this time. "Don't bring her into this."

"I'm not. It's you. You're being selfish."

"*I'm* being selfish?" She placed Faith into the stroller, and the little girl snuggled against the wool princess blanket Trish had bought her. Jamie buckled her in.

"You're missing out on the opportunity for a boatload of cash." Bob lowered his voice so that the woman swinging her child next to them couldn't hear. "These publishers pay stupid money. And I didn't even have to write the damn thing. They hired some flunky to talk to me for a couple of hours, and now I'm an author. It's the greatest racket going. Think of her college fund."

"How about I think about her life? I won't sell out my daughter, or myself." Jamie adjusted Faith's blanket and kicked off the stroller brake. "You do what you have to do. Nobody's stopping you." She pushed Faith toward Central Avenue.

Bob walked beside her. "Do you know what it would mean to have an exclusive on your story? Do you know how much they would *pay*?"

"You gave your own account of what happened, which was enough—and wrong, by the way."

"Well, what do you expect?" Bob jumped in front of her, and she stopped. "You wouldn't tell me what happened, which shouldn't surprise me. You didn't tell me anything even when we were married."

"Please, like you cared." Jamie maneuvered the stroller around him.

"Okay, you think my version of events is wrong? Fine. This is your chance to set the record straight."

"You really don't get it, do you? I just want to move on."

Bob gestured to the rows of colorful brick housing. "And move here, apparently."

"That's right."

"What about Edward? Maybe I should ask him."

"Edward wants to beat the shit out of you." Jamie said too loudly, attracting the attention of several moms who were loading their children into a minivan. She lowered her voice. "You completely misrepresented things—including Edward, *especially* Edward—in that book of yours."

"He's just pissed off that I got Grand's legal roundtable position and he didn't."

"Think whatever you want, but if I were you, I wouldn't go anywhere near Edward."

Bob threw up his hands. "What was I expecting? The Carter siblings—united in their idealism. Do-gooders, patriots, heroes . . . How is it possible for anyone to live up to their impossible standards?"

"It's not that hard actually . . ." Jamie said, but then took a breath.

She wasn't going to get pulled into an argument. "Listen, Bob, you must have known I wouldn't want anything to do with this book. I'm past all that."

"Jamie, who are you kidding with this strong and brave act? I saw the way you looked at the Escalade before you knew it was me in there. You looked scared shitless. You forget, I knew you before you became the hero of the world and the cover girl for *People* magazine."

"Did it ever occur to you that you don't know me at all?" she said.

"And who does, Jamie? C'mon. The Spanish guy from upstate?"

"Leave Reynaldo out of this." Jamie quickened her pace. "You don't know anything about him. Just like you don't know about anything that happened two years ago. That book of yours might as well be a novel."

"Oh, sure, tough girl. You probably showed more assertiveness in the last five minutes that you did our entire marriage. So, what? You're Ms. Big and Strong, now?"

"Maybe I am."

"Yeah, sure. Too bad all that fearlessness couldn't keep Bailino's dick from going inside you."

Jamie jerked the stroller to a stop. "You son of a bitch." She glanced at Faith, who was asleep, as if she could understand what Bob had said even if she had been awake. "Stay away from me and my daughter. If I see you again, I will not only call the police, but I will call Governor Grand and personally ask him to remove you from his legal roundtable."

"Bullshit." Bob's face reddened, and Jamie could tell she had gotten under his skin. That roundtable position in Albany meant everything to Bob and had gotten him a regular seat on the Sunday news shows. "You wouldn't have the nerve."

"Oh, no? Try me, asshole. I think that guy owes me a solid. And as far as I'm concerned, doing that would be all the gratitude I need." Jamie turned on her heel and continued pushing the stroller. She felt the eyes of the parents in the park and was fearful that they would recognize her. She didn't want to have to move again.

"Jamie," Bob called, his voice softer. "Wait, don't go."

She ignored him, the tears welling in her eyes. Bob had hit a nerve, too.

"He asked how you were doing again, you know," Bob called. "Governor Grand, I mean. I'll see him tomorrow, if you want me to . . ."

Bob's voice became a whisper, drowned out by the sounds of her new neighborhood as Jamie hurried down the city block. The traffic light turned green, and Jamie hurried the stroller across Central Avenue, turning onto a side street toward home and hoping that Bob would climb into his Escalade, head back to his life of bestselling books and talk shows, and leave her and Faith alone. She may have needed him once to hold her up, especially after her mother had died, but she didn't need his money or his help anymore, and as far as she was concerned, she never would again.

12

Reynaldo whistled as he pulled the rear tire off the raised SUV and switched it with the front tire, which was leaning against the wall of the garage. He hand-tightened the lug nuts for each wheel and moved to the other side of the vehicle.

Pedro pushed through the garage door and zipped up his overalls. "Well, you're here early. The birds aren't even up yet." He listened. "And you're whistling Miley Cyrus. You must be in a good mood."

"And why shouldn't I be?" Reynaldo performed a slow waltz with the back tire before pushing it onto the axle and securing it into place.

"What's with him?" Ricardo asked, marching into the garage behind Pedro.

Pedro shook his head. "Don't know. I think he's finally lost it. He needs a woman."

"Speaking of women . . ." Reynaldo tightened the last of the lug nuts. "How did it go last night?"

Ricardo ducked behind a clipboard, grabbed a set of keys, and headed toward a minivan parked outside.

"It went that well, huh?" Reynaldo asked.

"It didn't go at all." Pedro pulled on a pair of gloves. "The girls never showed."

"Smart girls," Reynaldo said. He pushed a button, and the raised car started its descent to the ground. "So what did you do?"

"Never mind that," Pedro said. "Why are you in such a good mood?"

"Why, you ask?" Reynaldo dug into his pocket and pulled out his cell phone. He swiped the screen and shoved it in front of Pedro's face.

"Geez, Rey, not so close." Pedro pushed Reynaldo's hand back and read the screen:

Jamie: Hi. It's so nice to hear from you. No, I don't hate you. How could I hate you?? Things were just a bit crazy back then. I understand that it was a lot to take in. I don't expect anyone, really, even Edward, to understand completely. I'm okay. Today was okay too. Trying to move on. Hopefully, this is the end. Or is it the beginning? :) Thank you for asking about Faith. She is good. A happy little girl. As it should be. Write to me again if you like. Your text brought a smile to my face. Jamie.

"Nice, Rey," Pedro said. "So you finally took my advice and called her. You should do that more often, *hermano*. Take my advice, I mean."

Ricardo drove the minivan into the second bay of the garage. "Did you tell him yet?" he asked Pedro through the open window.

"Tell me what?" Reynaldo said, crossing his arms. "Do I really want to know?"

"I hate to ruin your good mood, Rey," Pedro said.

"Consider it already ruined, Pedro. What is it?"

Pedro took a deep breath. "Papa's coming."

"What?" Reynaldo said as Ricardo rolled the minivan window up and locked the driver's side door. "When?"

"Today," Pedro said.

"*Today?*" Reynaldo said. "What do you mean *today*? Where is he staying?"

"Where else? By you, Rey." Pedro threw a dirty rag against the window of the minivan. "Stop being a scaredy-cat, Ricky, and come out of the car," but Ricardo put his hands to his ears, pretending not to hear him.

"How long have you known this?" Reynaldo asked.

"Known what?"

Reynaldo grabbed at Pedro, who ran to the other side of the minivan, but not before Reynaldo got a handful of his overalls and yanked him back.

"Easy, Rey, you're going to pull off my nametag," Pedro said, trying to shove him.

"What does it matter, *hermano*?" Reynaldo wrestled Pedro to the ground. "You go around pretending to be me anyway."

"All right, already, Rey, get off," Pedro said. Reynaldo let go of his brother, and they both sat on the floor. "Papa left a message on your house phone last week."

"Last week?" Reynaldo asked. "What did it say?"

Pedro shrugged his shoulders, and Reynaldo moved to grab him again. "No, really, Rey, I don't know. Ricardo"—Pedro pointed at Ricardo in the car window, but when their eyes met Ricardo ducked under the dashboard—"saw the light beeping, and he pressed the button, but when Papa started to talk, he leaned on it and erased the message."

Reynaldo sighed and lay back on the floor. He had to get rid of that old answering machine.

"Then last night, when me and Ricky were . . . waiting for the girls, he called again to remind you to pick him up from the airport tonight."

"Do you at least know the airline?"

"Southwest." Pedro rolled his eyes. "I'm not an idiot, Rey."

Reynaldo looked around the garage. It was a mess. His father was a stickler for clean workstations. He was going to flip. Reynaldo would have to fix the place up or else he and his brothers would have to endure lectures—mostly in Spanish—for the duration of his father's visit, however long that was going to be. "Okay, your punishment, *mi hermano*, is you and Ricardo get to pick up Papa."

"Oh, no, I can't be around him," Pedro said. "He smells like old people. Plus, he left the message for *you*."

"Ricardo can pretend he's me. Now that he's had practice, it should be easy."

"You know I get lost at the airport, Rey," Pedro said.

"Ah, you'll figure it out, *hermano*." Reynaldo slapped him on the back. "I have faith."

Reynaldo banged on the minivan's window until Ricardo rolled it open. "It's not my fault, Rey," he said.

"It's never your fault, Ricky. C'mon, let's go. We have things to do."

Reynaldo went into the garage office and took a look around. Suddenly, everything looked old and worn. Maybe now was the time to get his father to agree to some renovations, he thought. The guy was such a cheapskate. Business had been good, particularly after the incident with Charlotte Grand. Reynaldo had been asking for years to make a few changes—maybe bring in some vending machines. He even thought about selling Aunt Ro's fresh banana bread each morning; the smell alone could boost business. He gathered up a few old magazines as Pedro and Ricardo entered.

"Do we have time to paint?" Pedro asked.

"Very funny," Reynaldo said. "I'm going to run home, straighten up a bit, and come back," he said. "It shouldn't take me more than a few hours."

"It's going to take a few hours just to fix the toilet," Ricardo said.

"Toilet?" Reynaldo asked.

Ricardo's eyes grew wide, and he pointed at Pedro.

"Oh, did I forget to mention that?" Pedro asked. He stepped behind the office counter as if that would protect him. "I think there's something wrong with the toilet on the first floor of your house."

"Why doesn't that surprise me?" Reynaldo flipped the *We're Open* sign so that it faced outward. "Do me a favor, and try not to burn the place down while I'm gone."

"¡Aye, aye, *capitán*!" Ricardo said.

"He's joking, idiot," Pedro said.

"You're an idiot."

"If it makes you feel any better, you're both idiots," Reynaldo said and ran out the front door toward his car.

13

Paolo, a ratty blanket wrapped around him, was sitting on the patio listening to a tinny radio broadcast the day's news. He was always so damn cold. The chain-link fence that connected his Brooklyn backyard with the next rattled from a breeze, or maybe it was from old age or neglect. There was a time when the families on the block would sit out there this time of day to trade stories and drink wine. Nowadays, it was like a ghost town. People were spending so much time inside playing their dopey video games and binge-watching shows that they slapped themselves silly with sunscreen—even on rainy days—just to throw out the garbage. As a result, what was once a vibrant community now resembled a zombie apocalypse—dead gardens, unused pools, dirty and chipped birdbaths that even the sparrows avoided. Paolo couldn't remember the last time anyone used his hot tub, which sat in the corner of the yard like a discarded relic. He was afraid of what he might find under the lid.

"Did you walk to the corner yet today, Paolo?" Mary asked, setting a can of ginger ale with a bendy straw next to him. "You know the doctor said that Parkinson's advances more quickly if you just sit around. You need to move."

"I think *you* need to move," Paolo said. "To New Jersey might be nice."

"Very funny, Mister Grumpy." Mary was wearing a purple sweater and a long black skirt.

"Where are you going all dolled up?" Paolo asked.

"I'm going to run next door and see how Ellen's feeling. She got a little light-headed the other day when she was getting out of bed. Her doctor did a check-up, and everything seems to be fine, but he told her to take it easy. I thought I might bring her some soup."

"Okay, I didn't ask for her entire medical history."

"If you need me, I'll be right here." Mary pointed to the next yard.

"Yes, I know where Ellen lives."

"Of course, you do." Mary pulled Paolo's blanket tighter around him and kissed his head before returning to the house and pulling the glass sliding door closed.

Paolo returned his attention to the news station. As far as he could tell, the authorities had determined that the cause of the fires that had burned down all seven Upackk warehouses was arson, but there had been no suspects. Fire officials had located an incendiary device at three of the warehouses, and they expected to find the same device at the others. Paolo expected they would, too.

He tried to pry his fingers out from under the blanket, but it was like getting out of a straight jacket. The Parkinson's was progressing, and pretty soon he probably wouldn't be able to move at all and would have to rely on Mary for everything—a fate worse than death. He reached for the telephone next to him, nearly knocking over the can of ginger ale.

"Goddamn it," Paolo said.

"You all right out there?" Mary called from the second-floor window next door.

"Just peachy," Paolo called, and Mary disappeared behind a window shade.

Paolo placed the telephone on his lap and slowly pushed the buttons corresponding to the burnable telephone number Marco had given him. The phone rang and Paolo hoped Marco had the good sense not to pick it up. After five rings, a voice prompted him to leave a message. He considered using Gino's code—a secret language his brother had invented that was based on some old Navajo history—but

Paolo could never figure it out, no matter how many times Gino tried to explain it to him. Gino liked to complicate things too much. That wasn't Paolo's style. He decided to keep it straightforward, especially for Marco. After the beep, Paolo simply said, "Time for Phase Two."

"Who are you talking to?" Mary called.

"Would you shut your trap?" Paolo yelled. He tried to find the end call button, but Mary had gotten him so irritated that his shaking worsened. He decided to throw the receiver across the yard instead. "Is Ellen even home?"

"Yes, she's napping," Mary said.

"Not with all your racket she's not. The whole block is up."

"Oh, you always exaggerate." Mary ducked back inside.

Paolo leaned back in his chair. He wouldn't let Mary spoil his mood. This was it. Payback, at last. He reached for the can of ginger ale in order to propose a silent toast, thought better of it, and instead raised his empty hand into the air. A few more details, a few more bruises, bodily or otherwise, and soon the great Don Bailino would be no more. "I'll drink to that," Paolo said aloud and sucked on his thumb as if it were a straw.

14

The renovated cafeteria at the Stanton federal correctional facility reminded Bailino of a fast-food joint. Across the large room, yellow tabletops, resembling floating puzzle pieces, were surrounded by small, circular orange seats, making each table and chairs look like a cluster of planets revolving around a sun.

According to a *Washington Post* article that Bailino had read once, the design scheme was implemented three years ago and thought up by a French architect named Pierre Dubois, intended to foster good cheer among the inmates. Bailino thought that Dubois might be trying to disguise an American fat joke as high art. However, thanks to Katherine Grand, who trumpeted the redesign to any press outlet that would listen, the concept caught on and was to become the prototype for prison cafeterias across the country. Bailino was sure Dubois— wherever he was—was having the last laugh.

The lunch crowd seemed especially large as Bailino got on the back of the food line. During breakfast, fly larvae had been discovered near one of the trays of oatmeal, and the prison staff had had to clean and disinfect the entire kitchen, causing a domino effect of mealtime delays. As Bailino inched closer to the counter, he could smell the disinfectant, but thought the place looked as filthy as it had that morning.

When it was his turn, Bailino placed his orange tray on the metal tracks and slid it down toward the first food bin. A paper menu announced that the day's lunch would be Salisbury steak, mashed potatoes, string beans, and cherry pie. Bailino didn't know why they even bothered coming up with a meal plan. The way it was prepared, everything ended up tasting the same.

He got his food and sat at a vacant table on the far right-hand side of the room, which is where he had breakfast earlier that day. Even though there was no assigned seating in the cafeteria, prisoners tended to take the same seats at every meal. In a lifetime made up of mostly routine, choices were often forsaken, as if the inmates had forgotten that they could even make them at all.

The guard whom Bailino recognized as Hop stood at the exit, and he sat with his back toward him, facing the inmates. He took his spork out of the packaging and placed the thin paper napkin on his lap. Across the room, Alvarez and his cohorts were leaving the lunch line and taking over a set of tables near the center of the cafeteria.

"Let's go, gentlemen," Hop said, "we have to move lunch along to get the kitchen ready for dinner."

The inmates seemed edgy, perhaps because they had been thrown off their routine. Normally, there was a precision to prison that suited Bailino just fine—meals at nine o'clock, two o'clock, and four o'clock; showers at ten a.m. or six p.m. (the prison recently added a later time due to overcrowding); lights out at ten p.m. It reminded him of the army in that way—every day a replica of the last and the next.

Alvarez was sitting next to the middle-aged guy with the gray and jet black hair that Bailino had seen in the showers. Their eyes met, and the guy put on a black knit cap before he dug his spork into his cherry pie. Behind Bailino, a guard snickered, the unmistakable laugh of Jensen.

Bailino checked the time, looking at his wrist out of habit, but then glanced up at the clock on the wall, covered in bars. It was 4:15. He dug his spork into his mashed potatoes and sniffed at it when Alvarez began making a fuss across the room.

"Fuck you, Hernandez," Alvarez said, pushing his food tray toward the guy with the gray and jet black hair.

"Quiet down, Alvarez," Jensen called. Bailino could feel the guard take a few steps into the cafeteria.

"I got it," said Hop, who headed toward the pair just as Hernandez folded his arms and glared at Alvarez. Prisoners along the food line abandoned their places, ducking under the zigzag queue in order to get an up-close view of the rising tension.

"Knock it off, boys," Hop said, his voice sounding stuffier than it had that morning. Bailino suspected Hop was getting a cold.

Ignoring the guard, Alvarez stood up, his eyes on Hernandez, and before Hop could warn him again, Alvarez jumped across the table and threw a punch that landed squarely on the other inmate's cheek. This set off the rest of the men at the table, and soon prisoners from all corners of the room began to hoot, holler, and surround them in a sea of orange that knocked Hop over and onto the floor.

An alarm sounded, and guards charged as gravy-drenched mashed potatoes were launched as missiles into the air. Bailino was swept up in the tide—sweating, writhing bodies were all around him, punching and tearing at one another. He was grabbed from behind and pushed to the ground, and when he looked up, he saw the face of Hernandez, his black knit cap covering part of his eye, which had begun to swell where Alvarez had punched it. Hernandez smiled.

"Knock it off, you animals," Jenson was screaming, pushing his way through the inmates until he stood beside Hernandez, the two huddled over Bailino like football teammates.

"Now," Jensen said, looking around.

Bailino yanked his orange V-neck over his head and handed it to Hernandez, who threw Bailino his shirt and black cap, which Bailino pulled on just as Jensen slapped handcuffs around his wrists and pulled him up.

"Let's go, Hernandez," Jenson said, yanking Bailino toward the side of the room as more guards filled the cafeteria.

Bailino pulled the black knit cap over his ears, the way Hernandez had worn it, and kept his head down. Through the crowd, he saw Hernandez make his way to Bailino's table, pick up his spork, and eat what was left of his mashed potatoes. Alvarez's carefully landed punch caused Hernandez's eye to swell on the right side under his cheek, resembling Bailino's wound. If Bailino didn't know any better, he would have thought he was looking at himself.

"All right, show's over," Jensen called, and the inmates reluctantly returned to their seats and places on the food line. "Eat up!"

Hop sidled up alongside Jensen, pushing a handcuffed Alvarez in front of him. "Was it worth it, man?" Hop asked as the two guards led Alvarez and Bailino out the cafeteria doors.

The night shift guards were clocking in, making this section of the prison more crowded than it normally would be. Bailino spotted Phil going through the metal detectors and tilted his head in the opposite direction.

"You being a bad boy, Alvarez?" Phil snickered as a security guard handed him back his gun.

Alvarez ignored him as Jensen and Hop turned down another hallway and into the solitary confinement section of Stanton, affectionately known as the SHU. They stopped at the first door, and Hop slid his keycard through a tiny mechanism.

"Alvarez, if you keep this up, you'll never get out of here," Hop said, giving him a light push into the cell. "When was the last time you saw your momma?"

Alvarez silently stepped inside the tiny room. He and Bailino exchanged a glance before Hop closed the door, and Alvarez stuck his hands through a small opening. Hop unlocked Alvarez's handcuffs before sliding a metal cover over the opening in the door, sealing Alvarez inside.

"I got this, Hop," Jensen said, swiping his keycard for the next isolation cell. "It's almost four-thirty. Get outta here. You look like shit."

"You sure?" Hop rubbed his eyes. "I'd appreciate it. I think I'm coming down with something."

"Go on ahead," Jensen said as he opened the door to the next cell and pushed Bailino through.

"All this violence just be getting you boys in more trouble," Hop muttered as he took off down the hallway. "You boys need to think. Hear that, Alvarez? Hernandez?"

Jensen closed the cell door, and Bailino, like Alvarez, stuck his hands through the small waist-high opening so that Jensen could unfasten his handcuffs before sliding the metal cover shut.

The quiet of the solitary confinement cell sounded like a low hum. The SHU was one of the original sections of Stanton prison, and not much construction had been done to update it. Along the walls were remnants of the older, outdated forms of punishment—hooks, from which metal shackles once hung, a thick post to which men had been tied—all of which was simply painted over, perhaps remaining as a grim reminder to the inmates of how things could be worse.

Bailino put his ear to the tiny glass window on the door and listened. Within a few seconds, he heard it.

Shuffle, tap, pause, shuffle, tap, pause.

He took a step back as there was a click and the cell door opened.

"Let's go," Jensen said, standing nervously in the corridor.

Bailino stuck his head out and peeked at the security camera.

"It's taken care of," Jensen said.

Bailino gave him a questioning look.

"Look, I'd be in just as much shit as you if that camera was on." He handed Bailino a keycard. "It's a training card. The shifts are changing right now, but you haven't got much time before someone realizes that *A*"—he pointed to the camera—"that thing isn't working, and *B*"—he pointed to the keycard—"that a training keycard has been activated in this section of the prison. As far as I know, I put Hernandez in solitary and left. What happened after that will be anyone's guess."

Bailino nodded and hurried down the corridor, keeping as close to the walls as possible. He knew from the Stanton blueprints that the next surveillance camera was located around the next bend, but he only needed to travel a few more feet. He reached a narrow door, swiped the keycard, and slipped into a utility room, letting the door close softly behind him.

The room was dark, and he crouched down and felt along the right wall until he reached a perforated metal grating. He stuck the edge of his keycard into one of the grating's screws, rotating it counter-clockwise. It was already loose and moved easily. He did the same for the other screws and quickly pulled off the cover, setting it down quietly. He reached into the hole in the wall, felt around, and pulled out a flashlight. He turned it on.

There were five utility rooms in Stanton, two of them nearly on top of one another in this section of the prison. Beside Bailino, a large water heater kicked in—a radiator was calling for heat somewhere above him. He shined his light on the adjacent wall, where there was an air-conditioning apparatus and a shelving unit, behind which was a circuit box and a series of cables. Bailino reached into the duct again and pulled out a large plastic bag. Inside was a razor, a Phillips-head screwdriver, a change of clothes, a wristwatch, a pair of plastic eyeglasses, a small Ziploc baggie, and a visitor's ID badge—everything he had asked for. He immediately strapped on the wristwatch, a cheap dime-store model with a black band and a Hello Kitty face. Good enough.

He checked the time. 4:27 p.m.

Bailino clicked on the razor, whose buzz rumbled in the small metal-clad room, and moved it carefully across his head in a neat back and forth pattern, black and gray strands of hair falling within the scope of the flashlight. He continued until his head felt completely bald and put on the clothing that was in the bag—a pair of jeans, a gray polo shirt, socks, and a used pair of sneakers, size 10. He slipped the visitor's badge in his pocket, along with the eyeglasses.

He checked the time again: 4:30 p.m.

He pulled the large shelving unit forward. Behind it, wires and cables fed through a hole in the sheetrock, leading to an upper floor. Using the screwdriver, Bailino stabbed at the hole until it was about the size of a watermelon and pushed his head and the flashlight through; its beam revealed a large concrete chute that resembled—and once was, Bailino remembered—an elevator shaft. He returned the flashlight to his pocket and, using the cables and wires as a rope, pulled himself through the hole, his shoulders pushing past the worn sheetrock and forcing it to give. Once inside the chute, his legs worked to find leverage, and he managed to wedge the tip of his shoes into the concrete, holding onto the cables for support. He reached for his flashlight and shined it onto his Hello Kitty watch—4:39 p.m.

He lowered himself down the cables until he was only several feet from the soft earth below and let go, landing with a thud on the ground floor. He shined his flashlight toward the other side of the chute where the cables fed into another sheetrock wall and into what he knew to be the second utility room in the west wing. This time, he stabbed his screwdriver into the sheetrock below the cables and dragged it straight down to the floor, making a deep groove. He did that several more times in the same place until there was a long tear in the soft wall, and he pulled apart both sides of the tear, creating a makeshift door, and stepped through the wall.

Inside the dark utility room, he took out his flashlight and held his watch over the beam.

4:47 p.m.

Bailino brushed the dirt from his bald head and clothing as best as he could and dug the visitor's pass out of his pocket, attaching it to his shirt. He reached into his other pocket for the eyeglasses, which he put on, placed the screwdriver and flashlight on the floor, and waited.

Within seconds, there was a light knock on the door next to him. Bailino knocked back. Immediately, there was a click, and the door to the utility closet opened, filling the room with voices, a slit of light, and a puff of chilled air.

Bailino squeezed through the narrow opening and found himself face to face with a large, brightly lit Coca-Cola logo and a man with a baseball cap and glasses. The man reached into the back of the soda machine and pulled out a worn New York Yankees baseball cap, which he handed to Bailino just as a woman screamed from somewhere on the other side of the room.

"Are you all right, lady?" a kid in work boots and a flannel shirt was asking an old woman who had fallen near a water fountain.

Bailino put the cap of his head, slipped inside the room, and hurried toward the scene. "Let me help you," he said, holding out his hand.

The old woman was tiny and frail, her gray hair tinged purple in the fluorescent light of the waiting room. She wore a white knit sweater over a green polyester blouse that was frayed on the ends, a safety pin holding her cuff together where a button should have been.

"I'm so sorry to cause so much trouble," the old woman said, placing her crooked fingers into Bailino's large palm. "I don't know where my head is. I'm fine. Really." She smiled kindly to those who had gathered around.

"Is that yours?" Bailino asked, pointing to a plastic box of black and white cookies that had been lying on the floor beside her. He picked it up.

"Thank you," the old woman said. "I hope they're not ruined."

Bailino escorted the woman toward the building exit. A female guard watched them and slid open her bullet-proof glass partition.

"Are you all right, Mrs. Alvarez?" the guard asked the old woman with a look of concern.

"Just stumbling over my own feet, I'm afraid," the old woman said, blushing.

"Well, I'm sorry to have given you such bad news," the guard said. "I would have called you sooner, so you wouldn't have had to make the trip, but he was just moved to solitary."

Bailino could feel the guard glancing at him as she spoke, and he stood impassively beside Mrs. Alvarez.

"That boy is always getting himself into trouble," Mrs. Alvarez said, shaking her head. She picked up a pen with shaky fingers and signed out on a visitor's log as the guard scanned her badge. "Well, you might as well take these." Mrs. Alvarez motioned to the box of cookies that Bailino was holding. "Maybe you will enjoy them."

"That's very kind of you, but I can't accept them," the guard said with a smile as Bailino took the pen from Mrs. Alvarez and scanned the visitor's log. He stopped his pen at the name *D. Carter,* who had signed in at 3:35, just below Mrs. Alvarez's. He looked at his Hello Kitty watch and wrote *4:58* in the log-out box.

"Oh, I guess I'll take them home then." Mrs. Alvarez said. "And save them for another day."

"See you next month, Mrs. Alvarez," the guard said. She reached over to scan Bailino's visitor's badge, checking her computer screen. At the back of the waiting room, the soda machine guy had finished restocking the beverage unit and was pushing his hand-truck of empty bins through the building exit. It was a journey Bailino had seen the young man make many times through his Upackk warehouse.

"You're good to go as well, Mr. Carter," the female guard said. "Both of you have a nice night, now."

Bailino and Mrs. Alvarez pushed through the crowded reception area as an automated voice came over the loudspeaker: "Ladies and gentlemen, visiting hours at Stanton correctional facility are now over. Please make sure you have all your belongings, and kindly prepare to exit the building."

Bailino checked his Hello Kitty watch again: 5 p.m. on the dot.

Mrs. Alvarez rested her hand on his arm, and the two of them eased through the metal detectors, out Stanton's front door, and into the cool spring evening.

15

Phillip spread his paperwork across the old wooden table in the second-floor conference room, where he often came when he wanted to escape the mayhem of his days. It hadn't been a surprise to him that investigators had deemed Upackk's fires a result of arson, but the news had riled up the press, which had been relentless, and Katherine was threatening to go on strike unless he started interviewing press secretary candidates immediately. And he would, he promised, but first he wanted to prepare for his meeting with his legal roundtable, which was about three hours away.

Since its inception, the roundtable of lawyers had become an incredibly helpful sounding board and had tackled difficult and polarizing issues, including fracking, gun laws, education, and disaster relief, following the devastation his state suffered from Superstorm Sandy in late 2012. Over time, the group had gained much respect in both political and media circles and had come to be called "The Grand Slam" for its tendency to focus on four core issues at a time. Phillip also liked to think it was because, when it came to making recommendations on how to strengthen legislation already on the books, the group often hit it out of the park.

He pulled a sheet of paper from his briefcase. Today's four topics were to include voting districts and gerrymandering, small business tax breaks, state-mandated curriculums on bullying, and dog parks and the liability for dog bites. He liked to keep the topics eclectic, yet relevant to the communities he served, which could be difficult since the folks in northern Buffalo cared little about beach erosion at Montauk Point on Long Island. He scribbled *stricter building codes* at the top of the agenda—as he had discussed with the board of fire commissioners the previous day—and was about to jot down some additional notes when Katherine opened the door.

"I promise, I promise," Phillip said, "I'll get to it as soon as I . . ." He saw the look on his wife's face. "What is it?"

Katherine stepped into the room, followed by Special Agent Wilcox.

"Agent Wilcox," Phillip said, surprised to see the agent back at the mansion.

Wilcox looked both tired and frustrated. Without a greeting, he said, "He got out, sir."

It took a moment for the four words to crystallize before they bore into Phillip like a cannonball. He held onto the roundtable for support. "When?" was all he could muster.

"They believe it was sometime last night after dinner, but before lights out . . . sometime between four-thirty, when Bailino was seen in the cafeteria, and nine p.m., when the nightshift guards checked the cells."

When Phillip took office, his administration had sunk millions of tax dollars back into the prison system after years of neglect and decline. Bailino had broken out at full capacity. "How did it happen?" he asked.

"He must have had help," Wilcox said. "They're investigating now, but no one's talking. At this point, he's been gone for as many as twelve hours. He could be anywhere."

Phillip looked around the room, as if Bailino could jump out from any corner. "Why am I only hearing about this now, Agent Wilcox?" he asked.

"Apparently, prison officials spent all evening looking for an Alejandro Hernandez, whom they had believed to be missing," Wilcox said. "Not Bailino. They believed Hernandez had escaped from solitary. Turns out, Hernandez was in Bailino's cell, and it was Bailino who was gone." Wilcox shook his head. "Some kind of mix-up by the guards. Who knows? Maybe they're in on it. Obviously, Hernandez is involved, but, as I said, nobody's talking. At least not yet."

"They have no idea how he got out?" Katherine asked.

"They're piecing it together—a convenient security camera glitch, unauthorized keycard use. It looks like he got out through the visitors' wing. They're checking the security footage now. They found Bailino's clothing and hair in a utility closet."

"His hair?" Katherine asked.

"He shaved it off. They found a razor, too. They're scanning the security camera feeds for anyone bald and matching Bailino's physical description."

Phillip knew there was a long list of people willing to help Bailino out—some out of fear, some out of obligation, but most because Bailino had been good to them, and that went a long way. He suddenly had a thought. "Oh, my God—"

"I've already dispatched agents to both Edward Carter and Jamie Carter's homes, downstate, governor, if that's what you're thinking," Wilcox said. "My men contained Bailino for two years, before we handed him over to the goddamn BOP." It was the first time Phillip heard the usually unflappable Wilcox use a swear word; it made him uneasy. Phillip was beginning to think it was Don Bailino who had contained Don Bailino for two years, but he kept quiet. "He won't get to them. It would be stupid for him to go anywhere near the Carters. The only thing stupider would be for him to try to come here." Wilcox's cell phone rang. "Excuse me," he said and stepped into a corner of the conference room.

"Cancel the roundtable meeting," Phillip whispered to Katherine.

"Right, and schedule a press conference," she said.

"A what?"

"You want me to be your interim press secretary? Well, my advice is that you need to get in front of this."

"Get in front of it how?" Phillip asked.

"Talk to Jim Olsen at the *Times*. Talk to all the press. Say what you need to say as the governor of New York—that you were just informed that Bailino has escaped from Stanton prison and that you have full confidence that he will be apprehended."

"You know as well as I do that I can't say that—and that I don't know that." He glanced at Wilcox who was whispering adamantly into his cell phone. "Jesus, if Bailino had enough pull to get out of federal prison, who knows what he can do. I think you should get the kids up here."

"Phillip, there's a floor full of agents downstairs. The kids are—"

"I just need to see them, Katherine. I need them with me now."

Katherine knew when to argue with Phillip and when not to. She left the conference room as Wilcox clipped his cell phone back onto his belt.

"More bad news?" Phillip asked.

"I'm not sure. My men are at Jamie Carter's apartment in Queens. She's not there. And Edward Carter and his family aren't home either. They're not answering their phones, land lines or cells."

Phillip felt himself turning pale. He thought of Jamie Carter and the things that she told him had transpired at the log cabin two years ago, the things Bailino had said. It was clear he had been smitten, taken with Jamie who had shown such strength and grace in the most dangerous of circumstances. Phillip knew that was something his old friend would admire, but would it be enough for him to go after her?

"None of the Carters?" Phillip asked, incredulously.

"No need to panic, Governor Grand. At this point, no news is good news."

Not when it came to Don Bailino, Phillip thought.

"We'll find them—and *him*," Wilcox said. "Do you have any idea where Bailino might be headed?"

"You're asking *me*?"

"Sir, at this point, other than Jamie Carter, you are probably one of the few people—the few people *left*—who know Don Bailino best.

Any ideas as to where he might go, sir? Brooklyn contacts? Old Army buddies? Anything come to mind?"

Phillip's mind filled with possibilities, but anything he could come up with would only be a guess. Bailino was pretty private. He knew a lot of people, that was for sure, but as far as people who were close to him or whom he trusted, the list was short. Phillip had been his only real friend. Other than that, Bailino had been close to his father, who died long ago, and he had no brothers or sisters, no family to speak of.

"Think out loud, sir," Wilcox said. "It might help."

"I was just thinking about what's meaningful to him—or, at least, what used to be."

"And what was that?" Wilcox asked.

"Family. Family was important to him."

"He has no family anymore, though," Wilcox said.

"Unless . . ." What Wilcox had said before was right. It would be stupid for Bailino to go anywhere near the Carters, but even if Jamie, herself, weren't enough to tempt Bailino, she had something—or someone—who might.

"The baby," Phillip said, a chill creeping up his spine. "The little girl, Faith. He might go after the baby."

16

Faith toddled after a monarch butterfly that was teetering toward the parking lot. Jamie took the little girl's hand and gently guided her back to the picnic tables.

"C'mon, sweetie, this way," she said, diverting Faith's attention with her favorite toy—a simple red ring in the shape of a fat donut that the little girl liked to hold in her hand as if she were lifting a barbell.

"See, I told you this was a great idea," Edward said. He was wearing his chef's hat and pouring batter into a waffle iron connected to a portable generator. "She loves it here."

It had been the first mild day in what had been a wet winter, and weather forecasters were predicting a string of balmy days until the weekend. Jamie had been insisting that Edward spend the rest of his vacation at home with Trish, Peter, and Sara, since she was fine, and Faith was fine, but Edward had been adamant. The only way to get him out of her apartment was to agree to spend the day out east. She watched Faith scamper through the grass toward Peter and Sara. She had to admit: It was nice to be surrounded by family. She scratched at her leg, where a mosquito had bitten her ankle.

"Do you really have to carry that thing?" Edward asked, motioning to her ankle pistol holster. "You know how I feel about those things, and the kids are here."

"That's exactly why I'm wearing it," Jamie said.

"Brady Park isn't what I could call a hotbed of violence," Edward said.

"Not yet," Jamie said with a smile, nudging her brother.

Jamie had been pregnant the last time she had been to Brady Park, which was attached to the Massapequa Preserve and encompassed a picnic area, pond, playground, and sports areas. Being there always reminded her of her mother, who, when she and Edward were children, took them there nearly every day to bike, fish, or picnic. It was like being on vacation in a place far, far away from Long Island, and because money had been so tight when she was growing up, it was the only vacation her family ever really had.

"Order up!" Edward yelled, and Peter and Sara gathered around the picnic table as Faith toddled after them.

"Hey, young man," Edward said to Peter when he saw him texting on his phone. "Phones in the basket for today, remember? The Carter family is officially off-grid. God knows we need a break."

"I'll second that," said Tricia, who had returned from the car with syrup and a fruit platter. She plucked the phone from Peter's hands, turned it off, and placed it into the picnic basket with all of the other cell phones.

"When am I gonna get a phone?" Sara whined, pulling herself onto the picnic bench.

"When you're old enough," Peter said snidely.

"I'm only a year younger than you," Sara said.

"Enough you two," Edward said. He eased a waffle onto Peter's plate. "Hey, James, remember when Mommy used to bring us here for breakfast?"

"She did?" Tricia asked. "I thought we were the only lunatics who came here this early."

"Yeah, she'd pack up the cereal boxes, bowls, and milk and bring us down here," Edward said. "We thought it was so special, eating breakfast outside. We'd laugh and eat, and then I'd kick Jamie's ass in horseshoes."

"I don't remember that last part," Jamie said. She watched a set of bikers and joggers disappear over the small footbridge near Massapequa Lake.

"Whatcha got there, Princess?" Tricia asked Faith who was bouncing toward them with her red ring in one hand and what looked like a rock in the other.

"I hope that's not duck poop," Sara said and grabbed a colored bowl from a stack and poured herself some cereal.

"We gotta eat fast, guys," Tricia said. "We have fifteen minutes to get you to school."

"Do we really have to go?" Sara whined. "Aunt Jamie is here."

"I'll be here when you get home, sweetie," Jamie said. "Faith and I are going to stay the whole day."

"Yay!" Sara said, milk dribbling down her cheek.

"No cheering with your mouth full, young lady," Tricia said.

Jamie's niece and nephew ate the way Edward ate, like the meal would be their last. Sara and Peter shoved the rest of their food into their mouths and, still chewing, gathered up their backpacks.

"Don't forget your lunch money," Tricia said and spun into action—tightening backpack straps, plopping dollar bills into upright palms, checking zippers to make sure they were secure. Sara and Peter danced around her like an orchestrated ballet.

"See ya, Aunt Jamie," Sara said, slipping her arms through the straps of her backpack and giving Jamie a hug.

"See you later, Sara Banana," Jamie said. She high-fived Peter who started running toward the parking lot.

"Goodbye, Faithy!" Sara called, but Faith was busy poking the bark of a nearby tree with her finger.

Tricia placed the strap of her handbag over her shoulder. "Edward, I'll be back in a jiffy."

"I'll walk you to the car." Edward wiped his hands on his apron and lifted Sara into the air the way Jamie had seen him do it hundreds of times. "Be right back, James."

"Faith!" Jamie called. "Come get your bottle." Jamie waved the bottle in the air, but Faith looked uninterested. Instead, she made a beeline toward the open gate that led to the lake.

"Faith, no!" Jamie hurried across the grass and down to the rocky bank. She grabbed Faith's hand just as she was entering the lake area and nearly stepped on a pair of resting ducks. "Gotcha, you little speed demon," she said.

The wildlife, so accustomed to people, barely even acknowledged that they had nearly been trampled upon by a toddler. They stared lazily at Jamie and Faith before turning their attention to the lake. Before Jamie could get a good enough grip on her daughter, Faith broke free of her grasp and headed toward a napping swan.

"No, no, no, honey. She's sleeping." Jamie picked her up and put her fingers to her lips. "*Shhh . . .*" she said, and again the memories came flooding back with a rush. Holding Charlotte by the river. Watching the frog. Bailino watching them both.

A female jogger ran by and waved to Faith, but Faith was more interested in grabbing the feathers of the swan.

"Come on, honey. Let's go have your bottle. Yummy."

Across the pond, the trees swayed, their stubby green leaves waving like fingers. Jamie knew that within a month, a bright green canopy would cover the preserve, which, in the fall, became a crown radiant with color. She thought of her mother collecting leaves to bring home and make collages. She made a mental note to bring Faith back in six months to do the same.

Faith pointed at the sunlight bouncing off the water, and Jamie leaned forward. "Who's that?" she asked, pointing at Faith's reflection in the still water.

"Who dat?" Faith imitated, pointing. She was wearing her red ring toy like a bracelet.

"That's you," Jamie said.

"That you," Faith said, pointing to herself, her dark eyes wide and happy.

"You mean, *that's me*." Jamie said, poking Faith's belly and making her giggle. "Let's get some food inside there."

She placed Faith back on the ground and reached for her daughter's hand.

It was the last thing she remembered.

17

Thousands of tiny black embers rested along the hilly countryside and were all that was left of Upackk's headquarters and warehouse. From atop a nearby hill, Bailino surveyed the last of the firefighters who sifted through the hollowed structure of his building. His detachment surprised him. He remembered his enthusiasm, almost child-like in its intensity, when he purchased the struggling family-owned company years ago, and after all the hard work, the investments, the awards and honors, the upgrades and improvements, it was all gone with the strike of a match—or, rather, the blast of an incendiary device.

Bailino knew it would only be a matter of time. The Cataldi family had not been too happy with this "little side job," as Gino had called it, of Bailino's. Gino insisted it distracted him from business, but Bailino knew that the old man was jealous. Upackk had given Bailino a respect and credibility that Gino Cataldi craved and had never received outside the confines of his underworld. Bailino imagined his old boss would be tickled pink to know that Upackk, the fly in his ointment, had finally been swatted, but probably stunned that it had been his brother, Paolo, to have done the job—and not him.

Bailino adjusted his cap and sunglasses and returned to the gray Toyota parked about a hundred feet back near a turnoff from the main road. The car had been at the Alvarezes, registered to a long dead uncle, and Mrs. Alvarez insisted that he take it, also insisting that he eat a nice hot meal since the food at Stanton "wasn't fit for a dog." Bailino didn't want to disappoint the old woman, who seemed like she could use the company, so he ate and got a later start than he would have liked.

He looked at his Hello Kitty watch: 9:37 a.m. The Feds had probably spent most of the night monitoring the prison's security camera footage and were most likely at the Alvarez home already, but this wasn't Mrs. Alvarez's first rodeo. She knew what to do, and say, and he hoped the money he had given her would help Alvarez—if he ever managed to get out of Stanton—to get back on his feet.

Bailino stood at the end of a gravel path, where an old tire had been thrown onto a wooden stake, and counted fifty steps due east until he reached a small stream. The rivers of upstate New York weren't what they used to be, but Bailino's employees—many of them avid fishermen—swore up and down that some of the region's remotest waterways, like this one, made for some of their biggest catches. He jumped down on the embankment from the overpass and crept underneath, wedging himself between the dirt and the concrete above. He reached into a small crack, digging his fingers around a gray stone until it became loose and fell out, and pulled out a long black metal box.

Bailino sat down on the wet ground, unfastened the combination lock on the box, flipped the lid open, and surveyed the contents: a passport with Bailino's photo in the name of Tom Smith; eight thousand dollars in fifties and hundreds; a driver's license, prepaid phones, credit cards registered in the name of Tom Smith, two sets of car keys, two Smith & Wesson pistols, binoculars, a silencer, two boxes of bullets, and two mustaches— one pencil, the other porn star. One of the phones signaled he had a text message. He held the phone at arm's length, reminding himself to pick up a pair of reading glasses. Apparently, no amount of meditation would restore old eyes. He squinted at the small letters on the screen:

USER 1: got it

He carried the metal box back to the Toyota, stowed it in the trunk, and pulled out a shovel and a bottle of water he had purchased from a vending machine at the train station that morning. Checking the sun's position in the sky, he counted fifty paces northeast until he came to a small patch of grass among a cluster of oak trees. He plunged the shovel into the hard dirt, kicked it in with his foot when it wouldn't budge, and began to dig.

The dirt came up in small clumps that turned into bigger ones the further down he went. He kept at it until the smell hit him, and then he tossed the shovel aside and crouched down on his knees. With his hands, he pulled the earth away until his fingers touched something hard and narrow—a wrist. He wrapped his hand around it and pulled until the entire arm emerged from the dirt, and he fished around until he found the other arm, and pulled on both wrists until the corpse rose from its dirt shroud. Then Bailino stood up and gazed at what was left of the body of Leo Cataldi.

18

"Jamie . . . Jamie . . . Are you all right?"

The words floated to her as if she were underwater, and she awoke to find that she was dirty and wet. It was only when she saw Edward standing over her that she remembered where she was.

"Where's the baby?" she asked.

"I was just going to ask you that," Edward said.

"What do you mean?" A panic overtook her, and she struggled to stand, but the back of her head was throbbing. "Faith!" she screamed, the sound of her voice reinforcing the pain. She tried to raise herself up on her elbows, but landed back onto the dirt.

"What happened?" Edward asked, bending down to help her.

"I don't know." She reached for the pistol in her ankle holster; her gun was still there.

"What do you mean you don't know? Did you fall?"

"Edward, please . . ." Jamie tried to remember. She was standing with Faith by the lake looking at their shadows, and then the memory lapsed. She gazed out on the water. It was calm, but something caught her attention near the shore—Faith's milk bottle was lying on the rocks, the gentle lap of the water pushing it into the dirt. "Oh my God . . ." she pointed.

Upon seeing it, Edward yanked off his shirt and ran into the water, causing the nearby ducks to squawk in protest.

"Faith, Faith . . ." Jamie kept screaming, hoping her voice would attract the little girl's attention. She started crawling into the water. "Baby, come to Mommy!"

"Jamie, you stay there. I mean it. You're in no shape to swim. You'll drown." Edward took a deep breath and plunged under the water's surface.

Jamie tried to sit on her heels, but she had trouble lifting her head. She jumped when Edward burst through the water, coming up for air, before he plummeted back down.

"Faith," Jamie yelled. She felt the back of her head: a large knob of flesh protruded from under her hairline, and she thought she felt blood, but it was difficult to tell because she was wet.

Edward rose again from the water's surface and charged toward her. "I don't see anything." He wiped his face with his hands. "It's too murky." He waded out of the water and examined Jamie's head where she was rubbing. "Jesus . . ." He touched her welt with his wet finger. "That doesn't look like a fall, James. I'm calling the police." He ran back toward the picnic tables.

"Edward . . ." Jamie tried to stand, but fell again. She leaned her body against a fence post and pulled herself up as Edward raced back. "Hurry," she said.

"I'm trying. . . . I had to power up. Ah, here we go." Edward's screen lit. "Jesus, I have fifteen messages . . . And nineteen texts. What the—" He swiped the screen. "Oh, no." He fell to his knees, the sand sticking to his wet jeans.

"What is it?" Jamie asked.

Edward's face lost its color. He showed Jamie the phone screen. She squinted at the text, but her vision was blurry. "I can't read it. What does it say?"

"It's from Wilcox." He looked back at the screen. "It says, 'Where are you, Edward? I can't reach Jamie. Did you get my texts/ phone calls?'" He took a breath. "Bailino's out. Wilcox said to call him immediately. *Immediately* is written in all uppercase." He pointed to the screen.

Jamie's chest tightened as the bright blue sky swirled above her. She clutched at her throat, which felt like it was closing. "No . . ." She reached for the fence post, but missed.

"Hello, Nine-One-One," she remembered Edward saying as she fell onto the pebbled shore. "This is an emergency. We need help."

19

Bailino made good time—there had been no traffic on Route 87—so he decided to get off the nearest exit and run some quick errands. He parked the Toyota on a side street and picked up a few items at a local supermarket, including a pair of reading glasses. On the way back to his car, he passed a bar, a tiny hole in the wall called Billy's. The red neon sign blinked *Open*. He checked his Hello Kitty watch and decided he had time for a drink. He dumped his groceries onto the backseat of the Toyota and went inside Billy's.

The place was nice and dark, and pretty empty. A guy in a business suit, with his tie—and, apparently, his mood—loosened, sat at the bar, and a kid wearing a cut-off shirt and shorts was leaning against a wall next to a dartboard that had three darts sagging out of its bull's eye. Both were watching a small television on a high shelf nestled between bottles of liquor.

"What can I get you?" the bartender asked Bailino, placing a napkin before him on the bar.

"Scotch," Bailino said. He adjusted his black baseball cap that read *Meat Department*, which he also bought at the supermarket, and made sure his pencil moustache was properly affixed to his lip before taking a seat on one of the stools.

On the television, a reporter was standing outside a familiar site: Stanton prison. She was all dolled up in a pink linen suit that looked out of place in front of the gray building. "Sources tell us," she said with authority, "that a security camera captured this image at the Amtrak station in Albany early this morning." A blurry photo of a bald Bailino was shown on a station platform. "Authorities believe Bailino is trying to leave the country and is heading north toward Canada. All train service out of Albany and nearby stations has been suspended, and all early morning trains have been ordered to stop at a designated checkpoint, where we are told the FBI will be searching each cabin and passenger."

"I'd like to see that guy get away," the bartender said, placing Bailino's drink on a paper coaster in front of him.

"No shit?" the man in the business suit said. "Why is that?"

"Didn't know him, but my buddy is an Army veteran. Said that guy donated hundreds of thousands of dollars to military charities. Meant a lot to him."

"My cousin worked for his company," the kid in the cut-off offered. "Well, my second cousin. Said the benefits were *primo*. They even interviewed him on the news yesterday about the fires. Don't know what he's going to do now, though. Guy has limited skills."

"Yeah, well, my opinion is that Bailino is a fucking psychopath," the man in the suit said, taking a slug of his beer. "Charity or no charity, he's a killing machine. Blew a hole right through that young cop, may he rest in peace."

"Yeah, well, the guy is a war hero," the bartender said. "Maybe he's got PTSD."

"He's got a case of the crazies, all right," the man said, "but there ain't no medication for his kind. Shoulda gotten the chair if that Phillip Grand weren't such a pussy." The man glanced at Bailino with glazed eyes. "You hear what I'm sayin'?"

"Loud and clear," Bailino said and took a slug of his drink. He reached into the pocket of his jeans and pulled out a ten-dollar bill, which he left on the counter. The television was showing a photo of him taken three years ago at a Walter Reed Hospital charity event. ". . . However, it is believed that Bailino is now bald and may have a series of bruises on his face, although prison officials won't say, exactly, how those were obtained. . . ."

"Probably had the shit beat out of him in prison," the man said with a sneer.

"*Shhh* . . ." said the kid in the cut-offs. "I'm trying to listen."

"Governor Grand held a short press conference this morning to address the issue," the reporter continued. "He said, quote, Our first order of business is to apprehend Don Bailino. After the search is over, we'll go over the exact details and get to the bottom of how he escaped the Stanton Correctional Facility to ensure that this never happens again, endquote."

Bailino imagined it was Katherine Grand's idea to get on top of the story with a press conference. That woman would hold a press conference for a paper cut.

"The governor went on to say that . . . what's that?" The reporter put her hand to her ear and listened. A look of surprise came over her face. "It appears we have breaking news . . . News 2 is being told that a man by the name of Bernie Brooks was found dead this morning in his bedroom, the victim of an apparent gunshot wound. Police are not saying whether there is any connection between the murder of Mr. Brooks and the disappearance of Don Bailino, but we're told that Mr. Brooks was part of the escort that brought Don Bailino to Stanton prison yesterday. . . ."

"See what I mean?" the man in the suit said. "Guy went and killed a guard. Jesus Christ."

"You don't know if there's a connection," the bartender said. He was wiping a shot glass with a towel.

"The hell I *dooooon't.*" The man tapped his bottle onto the counter. "Another."

"I think you've had enough, Doug." The bartender slid the bottle from the bar and placed it in a sink behind him. "Can I get you anything else?" he asked Bailino.

"Nah," Bailino shook his head. "I've had enough."

"Well, trust me, pal, there's more to come," the man in the suit said as Bailino rose to leave.

"Are you kidding?" the kid in the cut-off said. "If that guy Bailino's smart, he'll squirrel himself away somewhere in the woods of Canada and never come back. They'll never find him."

"Nah, guys like that can't stop," the man in the suit said.

"Ya think?" the kid asked.

"It's in their blood." The man in the suit tightened his tie. "Trust me, I know how these people operate. We haven't seen the last of Don Bailino," he said as Bailino made his way toward the exit.

Outside, the air was warm, and Bailino didn't know whether to attribute the change in temperature to the sun or the scotch. He checked his Hello Kitty watch—12:28 p.m.—and crossed back to his Toyota. He pulled a banana from one of the grocery bags spread across the backseat, started the car, and drove west along country roads for about fifteen minutes, the bottles and cans clanking against one another in the grocery bags behind him. A small white church appeared on the right, and he pulled into its parking lot, which was deserted, and took the space closest to the building. He turned off the engine.

The church had seen better days. The painted white of the arched doorway was chipping, and the stained glass pattern of the Virgin Mary and child had lost much of its color. Bailino climbed the three crooked steps leading up to the front door and was reminded of the time, decades ago, that his father had stopped there with him to use the bathroom. That day with his father had probably been the last time Bailino was in a church, with the exception of Joey's baptism. He opened the front wooden door, startling a nest of baby sparrows hidden under the archway, and stepped inside.

Despite its outer facade, the church looked refurbished on the inside and still held that ominous medieval timbre that he remembered so vividly from his boyhood. He sat in the last pew and gazed at the large cross portraying the crucifixion of Jesus behind the altar. It was smaller than he remembered. He felt absently for the gold cross that once hung around his neck.

The door opened, and a man entered the church vestibule. He met Bailino's eye and stood in the back near the candles, most of which had burned down to nubs. The man lit a candle, threw some change into an old metal box, and returned outside. Bailino followed him.

The man walked toward a white minivan that was parked behind Bailino's Toyota. He grabbed the handle of its sliding door and gently opened it. Inside, sprawled across the middle seat, was Faith Carter, sound asleep.

Bailino caught his breath. The little girl was bigger than he thought she would be. Her hair, dark and straight, was shoulder length, and her nose was turned up slightly over her lips, which were wet and pouty. She reminded him of her mother.

"Why was she crying?" he asked, eyeing the tear stains on the little girl's cheeks.

"She cried most of the way." The man rubbed his head as if it ached from all the racket. "I guess it's to be expected when you take a little girl away from her mother."

Bailino nodded. "Everything went as planned?"

"Yes," the man said, but Bailino could tell he was lying—there was a slight hesitation before his answer. He waited.

The man took a nervous breath. "I know the instructions were not to hurt the mother, but the park had people in it—joggers, bike riders. The girl's brother and his family were right there. I had to work fast and couldn't take the chance that she would scream or anything."

"What happened?" Bailino asked.

"I had to give her a whack on the head," the man said. "I used a piece of wood I found lying near the picnic tables, but, honestly, she'll be all right. It's just a good-sized bump."

They both stood there, looking at the little girl asleep in the minivan, until the man said, "So . . . you got the money?"

Bailino nodded. He walked back to his car, with the man in tow, and reached into the glove compartment of the Toyota.

"You know, you're practically on every news station," the man said, leaning on Bailino's car door. He wiped his forehead with the back of his hand. "I'll tell ya, you got balls sticking around. If I were—"

The silenced gunshot ripped through the man's head, and his body crumbled to the ground.

Bailino tossed the Toyota's car keys next to the body and grabbed the keys that were dangling from the man's quivering fingers. He hauled the groceries out of the back of the Toyota and brought them to the minivan, popping the back door open and dropped the bags inside. He eyed the little girl—she was still asleep on the seat. He made a note to himself to buy a proper car seat and softly closed the door.

As he grabbed the handle of the sliding door to close it, he hesitated and returned to the back of the minivan. He reopened the door, reached into one of the grocery bags, and pulled out a T-shirt with Pennsylvania's new tourism slogan, *The State of Independence*. He snapped the back door closed and placed the T-shirt over the little girl, tucking the sleeves around her shoulders. He nudged the sliding door closed and got into the driver's seat, adjusting the rearview mirror so he could see her sleeping. Then he put the car into gear and followed the signs to Interstate 80, turning west toward Pennsylvania.

20

"I really wish you would go to the hospital, Jamie," Edward said. "I think you might need stitches."

"Or at least get a scan," said Tricia, who was standing next to him with concern.

"I don't want to go to the hospital," Jamie said. She was sitting on the picnic table, next to the waffle iron, where an EMT was holding an ice pack to the back of her head.

"I think your brother's right, ma'am," the tech said.

"I feel fine, really," Jamie said. "Where do I sign to refuse treatment?" The EMT shook his head and handed her the paperwork. She scribbled her name, keeping it to herself that her eyes hurt when she tried to read the small print.

"Keep that on there," the tech instructed. He adjusted the ice pack.

Edward climbed on top of the picnic table and sat. "I know what you're thinking, James, but he won't hurt her."

"You, of all people, don't know that, Edward," Jamie said. In her mind's eye, she saw Edward hogtied in the trunk of the Ford Flex, the blood oozing from the gunshot to his shoulder.

"We still don't know if he even has her," Tricia offered.

"He has her," Jamie said. "I know it."

"Even so, you have to *believe* that he won't hurt her." Edward put his arm around Jamie. "You *have* to."

"I agree," said Wilcox, who had his sleeves rolled up and was leaning on the picnic table surveying the park. He had flown into Republic Airport forty-five minutes ago with a team of agents who had dispersed like insects on the scene. "The baby's his insurance. He'll keep her safe."

Jamie wanted to believe that, but she knew better. She had seen the fire in Bailino's eyes. She knew what he was capable of. She'd seen him snap, from Jekyll to Hyde, from warm to ice and back to warm, in an instant. She'd seen him act on revenge and on a whim. Perhaps she was naive, but she believed she knew Don Bailino in ways that the FBI, with all their years of research and surveillance, didn't, and even *she* didn't know what he would do.

People gathered all around Brady Park, which for the past hour and a half had become a center of attraction in the usually sleepy village. Federal agents cased the picnic grounds and bike paths with dogs, which had spooked the ducks into the brush. Pairs of agents dotted Massapequa Lake, which was being dredged, but so far nothing—and no one—had been found. Women pushing strollers gathered around the police barricades, holding up their phones to record the action. Jamie thought she heard someone call her name and pulled her jacket tighter around her shoulders.

"Goddamn vultures, all of them," Tricia said, shaking her head. "Don't people have better things to do?"

"I think you should go home, James," Edward said.

"I agree with your brother," Wilcox said.

"How can I go home?" she asked.

"There's really nothing that you can do here," Wilcox said, his hard eyes softening. Jamie had always wondered what Wilcox thought of her decision to have Faith. She wondered if there were a part of him that thought she had been selfish—after all, the birth of Faith Carter had thrown a monkey wrench into the FBI's observation of New York organized crime, giving it, at least biologically, a new heir. However, over the past two years, he never said a word. "We've got it covered. I'll contact you the moment we hear anything," he said.

Jamie removed the ice bag from the back of her head and felt the area with her hand. The lump had subsided, but was still there, and still hurt. She climbed down from the table.

"Good. I'll go with you," Edward said, following her down.

"No, Edward," Jamie said. "I need to be alone."

"But, Jamie—"

"I'll have a car escort her home," Wilcox said, putting a hand on Edward's shoulder. "We'll watch her."

"I can drive," Jamie said.

"I prefer you didn't," Wilcox said.

"So do I," said the EMT, who packed up the rest of his gear and walked toward the ambulance.

"I'm fine. I need to be alone," Jamie said. "Please."

"Jamie," Edward said, "I don't think—"

"My men will follow you home then," Wilcox said. "I think we'd all feel better with a detail at your apartment, Ms. Carter. Just in case."

"He won't go there." Jamie watched one of Wilcox's men place Faith's plastic red ring, which had been lying in the grass, into a Ziploc baggie. She remembered the little girl had been wearing it by the lake—it must have fallen off or had been taken off. "I know he won't."

"Even so," Wilcox said with a look that told her she had no choice in the matter.

She sighed. "All right."

The parking lot had been cordoned off, and it took twenty minutes for Jamie to drive through the double-parked cars and people who had gathered along Lakeshore Drive and Front Street. She looked into the rearview mirror—the empty car seat made her heart wrench. Behind her, the pair of agents was following in a black sedan. She eased the car under the Long Island Railroad trestle and onto Sunrise Highway, which she rode west until she reached the Wantagh Parkway and took the northbound exit.

As the trees blew by her, her mind raced with questions: Why? Why would Bailino kidnap Faith? What had he to gain? He had taken Charlotte Grand two years ago to use as leverage in order to stay the execution of Gino Cataldi, but what had he to gain now? His fiery gaze returned to her mind's eye. *Revenge* was her first thought, and her stomach knotted. Or was it for insurance, as Wilcox suggested, in case the FBI caught up with him? Was it to hurt Jamie? To hurt Faith? To *raise* Faith? Jamie couldn't imagine the latter. He had been so eager to help Joey Santelli get away from the Cataldis. Why would he want to usher a baby into that life? Or had he escaped prison to start over and take his child with him?

She turned west onto the Northern State Parkway toward New York City and checked her rearview mirror—Wilcox's men were right behind her. Signs for the Cross Island Parkway emerged, and the word *cross* brought to mind Bailino's large gold cross hanging from his neck, slapping against her, the cold of the metal, the heat of his body. She tightened her grip on the steering wheel.

More cars filed onto the highway as the evening rush hour neared, and soon a sea of red brake lights coated the road, glinting in the setting sun. Her mind churned with images of plunging into the river with Charlotte Grand in her hands and Joey Santelli on her heels. Her throat constricted as if she were gasping for air again, and she opened the driver's side window, but the air was as stagnant as the traffic. She couldn't breathe.

Two SUVs merged behind her from the left lane, coming between her and the federal agents, and she followed them into the exit lane, using their bulk as a shield. Quickly, the agents discovered her maneuver and were twisting their vehicle in front of a sports car that moved up into the empty lane space and was blocking them. The agents were backing up their vehicle to merge onto the shoulder, and Jamie floored the gas pedal, careening onto the Cross Island Parkway, where, unlike the Northern State, traffic was moving. She skidded toward the first exit before the federal agents had gotten onto the on-ramp and made the first turn and then a series of left and right turns until she was lost somewhere along the side streets of a residential area in Queens. She pulled in front of two-story home, put the car in park, and waited, her heart thumping.

She had no idea what she was doing, but she couldn't sit there anymore, and she couldn't go home, not to an empty apartment. She knew Wilcox wanted to help her, but she wouldn't be babysat. She needed to do something.

After ten minutes when she hadn't seen the agents' car, she imagined they had stayed on the Cross Island or perhaps were at the side of the road calling Agent Wilcox. She opened the passenger window and tossed her cell phone over a white fence, and also reached into her glove compartment, took out her E-ZPass, and threw that over the fence as well.

Absently, she rubbed her legs together and felt the hardness of her gun against her calf. A lot of good that thing had done her. She took a deep breath and leaned back against the car seat, the back of her head tender with pain. Why hadn't Bailino killed Jamie? Why had he hit her on the back of the head and taken the baby? Was it a test? Was Jamie supposed to go looking for him? If so, where?

She had a thought and eased back onto the road, snaking her way through the neighborhood until she reached a main street with stores, restaurants, and lots of evening foot traffic. She parked in a municipal lot, ran toward an ATM vestibule at one of the local banks, and withdrew five hundred dollars from her bank account, knowing that the transaction would give away her location, but she didn't expect to be there long. She hurried back to her car and drove along more back roads until she met up again with the Cross Island Parkway and got on the northbound on-ramp.

Traffic was still moving steadily, and she drove the speed limit. No one seemed to notice her, and nothing was out of the ordinary. She merged into the right lane and took the exit for the Throgs Neck Bridge. Her tires rumbled over the metal grooves—it was the first time she had been on a bridge in two years, since around the time she, Reynaldo, and Charlotte crashed into the guardrails of the Albany County Bridge fleeing Bailino's Ford Flex. She cleared her mind and focused on the road. *Just go.*

Once on the mainland, she slipped her money to the toll booth attendant, keeping her head cocked to the side and away from the security cameras, although there was nothing she could do about the license plate. Then she followed the signs toward Interstate 95 and slowly exhaled. If she had learned anything from Bailino, it was that she was in control of what happened to her. She wasn't going to sit around and wait. She wasn't going to be babysat, by Wilcox or by Edward. She was going to find her little girl—or at least try. And she knew of only one way to start. She was going to Boston.

21

Reynaldo felt something wet and prickly on his cheek. He opened his eyes. A big, hairy snout with white whiskers was sniffing along the bridge of his nose.

"Who are *you*?" he asked the mangy dog lying next to him. He ran his hand down and around the mutt's floppy ears, making its tail flap like a windshield wiper, and grabbed the tag dangling from its collar. It read: *Maricón, ID# 37843-32*.

There was only one person he knew who would name his dog Maricón.

"Papa?" Reynaldo sat up, and the dog nudged his nose under his armpit. "You're a friendly one." He patted the dog's head. "Either that, or you're hungry."

Reynaldo put on his slippers and, with the dog padding beside him, walked out of his bedroom and across the hall to the master bedroom. The room was empty. A luggage cart was opened neatly on a chair, and several pairs of shoes and slippers had been laid out below it.

"Papa, where are you?"

Reynaldo had waited all night for his brothers to bring his father to the house after Pedro texted that they were taking him out for a late dinner, which was Pedro-speak for bar hopping. At seventy-one, Hector Rodriguez could drink anyone half his age under the table, and Reynaldo was pretty sure he *had* since they had never come home.

"Reyito," his father called. "I'm down *aqui*."

At the sound of Hector's voice, the dog left Reynaldo's side and eased smoothly down the stairs like a centipede. Reynaldo followed behind, stopping on the bottom step. He blinked his eyes a few times. All the shoes and sneakers that were usually piled in a heap at the front of the living room had been neatly arranged on the shoe shelves. His jackets had been hung on the coat rack, the tabletops dusted, and the glass of the windows, framed photographs, and china cabinet wiped clean. Years ago, after a night of carousing with the guys, Hector Rodriguez liked to make it up to Reynaldo's mother by straightening up the house—he was what his *mamá* had called *a drunk cleaner*. It was a tendency that had probably saved their marriage. Apparently, old habits were hard to break.

"*Buenos días*, Reyito," his father said when Reynaldo walked into the kitchen. "I see you've met Mari."

It had been nearly two years since Reynaldo had seen his father, and it was as if time had stood still. He was sitting at the kitchen table in his white wife-beater T-shirt, his curly gray chest hairs peeking over the top of the scoop collar, his reading glasses at the end of his long nose to read the newspaper, his hands bejeweled with rings.

"How was your flight?" Reynaldo reached into a cabinet for a coffee mug.

"Bumpy," his father said, folding the paper and placing it on the table. A look of seriousness came over him. "Listen, Reyito, we have to talk."

Reynaldo's heart sank a little. It had been his father who told him that his mother had been killed in a car accident across from Crain's Grocery more than twenty years ago, and he had done so by uttering those same words, which Reynaldo had come to associate with unfortunate events. "What is it, Papa?" Reynaldo sat down at the table and reached for his hand. "Are you sick?"

"Sick?" His father pulled his hand away. "What is wrong with you? I'm as healthy as a horse."

"Oh, *bien*, I thought, well, because of the sudden visit that maybe—"

"Stop changing the subject." His father slipped a piece of toast under the table for Maricón as the front door opened and slammed, and Pedro burst into the kitchen.

"*Buenos días*, Rodriguezes," Pedro said. He had taken a shower and was already dressed in his garage jumpsuit. Pedro was never out of bed before nine o'clock.

"To what do I owe this honor?" Reynaldo asked.

"What you say, Rey? I'm always up this early for work." Pedro smiled at his *papá*.

"*Sure* you are," Reynaldo said.

"Can you believe it, Rey?" Pedro said, jamming a piece of toast into his mouth. "We're going to have a new *mamá*!"

"A what?!" Reynaldo stood.

"Now, now, Pedro," his father said, "I didn't have a chance to tell Rey yet."

"I already have a *mamá*," Reynaldo said, crossing his arms.

"You know what I mean, you big dummy." Pedro knelt down to pet Maricón, who licked the crumbs from Pedro's lips. "Papa is getting married."

"Married?" Reynaldo asked. "To who?"

"A wonderful woman," his father said and leaned back in the kitchen chair, puffing out his chest like a peacock. "Her name is Pearl, and she is a Latina princess."

"You say that about all women," Reynaldo said.

"I do not, and there you go again changing the subject. What? No congratulations?"

"Yeah, Rey," Pedro said. "What gives?"

"Nothing," Reynaldo said, his cheeks reddening. "I'm just surprised, that's all."

"Why?" His father stood up, adjusted his T-shirt over his jeans, and put his mug into the sink. "You think no woman would want me? You think I should just shrivel up and die since your *mamá* is gone? It's been twenty years. You think I'm like you?"

"What's that supposed to mean?" Reynaldo asked.

"I know all about your whining and wasting away over a woman," his father said. "*Qué patético.*"

Reynaldo glared at Pedro who made himself busy rubbing Maricon's belly.

"Now who's changing the subject," Reynaldo said. He grabbed a piece of toast, murmured, "Congratulations," and strode out of the kitchen. He marched back up the stairs and slammed the door to his bedroom, causing the model planes that were hanging from the ceiling to sway.

He sat on his bed, shoved the toast into his mouth, and chewed until the planes stopped swinging. The night before had been the first night he had slept in this room for many years, leaving his usual perch—the living room sofa—so that his *papá* could have some privacy when he arrived. He gazed at the model planes, cobbled together with such care, and at the old Hardy Boys books and *Star Wars* posters lining his walls, all worn with age. *This is the perfect room for me,* he thought with embarrassment. *A little boy's room for a little boy.*

There was a knock at the door. "Rey?"

"Pedro, not now." Reynaldo flopped back onto the bed.

The door opened, and Maricón came running into the room and onto Reynaldo's bed. The dog circled around a few times before plopping himself down beside Reynaldo.

"Rey, what gives? You no happy for Papa?" Pedro put the newspaper down on the bed. "Here, I brought you this, so you have something to do while you pout."

"I'm not pouting, Pedro."

Pedro scratched behind Maricón's ears. "Rey, *mamá* has been gone a long time."

"I know, it's not that. I *am* happy for Papa. It's just . . ."

"I know, you're mad that they're making you move . . ."

Reynaldo bolted upright, scaring Maricón, who jumped onto the floor. "They're *what?*"

Pedro's face froze. "Please don't tell me I'm like Britney Spears and, oops, did it again."

"I'm *moving*?"

"*Shhh . . .*" Pedro closed the bedroom door. "Papa and Pearl are tired of having sweat in all their creases and want a place for themselves so they can have old people sex and not bother the people in the next room. The walls in those senior communities are paper thin."

"Pedro, please," Rey said, covering his ears.

"No, seriously, that's what Papa told me last night. Apparently, Pearl is pretty loud."

"I can't hear you," Reynaldo said with his hands pressed tightly against his ears. "*La la la la la . . .*"

"You're being childish, Rey."

"Talk about the pot calling the kettle childish," Reynaldo said. "So I'm supposed to just up and go, because Papa wants to—"

"Maybe it's for the best, Rey, no? Maybe you are one of those people who need a little push." Pedro opened the door so the dog could leave, but Maricón sat on the floor looking up at him. "Look, Rey, I love you, you know that."

"But . . ."

"Well," Pedro pointed to the newspaper, "you are very much like this newspaper, *hermano*. Full of knowledge, but always a day behind. Somehow, sometime, you became the old man around here, not Papa, you know?" Pedro pointed to the walls. "There's no room to grow when you live in the same room that you used as a boy. And, plus," Pedro pressed on the mattress, "not much room on this thing for anything more than sleeping, which leads me to . . .Wherever you move to, make sure you have an extra bedroom big enough for a king-sized bed. I like to—"

"Out, Pedro," Reynaldo said.

"You're right. Too soon," Pedro said, whisking the dog out of the bedroom and closing the door behind him.

Reynaldo leaned back against his wooden headboard and pulled the newspaper toward him. The large front-page headline read, "The Con Don: Stanton is Bailino's New Home." A color photo showed

Bailino being led into the prison surrounded by corrections officers. Reynaldo thought of Jamie. Maybe this was all a sign, that it was finally time to go to New York City—sell the garage, make a fresh start, and tell Jamie he loved her, because he knew he did. Across the room, the large world map that hung on the wall stared at him. "You will keep track of all the places you're going to see, Reyito," his mother had said, handing him a plastic square container filled with thumbtacks. Decades later, there were still only two red thumbtacks in place—one for a school trip to New York City, the other for Miami to visit his *papá*.

His stomach rumbled, but he wasn't ready to face his father. He had acted badly, and even though it was only once in a lifetime of Hector Rodriguez acting badly, Reynaldo thought he should have known better. He pushed the newspaper to the floor. His *mamá* would have wanted his father to be happy, for all of them to be happy. Who was Reynaldo to deprive someone of love? He knew, firsthand, how lonely life could be. He was going to apologize to his father.

Reynaldo sat up on the small bed and accidentally pushed the power button on the television remote control. As the old set warmed and crinkled to life, a word—in big, bold lettering—appeared across the television screen: ESCAPED.

22

Phillip finished reading his cell phone screen and ran his hand through his hair. He had been right, but he had been too late.

"What is it?" Katherine asked. She was standing at the edge of the bedroom in a pair of plaid pajama pants and a T-shirt. "They haven't caught him?" When Phillip shook his head, she asked, "There's more, isn't there?"

"The baby . . ." Phillip said in a small voice. "Jamie's baby . . . Faith . . . is missing."

Stunned, Katherine sat down on the edge of the bed and folded her hands neatly on her lap. "But Wilcox said Bailino would be stupid to go near the Carters."

"It would have been," Phillip said. "I agree with him."

"Well, you were both wrong."

"I'm not sure we were."

"What do you mean?"

The sound of giggling children carried across the bedroom followed by sing-songy music. Phillip peeked down the hall toward Charlotte's room, where she and Philly were playing with a jack-in-the-box that Rosalia had given them. He found comfort in their happy faces.

"Phillip?" Katherine asked.

"There's no trace of Bailino anywhere near Long Island."

"What kind of trace?"

"Anything—surveillance footage, DNA, blood samples . . . Jamie

Carter was hit on the back of the head while she was at a park, and when she came to the baby was gone."

"Oh, my Lord," Katherine covered her mouth with her hand. "Is she—?"

"She's all right," Phillip said. "Wilcox's team managed to get a partial fingerprint off a red ring toy that the baby must have been holding, but the fingerprint wasn't Bailino's."

"Whose was it?"

"They don't know. Nobody in the system."

Katherine pulled a plaid skirt and white blouse out of her closet and quickly got dressed. "Could the child have been taken by someone else? Could this be a completely unrelated incident?"

"That would be too coincidental, I think, don't you?"

She tossed her pajamas onto the bed. "Bailino had help then . . ."

"Yes."

Phillip imagined Katherine, too, was thinking of Maddox, their dutiful press secretary who had double-crossed them and gotten Bailino inside the Executive Mansion two years ago so that he could kidnap Charlotte. Bailino seemed to have people who would do his bidding everywhere.

"Daddy, Daddy! Watch this!" Charlotte said, running into the room. She was holding Philly's hand and placed the jack-in-the-box on his bed. She cranked its handle, her little tongue sticking out of the corner of her mouth, until a clown popped out and her little brother cackled. "He likes it!" she said, beaming.

"That's great, sweetie," Phillip said.

"C'mon, Philly, follow me!" Charlotte squealed and ran back toward her bedroom with Philly in tow.

"Maybe we should visit with Ms. Carter," Katherine said. "Is she at the hospital?"

Phillip shook his head. "There's more. Jamie has disappeared," he said, "but it's not what you think. She was being escorted back to her apartment by two of Wilcox's men. Wilcox insisted that his men ride behind her, as an escort. For protection."

"How much protecting can you do from another car?" Katherine said, throwing up her hands. "He must know that by now."

"Wilcox said he wanted one of his men to ride with Jamie, but she wouldn't allow it," Phillip said. "He couldn't force her, Katherine, but now he knows why perhaps she wanted to be alone. She lost them on the highway. Wilcox said he never even considered the possibility that she would go anywhere but home."

"It amazes me why anyone would underestimate that woman," Katherine said. "Did they try tracking Jamie's cell phone?"

"Jamie tossed it. They found it in a backyard somewhere in Queens. Scared the heck out of some old couple when a bunch of federal agents showed up at their door."

"What about E-ZPass?"

"Tossed that, too. Wilcox had agents spend the night going through security footage throughout the area, including at the Whitestone and Throgs Neck Bridges' toll stations. They found a shot of her crossing north on the Throgs Neck at around six-thirty. From there, it's anyone's guess where she is."

Katherine considered the information. "Do you think she's coming *here*?"

Phillip shook his head. "Why would she? And leave Edward? She knows better than anyone how dangerous that man is."

"She also probably knows better than anyone how to find him," Katherine said, "which is what I suspect she may be trying to do."

Phillip knew Katherine felt a sort of kinship with Jamie Carter. Although Katherine didn't bond easily with many people, especially women, she had liked Jamie Carter from the moment she had met her.

"You and I both know what it's like when your child is in danger, and all you're told is to stay calm and sit at home," Katherine said. "I wouldn't wish it on anyone."

"Sir?"

Brandon stood in the doorway. He and several other federal agents had stayed on following Bailino's escape from Stanton. Even though Wilcox had been sure Bailino would not come anywhere near the Executive Mansion, he kept a handful of agents there, just in case. And after what had happened to Faith Carter, Phillip was glad he had. "What is it, Brandon?" he asked.

"Reynaldo Rodriguez is here to see you, sir."

❀

Reynaldo was pacing in the public lobby.

"He's out?" Reynaldo asked, panicked, as soon as Phillip arrived.

"Son, calm down." He ushered Reynaldo upstairs into his private office and closed the door. He pulled out a chair, but Reynaldo refused, choosing to stand.

"I can't reach Jamie," Reynaldo said.

"I know."

"You know?" Reynaldo's eyes grew wide. "What happened to her?"

"Nothing, nothing," Phillip said. "She's all right, as far as we know . . ."

"As far as you know? What does that mean? Where is she?"

"We don't know."

Reynaldo looked wild with fear. "And the baby? Where's the baby, Faith?"

"We believe—well, Special Agent Wilcox believes—that . . . that Bailino may have Faith."

The words looked as if they had borne a hole through Reynaldo. He held onto the governor's desk for support. "You have to find her."

"Reynaldo, we're doing everything we—"

"He has done horrible things."

"Son, I know he has, and please know the FBI is—"

"Wait, that's right." Reynaldo caught his breath. "You two knew each other. You have a history."

"That was a long time ago," Phillip said. "Don Bailino and I are far from friends. I'm in just as much danger as anyone, I—"

The office door burst open and in ran Charlotte.

"I knew you were here, Rey Rey! I knew it!" she said, jumping up and down with excitement. She was followed by Katherine and Rosalia, who was holding Phillip Jr.

"Charlie," Phillip said, "you're not supposed to come into Daddy's office without—"

"But it's Rey Rey!" Charlotte squealed. She launched herself into Reynaldo's arms.

"*Carlota* . . ." Reynaldo feigned a smile. Charlotte ran her hands through his thick, wavy hair. "Don't you look pretty today."

"I'm wearing my flag pin even though there are no TV cameras," she said proudly.

"Rey? What are you doing here?" Rosalia said. She placed Philly on the floor, and the little boy toddled toward Reynaldo's legs. "I didn't know you were coming." She studied his face. "What's the matter?"

"Nothing, *tía*, I'm fine."

Charlotte got close to Reynaldo's face, too, mimicking Rosalia. "Yeah, Rey Rey, what's the matter?"

Reynaldo clasped the little girl's chin. "Nothing, *tía* junior," Rey said, and the little girl giggled.

Rosalia crossed her arms. She was at least a foot shorter than Reynaldo, but Rosalia could be intimidating when she wanted to be, particularly when it came to her family, or Phillip's. "Reynaldo Rodriguez, don't you lie to your *tía*."

"Yeah, Rey Rey," Charlotte scolded. The little girl was looking up at him with big blue eyes. He kissed her forehead.

"Papa is here, *tía*," Reynaldo said. "He's visiting."

"Hector?" Rosalia rolled her eyes. There was no love lost between his father and his aunt, who had told Reynaldo's mother many times that Hector Rodriguez was a no-good philanderer and a drunk, but Reynaldo's mother had had a soft spot for her husband ever since he retrieved her sandal when it had fallen down a well when they were six years old.

"He's getting married. I thought I should come and tell you

the news in person." Reynaldo glanced at Phillip, who nodded, corroborating the lie.

Rosalia appeared astonished. "*Marido?* At his age?"

"Congratulations," Phillip said with a small smile.

"Congratulations? That means ice cream!" Charlotte cheered.

"Dear, it's the morning," Katherine said. "We don't have—"

"But, Mommy, you said for a special occasion ice cream is okay," Charlotte pleaded.

"Yes, but, I don't think this is quite—"

"But you always say we can!" the girl debated like a seasoned lawyer.

Katherine looked to Phillip for support, but he needed to distract and calm Reynaldo Rodriguez for a few minutes, and he couldn't think of a better person to do it than Charlotte Grand. "Well, Charlie, your mother is right," he said. "Ice cream is—usually—not for the mornings . . ."

"Usually?" Katherine asked.

". . . But I think we might be able to make an exception for today."

"Yay! Did you hear that, Rey Rey?" Charlotte cheered. "I want chocolate!"

"You better not say no, Reynaldo," Phillip said, putting his hand on Reynaldo's shoulder. "She's pushy like her mother that way." He winked at Katherine, who didn't appear angry, and he was thankful that she was giving her husband the benefit of the doubt for not backing her up.

"C'mon, Rey Rey, let's go," Charlotte said. She climbed down from Reynaldo and took his hand. "C'mon, Philly," she said, reaching for her little brother, who placed his tiny hand into his sister's other palm. "Ro Ro will take us to the kitchen."

Reynaldo took a reluctant step with Charlotte, but his eyes were fixed on Phillip.

"Go on ahead, Reynaldo," Phillip said. "Spend twenty minutes with the kids. We'll talk in a little while, I promise. I'll explain everything."

The children left Phillip's office as quickly as they had come, along with Reynaldo and Rosalia who looked as if she were still reeling from the news about Hector Rodriguez. When they were gone and before Katherine could say a word, Phillip said, "I had to distract him, Katherine. He's beside himself about Jamie."

Her cell phone rang. She pulled it from her pocket and rolled her eyes before swiping the screen. "Yes, Jim," she said into the phone and then mouthing *I'll be right back* to Phillip. "What can I do for you?" Katherine eased herself out of Phillip's office, closing the door.

 The office became suddenly quiet. Phillip walked over to the bookshelf on the far wall, pulled out a book, and blew the dust off the top. He opened to a middle page where an old Polaroid photo had served as a placeholder for more than two decades. The photo, taken during Family Day, showed him and Don Bailino the day before their graduation from Army boot camp. The two men had their arms around one another, wide smiles on their faces, as if they were about to conquer the world. It was the last photo they had taken together, and one of the only.

Phillip looked at the youthful features on the young men, and he wasn't sure whether it was Bailino he barely recognized or himself. So much had happened to both of them over the years, courses mostly dictated by their lineage. Did their friendship hold some kind of meaning, Phillip wondered, as both Wilcox and Reynaldo seemed to suggest. Did Phillip know more than he realized? After all, he had been right about Don going after Faith Carter. However, the Don Bailino he knew once would have never kidnapped a child. The Don Bailino he knew would have never abducted and raped a woman or killed a police officer in cold blood.

Or would he have?

23

Bailino pulled up in front of the home his father used to refer to as "the country house." It looked more like a haunted house. Weeds had grown high across the first floor windows, which were dirty and cracked. Paint peeled in large sections from the wood siding, and all along the roof tiles had fallen or were destroyed by tree branches. Two rusty bicycles and an old tire lay on top of a large patch of dirt beside the front entrance, where Bailino remembered gardening with his father as a kid. Across the property were beer cans, hay, and remnants of old campfires. Yet, even with all the disarray, there didn't seem to be any discernible fresh tire tracks or footprints. No one had stepped foot near this property for a very long time.

"Mama?" a small voice said from the backseat of the car.

In the rearview mirror, Bailino saw little Faith Carter sit up and rub her eyes. She had slept for the entire ride through Pennsylvania, although she had shifted around quite a bit. Bailino left a bottle back there for her in case she woke up during the trip, but she had been out cold. He saw her pick up the bottle and furrow her brows at it, probably realizing it wasn't the one she was used to.

"Mama?" she said again before plunging the bottle into her mouth.

Bailino got out of the minivan and stretched his legs. He glanced quickly at the lake and the trees, the natural barriers that had done an adequate job of protecting the house from winter storms as well as prying eyes. It was quiet. No breeze. No sound. He took off his cap, his phony moustache, and glasses, and opened the sliding door to the minivan.

"Hi," he said with a smile.

The little girl cried instantly—a powerful wail that seemed to ricochet through the trees.

"*Shhhh . . ..*" he said. "It's all right. *Shhhh . . .*" He reached inside the minivan, but Faith pulled back, hunkering down in the well of the backseat.

Distrustful, he thought. *Good girl.*

"It's all right, cupcake. Don't cry," he said in a tender voice. "*Shhhh . . .* I know, I know, honey, you want mommy, right?"

The little girl stopped crying at the word *mommy* and nodded her head.

"She's not here right now, but let's get something to eat until we see her again, okay? Do you want to eat?"

Tiny tears dropped from Faith's eyes to the tops of her cheeks. She shook her head no.

"No? Well, let's see what we have anyway . . ."

Bailino popped open the back door, rifled through a grocery bag, and pulled out a packet of Oreo cookies. He ripped open the bag and held it out to her. The little girl studied him, her gaze dark and serious. She shook her head no.

"You don't like cookies?" he asked. "Okay, let's try something else."

He searched another bag and pulled out a package of Twinkies. He held it up.

The little girl shook her head again.

"I don't blame you," Bailino said and put the package back.

He heard a noise and quickly turned around, pulling his gun from the front of his pants. He scanned the tree trunks for the slightest movement or misshape, but saw neither. By the time he turned back, the little girl had come out of the well of the seat and was reaching into one of the grocery bags. She plunged her hand inside the bag closest to her and moved around packages of diapers and jars of baby food until she reached a pint of blueberries. She looked up at him with big dark brown eyes and held it toward him with both hands.

He smiled. "Good choice. Very healthy, but we have to wash them first, okay?"

Faith nodded her head, showing she knew the drill, although her eyes still bubbled with tears. Bailino put the blueberries back into a bag, threaded the handles of three grocery bags through the fingers of his left hand, and closed the back door. He came around to the backseat and this time, instead of reaching in for the little girl, he stood where he was and held out his hand. "Come, Faith," he said. "Let's go into the house."

The little girl was perched on the edge of the seat. She stared at him.

"We can't eat them out here," Bailino explained. "We need to go into the house where we have a table and some chairs. Let's go into the house where it's safe."

Faith looked around at the trees, the house, and the barn that was located across the property as if seeing them for the first time and brightened. He got the feeling that she liked being outdoors.

"Hey, maybe we can rig that old tire into a swing," Bailino said. "You like to swing?"

The word *swing* made the little girl brighten even more. She stared at him, her dark eyes like lasers, and took a step out of the minivan, grabbing hold of the T-shirt and bottle that was lying on the seat. Cradling them in one hand, she reached up for Bailino's hand. Her little palm felt like an overripe peach that would squish if he squeezed too firmly.

"Good girl," he said.

He led her toward the house, four of her tiny steps equaling one of his, and waited on each rickety stair until Faith caught up with him. They continued that way until they reached the front door.

"I have to let go for a minute, okay," he said. The little girl nodded, dropped his hand, and returned the bottle to her mouth.

The shiny new deadbolt Bailino had installed a few years before looked out of place on the old oak veneer door, which had scratch marks at the bottom, presumably from tiny critters trying to get inside. He looked closely to make sure it hadn't been tampered with before sticking in his key and pushing it open. A whiff of stale air slapped him in the face.

"Let's go, little one," he said, reaching for Faith's hand again, and she slipped it into his palm, her dark brown eyes wide as the two entered the home.

He was surprised that the little girl wasn't put off by the look of the place. Dust coated every surface of the house like dirty snow, and cobwebs hovered in corners and across doorways. The white sheets covering the furniture appeared like ghosts, but Faith pressed on, undaunted. Bailino put the grocery bags on the counter and pulled out a chair at an old dining room table.

"You're going to sit here, okay?" he said, wiping the dust from the chair.

The little girl examined the seat and lifted her hands into the air.

"You can climb up there on your own, can't you?" he asked.

The little girl kept her hands raised.

"All right, up you go." He picked up her tiny body, which felt light but solid, and sat her on the chair. "You stay right there, okay?" he said.

Bailino turned on the water faucet, which sputtered to life, brown water spitting from its mouth.

"Ewww . . ." Faith said, scrunching her face.

"I know, right," Bailino said. "That's pretty gross."

When the water cleared, he stuck the pint of blueberries under the stream. He reached into a cabinet, brought down a plastic bowl, the blue one decorated with Superman that used to be Joey's favorite, wiped it with his shirt sleeve, and poured the blueberries inside. He brought them to the table.

"Good?" he asked.

The little girl brought her face close to the blueberries to examine them. She nodded and shoved a handful into her mouth.

"Not too many at once, now," Bailino said. "I'll be right back."

He returned to the car to pick up the rest of the groceries. As he was grabbing the last of the bags, Faith appeared at the front door and was watching him.

"You okay?" Bailino asked.

The little girl nodded. She appeared to be checking on him.

"I'll be right there." He closed the minivan's back door and brought the bags into the house, dropping them inside the front door.

Faith scrambled back onto her seat and reached for another handful of blueberries.

"I knew you could get up there on your own," Bailino said with a smirk. He grabbed hold of the front door knob and took one last look at the property. "Now, let's see if we can find us some rope," he said as he closed the door shut, engaging the deadbolt with a click.

24

J amie stood on Massachusetts Avenue gazing up at the buildings of the Massachusetts Institute of Technology. She felt drained. By taking ancillary roadways, it had taken her three times as long to get to Providence, Rhode Island, where she had ditched her car and traveled by train north to Boston—a long night, to say the least. And now that she was standing before one of the foremost private research institutes in the world, her plan to find her daughter suddenly seemed childish and farfetched.

It had been two years since she'd seen Joey Santelli, someone whom she never expected to see again. He would be about twenty years old now—a man—and she wasn't sure if she'd recognize him. Or if he was even there. She knew he was still enrolled at MIT, thanks to the good reporting of the tabloid press, but for all she knew he was studying abroad, had taken a semester off, had dropped out, or, given his family history, had succumbed to something far worse.

All this time, the media had left Joey virtually alone, choosing instead to focus on the main attraction, the rape child of Don Bailino—whom they dubbed Baby Bailino—ever since they had gotten wind of Faith's conception. Joey Santelli had become the sideshow. Although he had been taken into custody after he was discharged from Albany Memorial, he was shortly released and was never indicted as an accessory to the kidnapping of Charlotte Grand or the murder of Mark Nurberg or anyone else. Jamie couldn't say that she was surprised; she assumed that Bailino had made some kind of deal to save his son. She thought about that moment in the log cabin bedroom when Joey told Bailino that his mother had told him that he was his father. Jamie hadn't noticed the resemblance until that moment. Then it became all she saw.

For the past two years, she had tried unsuccessfully to forget about Joey—still never sure whether he had jumped into the river that day to save her or hurt her. She'd be lying if she didn't admit she had developed a soft spot for the kid, particularly after Faith was born. Children couldn't control who their parents were—that had become painfully obvious. Plus, like it or not, Joey was her daughter's half-brother.

Jamie pulled down on the baseball cap that she had picked up at the Providence train station and tucked her hair behind her ears. She knew that the FBI was lurking around, unseen, on the off-chance that Bailino would visit Joey, which is the last thing Jamie thought he would do. She didn't think they expected her to be there, but she didn't know. Although she had nothing to fear from the FBI—after all, she had done nothing wrong—she wanted to stay off their radar.

The college students walking in and out of the buildings all looked the same to her. They seemed happy and young and inspired, lugging backpacks, cups of coffee, and smartphones, ear buds dangling from their ears. Jamie followed a student she thought looked enough like Joey into a sandwich place, but discovered it wasn't him when he placed his order in Spanish. She tailed a group of girls to a crowded coffee shop, which was mobbed with morning traffic, but she had no luck there either. She kept her head down and followed two professorial-looking women into a library, but she was unable to enter without student identification.

After an hour of dead ends, she plopped down on a bench outside the library. At this rate, she would be there for weeks. *There had to be a better way*, she thought and had an idea. She reached into her purse and took out the prepaid cell phone she had purchased in Providence. She activated it, clicked to Google, and searched for *Santelli Instagram*. Most teenagers and young adults had social media accounts. She hoped Joey did, too.

More than a hundred entries came up. *Damn.* She narrowed the search by adding *MIT* and *Boston*, and that lessened the list to three. She clicked on the only one who wasn't a woman, and up came the profile of Joey Santelli. His bio read simply:

Joe. Some men ARE an island.

His home page featured a series of photos, most of them selfies taken at various Boston attractions—the Bunker Hill monument, Faneuil Hall. A few featured MIT landmarks, including the Nuclear Research Reactor and the Great Dome. He was alone in all of them. He looked older to Jamie and tired; he let his beard come in more fully and left it unshaven. She scanned all two hundred of his photos, hoping she'd find an address or a dorm room or something. She didn't, but what she did find was a consistent setting—a good twenty of the photos were taken on what looked like a grassy quad with a line of trees in the foreground of a white building.

"Excuse me," Jamie said to a young redhead who was lying near her on a blanket and reading a textbook on quantum physics. "This is a friend of mine. I'm supposed to meet him in a little while, and I forgot where he said, but it's here." She pointed to the photo. "Do you recognize this area?"

The redhead took a look. "Sure," she said cheerily. "That's Killian Court. It's actually right over there, right around the bend. You were close." She smiled.

"Thank you." Jamie followed the young woman's directions. Within minutes, she found herself at the scenic setting, not far from the Great Dome. It was actually a lovely place to sit, think, or study, and she could see why Joey spent a lot of time there—a patch of tranquility in the center of a bustling university campus.

She found a spot under the shade of a tree, plopped down to the ground, and waited.

❀

"Jamie . . ."

She opened her eyes to a tall, lanky silhouette. Someone was tapping her shoulder. Dreamily, she answered, "Edward, I'm fine."

"Jamie, it's me."

Jamie focused her eyes and realized the words were coming from Joey Santelli.

"You shouldn't be here." Joey was looking around. "They're watching me."

"What time is it?" she asked, sitting up.

"It's two o'clock."

Jesus, she'd been asleep for three hours. She wiped her face, which was full of dirt and saliva, with her hand.

"What are you doing here?" Joey asked.

His face seemed different. Older. The square jaw. The jet-black hair. Jamie didn't know what frightened her more—that Joey looked exactly like Bailino, or that he looked a lot like Faith. "How did you find me?" she asked.

"Some girl said you were looking for me." Joey scanned the quad. "I think she's gone, but she said she recognized me from the photo you showed her. What photo?"

"Never mind. Where is he?" Jamie whispered. She pulled her baseball cap firmly onto her head.

"*Shhh . . .*" Joey bent down. "I've already been through this with the Feds." He said the word *Feds* with distaste, the way Bailino said it. "I don't know."

"Bullshit. I know you do."

"I *don't.*"

"You're the only family he has," Jamie said.

"Which is exactly why he wouldn't tell me where he is." Joey quickly reached into his backpack and pulled out a coding textbook. He flipped it open and pretended to show Jamie something on a page. "You need to leave." He closed the textbook and placed it into his backpack. "He won't come near you. Don't worry. You're safe. Good-bye." He stood up abruptly and began walking away.

"Wait," Jamie called.

Joey put his hood over his head and kept walking.

"Wait," she called louder. "He has her."

Joey stopped.

"My baby . . . He has Faith."

"What do you mean he has her?" he asked, hurrying back.

"She's gone." Jamie told him what had happened the day before. She was surprised that Joey seemed surprised.

"Are you sure *he* has her?" he asked. "Did you see him?"

"Who else would it be?" she whispered. "You know as well as I do what he's capable of."

Joey sat back on the ground. He opened his backpack, took out another textbook, and stared blankly at an open page.

"You know nothing about this?" she asked.

Joey shook his head.

"I don't believe you. Where is he?"

"I *don't know*," he repeated, adding under his breath, "He can be anywhere. The log cabin's gone."

"I know." Although the demise of Upackk had dominated the media coverage, there was a mention that Bailino's home had burned down, too, the place where he had held Jamie and Charlotte. The news had given Jamie no solace—even if the log cabin was no longer there, it would live on indefinitely in her mind.

"I really can't help you," Joey said. "The Feds think he's leaving the country."

"Is that what you think?" Jamie asked.

Joey stared off toward the Great Dome.

"Can you tell me anything?" she asked. "*Anything* that might help me?"

Joey flipped through the textbook. It was a guide to American

History, and he was staring at a map of the original thirteen colonies. She thought she detected something, a tiny movement of his gaze. "What is it?" she asked.

He shook his head. "Nothing. I don't think it's anything."

"Anything can be something," Jamie said.

"You really should go home. This isn't a game, Jamie."

"I am *not* going home without my baby. If you can't help me, then I'll find someone who will."

Joey closed the book. "Listen, I really don't know where he is. Honest." He put his right hand up and his left hand on his textbook as if he were taking the witness stand. "But when I was little he used to take me to this place in Pennsylvania, a place his father bought way back when as insurance."

There was that word again, Jamie thought. *Insurance.* "Where is it?" she asked.

Joey scanned the quad and lowered his head. "It's in a town called Little Gap, not far from Bethlehem."

"Do you have an address?"

He shook his head. "No, I was only there a few times when I was thirteen or fourteen. The house is this really light blue. It's right near a lake on one side, and it's surrounded by a thick forest on the other." His gaze drifted toward the trees. "I remember it had this tire swing in the front, a big barn on the property with a silo and everything. I used to pretend it was a castle. I loved it there. It was away from everything, everybody."

"Nobody knows about it?"

Joey shook his head. "Just me. Not even my mom. He made me promise not to tell. Said it was our secret. Said he might need to get away someday."

That must be it, she thought. *And, if not, it was worth a try.* "Thanks," she said and stood up.

"Wait." Joey returned his textbook to his backpack. "Where are you going?"

"Where do you think?" she said.

"You're just going to go there, with no address? Just wander around the town?"

"What else am I supposed to do?" she said. She felt her eyes fill with tears.

"Do you have a car?"

"I left it in Providence and took the train here. I'll take a train back and get it."

"They probably already found it by now. Here . . ." He reached into his backpack and pulled out a set of keys. "Take my car. It's parked in Jamaica Plain. It's a ways from campus, but I wanted it far enough away, but accessible, just in case."

She wanted to ask *just in case of what*, but didn't. "No, that's okay, I don't—"

"Please. Take it. It's the least I can do. I don't use it. I never leave Boston, and when I'm in the city I just take Uber or public transportation. They follow me everywhere I go."

"Who's following you?"

"It doesn't matter. Just go."

"What makes you think they won't follow me?"

"They won't, not if they don't know you're here, and not if they see me." He gave her the make, model, and color of the car and put the keys on the ground; she discreetly took them. "Take the T to Jamaica Plain. It's parked on Greenough Avenue. I have friends who live over there."

"What are you going to do?"

"I'll take a walk on Massachusetts Avenue. There's a Starbucks there where I like to study. I'll stay out in the open."

"Yeah, I saw that Starbucks in the Instagram photos."

Joey smiled. "Ah, Instagram. That's how you found me? Nice. I'll sit there for a half hour or so. That should give you enough time to get out."

"Thanks," Jamie said. Now that she had spent a little time with him, she saw how young Joey still was underneath the stubbly beard. He was trying to get his life started, just like she was.

"You're welcome." He put the earbuds into his ears. "Be careful, okay?"

"You too."

She had the urge to reach for his hand, but didn't. Instead, each of them stood, hunched their shoulders, and walked across the quad in opposite directions.

25

Paolo shuffled toward the Knights of Columbus beside Mary, who was hauling his oxygen tank cart beside him in a pair of three-inch-heeled clogs that matched her snazzy purple dress.

"Do you want me to ask Adriano to pull that?" Paolo said. "You look like you're defying the laws of gravity in those shoes."

"I got it," Mary said.

"You do realize this is only Bingo, right?"

"Yes, I do, because it's the only place you take me." She rolled her eyes.

At the entrance to the building, which was located next to a busy McDonald's drive-thru populated by kids who looked barely old enough to walk let alone drive, Marco stood solemnly like a bouncer, dressed in a black suit that was too baggy even for his large frame. He waved when he saw them coming.

"Hi, Aunt Mary," Marco said, kissing Mary on both cheeks and relieving her from oxygen tank duty. "My mom is at the back table with Cousin Eddie."

"Thank you, dear," Mary said. She yelled in Paolo's direction, "I'm going to—"

"Yeah, I heard him. I ain't deaf. Go, go," Paolo said with a dismissive hand. "Get me a seat before it gets too crowded and I have to sit near the air conditioner like last time. I almost got pneumonia."

"Everything's *my* fault," Mary muttered and made her way through the gathering of people.

The Knights of Columbus was already crowded. Long tables were set up in rows underneath a neon-lit Bingo board, and a large sphere of balls was erected at the front near the bar. Membership at the Knights soared last year after a local billiards place closed down, and holiday Catholics had nowhere else to go for some good, wholesome fun. The influx of people spurred the organization to finally splurge on some new activities, including Pokeno, Pictionary, and a new Bingo set. Paolo could barely read the numbers anymore on the old Bingo cards, so he was thankful for the investment.

"What's with the pink?" Paolo asked, looking around. Pink streamers crisscrossed the large room like a canopy, and big cardboard pink stars and hearts hung down like spiders from the drop ceiling. "It looks like a bubble gum factory exploded."

"There's a Sweet Sixteen here tomorrow," Marco said.

To add to the cash flow, the Knights had also been renting out their party room for community events, and Marco, since his retirement from Cushy Jobville, had been working part-time as a bartender. Paolo figured the place was probably making a killing with Sweet Sixteens alone, since most of them were more lavish than weddings.

"Remember to keep your hands to yourself, kid," Paolo said. "Those girls are young. One false move, and the next thing you know you're stuck in jail for the rest of your life."

"Or you're getting married," Marco said.

"That's what I said."

Paolo made his way toward a door near a large aquarium—another by-product of the Knights' recent windfall—that was decorated with a Roman ruins motif. A pair of kissing gouramis was chasing one another in and around a set of faux crumbling columns. Paolo knocked on the tank with a shaky finger telling them to knock it off and was startled to see two goons standing behind it next to the door.

"Jesus, you scared the crap out of me," Paolo said to the men. "They inside?"

They nodded and parted slightly so that Paolo could pass to the next room, but then closed the gap before Marco could enter.

"Just you," one of the men said.

"For Chrissake, Benny, he needs to wheel the oxygen," Paolo said.

Benny's dull eyes focused on Marco, who looked to the ground, and he took a small step aside.

"Thank you," Paolo said. "Charming as always, I see," and he and Marco stepped across the threshold.

Inside the small kitchen, pink goody bags, platters of pink cookies and donuts, and large pink LED centerpieces covered nearly every table and floor surface. Paolo fought his way through bunches of pink, white, and silver balloons toward the end of the room, where two old men were sitting around a small table, a platter of cold cuts and antipasti between them. Paolo maneuvered toward the open seat at the table and carefully sat down as Marco dragged his oxygen tank behind him into a corner.

"Excuse my not getting up," said the old man sitting across from Paolo who was gnawing on the end of piece of Italian bread.

"Wouldn't want to put you out, Sal." Paolo adjusted the oxygen tubes in his nose and boosted one of the tank's valves. The short walk from the car to the building had already taken a toll on him.

"Let's cut to the chase," said the other old man.

"By all means, Vincent," Paolo said. "Wouldn't want to hold you up. I'm sure you have a busy social calendar."

Vincent added a squirt of Gulden's mustard to the top of his pastrami and took a bite. He motioned to Marco, who was standing behind Paolo. "Okay to talk in front of him?"

"Jesus, between you and Benny . . ." Paolo said. "Of course, Vincent. He's my nephew."

"Not by blood."

"He's fine," Paolo answered with a grunt. "I'll vouch for the shmuck. Please continue."

"In a nutshell?" Vincent said. "You should have taken care of this a long time ago, Paolo."

"You mean Gino, Vincent. *Gino* should have taken care of Bailino a long time ago. But he didn't. Had some sort of bromance with the guy, and now he's our problem."

"You mean, he's *your* problem," Sal said. He ripped the inside of the bread out with his hands and tossed it into his mouth.

"Sal," Paolo said, "I'm sure you know who you're dealing with. Bailino isn't only dangerous to the Cataldis. He's dangerous to all of us. He knows a lot of shit."

"Feds think he fled the country," Vincent said.

"That fucking guy wouldn't leave this country if you paid him," Paolo said. "He's got a hard-on for the United States of America. Goddamn war hero. He's here. *Somewhere*. We just have to find him."

"Frankly, I still don't see the big problem," Vincent said. He took a swig of his espresso drink. "Why was it necessary for us to all be here?"

"Me either," Sal said, "although I don't mind a little Bingo, but the guy didn't say shit to anyone about anything. Told the cops it was all his idea, wasn't working for anyone. Didn't name names. Sucked it up."

"How do you know all that?" Paolo asked.

"I have my sources." Sal wiped his mouth with a pink cocktail napkin. "The guy didn't even implicate your grand-nephew, Joey. He could have, but he didn't. Frankly, I don't see the problem. If you ask me, this is personal."

"And you had to go and fucking burn down the goddamn company warehouses," Vincent said. Tiny pieces of pastrami spit out of his mouth as he talked. "It had started to quiet down around here since they got Bailino. Now, I've got unmarked vans following me everywhere I go."

"It's like the goddamn 1970s all over again," Sal said.

"Gentleman, please." Paolo held up his shaky hands. "The warehouse thing was to send a message. And unless both of your

Alzheimer's have kicked in, we do that kind of shit, remember?" Paolo took his breathing tube out of his nose to hack up some loose phlegm, which he spit into a pink napkin.

"Be serious, Paolo, it's been years," Vincent said. "I'm too busy with my great-grandchildren to be running around like that anymore. I can barely keep up with them brats. And, frankly, I never had a problem with Donny. And I was a fan of his father, Patsy Bailino. He was a stand-up guy."

"Don Bailino killed my nephew Leo." Paolo shimmied his breathing tube back into place. "You realize he's trying to do this, trying to isolate the Cataldis from the other families. He knew this would happen."

"Well, then, he's even smarter than I thought he was," Vincent said, standing up. "I got no beef. I think this meeting is over."

"Let's go play some Bingo!" Sal said with as much energy as his shriveled body could muster.

"Wait a second, gentlemen, I don't think you're seeing the big picture. . . ." Paolo motioned to his oxygen cart, and Marco inched it closer to the table so he could turn the valve even higher. "Look what's become of me." He gave the cart a tiny push. "I have to lug this thing around with me everywhere I go, and most days I'm lucky if I can wrap my fingers around the goddamn television remote control, the Parkinson's is so bad. Vincent, you're on your second pacemaker. Sal, you beat cancer twice, right?"

"Damn right," Sal said, "but what does it have to do with—"

"My point is how much time do we have left, gentlemen? What is our quality of life? What will become of these three dynasties? Who will run them? Him?" Paolo pointed to Marco, who looked embarrassed. "I ain't seen any of your kids around. Sal, your grandson makes YouTube videos on how to knot a necktie."

"I don't know where my daughter went wrong with that kid," Sal said, shaking his head.

"It's not just him, Sally, it's everyone. It's a different world today. Kids are selfish, and self-centered. No offense, kid," Paolo motioned to Marco, who looked at the floor. "They take more photos of themselves in one day than I have of my entire family for years. They've forgotten how to say please and thank you or how to look someone in the eye when they speak. They're not interested in us, in *this*." He threw his shaky arms into the air. "This is it for us, my old friends. The last supper. Whether we want to admit it or not, this thing dies with us. And I don't know about you, but this isn't the way I want to go out. Like an old man."

"We *are* old men," Vincent said.

Paolo sighed. *Stupid old bastards*, he thought. He decided to change tacks.

"Vincent," Paolo said, "Gino was good to you."

"Yes, he was," Vincent said with a nod.

"And, Sal, if it weren't for Gino, you'd never have gotten in with the New York State Gaming Commission."

"Gino was always very generous to me," Sal said. "It's true."

"In the end, Gino deserved better than what he got, and why? Because the person he entrusted to do right by him fucked up. As far as I can see, this matter isn't about Don Bailino. Or Pat Bailino. This is about Gino. It's about honoring his memory. It's about loyalty and making good on the promises, the pacts, our families made long ago when we were just little shits running around here, eating free bologna from the butcher."

"Good old Mr. Peterson," Vincent said. "Made the best damn macaroni salad."

"We have a history, gentlemen," Paolo said, "and I don't think it's asking very much for you to return the favor."

"You're laying it on a little thick there, Paolo," Vincent said when a buzzing sound came out of Marco's pocket.

"What the fuck?" Paolo exclaimed. "You're supposed to drop your cell phone outside, nitwit."

"I did," Marco whispered, his cheeks reddening. He fumbled inside his coat. "This is the prepaid." He lifted the phone from his pocket, swiped the screen with his index finger, and stared at it.

"Well?" Paolo asked. "Who the fuck is it?"

Marco hesitated.

"Don't you want to share it with the class?" Sal asked with a toothless chuckle.

Marco held the cell phone in front of Paolo's face, but Paolo swatted it away. "How am I supposed to see it without my glasses?" he said.

Marco reached into Paolo's shirt pocket and placed his glasses on the bridge of his nose.

"Give me that," Paolo said, grabbing for the phone. Marco placed it into Paolo's trembling hand and turned the screen toward him. "I can't see nothin'. Damn thing is dark."

"Oh." Marco swiped the screen with his finger, and it glowed with the image of Leo Cataldi's dead, dirt-covered body lying in a ditch. The accompanying text message read:

YOU SAID YOU WANTED TO KNOW WHAT HAPPENED TO HIM. THOUGHT A PICTURE WOULD BE WORTH A THOUSAND WORDS.

The slight tremor in Paolo's hand became a jolt until it shook so violently that Marco had to hold it in place. "That fuckin' prick," Paolo muttered.

"What is it, Paolo?" Vincent asked. He and Sal shuffled toward Paolo's side of the table, and the three old men peered at the tiny phone screen as Marco struggled to hold Paolo's hand steady. Suddenly, the phone beeped again, and the screen revealed a new image: It was the same photo as before, except this one showed Leo's body engulfed in flames. The text read:

GUESS THIS MAKES TWO THOUSAND WORDS.

"That fuckin' son of a bitch." Paolo swatted the phone away. "Jesus," Vincent said.

"How the fuck did he get out of Stanton anyway?" Sal asked.

"How did he get this number?" Marco asked.

"Does it fucking matter?" Paolo put his hands on the side of the table and pulled himself up to a shaky stand. "Bailino first lets Gino die, and then he doesn't even let my niece get the chance to give her brother Leo a proper burial," he said. "I don't care who a man is, what he's done, he deserves to have the appropriate sendoff with his loved ones around him. Even Gino—who was executed by the state—had that right. But, you know what?" He nodded toward Vincent and Sal. "You're right, you're both right. . . . This is my cross to bear. Not yours. Let's go, Marco." Marco swung the oxygen cart out from the corner and held onto Paolo's arm. "Good-bye, gentlemen . . ." he said, shuffling away.

"Jesus Christ, you don't have to be so dramatic, Paolo." Vincent threw his hands into the air. "All right, already. I'm in."

"What the hell?" Sal said. "I'll probably be dead in a year anyway."

Paolo's lips twitched into a small smile. He turned and faced the two men at the table. "You still got those contacts at the Bureau, Vincent?" Paolo asked. "I need to know what they know."

"I'll find out what I can," Vincent said.

"And, Sally, I need to find the bastard. Your cousin still got access to those interceptors?"

"You kiddin'? He can tell you every time a burner is turned on anywhere in the eastern United States. I don't take a shit anymore without the phone in another room and the window shades closed. Goddamn eyes are everywhere."

"Good, good. Oh, and one more thing," Paolo said.

"What's that?" Vincent asked.

"Do either of you have any ties in Boston?"

26

Jamie awoke with a start. A tiny scraping noise caught her ear, and she hoisted herself up from the backseat of Joey's car, scaring away the robin that had been hauling a twig across the trunk.

She leaned back against the seat and rubbed her eyes. Outside, the green cornfield rose up on all sides of the small patch of dirt on which she had parked, the stalks bending in unison around the car as if they were waving. The night before, she had spent hours driving in and around Little Gap looking for a light blue house with a tire swing near a barn located on a lakefront. She knew the description wasn't much to go on, but it was all she had, and whatever high hopes she had about finding it had waned by sundown. She pulled out the map that she had purchased at a local visitor's center onto her lap. According to the layout, there were seven bodies of water in town, and she had managed to visit five of them already, but found nothing—only large families living in what looked like happy households, which made her yearn for her daughter even more. She marked each of them with a big X.

Two to go, she told herself and hopped into the front seat.

She laid the map on the passenger seat, started the engine, and pulled out onto the dirt road. She couldn't remember the last time she ate anything. She fumbled through her purse, found a stick of chewing gum, and stuck it in her mouth. After driving through what felt like miles of cornfields, she turned off onto a tiny road that led straight to an inlet opening into a large swath of blue, which, according to the map, was Little Bear Lake. With the car still running, she opened her door, stepped out onto the pebbled sand, and gazed out upon the still blue water.

The lake was a wide, almost perfect circle that was surrounded by fields and farms on one half and forest on the other. As was the drill, Jamie looked for a light blue house and barn, but, as was also the drill, she didn't see any, and she was beginning to think she never would. She sat back down in the driver's seat, picked up the map, and put a big X through Little Bear Lake. That left only one more body of water: A tiny one called Cub Creek located somewhere northwest.

She put the car into reverse and was about to back out onto the road when she noticed a plume of black smoke rising into the air above the tree line to her left. She put her hand across her brows to shield the morning sun from her eyes. The smoke's curly column was narrow and slowly thinning—as if it had been a campfire that had already been snuffed out.

Jamie backed out on to the road and followed a series of dirt paths around Little Bear Lake, trying to keep the smoke's plume, which was fading fast, within her sights. After a few minutes, she lost it, but found herself on the other side of the lake, near a wooded area thick with trees and a narrow body of water that she hadn't been able to see from her previous vantage point. She parked her car in an empty lot reserved for family camping, climbed over a metal divider, and walked toward the dense woods.

The tops of the trees blocked out the sunshine, making it about ten degrees cooler under the leafy canopy, and Jamie wrapped her arms around herself to stem the chill. It was quiet; she could hear her every step across the rocks and branches as she trekked deeper and deeper into the woods. As far as she could tell, there were no remains of a fire, but she could now smell traces of one somewhere up ahead.

She kept walking until she saw the end of the tree line, and as she emerged back into the bright sunshine, she was stunned: About twenty yards ahead was a house beside a barn with a silo overlooking the lake on a secluded lakefront property. The house may have been light blue once, but it had been so weathered and forsaken that it was now a dull gray. A tire lay limply across the front yard and was attached to a rope that was slung over the branch of a tree as if someone were going to erect a swing. She imagined young Joey Santelli swinging on that tire as a boy many years ago. *Could it be?*

She took another step forward, but noticed a minivan parked behind a small shed, and she hid behind a thick, knotted tree. She peered around the trunk to look at the license plate: It was from New York.

Her heart raced. She searched the cracked windows of each of the home's levels, but they were boarded up diagonally with planks of wood as if preparing for a hurricane. She thought of her daughter somewhere inside the old house under Bailino's care, and she suddenly felt vulnerable and alone. She rummaged through her purse for the prepaid phone. She turned it on, and the battery icon immediately began blinking—*damn*, she had forgotten to charge it. She began to dial as the front door to the home creaked opened, and she pressed her body so tightly up against the bark of the tree that its edges felt like blades across her back. She put the phone into her pocket, reached down into her ankle holster, and pulled out her pistol with a shaky hand.

She waited, but didn't hear anything behind her—no rustling, no footsteps. She peeked back toward the front door and stifled a small gasp: Standing partially across the threshold was Don Bailino, his intense and familiar stare firmly upon her. Although he looked a bit different—his hair was cut very short, almost to the scalp, and his face seemed bulkier than before—she knew immediately that it was him, and her body trembled. She hoisted the pistol and pressed harder against the tree for leverage, keeping her eyes on him. They stayed like that for some time until Bailino took a small step forward, revealing his whole body and what he held in his massive arms: the tiny body of Faith, who had a baby bottle to her lips and was rubbing her eyes.

"Faith!" Jamie screamed, leaping out from her hiding place and keeping the gun steady.

The little girl's head turned in the direction of her mother's voice.

"Toss the gun," Bailino said, producing a gun, which he held to the little girl's head.

"Mama!" Faith yelled when she spotted Jamie.

"Let her go," Jamie yelled, moving slowly toward them. She had taken shots at this distance before at the shooting range, but her arms were shaking, and she couldn't risk missing him—or worse, hitting her daughter.

"I said toss it." Bailino's eyes were like laser beams on hers. "I'm not going to say it again."

Jamie arms buckled. Faith's face was dirty with tear and milk stains. She lowered the gun and tossed it behind her into the forest. When she did, Bailino stepped back, disappearing somewhere inside the house, and she made a mad dash toward the front door, bounding up the front steps and across the threshold until she was inside. The old home was dark, lit only by a lantern sitting on a table that was covered with coloring books and crayons.

"Close the door," Bailino said. He was standing near the far wall, below an iron spiral staircase, the gun still aimed at the little girl.

"Mama!" Faith said. She leaned forward in Bailino's arms, but he pulled her back.

"Give me my baby," Jamie said.

"I said close the door," he said.

"Mama!" Faith called more desperately, squirming in Bailino's arms and dropping her baby bottle, which rolled across the old wooden floor beams.

"Give her to me," Jamie cried. "She wants me." She ran to the front door and slammed it closed. The moment it shut, Bailino put Faith on the floor, and the little girl hobbled happily toward her mother.

"Mama! Mama!" she cried and held up her hands.

"Oh, sweetie." Jamie lifted Faith in her arms, and as soon as she had a firm hold on her, she reached for the doorknob to the front door, but Bailino stepped in front of her.

"I can't let you do that," he said.

"Please, let her go. She's an innocent little girl. I'll stay. Let me bring her somewhere, to safety."

"How did you find me?"

"Please . . ."

"I asked how you found me."

Jamie ran toward the center of the room, which was grim and looked largely untouched for a very long time with the exception of tiny spots of color—a purple sippy cup in an old wooden dish rack, a bright yellow bib hanging over the back of a chair, a baby jar half filled with carrots.

"Answer me, please," Bailino said.

He walked toward her, and Jamie pulled a chair out in front of her to block his way. She boosted Faith in her arms and ran randomly toward a room, slamming the door shut and locking it. She felt along the wooden wall for the light and flicked it on, but nothing happened— the bulb was missing from the broken wall sconce. Red-tinged sunshine poured into the room from a small stained-glass window, and Jamie realized she was in a bathroom. Leak marks dotted the ceiling near the outer walls, and the toilet was empty and brown with rust stains; a bucket filled with water was beside it. The only other exit beside the small window was a wall-mounted bathroom fan that had large rusted blades and was missing its chain. There was no other way out. She pulled down the lid of the toilet seat, which swiveled precariously on the porcelain base—one of its screws being loose—and sat down.

"Were you followed?" Bailino asked through the door.

"Mama, mama!" Faith said excitedly, pointing to the stained-glass window.

Jamie brushed the hair out of her daughter's face and quickly looked her over. She checked the top of her head and each of her limbs as Faith's dark brown eyes surveyed the bathroom. She seemed unharmed. "Are you okay, Faithy?" she whispered.

"She's fine," Bailino said, and the bathroom door clicked and opened, and he was standing over her. He stuck a key into his pocket. "I'm going to ask these two questions one more time, understand?" he said. "Were you followed?"

Jamie shook her head and held Faith close.

"I need an answer," Bailino said.

"No," she said. The tears gathered in the corners of her eyes. "I can't do this again," she said. "If you're going to hurt me, all I ask is that you let her go. She's done nothing. She is an innocent in all of this."

"What makes you think I'm going to hurt you?"

Bailino's face was badly bruised, his eyes hidden partially behind cuts and swellings that had begun to heal but were fairly recent.

"Why are you doing this?" she asked.

"How did you find me?" Bailino said.

Jamie pulled Faith closer to her. "Joey," Jamie said softly, her lips brushing the little girl's cheeks.

Bailino nodded. He leaned against the door frame and crossed his arms. "You called him?" he asked.

Jamie shook her head. "I saw him."

"Where? At school?"

"Yes." Jamie's heart was pumping hard and fast, but she tried to steady her breathing, keeping her gaze steady on him.

"How is he?" Bailino asked.

"Joey? Okay, I guess . . ." she said. "He's being watched. . ."

Bailino nodded. He reached behind him, and Jamie braced herself against the toilet, but his arm returned with the baby bottle that Faith had dropped. He held it out, and the little girl reached for it, but Jamie grabbed it first. She sniffed it.

"It's milk," Bailino said. "Two percent."

Faith grabbed it out of Jamie's hands, stuck it into her mouth, and leaned against Jamie's chest.

"How did you get here?" Bailino asked.

"Please, can I just—"

"*How* did you get here?"

Jamie took a deep breath and exhaled. "Joey gave me his car," she said.

"Where is it?"

"It's parked on the other side of the wooded area."

Bailino absorbed the information. "E-ZPass?" he asked.

Jamie shook her head. "No."

"GPS?"

"Not that I know of," Jamie said.

"Phone?"

"I got rid of mine and bought a prepaid."

He nodded. "Where is it?"

It was all flooding back to her—the direct questions, the way he used his eyes, his tone, and his body as intimidation. Conversations were warfare for Don Bailino—a way to gauge and decipher. She knew she had no choice; she reached into her pocket, fished out the phone, and handed it to him. He put the phone in the pocket of his jeans.

"Good girl," he said. "Did you use it?"

"No," she said.

Bailino cocked his head to the side as if he heard something. When he did, his white T-shirt moved from his shoulder, revealing a large surgery scar—ragged and red—right where Jamie had shot him, and that night in the deserted playground played back in her mind. She had witnessed him do horrible things to people who had done far less to him than she had.

"Please," she tried again, caressing the top of Faith's head, "can you—"

"*Shhh . . .*" Bailino was still listening for something. He reached into the waistband of his pants and pulled out a small handgun.

Jamie grabbed Faith and backed away toward the rusted bathtub. "Please, I didn't—"

"Wait here," Bailino ordered and closed the bathroom door, and before Jamie could follow after him, she heard the door lock with a click.

27

Special Agent Wilcox was talking on the phone at the head of the conference table. Phillip watched his facial expressions turn from serious to incredulous back to serious again. He hadn't expected to see Wilcox back at the Executive Mansion so quickly, but just as Phillip managed to convince Reynaldo to go home, promising to keep him updated regularly, Wilcox had returned from Long Island, bringing with him an army of federal agents.

Wilcox also returned with news: The FBI had discovered the body of Leo Cataldi, which had been burned and lying in a ditch not far from Upackk's headquarters in Albany. Leo had been missing and presumed dead by law enforcement, who generally believed the body to be floating somewhere in the Atlantic. Wilcox explained that since Bailino's escape, the FBI had been probing burners, or disposable phones, in the Albany area—including records of when a phone went online, when it stopped being used, and its total number of calls. They also monitored areas for phones that were used for a standard amount of time—say, twelve or twenty-four hours—and then went dead just as another burner in the area went online. The presumption, Wilcox said, was that Bailino—and perhaps even Jamie Carter—was cycling through cell phones as a counter-surveillance tactic. Earlier that afternoon, Wilcox's men had tracked a lead to a burner that took them right to the body of Leo Cataldi. When they got there, a prepaid cell phone was lying next to the grave. Wilcox believed that Bailino had led the Feds right to the site.

"I didn't think there'd be much to go on with the Cataldi body," Wilcox said, hanging up the phone, "but because the body was somewhat damp, it didn't burn for long—probably just long enough for Bailino to make his point, which we found on his phone."

"What do you mean?" Phillip asked.

"Images of the body were sent to another telephone number downstate in Brooklyn, another burner. We're assuming it was to a member of the Cataldi family or another one of the families." Wilcox gave a quick explanation of the surveillance tactics used in determining the receiving cell phone.

"Why would Bailino lead you right to the body?" Phillip asked.

"Frankly, nothing about the guy surprises me," Wilcox said. "Unfortunately, there was nothing at the crime scene, as far as we could see, that will tell us Bailino's whereabouts, other than that he was at the location of the body at the time the phone calls were made—we know he was there because I just got the official ID on a pair of prints we found on the phone. Plus," Wilcox tapped the legal pad he had been writing on, "preliminary forensics also tells me it looks like we found Bailino's DNA under Leo Cataldi's fingernails. Apparently, there was some kind of struggle before Mr. Cataldi was killed, which, we believe, was about two years ago."

"Around the time of Charlotte's kidnapping," Phillip said.

"Exactly. And it all lines up with Jamie Carter's testimony about how things went down. It's a missing puzzle piece."

"So then you have probable cause to arrest Don Bailino for the death of Leo Cataldi," Phillip said.

"Yes, we do," Wilcox said with assurance, "but, at this point, it looks like we'll just be adding Leo Cataldi to an already lengthy list. Although," he added, "if Bailino is found guilty of the additional homicide—and I believe he will be, once he's captured—it *is* possible that the prosecutors will push for the death penalty this time around."

Phillip studied Wilcox's expression, trying to figure out whether the agent was intimating that Phillip should have pushed harder for the death penalty the first time, despite Bailino's plea agreement. As always, though, Wilcox was hard to read. "Bailino already made a deal," Phillip said.

"All bets would be off at that point," Wilcox said. "New crime, new punishment."

There was a knock on the door, and Katherine stuck in her head. "May I?" she said.

"Of course, Mrs. Grand," Wilcox said. "Come in."

In addition to maintaining open communications with the governor's office regarding the ongoing organized crime investigations in the state, and with the Cataldi family, in particular, Wilcox had extended the same courtesy to Katherine, the state's first lady. This was virtually unheard of in law enforcement circles since hers was an unofficial position politically. Phillip imagined that somewhere along the way Katherine Grand had earned Special Agent Wilcox's respect. She came into the conference room holding a laptop computer and closed the door behind her.

"Any news on Bailino's whereabouts?" she asked.

"Not yet, I'm afraid," Wilcox said.

"Nothing further on that photo taken at the Albany Amtrak station yesterday morning?" Katherine said.

"Probably a red herring, to throw us off," Wilcox said. "It looks like he's sticking around."

"Great," Katherine sat down at the conference table, "shutting down one of the busiest transit areas in the country for nothing. The press will have a field day with that one." She opened her laptop computer on the table. "So he can be anywhere?"

"Maybe he'll just stay in hiding," Phillip said. "He managed to do what nobody—including Gino Cataldi—was able to do before him, escape from Stanton prison. Why risk getting caught?"

"But with a baby?" Katherine asked. "If what you believe is true, that Don Bailino has Faith Carter, how does one keep a low profile with an infant that all of America is looking for?"

Wilcox's walkie-talkie unit crackled, and a series of codes came through that sounded unintelligible to Phillip, but Wilcox answered in kind. He replaced the unit on his belt. "I do believe that Bailino will lay low," Wilcox said, "at least for now, until he feels the time is right to strike."

"Strike whom?" Phillip asked.

Wilcox reached into a briefcase that was at his side, pulled out a manila folder, and opened it on the conference table. Inside were photos of three men—he fanned them out on the tabletop. "These were taken last night outside the Knights of Columbus in Brooklyn," he said.

Phillip and Katherine peered down at the images. Phillip recognized the three figures immediately—Salvatore DeGrassi, Vincent LaPazza, and Paolo Cataldi, the heads of the three remaining organized crime families in New York.

"Brooklyn?" Phillip asked. "Didn't you just say that Don Bailino's photos were sent there?"

"What photos?" Katherine asked.

"Yes, exactly," Wilcox said. "Mrs. Grand, as I told the governor, we believe that Don Bailino transmitted two digital photos of Leo Cataldi, whose body we found early this morning, to one or all of these men last night."

Katherine studied them. "Do you think it's some kind of challenge?" she asked.

"Or goading?" Phillip said.

"We think it's probably a little of both," Wilcox said. "We know that there's no love lost between Paolo Cataldi and Don Bailino. There seemed to be some sort of power struggle between the two men for years. If you were to liken them to the old *Godfather* movies, Paolo Cataldi would be your Fredo." Wilcox put the photos away and returned the folder to his briefcase. "Things had always been tetchy, and I can only imagine they got worse since Gino Cataldi's— and now Leo Cataldi's—death. Based on the evidence we found at Bailino's Upackk headquarters in Albany and several of the other warehouses, we're pretty sure Paolo Cataldi was behind the fires of Upackk. The modus operandi matches other arson crimes he was charged with in the early 1980s."

"Could Bailino be forming an alliance with the other families?" Phillip asked.

"We still don't know. We can pin the call to a specific geographical area, but not a specific person," Wilcox said.

"Are you going to arrest Paolo Cataldi for arson?" Katherine asked.

"We're still deciding on the best protocol," Wilcox said. "Truth be told, we think the old man did us a favor."

"What do you mean?" Katherine asked. "The way I see it, the fires incited Bailino to escape from prison. Without them, none of this would have happened."

"We don't believe so, ma'am," Wilcox said. "We believe Bailino had things in place to escape from Stanton from the get-go. He never had any intention of staying."

"Any idea yet on how he managed to escape?" Phillip asked.

"We're continuing to interview the prison staff. He had help, that's for sure. It's ongoing, but our priority now is to capture the fugitive before . . . well, to put it mildly, before things get even worse," Wilcox said. "We already have one guard dead whom we believe to be the victim of Don Bailino. No DNA yet, but we're told by fellow COs that Bernie Brooks had some words with Bailino on the transport to Stanton. As I'm sure you know, Governor Grand, Don Bailino isn't one to let things lie. Before the fires, Bailino may have been planning to escape for his freedom, but we believe the fires may have changed that, and now Don Bailino is out for—"

"Revenge," Phillip said.

"Correct, governor," Wilcox said.

Katherine seemed unconvinced. "Do you really think he would risk everything for revenge?" she asked.

"Yes," Phillip said without hesitation.

"But revenge against whom?" Katherine asked. "Cataldi? The other bosses?" She looked at Phillip. "Us?"

"Everyone," Phillip said. He walked over to the second-floor window and stared out at the American flag being hoisted atop the flagpole on the front lawn. He had watched the same routine every morning on the Army's forward operating base from his tent. There were not many things that Phillip wanted to remember about his time serving in America's armed forces, particularly those years spent in the Middle East, but the clear nights in the desert when the sky was starry and the gunfire had ceased was one of them. Phillip and Bailino would walk the perimeter, gazing up at the constellations as if they could tell their futures. "Anyone can be an adversary, Phil," Phillip remembered Bailino telling him one night as they looked out into the black desert. "It doesn't matter what color uniform you wear, as far as I'm concerned, if you're not with me, you're against me." *On what side would Bailino see him now?*

"He'll go after anyone he deems to be an enemy," Wilcox said. "However, I don't want either of you to worry. This place is more secure than Fort Knox."

"Are you saying that you consider us to be one of Bailino's enemies?" Katherine asked.

"I'm saying not to worry," Wilcox said. "And as for the Brooklyn-based families, the thing is, we've been following Cataldi, DeGrassi, and LaPazza for years. The old heads don't get together much anymore. Too old. Too sick. Too bored. What happened last night was rare. I'm assuming it was to talk about Bailino."

"So you think Bailino's heading to Brooklyn?" Katherine asked.

"Maybe. It'll be tough, though," Wilcox said. "We've got a heavy presence downstate, but Bailino knows the borough well, so it's possible. But knocking off these old birds one by one will only bring attention to him. His best bet would be to kill them off in one fell swoop."

"Looks like he missed his chance," Phillip said. "What are the odds of them being in one place again?"

Wilcox stepped toward Phillip, his long, slender frame as straight as a board. He crossed his arms. "Actually, that's where we were hoping you could come in, Governor," he said.

"Me?" Phillip asked.

"Cat and mouse can be played in a variety of ways," Wilcox said.

Phillip thought he detected a gleam in the agent's eye. "I don't follow," he said.

"The way I see it, if the cat can't find the mouse," Wilcox said, "then we need to get the mouse to go to the cheese."

28

At least twenty minutes had passed since Bailino had locked Jamie and Faith in the tiny bathroom, and, without any ventilation from the broken wall fan, it was getting hot. Jamie turned on the water faucet and placed Faith's hand under the stream to help her cool off. The pressure was poor, and the water temperature was tepid at best, but it was all they had. She had been trying to figure out if there was a way to get out through the stained-glass window when the bathroom door opened, startling her, and a blast of cooler, but stale air rushed inside the room. Even in a house full of rickety old sounds, Bailino seemed to be able to move around surreptitiously.

"You should eat something," he said, putting the gun inside the waistband of his pants, and stepped away from the door.

Jamie held onto Faith, who was sitting on the edge of the sink. The clanking of pots and pans and another *whoosh* of running water emanated from the kitchen, and Faith lifted her hands for Jamie to pick her up.

"Go?" the little girl said once she was in Jamie's arms, pointing out the bathroom door, and it dawned on Jamie that Faith was showing no real fear of Bailino, not the kind of fear that little children would have of strangers or of danger. If he had harmed her in any way, Jamie believed she would have been able to detect it in her daughter, or at least she hoped that she would. Still, she knew that just because

Bailino hadn't hurt them already didn't mean he wouldn't. She turned off the water faucet, tiptoed to the bathroom door, and peeked into the dining area.

On the table was a teddy bear, a rattle, and a ceramic bowl of fruit that looked wet and washed. A box of milk, the kind that didn't need refrigeration, was next to the bowl, along with Jamie's gun, which Bailino must have retrieved from the front of the house.

"Next time," Bailino said, "don't hesitate. Take the shot." He caught her eye before she could look away.

Faith straightened her body, signaling that she wanted Jamie to put her on the floor.

"No, I want to hold you," Jamie whispered.

"I think she wants to get down." Bailino reached for a package from a cabinet.

"I'd rather hold her," Jamie said, a little too boldly. She was surprised at the familiarity in her voice despite her fear, but Bailino didn't seem fazed and pulled the plastic from a small box of chocolate chip cookies.

"Suit yourself." He placed the cookies onto a plate and set it next to the bowl of fruit on the table.

"Baba?" Faith said, pointing to the bathroom floor where her empty milk bottle was lying next to one of the clawed feet of the bathtub. Jamie picked it up and gave it to her.

"Down?" Faith wrapped the bottle under her arm.

"Not now," Jamie whispered.

"Down, down," Faith said again with more force. She narrowed her big brown eyes at her mother.

"She's a tough cookie, that one," Bailino said. He placed an apple juice box on the table next to the cookies. "Reminds me of someone." He smirked.

"Are you going to kill me?" Jamie asked.

"Well, seems like old times," Bailino said. "Answer's still the same, although I just might if you don't come out of the bathroom."

Faith leaned forward in Jamie's arms, causing Jamie to take a step forward. With Faith's pointer finger leading the way, she padded toward the table of snacks, casually glancing at the front door to the house. It was closed, and presumably locked.

Bailino grabbed another juice box from a package on the counter and held it out for Jamie. "This one's for you, if you want it," he said. "I didn't know you were going to be here, or else I would have bought some chocolate milk." He smirked again.

"Thank you," she said as politely and unfamiliarly as possible, took the juice box from him, and sat down with Faith on her lap at the table. Faith put down her bottle and reached for a chocolate chip cookie and a juice box. She fumbled with the plastic straw, and Jamie helped her punch it through the aluminum hole at the top. Faith puckered her pouty lips around the straw and sucked so hard the sides of the juice box caved inward.

"Somebody was thirsty," Bailino said, sitting down across the table from them. He reached into the bowl of fruit, plucked out a cherry, and popped it into his mouth, pulling out the stem between his teeth. He placed the stem on a napkin. "She looks exactly like you, you know," he said, his eyes scanning Jamie's face. "She's beautiful."

At the word *beautiful*, Jamie looked down. The word brought to mind the last thing Bailino had said to her after she shot him twice. *I love you. . . .* She had thought about those three words many times over the past two years—what they meant, why he had said them, since there was no way he could really love her, but why he thought he did. And if she were being honest with herself, she knew that those three words were what she held onto when she had decided to have this baby, when she was feeling scared and alone, when Reynaldo—and even Edward—had looked at her like she was crazy. The thought that in all that ugliness perhaps there was a glimmer of goodness—a kind thought, an honest care—might be enough to allow her to live her life beyond those four days in April 2012. She tightened her hold on her daughter.

"Are you still freelance writing?" Bailino asked.

Jamie shrugged her shoulders.

"Have we really forgotten how much I detest indirectness?" he asked.

Jamie lifted her eyes. "Not really. It's hard to write articles about other people when your clients seem to think that it's *you* who's the story. I lost some clients. Others I dropped."

"How do you get by?"

"Dipped into savings. We're okay," she said, smoothing Faith's dark hair.

Bailino nodded. "Why didn't you write the book?" He reached for another cherry.

"Book?" Jamie could smell cherry juice, and her stomach rumbled. Bailino pushed the bowl of fruit toward her. Tentatively, she plucked a cherry out for herself.

"I got at least three requests from some shmucks to sign over the rights to my story so they could make a Lifetime movie about what happened," Bailino said. "I'm sure you—being a writer—were inundated with requests of your own." He placed the cherry's stem neatly next to the other on the napkin.

"I was," she said, "inundated, I mean. It's weird . . . I waited my entire life for a publishing company to knock on my door and ask me to write a book. And when someone finally did, I said no."

"Why say no, then?" Bailino asked, his eyes curious. "I'm sure they offered you a lot of money."

"They did. *A lot* of money. More than I ever thought I'd see. And part of me thought—well, some people said—it was selfish of me to say no, that I should be thinking about *her*," Jamie motioned toward Faith, "about college and all that—all that money would buy a lot of things that we might never have. But . . ." She shrugged and bit into the cherry. "That kind of stuff doesn't really matter to me, to be honest. And that wasn't really the kind of book I wanted to write. It didn't matter anyway. They found other people to write it for them."

"Four, actually. They banged those puppies out fast." Bailino shook his head. "Apparently, they didn't need us at all to tell our story."

The *our* of Bailino's statement hung in the air like an invisible line connecting them. "You read them?" she asked quickly, as if new words would make the old one disappear. "The books?"

"Every one."

Jamie felt her cheeks redden. She hadn't been interested in reading any of the versions, although she did glance at a few excerpts on various websites—it was hard to avoid them for a time. Without much to go on, since both Bailino and Jamie had refused to talk to the press, and because Jamie had also refused to get a DNA test done on Faith, the writers had created a very vivid portrait of what they thought happened at the log cabin two years ago. Bob's version of events, of the four, had been the most graphic.

"That ex-husband of yours has quite an imagination," Bailino said with distaste.

"Ironic, since he didn't have much of one while we were married," Jamie said.

Bailino smirked again and leaned back in his chair. The two watched Faith pull apart the chocolate chip cookie, her fingers covered in goo.

The back of her head stung, and Jamie touched it absently. She put her hand down when she saw Bailino watching.

"Sorry about that," he said. "It wasn't supposed to happen. Good help is hard to find." He plucked another cherry. "He's not gonna bother you anymore."

Bailino had said the same thing to her about Leo Cataldi. She kept her eyes cast downward, although she remembered how hard it was not to look at him. It was as if his eyes commanded hers without his saying a word.

"Faith is a pretty name," Bailino said. "What made you decide on it?"

Jamie shrugged. "It was something my mom used to say, to always have faith—it was one of the many things she said. So when I got the chance, I did."

Bailino held a cherry out for Faith, and Jamie's impulse was to seize it, but she let the little girl reach for it. Faith looked up at Bailino with her dark brown gaze, and he returned it, his eyes softening as she reached for the cherry with her sticky fingers. Jamie held the stem while the little girl nibbled at the fruit.

"Thank you," Bailino said, his eyes returning to Jamie's.

"For what?" she asked.

"For having her," he said, but then cocked his head again to the side.

"What is it?"

"*Shhh . . .*" he said, listening. "I thought I heard something." He was looking toward the window over the kitchen sink.

For a moment, Jamie hoped that the FBI had followed her or had somehow gotten Joey Santelli to give up the details on Bailino's Pennsylvania house. Would they stumble upon it as she had?

"Are you sure you didn't use your phone?" Bailino asked, pulling her cell phone out of his pocket. "Wait, is this thing on?"

"Yes, it's on," Jamie said, "but I didn't—"

A loud *bang* shattered the glass over the kitchen sink, and the ceramic fruit bowl on the table burst into pieces, shooting out in every direction.

Bailino leaped across the table. "Get down," he yelled, pulling Jamie and Faith to the floor and his gun out of his waistband.

Faith was shrieking, her face mottled with red, and grabbed onto her mother tightly as Jamie crouched under the table, clinging to the iron stand, Bailino's strong chest pressing against her.

"Stay there," he ordered. He got up and ran to the side of the shattered window. A shadow passed by, and Bailino ducked down and tiptoed past the sink toward the front door. He put his ear to the wood before slowly opening it and peering outside. Then he put his finger to his lips, signaling for Jamie to be quiet, which seemed absurd since Faith was screaming her head off, and slipped onto the front porch.

Jamie wiped the bits of ceramic from Faith's shirt and out of her hair. The little girl was heaving, but otherwise looked all right, and Jamie pressed Faith's head to her neck and patted her back to calm her, hoping the little girl wouldn't hear Jamie's racing heart. Jamie knew exactly what that popping sound had been. She remembered it well. The bullet had missed Bailino by no more than a foot.

"Home, mama," Faith cried, her voice muffled by Jamie's shirt.

"I know, baby," Jamie said. She spotted her cell phone on the floor among the fruit and broken pieces of bowl. She reached for it and pressed the power button.

"C'mon, c'mon . . ." she said as the screen lit up and a large red hourglass battery icon began to blink. *There was still power.*

With Faith in her arms, Jamie got out from under the table and ran to the front door. The tree line wasn't far ahead, and she wondered if she could make it to the wooded area—she still had the car keys in her pocket—but another gunshot, this time at the front of the house, made Jamie backtrack into the dining room. She ran into the room next to the bathroom, a child's bedroom with faded posters of Mickey Mantle and Jackie Robinson on the walls. An empty bookshelf held a dusty framed eight-by-ten photo of a woman in a polka-dot bikini. The woman was holding a little boy—a boy who looked identical to Faith.

Jamie ran toward a window, which was double-hung and big enough for her to climb out, but, as with the rest of the house, was boarded up with a big X of wood. On the bottom right, one of the four panes was broken, and Jamie bent down to look outside. She didn't see anything beyond the pebble and dirt lakefront and the blue of the water.

"Home, mama," Faith screamed again as Jamie sat down on the floor underneath the broken window pane.

"We're going home, I promise," she said. She placed her daughter on her lap and dialed Special Agent Wilcox's phone number. "Please don't die, please don't die," she said, putting the phone to her ear and hoping the battery power would hold out. The little girl's cries seemed even louder in the small bedroom.

On the third ring, she heard a click and then, "Special Agent Wilcox."

"It's Jamie Carter," she yelled into the receiver so that he could hear her on top of Faith's voice. "Are you there?"

"Jamie? Where are you?"

"I'm—"

Jamie's head jolted backward as someone grabbed her neck from outside the window, pulling her back by her hair. She dropped the cell phone and Faith tumbled to the floor as Jamie's head banged against the window ledge right where she had been hit before, the knot of skin under her hair feeling as if it were slicing open. She scratched at the hairy knuckles gripping her throat and tried to rise up on her legs to gain some traction, but the hold was tight.

"Mama! Mama!" Faith wailed, but Jamie couldn't see her daughter who was somewhere underfoot. She clawed and pulled at the fingers around her neck, one of which had a gold ring that was cutting into her skin, when a window pane shattered next to her and another hand pushed into the bedroom, this one carrying a handgun.

"Noooo!" Jamie screamed and threw her body down, pulling the hand down with her. She planted her feet and kicked the gun, which slid across the floor and under the twin bed.

Without the gun, the other hand reached around Jamie's throat, the two hands working like a clamp, and Jamie could no longer breathe at all.

"I'll kill you, bitch," a deep voice muttered, and she felt herself losing consciousness when suddenly the hands let go and Jamie fell onto the floor, gasping for breath. She inhaled the dusty air of the old carpet as Faith's screaming face clawed at her cheeks.

"Mama!" Faith climbed onto Jamie's back as Jamie got up on all fours and put her head to the floor, trying to suck air into her lungs. She reached out for her daughter and saw Bailino through the broken window pane wrapping a piece of twine around a man's neck like he was winding a yo-yo. Pulling Faith into her arms, Jamie inched back toward the far wall as the man's face turned purple and Bailino slammed his head into the dirt lawn over and over until he twisted it back with a jerk. The man's body lay twitching on the ground, and Bailino picked up the man's limp arm, ripped the ring off his finger, and stuck it in his pocket. Then he rummaged through the man's pockets and pulled out a cell phone. Bailino looked at the screen, stood up, and disappeared from view.

Jamie's throat was on fire, and she opened and closed her mouth trying to draw enough saliva to swallow when Bailino burst through the bedroom door.

"Are you all right, sweetheart?" he asked Jamie. "Let me have her." He tried to pull Faith from her grasp.

"No," Jamie wheezed and tightened her hold on Faith.

"Let her go, hon," Bailino said calmly. "I need to see if you're all right." He lifted Jamie, with Faith on her lap, into the air and onto the twin bed. "Sit over here, cupcake," he said, plucking Faith from Jamie's grip and moving her toward the wall. He gently pushed up on Jamie's chin. "We're going to have to get something to put on that." He ran his fingers lightly on the raw skin.

"Don't . . ." Jamie said.

"It's going to burn for a few days, but you'll be all right. Can you swallow?"

"I don't know." She squeezed her lids shut to keep tears from falling onto her cheeks, but she felt them lacing her eyelids.

Bailino reached around her head and placed his hand between Jamie's head and the pillow and felt the skin under her hair. "Does that hurt?" he asked.

"Yes," she whimpered. "Please don't—"

"Can you walk?"

"I'm not sure, I—"

"We need to go, sweetheart." He stood and tugged on her arm as if he were a parent trying to wake her for school. "Up, up, up, up. We don't have much time."

"I can't," Jamie croaked. She reached for Faith's hand and pulled the little girl beside her. "You can just leave us here, can't you? You can go. I won't tell anyone I saw you. I promise. I'll say I found Faith here. Unharmed and alone."

"I'm afraid I can't do that," Bailino said.

"Why?" she asked, her voice cracking. "I don't understand what—"

"Honey, you see how easily I got this kid from you on Long Island. They'll get to her."

"*Who* will get to her? Why was that man trying to shoot you?"

His eyes were a restrained wild, reminding her of an animal caged at a zoo. It was hard to believe that the man looking at her now, the one she had watched choke a man to death, was the same sweet-faced little boy in the photograph behind him.

"Sweetheart, that man . . ." Bailino ran his hand over the razor stubble on his cheeks. "He wasn't trying to shoot *me*."

"But . . ." Bailino's words traveled to her as if through a fog. "I don't understand."

"I think you do," he said, "and we really have to go. If that guy was alone, and from what I could see he was, it won't be long until others come looking for him—and for *her*." He tilted his chin at Faith, who had calmed down, but was still crying as she lay her head on Jamie's arm.

"Why would anyone want to hurt a little girl?" Jamie asked.

"They don't," Bailino said. "They want to hurt *me*." He tugged again on her arm. "Let's go."

"But I—"

"You gotta trust me," Bailino said. "I have never lied to you. Not then. Not now. And right now, we need to go."

Jamie knew that Special Agent Wilcox or his men would be there soon. She had gotten through to him. Wasn't that enough to perform some kind of trace? Hadn't Bailino said the same thing himself? She could try to stall Bailino until the FBI arrived, but what if Bailino was telling the truth? What if more men were coming to harm Faith? Could it be possible that Bailino had abducted Faith not to hurt her, but to *protect* her?

As if reading her thoughts, Bailino said, "I know these men, hon. The only reason they haven't tried to hurt Faith before was . . . Well, they were waiting. For me to get better, for me to be put back together so that they could take my life apart, piece by piece. That's what they do. She's not safe, not with the FBI, not with New York PD, and, frankly, depending upon what *he*"—he motioned to the dead man outside—"saw, I'm not sure you are anymore either."

"What do you mean?" she asked.

"We need to go," Bailino said. "Okay?"

Jamie felt the weight of his gaze. For two years, she had lived in fear of those eyes, had had nightmares about them and their reign of terror. She didn't have a choice then, and she didn't have a choice now, she knew that, but for some reason Bailino was giving Jamie the *illusion* of choice. He wasn't forcing her to go with him, at least not yet. He was asking.

"Let's keep her safe," he said and held out his hand—the same hand that had grabbed her in midtown Manhattan, that had held her down onto a bed, that he had slipped between her thighs when he slept beside her. Her mother's words, as they often did in times of crisis or uncertainty, floated to her in a whisper: *Driving is easy—go when it's green, stop when it's red. The real trick is learning to live your life that way.* But in which direction was she supposed to go?

Faith was looking up at Jamie with big bloodshot brown eyes as if she too were waiting for her to do something. Jamie weighed her options and realized she didn't have any—Bailino, despite what he said or how he asked, would never let her stay. However, that wasn't what was most troubling. What was most troubling was that *she believed him*. She believed others were coming. She believed he could protect them—more so than anyone else. And that meant that she had to trust him.

Jamie took a deep breath. "Okay," she said.

"Good girl. Can you walk?" he asked, helping her into a sitting position.

"I don't know," Jamie whispered. "I think so." She reached down for her cell phone, which was on the floor.

"Leave it. It's not good to us anymore," Bailino said.

"That man . . ." Jamie said. "He found Faith because of *me*?"

"Let's just say for future reference, you don't need to make a call from a cell phone to alert someone to your location. Just turning it on will do the trick." His eyes softened. "Don't worry about it, okay? Rookie mistake. C'mon, let's go."

"Where?"

"I have a few places in mind. My father didn't trust those goddamn bastards either." He pulled gently on her arm to help her stand.

"Wait, please just give me a minute," Jamie said. "I'll be right there."

"Sweetheart, we don't—"

"Please," Jamie said.

Faith put her hand into her mother's. "Peas," she added in a little voice and looked up at Bailino.

Bailino sighed. "Okay, *one minute.*" He dropped Jamie's hand and held his hand out for Faith. "Come on, cupcake, let's get your coloring books. It's time to go bye-bye."

"She can stay with me." Jamie rested her hand on Faith's arm.

"She's safer with me. Let's get your crayons, sweetie," Bailino said, drawing Faith's attention again. "Okay?"

Faith thought about it, her large brown eyes tightening in the corners. She looked at her mother for approval, and Jamie, to her own astonishment, found herself nodding. The little girl put her hand in Bailino's dirty palm.

"Good girl." Bailino led Faith toward the dining room, her tiny legs hurrying to keep up with his.

"Come, mama!" Faith said, looking back at Jamie.

"I'll be right there." Jamie forced a smile. "Don't forget your baba."

When they were out of the room, Jamie crept down onto the floor and reached her hand under the bed. She felt around until she found the handgun she had kicked there and pulled it toward her, the dust and cobwebs clinging to it like powder. It was larger than the one she carried, and she wrapped her hand around the massive grip. What was stopping her from shooting Bailino now, as she had practiced, and taking her daughter away to a safe place of her own choosing?

There was a moment two years ago when Leo Cataldi had

pinned Jamie down to the floor of the log cabin bedroom, and all she could think about was Bailino coming to her rescue—how absurd it had seemed to seek protection from the person who had done her the most harm. She felt the same way now—that a flip of circumstance had turned her fiercest adversary into her strongest ally. She slipped the oversized gun into her leg holster as best she could.

"Mama?" Faith called again from the other room as cabinet doors and drawers were opened and closed.

"Yes, baby," Jamie called, pulling down the cuff of her jeans. "I'm ready."

29

Reynaldo slammed the car door and ran toward his house. It had taken him twenty minutes to coax his aunt back into the Executive Mansion. Since hearing about Jamie on the news, she kept insisting that Reynaldo stay with her.

"You'll be safe here, *Reyito*," she had said. "Governor Phillip's men will protect you."

"I'll be fine, *tía*," Reynaldo had said, escorting her up the long driveway. He had felt bad rushing her, but he needed to get home. "I'm not afraid. Please, go, take care of little Charlotte and baby Phil. They need you."

"Are you sure, I just—"

"*Tía*," Reynaldo wrapped his aunt in a hug, "I need to go. I will be careful, and I will bring a jacket, I promise." He forced a smile.

"I'm afraid you will need more than a jacket, *Reyito*." She kissed the top of his head and whispered a sweet "*te amo*" as Reynaldo handed his aunt to one of the federal agents hovering outside the front door who guided her inside the mansion.

Reynaldo raced up his front steps. When he opened the front door, a startled Pedro was sitting on his living room couch watching television.

"Rey, what are you doing home?" he asked in a voice that told Reynaldo that Pedro didn't expect to see him. Reynaldo could only imagine what his brother was up to in order to warrant such a guilty face, but right now he didn't have time.

"Can't talk, Pedro, I need to get some things."

"From where?" Pedro jumped up from the couch and blocked the staircase.

"*What the* . . . Pedro, I don't have time for games."

"WHAT DID YOU SAY, REY?" Pedro shouted. He waved his hands wildly as if guiding a plane to a hangar.

"Pedro, what is wrong with you?"

"NOTHING, WHY?" he shouted again.

"Then let me pass." Reynaldo tried to take a step up the staircase, but Pedro stepped with him as if they were dancing.

"WHAT'S THE RUSH?" Pedro yelled. "TELL ME ABOUT YOUR DAY."

"My *what*?" Reynaldo said. "Since when do you care about my day?"

"WHAT ARE YOU TALKING ABOUT, REY? I ALWAYS ASK YOU ABOUT—"

"Are you wearing Ricky's pants again, *hermano*?" Reynaldo shook his head and pulled at the waistband of Pedro's pants.

"Am I . . . ?" When Pedro looked at his crotch, Reynaldo snuck under his arm, taking the rest of the stairs in threes.

"You always fall for the same trick, *hermano*." Reynaldo hurried across the landing toward his bedroom.

"Wait, Rey!" Pedro clambered after him. "You don't want to go up there."

"Why is my door closed?" Reynaldo asked and flung the bedroom door open, startling his father and a woman, who were lying naked on top of the Teenage Mutant Ninja Turtles comforter. They immediately started covering themselves up.

"Papa!" Reynaldo said and covered his eyes with his arm.

"I told you that you no want to go in there, Rey," said Pedro, who was out of breath by the time he reached the bedroom. He put his arm on Reynaldo's shoulder.

"Does no one knock around here?" Reynaldo's father asked. He was holding the comforter over his and the woman's bare chest.

"In *my* room?" Reynaldo asked. "It's still mine—at least for now."
He hurried toward his chest of drawers.

"Rey, I'd like you to meet my fiancée, Pearl," Rey's father said
with ease and a broad smile as if they were all meeting at a restaurant.
Pearl waved her hand out from behind the comforter.

"Hello." Reynaldo grabbed a duffle bag from a chair and began
stuffing clothing into it.

"I would have told you she was coming if you hadn't locked
yourself in your room and then ran out of the house before," his father
said, stepping out from the blanket. He stood naked in the middle of
the bedroom.

"*Ay*, Papa, *por favor*, put on some clothes," Reynaldo said, averting
his eyes.

"Why? I have nothing to be ashamed of," his father said.

"You certainly don't, Hector," the woman said with a giggle.

"You never see Papa's *pene* before, Rey?" Pedro asked, unfazed.
"Where you been?"

"Where are you going now?" Hector asked Reynaldo, who was
stuffing balls of socks into his bag.

"New York City," Reynaldo answered.

"New York City?" Pedro asked. "For what?"

"I don't have time to explain." Reynaldo opened a closet and
reached for a box on the top shelf.

"If you're looking for money, there isn't any there," Pedro said.
He picked up an Encyclopedia Brown book from Reynaldo's old book
shelf and nervously leafed through it.

"Why does that not surprise me?" Reynaldo said, putting the
box back.

"Is this about Jamie, *hermano*?" Pedro said. "I heard the news.
I'm sorry."

"What news?" his father asked.

"It was on the news," Pedro said. "The *policía* say—"

"No," his father put up his hand," "I want to hear it from Rey . . ."

"I can't. I have a lot on my mind," Reynaldo said, continuing to pack.

"You have had a lot on your mind since you were a little boy," his father said. "So much that I'm surprised you're even able to stand up straight."

Reynaldo stopped moving. "She is missing," he said. "Jamie. She is in trouble. I fear that . . . that she may be with . . . *him*. I have to help her." He threw up his hands. "I can't just sit here. I have to find her." Reynaldo stuffed a pair of underwear into the bag. "I have to do *something*."

"*Reyito*, you can't just go," his father said.

"Why not?" he asked. "That's exactly what you did. *Go*."

"That's not fair," his father said, "I—"

"You announced on a Monday you were leaving and were gone by Wednesday," Reynaldo said. "Just like that." He snapped his fingers. "And we all had to fall in line. Well . . ." Reynaldo looked at Pedro. "Some of us more than others."

"What's that supposed to mean, Rey?" Pedro asked, crossing his arms.

"Enough, Pedro," his father said. "Okay, Rey, what are you going to do when you get there? To New York City?"

"I'll figure it out." Reynaldo stuffed a sweatshirt into his duffle bag, keeping his promise to his aunt.

His father touched Reynaldo's arm. "*Reyito*, stop. Maybe you should give this some thought."

"There's nothing to think about," Reynaldo said.

"Rey, the FBI is looking for her. They will find her," Pedro said.

"Your brother is right, *Reyito*," his father said. "Let the police do their job. You have your own job, your own responsibilities."

"That's just it, Papa. This *is* my responsibility. Not because *you* told me it was, but because *I* told me it was. The garage is fine. Pedro will take care of it."

"Pedro is not good with numbers," his father said.

"Well, he'll have to learn." Reynaldo squeezed his duffle bag closed so he could zipper it. "What's the difference if I stay here anyway? Since you're *selling my house*."

"It's *my* house." His father folded his arms. "I can do what I want with it. And, what, you think I'd leave you with no place to live? I'm not a monster, despite what you think."

"I don't think you're a monster."

"Maybe I should go downstairs, Hector," Pearl said. As she dropped the blanket, Reynaldo was about to cover his eyes, but realized that Pearl had put on his father's Hawaiian shirt and a pair of wrinkled shorts. She came over and refolded one of Reynaldo's T-shirts that had fallen onto the floor and placed it on top of the duffle bag. "I'm sorry we had to meet this way," she said with a smile. "I care for your father very much."

"Thank you," Reynaldo said. He unzipped the bag and as he added the T-shirt to his belongings, the downstairs front door opened and Ricardo came running up the stairs with Maricón scrambling behind him.

"I saw Rey's car. What did I miss? What did I miss?" Ricardo yelled. "And why is Papa naked again?"

"Please put on some clothes," Reynaldo said.

"Stop changing the subject, Rey."

Reynaldo dropped the duffle bag onto the floor. "Papa, I don't think you are a monster. I love you, and you are right. This is your house. Yours and *mamá's*, but she's gone. And you are not here, and who has been taking care of it?"

"I never asked you to, Rey . . ." his father said.

"I know you didn't. But I didn't ask for it either. You want to know the truth, Papa?" Reynaldo said. "I'm happy you are selling this house. What Pedro said to me earlier today was the truth."

"It was?" Pedro asked. He stuck his tongue out at Ricardo.

"I do need a push," Reynaldo said. "I need to act, not react. I *love* Jamie. I need to find her. I need to help her. And I need to go." Reynaldo picked the duffle bag up. "I am happy you found someone to love, Papa. Now, please let me find someone, too." He started toward the door.

"Wait, Rey . . ." Pedro said, blocking the way.

"Let him go, Pedro," his father said. "Your brother has to do what he has to do."

Pedro stepped aside, and Reynaldo stopped in front of him. He pointed at Pedro's pants.

"You really are wearing Ricardo's pants, you know," Reynaldo said.

"I'm not falling for that again, Rey."

"No, seriously, I'm not kidding."

Pedro looked at his crotch, and Reynaldo laughed.

"And Papa thinks *I'm* the dumb one," Ricardo said with a shake of his head.

Reynaldo reached his arms around Pedro and Ricardo's necks and pulled them in for a hug. "I'll be in touch soon. I am going to run to the garage to pick up a few things before I head out. You can always call me if you need me."

"We'll always need you," Pedro said, kissing Reynaldo's cheek, "but right now Jamie needs you more." He smiled.

"Be well, my son," his father said, finally pulling on a pair of boxer shorts. Pearl sat near him on Reynaldo's bed.

Reynaldo bent down to pet Maricón on the head before tossing his duffle bag over his shoulder. He took one last look at his boyhood bedroom, and his boyhood family, before charging down the stairs toward his car—and, perhaps for the first time, his future.

30

aith tugged at the map, splitting it along the center crease.

"Be careful, Faithy," Jamie said.

She pulled the map out of her daughter's hands and placed it beside her on the passenger seat of Joey's car as Bailino turned onto another dirt road, the tires kicking up dust as if the vehicle were a twister.

Bailino had insisted on taking Joey's car as a precaution. He said the man who found the house may have given the make, model, and license plate number of the car parked in the driveway to his associates. They trekked as much food and items as they could through the woods, but there wasn't much—the supplies they had wouldn't last very long.

From what Jamie could tell, Bailino was driving southeast. They passed Pittsburgh about twenty minutes ago and were starting to see signs for West Virginia. She had asked several times where they were heading, but the answer was always the same: "It's better if you don't know for now."

Faith reached out toward the car dashboard and pulled at the knobs for the radio.

"Not now, honey," Jamie said, pulling her hand back. Her hand grazed the Hello Kitty watch that Faith was wearing on her wrist, a gift Bailino had given her before they left the house in Pennsylvania.

"Push?" Faith said, furrowing her brows.

"She can put the radio on if she likes," Bailino said.

Faith looked at Jamie, who shrugged her shoulders, and the little girl started pushing all the buttons she could reach. She grew frustrated when nothing happened, so Jamie took the little girl's finger and pushed the large knob on the left, and the dashboard lit up with LED numbers; music began to play.

"Yay," Faith clapped.

Bailino smirked. "It's the little things," he said.

"My brother says I can't always give her what she wants," Jamie said. "He says I give in to her too much."

"Do you?" Bailino asked.

"Probably."

Bailino reached for a bottle of water he had in one of the driver's side door pockets. "How is he? Your brother?"

Jamie stiffened, wondering if Bailino was obliquely referring to Edward's gunshot wound. She wiped the image of Edward crumpled in the trunk of Bailino's car from her mind, reminding herself that the man who had done that to him was the same one in whom she was now putting her trust. "He's okay," she said. She thought of how worried Edward must be, going through all this again, not knowing where she was. The first moment they had, when they were safe, Jamie had to call him.

"How's his shoulder?" Bailino asked.

"He's recovering," she said and wondered for a moment if Bailino were going to apologize. She wouldn't know what to say if he did, and, ironically, was hoping he didn't. She decided to keep it light. "He says it hurts when it rains, so he's always telling me the weather. Edward's like a walking weather station."

"Eddie," Faith said, looking around the car and out the window. "Where Eddie?"

"Uncle Edward's home, honey," Jamie said.

"He's good to her?" Bailino asked. "Your brother?"

Jamie nodded. "Edward adores her," she said.

"Good," Bailino said.

Faith pushed another radio button, and the staticky voice of a news anchor blared from the speakers. ". . . Sunny, a high of seventy-five on Saturday, showers on Sunday." The news station's ID played, followed by the rat-a-tat-tat of a typewriter. "Here are today's headlines. In local news, this morning Pittsburgh police issued a Silver Alert for seventy-five-year-old Albert Calhoun, who was last seen at a Wal-Mart on Summit Park Drive in Pittsburgh. Mr. Calhoun is believed to suffer from dementia. He is wearing a blue plaid shirt, navy blue shorts, white socks, and brown sandals. Anyone with information is asked to contact the Pittsburgh Police Department at . . ."

"I guess it's a slow news day," Bailino said.

". . . In national news, the manhunt continues for Don Bailino, who escaped the Stanton Federal Correctional Facility on Tuesday . . ."

Faith reached for another button, but Bailino held out his hand. "One second, cupcake," he said.

". . . While authorities first suspected that Bailino had fled the country, they now believe he is in the Northeast. The FBI also announced that it believes Bailino to be behind the abduction of Jamie Carter and her daughter, Faith. Bailino is believed to be the little girl's father, having raped the Massapequa woman in the spring of two thousand and twelve . . ."

Jamie stared straight-ahead, avoiding eye contact with Bailino. She ran her hand through Faith's hair.

". . . The little girl was abducted sometime around eight-thirty a.m. yesterday. Right now, law enforcement is working with the Federal Bureau of Investigation on the following up of all leads. Earlier today, Robert Scott, the ex-husband of Jamie Carter and author of *Bondage: The Unauthorized Jamie Carter Story*, the bestselling book that detailed the abduction of Jamie Carter and Charlotte Grand, was seen leaving the FBI field office in Albany. Mr. Scott told local media that he had been asked to aid the investigation in a consulting capacity . . ."

"I should have taken care of that guy when I had the chance," Bailino sighed.

". . . Bailino is now at the top of the FBI's Most Wanted List.

Anyone with information about Don Bailino's whereabouts, or that of Jamie or Faith Carter, is asked to contact the Federal Bureau of Investigation at 1-800-CALL-FBI. The FBI cautions that Bailino may be armed and dangerous, so it is advised not to approach him directly. Instead, call the FBI immediately . . ."

"Please, NYPD will shoot me on sight," Bailino said.

". . . In related news, Phillip Grand, the governor of New York, who is believed will announce his bid for the Republican nomination for U.S. president after this fall's mid-term elections, held a news conference this morning to say that he continues to be in contact with the FBI regarding the investigation into how Bailino escaped and the ensuing manhunt. He noted that the FBI will be bringing the alleged heads of the three remaining organized crime families tomorrow for questioning in its Albany field office. . . ."

Bailino suddenly swerved and pulled over to the side of the road, causing Jamie to thrust her feet toward the dashboard to steady her and Faith.

". . . Each of the three men will be questioned in connection to Bailino's prison break. The governor would not say if he would be privy to the interviews, only that they would take place. More on this story as it develops. In sports . . ."

Bailino turned off the radio. "Well, I'll be damned," he said.

"What?" Jamie asked as Faith reached her hand toward the dashboard to turn the radio back on. Jamie expected another non-answer and was surprised when Bailino said more.

"Looks like the Governor of New York just did me a favor."

Bailino turned the steering wheel hard, making a U-turn, and got back on the road, this time driving in the opposite direction toward traffic signs for New York.

31

After hours, the Executive Mansion always reminded Phillip of a tomb, a large crypt filled with the ghosts of governors past. After Charlotte's abduction two years ago, he had gotten into the habit of walking the halls after everyone had gone to bed, patrolling the grounds like some sort of night watchman or perhaps seeking divine counsel from the men displayed in the various portraits hung throughout the mansion. He wondered, *Would Teddy Roosevelt, a national hero during the Spanish-American War, have clamped down on immigration? Focus on reviving a crumbling infrastructure? Would he have given LaGuardia Airport a facelift? Or Bailino the death penalty?*

The past few nights, however, the buzz of the federal agents made the building seem less like a crypt and more like a hive—particularly tonight, when Jamie Carter's call to Special Agent Wilcox had sent the agents into a frenzy. Phillip needed more than divine counsel. He needed a life raft.

He was sitting on the top step of the staircase connecting the mansion's second and third levels. Moments ago, Wilcox had rushed out the door with a gaggle of agents after the FBI was able to pinpoint Jamie's location to western Pennsylvania. Phillip had been hopeful, thinking perhaps Bailino had let her and her daughter go—if, indeed, he had them, as was the assumption following the call. However, when Wilcox, at Phillip's insistence, played for him the conversation he had had with Jamie, Phillip's optimism had dimmed. The phone had fallen to the ground only seconds following the connection, and Jamie sounded distressed, like there was some kind of struggle. There was a series of thumps and shattered glass and the continuous cries of a child, presumably little Faith Carter, before the connection ended. The notion of something happening to either Jamie or Faith had been a real threat all along, but the thought truly hadn't occurred to Phillip until he heard that message—it was as if his own daughter had been taken again. Wilcox had played and replayed the recording for the federal agents, believing to have heard a man's voice, barely audible, before the line died. He sent the recording out for analysis before taking off for the helipad.

"There you are, Phillip," Katherine said, climbing the stairs. "I've been looking for you."

"What is it?" he asked, trying to decode his wife's tone. He couldn't tell if she had bad or good news, but he knew she had some kind of urgent news—her normally straight posture was bent forward at the waist—and Wilcox knew he could talk to Katherine as if she were Phillip. They were a team. "Does Wilcox have them?"

Katherine shook her head. "Unfortunately, no. The phone turned out to be in an old house in Pennsylvania. Lying on the floor. Wilcox said the house looked like it hadn't been lived in for years. No one was there."

"No one?" Phillip asked.

"A man had been strangled in the backyard. He was lying on the ground. Wilcox said he recognized him as one of DeGrassi's people, but forensics is examining the body. Jamie, the baby, and Bailino or whoever was with them were gone."

Phillip processed the information. "Pennsylvania, you said?" He felt a tiny wisp of memory materialize. All day, Phillip had been thinking about what Wilcox and Reynaldo Rodriguez had said and whether he knew more than he realized. He had spent hours rummaging through old documents and photographs, but so far had come up with nothing.

"Yes," Katherine said. "In a town called Little Gap. Wilcox said the property is owned by some corporation. They're working on any principals."

"What's the corporation's name?" Phillip asked.

"I don't know. Why?"

"Just wondering," Phillip said, hoping the name would spark something. He stared up at the portrait of George Clinton, who was considered the father of New York State and had served as governor for twenty-one years—the longest of any chief executive in the state's history. The painting, on loan from the state capitol's Hall of Governors, hung over the second-level landing and was one of Phillip's favorites, depicting the former governor in the grand style of European painting with Greco-Roman columns and rich drapery. Phillip usually felt a kinship with Clinton, who had been an ardent patriot and defended New York as a Brigadier General during the Revolutionary War, but lately Phillip felt like he had let him down. "The kids okay?" he asked.

"Yes, all changed and tucked into bed. Rosalia's in her room praying, fumbling, doing whatever she does with her beads. That'll keep her busy for hours." Katherine tucked a wisp of hair behind Phillip's ear. "How are you holding up?"

"I should be the last person you're worried about right now," he said.

"Phillip, everything that can be done is being done. You know that." She sat down next to him on the step. "Are you having second thoughts about Wilcox's plan?"

"What makes you say that?"

"You're hiding again." She smiled.

Phillip shrugged. "I think it's a shot in the dark. Bailino's too smart. And if he was in western Pennsylvania, would he really drive all the way back here just for the chance to get rid of Paolo Cataldi or any of the others? He knows the FBI would be all over him."

"Bailino strikes me as a person who thinks methodically about whatever he's doing and who doesn't care about the FBI," Katherine said. "He'll do what he wants, or what's most effective. In fact . . ."

Katherine leaned forward again—she had something important to say. "I was thinking perhaps it might be good advice for you to do the same."

"What do you mean?"

"I mean . . . I think we should go forward with the national campaign, form an exploratory committee, get the ball rolling."

"You mean the presidency? Now? Before my re-election as governor?"

"Phillip, hear me out. You know as well as I do the importance of taking charge of your brand. Let's not let this Bailino mess define it—define *us*."

"What happened to not announcing while New York is burning?"

"We're not announcing anything, Phillip, we're just setting the wheels in motion. And New York isn't burning anymore. The fires have been put out. In fact, New York needs to be rebuilt. The whole country does."

"Katherine—"

"This Bailino thing has people talking again about guns and gun control. About illegal immigration, getting in and out of the country. About our overcrowded prison system. All the issues that you've embraced and fought for over the past ten years. Did you know that Senator Howard, that prick, is already out there clamoring for more gun control laws? Like he gives a damn."

"We need enforcement of our gun control laws, not more of them," Phillip said.

"Exactly. But Howard isn't the only one jumping in front of this Bailino thing. It seems like the entire Congress, both sides of the aisle, is jockeying for position in the national race. We can't sit tight for too long. Rumor has it that Howard may be tossing his hat into the ring very soon."

"Burt? He said he wasn't running for president."

"They all say that, Phillip, before they do. You know that. If Howard does announce his candidacy and continues droning on and on about gun control, it won't be good for your campaign." She brushed his bushy eyebrow hair with the pad of her thumb. "It's time to get out there, Phillip. It's *your* time."

Phillip stared at the portrait of George Clinton. "Katherine, I've been thinking, and . . . Well, I was actually thinking of postponing the announcement."

"Postpone?" She appeared stricken. "For how long?"

He took a breath. "Indefinitely."

"What?" Katherine took her hand away from Phillip's face.

"At least until after the gubernatorial election in November."

"I'm not sure that's such a good idea."

"Why not?"

"Because . . ." Katherine stood up and paced the small landing. "There's a possibility, a real possibility, that Jamie and Faith Carter may not come out of this."

"Katherine!" Phillip yelled, his voice sounding like a roar in the narrow stairwell.

"I'm being honest, Phillip. You heard that recording as I did."

"We don't know what that was . . ."

"But we do know it wasn't good. And there's a very real chance that this can go horribly wrong. You know I care for that young woman and that I know she is the reason our daughter is safe and sound, but we can't protect her right now. We can only brace ourselves for what outcome this situation will lead to."

"Outcome?"

"Phillip, this mess with Bailino can go on for a long time. Months. Years. We may not hear anything at all. Waiting will only hurt us. If we charge ahead full steam, whatever happens with Bailino won't affect us."

"Won't affect us?" Phillip ran his hand through his hair so hard that he was surprised he didn't see strands floating to the floor. "This *hasn't stopped* affecting me. For two years it's all I've thought about— what happened and how to keep it from happening again." He, too, paced back and forth on the small landing. "I refuse to give up on Jamie Carter. For what? A political office? Did Jamie just give up on our daughter to save her own skin?"

"I'm not giving up," Katherine stressed. "All I'm saying is that maybe you would be doing Jamie Carter more good if you stopped moping around." She pointed to the portrait of George Clinton. "And staring at dead presidents."

"The last thing Jamie Carter needs is *my* help, Katherine. If you don't recall, Jamie Carter is in this mess because of me—because of *me*."

"No," Katherine barked. "She's in this mess because of one man. And that's Don Bailino. Not you. Stop taking responsibility for everything."

"But isn't that exactly—*exactly*—what leaders are supposed to do, Katherine?" Phillip was flailing his arms in the air. "Take responsibility. Brainstorm solutions. Solve problems. *Lead.*"

"Lead from where? From *here*?" Katherine asked, pointing to the landing. "I didn't think leading from behind was your style," she said with sarcasm.

"It's more like yours," Phillip said. "You've been leading from behind me for years."

He could tell the barb hit its mark, because Katherine caught her breath. Her eyes got very small as if her lids were straining to keep them in their sockets.

"Maybe we should continue this discussion another time," she said calmly, but through gritted teeth. She smoothed out her pajama shirt with her palms. "I'll be in our bedroom if you need me."

Before Phillip could say anything more, Katherine strode up the stairs and down the hallway until Phillip could hear the door to their bedroom slam closed. He sat back down on the landing and leaned his head against the banister. His heart was slamming against his chest, the blood pumping in his ears. It had been a long time since he and Katherine argued—if he had to guess, he'd say it was probably about two years' time. He knew Katherine was doing what she did best—look out for Phillip's future—but what perhaps she didn't realize was that if something happened to Jamie Carter, or her little girl, there would be no future. His career might somehow recover, but Phillip knew that he never would.

"Daddy?" Charlotte stood at the top of the second-floor landing. She was wearing pink footie pajamas, her blond stringy curls dangling in her face. "Were you and mommy fighting?"

"Oh, sweetie, did Mommy and I wake you?"

Charlotte rubbed her eyes and nodded. "But that's okay," she said. "Mommy says people who sleep too much are lazy."

"She does say that, doesn't she?" Phillip said. "C'mere, Charlie." He reached out his hand, and Charlotte tiptoed down the short flight of stairs and folded into her father's arms. Up close in her pajamas, she reminded Phillip of a younger version of her mother.

"Did they find the bad man yet?" Charlotte asked.

"Bad man?" She had said the words as if they were innocuous, like she was saying *peanut butter*. "What bad man?"

"The one who took the people away."

As far as Phillip knew, Charlotte didn't remember anything about her abduction by Bailino. He had resisted sending her to a psychologist despite Katherine's insistence and the recommendations of her pediatrician, choosing instead to simply move forward and shower her with love and affection, which he believed in more than years of therapy with a paid stranger. Still, he always wondered if a tiny part of her remembered anything about those four days in captivity. "Who told you about that?" he asked.

"I heard the men in the black talking downstairs."

"Oh," Phillip said. He was always amazed by what children picked up when they seemed to be uninterested or busy doing other things. "What did you hear, sweetie?"

"I heard that he was going to Pennsylvania and that he took people. Didn't we go to Pennsylvania, Daddy, once?"

"Yes, sweetie, we did, but . . ." He tilted Charlotte's chin up. "I want you to look at me."

Charlotte looked up at Phillip with her big, inquisitive eyes.

"I just want you to know that you should never worry. That

Daddy and Mommy will protect you and Philly. And those men? The ones who are here, the ones in the black, are good at protecting, too, that's their job, okay?"

"Okay, Daddy, but just in case, Ro Ro said in my prayers that I should pray for people, too, because if they are in trouble, my prayers will find them and help them. Is that true?"

"Yes, I believe that's true," Phillip said.

"But how do my prayers know where to go?" she asked.

"Well, it's kind of like taking medicine," Phillip said. "When you're sick and Mommy gives you medicine—"

"Ro Ro usually gives me medicine, Daddy."

"Well, when Ro Ro gives you medicine, the medicine knows if it needs to go to your head or your lungs or even your feet." He tickled the bottom of Charlotte's foot through the plastic bottoms of her pajamas, and she giggled. "Same thing with your prayers. They go straight where they need to go."

"How do the prayers get out of the house, though? What if it's cold and the windows are closed? Can they go through glass?"

"Yes, and walls, too," Phillip said.

"Like magic?"

"Exactly, and when you're a good person and you think really, really good thoughts, your prayers are extra-special, so I bet that your prayers are really going to help somebody out there. Somebody who needs them."

"Do you pray, too, Daddy?"

"All the time," Phillip said.

"Well, I bet your prayers are the most powerful prayers in the whole world!" Charlotte lifted her arms and traced a big circle in the air with them. "Because you are the goodest person I know."

Phillip kissed the top of his daughter's head. "Why don't we go back to your bedroom, and together we'll send out some super-duper powerful prayers?"

"The two of us?" Charlotte brightened. "But Mommy says I'm supposed to learn how to go back to sleep by myself."

"Yeah, well, I have a feeling Mommy won't mind me sleeping with you tonight."

"Really? A sleepover!" Charlotte shouted and wrapped her arms around Phillip's neck, before putting her finger to her lips. "*Shhh*," she whispered. "We can't let Philly know. He might get jello."

"*Jealous*, cutie." Phillip lifted Charlotte into the air. He took one last look at Governor Clinton, who had gotten quite an earful that night in the usually quiet stairwell. "But don't worry," he told his daughter. "It'll be our little secret—between you, me, and Governor Clinton." Phillip motioned to the portrait.

"Don't be silly, Daddy." Charlotte rolled her eyes. "He's not the governor. *You* are."

"That's right. I am," he said, carrying Charlotte to her bedroom. "It's my second-favorite job."

"What's your first-favorite?"

He kissed her forehead. "Being your daddy."

32

B ailino crossed into New York with little fanfare. A small sign,
barely noticeable on the side of the road even in the bright
morning sun, heralded *The Empire State* in tiny white block
lettering against a faded green background. The bottom of the sign
read, *Phillip S. Grand, Governor*, beside which a tiny *I ♥ New York*
insignia was etched.

Bailino still got a bit of a jolt when he saw Phillip's name on
things—signs, monuments, parks, newspaper articles—even though
it had been almost eight years since Phillip began serving as governor
of New York. It was like running into an old classmate where you
least expected to. Bailino remembered how hopeful and idealistic
Phillip had been when the two of them met in the army, a far cry
from the jaded distrust that had been instilled in Bailino from the
time he was a boy. The bond between them had been as immediate
as it was magnetic, spurred on by a curiosity each man had about the
other's point of view and vastly different upbringing, and eventually
cemented by their ability to welcome, perhaps *crave*, that disparity. It
was probably more for those reasons than anything the army threw at
them that Phillip Grand and Don Bailino became friends—as well as
the men they were today.

Bailino was sure that Phillip knew he would sense that he was
being lured into a trap with this sudden tête-à-tête with the heads
of the families—and he probably also knew that Bailino wouldn't let

an opportunity like that go by. The question was: What was Phillip's intent? To help or hurt him? Was he on his side, or not?

Bailino looked over at Faith, who was lying under Jamie's protective arms clutching his Hello Kitty watch, which was strapped across her tiny wrist, the two of them lulled to sleep by the hum of the engine and the bleakness of the tedious rural landscape. This wasn't how he had planned things, but this last-minute detour would get the job done faster, and the faster Bailino got rid of Paolo Cataldi, the safer Faith and Jamie would be.

He did a quick check of the time on the car dashboard and of his mirrors. He hadn't seen anyone following them—many of the roads they had taken were well off the main thoroughfares, so there had been few cars, making it easy to spot a tail. Now that they were on the brink of the early morning rush hour, though, it was a bit more crowded, and with more cars on the road, there was more of a chance of being spotted. Plus, they couldn't drive much further without a car seat—Bailino wasn't worried about the little girl's safety, but having Faith in the front seat, and not strapped like a Frankenstein monster into some contraption in the back, was attracting unwanted attention from other vehicles, and that was the last thing he needed. He needed for them to be invisible.

He checked on the handgun in his pocket and tightened his grip on the steering wheel. Despite the circumstances, it felt good to drive again. He didn't know what he liked more—harnessing the power of an engine or being in full control of his destination.

"Mama?" Faith said. She was sitting on her mother's lap and lightly slapping Jamie's cheek.

"Let her sleep, cupcake," Bailino whispered.

"I'm not sleeping, I'm up," Jamie said, wiping the drool that was coming out of the corner of her mouth with the back of her hand.

It had only taken seeing Jamie Carter in the woods outside his Pennsylvania house for intense feelings to come roaring back to Bailino, feelings that he thought he'd put to rest. He had spent a good chunk of his recuperation trying to disconnect from the woman he had dragged into his life, and into this mess, but there was something about her that he couldn't shake—a kindness, a vulnerability, coupled with a strength of spirit. She was tougher than he thought most people—including him—gave her credit for, and, despite the healing bullet wounds in his chest and clavicle, that shit seriously turned him on.

"Eat?" Faith asked Jamie. She grabbed both sides of her mother's face to get her attention, so that their noses touched. "Kickin' nuggets?"

"I don't think we have chicken nuggets," Jamie said. She leaned over and rummaged through the bags in the backseat.

"I need to stop for gas anyway." Bailino looked in his rearview mirror and made a turn onto another rural road. "You hungry?"

"Kickin' nuggets," Faith said again in Bailino's direction.

"We're fine," Jamie said.

Jamie looked tired and had a deep sadness about her now. Bailino thought of the polite, smiling woman he had seen searching for a chair that day in Bryant Park. He had the urge to reach over and hold her hand. "It's going to be okay, you know," he said instead.

"I don't think it will." He could tell she was stifling a sniffle.

"Look at me," he said, and she turned her face, which, despite its troubled pallor, had a natural cherubic shape. "I promise you."

"Can you really make that promise?" she asked, her eyes returning frontward. She parted Faith's hair with her fingers so that her bangs were out of her eyes.

"I can, and I will, so I suggest that, this time, you stick with me."

They drove on in silence for a few minutes, Faith staring at both of them as if she were hoping that at least one of them would eventually remember that she had asked for chicken nuggets.

"We should talk," Bailino said finally.

"What do you mean?" Jamie asked, her eyes, like spotlights, returning to him.

Bailino liked when she looked at him; her gaze was intense and reminded him of his father—and also of Faith. He tightened his hold on the steering wheel as they drove over a rough patch of asphalt. "You need to know what to do if something happens to me."

"I thought I was sticking with you?"

"You are, but I have a lot of people who want to see me dead, from the NYPD to some old Brooklyn friends, and if that happens, I need you to take the kid and go out west."

"Out west?"

Bailino checked his mirrors. "Years ago, my father bought property across the country. He was a big believer in investments, particularly in owning land—something he could feel, walk on. He had lived in apartments all his life, always having to keep quiet so that he didn't wake the landlord, so he bought land wherever and whenever he could. Can you imagine a man's dream is to be able to stomp like mad in his own home and not have to answer to anyone about it?" He looked at Jamie, and he thought he caught a flicker of recognition in her eyes. "So he bought a lot of land—the further from Brooklyn the better, although if he could see what eventually became of Park Slope he'd be stunned. . . . Anyway, I inherited the land after my father was killed and used most of it for Upackk's distribution and fulfillment centers—a lot of the land he purchased back then was located in large lots, big open spaces perfect for commercial development. Even though the factories are gone now, the land is still there, still worth something."

"I'm sorry," Jamie said.

"For what?"

"About your dad."

"Oh." Bailino said. "Thank you." He signaled his blinker and changed lanes. "As Upackk grew, I was able to invest in some additional properties, which I bought under an umbrella corporation, and various subsidiaries, including my father's Pennsylvania house. I needed to keep the purchases quiet for a lot of reasons." Bailino glanced into his rearview mirror. The road was getting a little too crowded for his taste, and he turned onto another road with less traffic. "There's a property out in Cody, Wyoming. It's near the

Wyoming/Montana border. I built a house there a few years back when I was . . . Well, when I thought I was getting out of some businesses. Thought I might retire there. My father said he always imagined waking up to sunshine and a view of the mountains instead of a window fan and a fire escape. He thought that would be enough. Sounded good to me, too."

Jamie shifted in her seat as if she were uncomfortable. Faith let out an exasperated sigh and laid her head on Jamie's chest.

"I have a guy subletting the house now. A single guy who's an architect or something. He has no idea who I am or who he's paying rent to. For all he knows, it's Donald Trump. He's quiet, doesn't give me any trouble, and doesn't ask any questions. Perfect tenant. I phoned him the other day that my work was bringing me out west sometime soon—didn't say when—and that I would be using the guest house. I told him that it would be me and my daughter." Bailino glanced at Jamie. "That's before I knew you would be with us. And that's also before I heard the news report about Grand and the meeting with the families."

"You were going to take her to Wyoming?"

"She would have been safe there, honey. Right now, the biggest threat to you is Paolo Cataldi. Do you know that name?"

Jamie nodded.

"He's old and probably couldn't find Wyoming on a map, but he's still got some tricks up his sleeve, the old bastard. And, worst of all, he's got something to prove. He's been riding shotgun to his brother for his whole life, and now that Gino's gone, he's eager to show the world what he's made of, which isn't much, but given the chance, he will hurt you—to hurt *me*. He will hurt Faith—to hurt *me*. The only way to stop him is to hurt him first. And I know how."

"You can't just go to the police?"

"I'm a wanted man, hon. You heard that news report—I'm *the* most wanted man, which, if you think about it, is pretty ridiculous considering all the goddamn terrorists who are running around. And I told you, there's no love lost between me and the NYPD or the state troopers. The first shot they get, they're going to take. So, if anything happens to me, you need to go there. To Wyoming. Remember this address: thirty-three Cooper Court. Say it."

"Thirty-three Cooper Court," she said.

"Right. You take this car and go. The guest house is completely set up. There's money. There's food. The tenant will have the key. Tell the guy you're my wife, that's my daughter. Plan B will kick into action, and you don't come out until you know Paolo Cataldi is dead. When he is, you'll be safe. Understand?"

"And what if he's not?" she asked. "Dead, I mean."

"He will be," Bailino said.

Jamie furrowed her brow and shook her head. "I don't think I can do it."

"I know you can."

"But what about the others?" she asked.

"What others?"

"The other heads of the families? Or anyone else? Won't they come after us, too?"

Bailino shook his head. "With Paolo gone, they'll probably go back to their nights spent watching *Wheel of Fortune* and railing about Obama." He lifted Jamie's chin with his hand. Her skin felt soft and cool. "And if they don't, I have Plans C and D. Trust me."

"Okay," she said, and Bailino could feel the quivering vibration of her voice through her skin, arousing him. He quickly removed his hand.

"Good girl."

He turned onto a desolate road with overgrown fields on both sides as far as the eye could see and realized he was back in familiar territory. Years ago, this stretch of road had run through a fifty-acre equestrian estate owned by an old bootlegger who spent more time at the track than he should have. Bailino had given him a part-time job as a packer, but years of gambling losses got the best of him— he was forced to sell off his property, piece by piece, including the horses and all the gear. Bailino didn't know what had become of the guy. He searched the eastern end of the property and could still see the remnants of a rundown old barn to his right, but otherwise the land was vacant. In a pinch, Bailino knew he could bring Jamie and the baby there.

A horn blared, startling Faith who wrapped her arms around her mother's neck, and a red sports car came up fast in Bailino's rearview mirror. The driver, who looked like a young kid in a graphic T-shirt and a backward hat, was smoking a cigarette, which he hung out the window.

"Is it . . . anyone you know?" Jamie asked, concerned.

"I don't think so," Bailino said. The sports car weaved back and forth, waiting for a chance to pass Bailino on the two-lane road. "Just some idiot."

"Kickin' nuggets?" Faith asked again, making sure her request hadn't been forgotten.

"Honey," Jamie said, "I—"

The red sports car roared, this time causing Faith to yelp in fear, as it crossed the double yellow line and accelerated until the driver was in line with Bailino's window. The two glanced wearily at one another and exchanged middle fingers before the sports car cut Bailino off and began riding up the rear end of an old truck that was up ahead on the road.

"Asshole," Bailino muttered.

"*Asso*," Faith repeated.

The sports car began weaving, waiting for oncoming traffic on the other side of the road to clear. Once it did, it crossed the double yellow line again and passed the old truck, but as the two rounded a curve, a light blue Oldsmobile town car emerged from the oncoming traffic side beeping its horn. The sports car slipped back over the double yellow line just in time, but clipped the back of the Oldsmobile, causing the driver to lose control of his car and crash into a gully on the other side of the road.

"Fuck," Bailino said, hitting the brake and skidding to a halt on the shoulder. The sports car and the old truck also stopped, the kicked up dust the only thing left moving on the desolate road.

Bailino took the keys out of the ignition and raced out of the car as the sports car and the truck took off. He ran across the two-lane road toward the Oldsmobile, whose engine had begun to smoke. Bailino peered inside the Oldsmobile's front window; the driver was slumped over the steering wheel. He picked up a large rock from the ground, threw it hard at the back window, shattering the glass, and reached his arm around to open the driver's side door. He reached for the neck of the driver, who looked like a man in his sixties, to feel for a pulse. When he didn't sense one, he pulled the guy out of the car and onto the pebbled ground and put his ear to his chest. He began administering CPR when a green Hyundai pulled behind Joey's car. A stout woman wearing a brown raincoat got out, just as Bailino was able to detect a heartbeat.

"What happened?" the woman called, running across the road with her cell phone in hand. "Did you dial 911?"

Bailino pulled his baseball cap down and brushed past her, hurrying back toward Joey's car.

"Wait! Sir?" the woman called, but Bailino slammed the door and sped down the road, leaving the woman in his wake.

After a few minutes, Bailino tossed his baseball cap out the window and reached into the glove compartment for a cap in a different color.

"Is he going to be all right?" Jamie asked. "That driver?"

"I don't know," Bailino said. "I got him breathing, but just barely. If an ambulance gets there in time, maybe. I'd like to take that kid in the red sports car and wring his neck."

"Why did you stop?" Jamie asked.

Bailino glanced at her. "You thought I should just leave him?"

"No, I thought it was . . . I mean, I thought it was . . . well, nice, but . . ." Bailino could tell she was struggling to find the right words. "It just . . . I don't know, wasn't smart—no, I don't mean that . . . I mean, if you don't want to be recognized—"

"So you thought I should just leave him there?"

"I'm not saying that," Jamie said. "Forget it."

"No, tell me."

Jamie took a long breath. "What I mean is . . . Well, when I was little, I used to bring home all kinds of wounded animals—turtles, frogs, cats, even though I was allergic. I thought I could help them all, but what happened was the more time I spent with one, the more the others didn't thrive. I was so sad, but mom said to me, 'You can't save them all.' You know what I mean?"

Bailino merged back onto one of the main roads, trying to get lost in traffic for a while to be sure no one was following him. "I know what you're saying," he said. "The truth is I don't know how to answer your question."

"You don't have to explain anything to me, I—"

"I know I don't," Bailino said. "And I know a little something about not being able to save them all myself." He glanced in the rearview mirror. "I've become accustomed to making quick decisions. It's one of the reasons I'm still here—think fast or don't think at all. I tend to rely on instinct, and my instinct told me to see if that guy was all right."

A flock of seagulls flew overhead in V formation, and Faith pointed to the birds, her finger making tiny marks on the window glass.

"Is that why you . . . ?" Jamie asked, her voice trailing off.

"Is that why I what?"

Jamie stroked the back of Faith's head. "Is that why you took me in Bryant Park that day?" she asked. "Instinct?"

"Yes," he said without hesitation. "And my instinct wasn't wrong."

A sign for a rest stop approached with details on gas and food.

"Still hungry for chicken nuggets?" Bailino asked Faith.

Faith bolted upright at the question. "Kickin' nuggets," she said, nodding.

"Kickin' nuggets, it is," he said, putting on his blinker and merging into the exit lane.

33

"Don't forget to pack your long-sleeved sweater," Mary said. "I hear it gets cold at night in Albany."

"Now who the hell told you that?" Paolo asked with a grunt. He was standing in the middle of the living room, surrounded by luggage Mary had packed for him that he was sure he wouldn't need, and was afraid to move for fear of tripping. "Your *peeps*?"

"You leave my peeps out of this." Mary brushed lint off his suit jacket.

"This ain't no sightseeing vacation, I told you." Paolo shuffled his feet, kicking a dent into one of the leather suitcases. "This is business. I'll be in my room when it's dark. You know I get tired after dinner." She fumbled with his tie. "Do I really have to wear this thing? I feel like I'm choking."

"How many times do you get to visit the governor?" Mary asked, pressing the tie under his suit jacket.

"You really aren't understanding what this trip is about, are you, Swifty?" Paolo said. "I ain't exactly being invited for tea. And I don't really think the governor is going to be there. This is the FBI field office."

"I know you're excited," Mary said. "You can't fool me."

He grunted again, even though it was true: This was the first time the Feds, the governor, or anyone in government or law enforcement had taken an interest in Paolo, who usually got no closer to the media spotlight than his living room couch. Gino had always been considered the face and brains of the organization; no fewer than three true crime books—two of them by former FBI agents, one by a rat who was now deceased—had been written about him. Meanwhile, Paolo had gotten better grades in school, was the better organizer, and was, as far as he was concerned, better looking, all of which had gotten trumped by birth order. "This is a bullshit meeting anyway, and Grand knows it." Paolo pulled at his neck. "Enough with the tie, already."

"Well, even so." Mary patted down his jacket. "You look very handsome."

Marco entered the living room huffing and puffing like he had just run a marathon.

"Boy, you're taking a lot of suitcases for an overnight trip, Uncle Paolo," he said, reaching for the three remaining bags that were at Paolo's feet.

"Yeah, well, speak to my personal assistant," Paolo said, motioning toward Mary. "Apparently, we're going to be asked who we're wearing on the red carpet."

"What's this one?" Marco asked, fiddling with a long, narrow case. "You plan on playing pool?"

"Just put the damn thing in the car, would you?" Paolo said.

Marco threw the strap of the carry-on bag over his head, and wheeled the other two out the front door.

"You sure you don't want me to come with you?" Mary asked. "You know how you are with directions."

"How hard could it be?" Paolo asked. "We're going due north. If we hit Canada, we'll know we've gone too far." He nudged Mary with his elbow, and she made a face at him. "Plus, Marco and Adriano will be with me. Adriano's good with directions. And Marco knows the locations of all the McDonald's this side of the Mississippi." Paolo laughed until he started to cough. He held onto the edge of the wall molding as Mary fixed the breathing tube in his nose.

"Don't forget to take your medicine," she said. "Twice a day. An hour before your meal, or two hours after, if you forget."

"I know, I know . . ." Paolo said.

Marco came back into the room, and Paolo stood there awkwardly while Mary planted a kiss on his forehead. "Not in front of the kid," Paolo said.

"I love you," Mary said.

"Yeah, well," Paolo said, "don't get into any trouble while I'm gone."

Outside, the air was cool, and Paolo felt a chill run through him. These days, he was always cold, and nothing—a hot shower, a heating pad—seemed to help. He dragged his oxygen tanks toward the town car. As he approached, Adriano got out of the driver's seat and opened the back door—the guy had let Marco carry all of the luggage into the car. Smart.

"Let me help you with that, Uncle Paolo," Marco said.

"It's about time," Paolo said, forking over the handle to the oxygen cart. Marco slipped the cart into the well of the backseat of the town car. Paolo waved to the two sedans parked in front of and behind his car and climbed in.

"Who's that, Uncle Paolo?" Marco asked as he stepped into the passenger seat.

"Feds. Looks like we got an escort," Paolo said. "Would you put the heat on? I'm freezing my ass off back here."

"It's seventy-five degrees today," Marco said.

"So? I'm fuckin' cold. Put it on."

Marco pushed a few buttons as Adriano slid back into the driver's seat. "That all right?"

"You sure you know where you're going?" Paolo asked.

"Always," Adriano said and put the car into gear.

The town car eased onto the road. They passed the Knights of Columbus and the supermarket, and then the office of Paolo's primary care physician—he knew the address by heart, because he'd been there so damn much lately. He looked at all the faces on the street, the dark foreigners who had infiltrated the neighborhood while he was busy growing roots into his armchair and the Parkinson's ate away at his mobility.

The red open-frame structure of the old Coney Island

Parachute Jump came into view over the rooftops in the distance. Paolo smiled.

"You know, I took your Aunt Mary on the Wonder Wheel once," Paolo said. "Mary was scared to go on one of the moving cars—she wanted to sit in the cars that don't go nowhere. I tricked her into going into the moving one." He smiled at the memory.

"Did she like it?"

"Hated it. Threw up all over me on the first turn."

They drove onto the Belt Parkway toward the Brooklyn-Queens Expressway and passed lower Manhattan and the Freedom Tower. "They finally finished that goddamn building," Paolo said. "Took them long enough."

"I should take you there, Uncle Paolo," Marco said, "into the 9/11 museum. It opens next month."

"No thanks. There's enough sadness in my own house."

Traffic slowed down on the Expressway, and Paolo leaned back in the seat. He wondered if Vincent and Sal were already up there. He didn't expect anything to come of this dopey meeting. He knew the Feds had nothing on him. If they had, he'd be making this trip in handcuffs. He also knew this would be some kind of dog and pony show for the media in the hopes that Bailino would show. And he probably would. *Guy's stupid enough to try and take us all out at once,* Paolo thought. That was exactly what he was counting on.

"Uncle Paolo, the news just said they think Bailino's back in New York," Marco said. "Should I turn it up?"

"Nah. They don't know shit." He smiled, thinking of the message that DeGrassi's guy, Frankie Fish, had relayed to him from Pennsylvania before Bailino killed him, or so the news reports had said. It was the best piece of news he'd received in years. For all his greatness, his accolades, and his respect, Gino could never find a way to bring down the Great Bailino, and, after all these years, it was Paolo who had finally found Bailino's Achilles' heel. He thought it would be the kid, the little girl Faith, the heir to Bailino's throne, but, based on what Frankie Fish had seen, it wasn't. Turns out, Bailino was in love.

34

"This is never going to work."

Katherine was pacing Phillip's office in her stockinged feet. It was unusual for her not to wear heels in the presence of Wilcox, or any colleague or associate, but many of the Executive Mansion's employees and staff members had become comfortable with Wilcox's team of federal agents hanging around over the past two years, and it seemed that, although she would probably deny it, Katherine had, too. "Frankly, I think Bailino is far, far away from New York by now, but if he is around, he will see right through this scheme," she said.

"Maybe so," Wilcox said. He, too, looked more casual than usual, his blue blazer draped across the back of a chair, his tie slightly loosened. He was leaning against Phillip's bookcase, his arms folded across on his chest. "But even if he knew what we were up to, I think the bait is too precious to pass up."

Katherine glanced at Phillip, who nodded his agreement. As was their habit, the two of them had woken up this morning as if the argument from the night before hadn't happened. Some couples never went to bed angry. He and Katherine never woke up angry.

Charlotte squealed with glee somewhere in another part of the mansion, and the sound gave Phillip a momentary feeling of happiness. This state of waiting, of being out of control, was both familiar and unwanted, and while he wasn't completely comfortable with Wilcox's plan, at least he felt like it was an attempt to do *something* to return Jamie and Faith Carter home safe. The problem was that there were just too many variables, most notably Bailino's unpredictability. Would he bring harm to his own daughter or risk her safety to settle old scores? Did he feel he had nothing to lose? Or everything? Phillip didn't know.

"Is that new?" Wilcox asked, motioning to the wood and glass display case on Phillip's desk containing his antique gun. "I don't remember seeing it before."

Phillip nodded. "It was a gift from my father a couple of Christmases ago."

"Phillip's father considers himself to be a regular Teddy Roosevelt," Katherine said. "Or maybe he considers Phillip to be one. I can't decide."

"It's a nice piece," Wilcox said. "Is that a flintlock pistol?"

"Model 1805 flintlock pistol," Phillip said. "You have a good eye. It was made at Harper's Ferry Armory in Virginia—the first American manufactured military pistol. Supposedly, this gun was used in the War of 1812, or at least that's what the seller told my father." He shook his head. "Groups of soldiers firing at one another while on horseback. Things seemed so much simpler back then."

"I'm not so sure," Wilcox said when his cell phone buzzed. "Wilcox," he said, putting it to his ear. He listened and raised himself off the bookcase. "DeGrassi, LaPazza, and Cataldi just arrived at the field office." Wilcox placed the phone in his pocket. "My men escorted each of them up from downstate. No problems on the road." Wilcox said that last part as if he were disappointed. "They made it up in under three hours."

"Do you really expect Bailino to go anywhere near Cataldi when he is surrounded by federal agents?" Katherine asked. "It's not smart, which makes it seem out of character for him."

"He's done this type of thing before, gotten past guards and security staff." Wilcox said. Without having to mention Charlotte's abduction from the Executive Mansion two years ago, he made his point clear. "Maybe he will, maybe he won't. We don't know, Mrs. Grand, but if he does, my men will be ready."

Wilcox slipped on his blue blazer. Phillip did the same.

"And where do you think *you're* going?" Katherine asked Phillip.

"To the field office," Phillip said.

"Like hell, you are." Katherine stepped in front of him, blocking his path to the door.

"Weren't you just telling me last night that I should be more active?" Phillip asked.

"Yes, in terms of your career, not this. You should be as far away from that place as possible," she said. "Have you forgotten who these people are? And that it was because of *you* that Gino Cataldi was on death row? The last thing our children need is a father who has been abducted—or worse."

"Katherine, you're being dramatic," Phillip said. "I'm perfectly—"

"She's right, Governor," Wilcox said. "I advise that you stay here. This is the safest place for you. For all of you."

"Safer than an FBI field office?" Phillip asked.

"We'll keep you informed with our progress," Wilcox said, already heading for the office door.

"I'm *coming*," Phillip called, and Wilcox stopped. "I'll be right behind you, Agent Wilcox. Give me five minutes." He held his palm, fingers spread, for emphasis.

Wilcox glanced at Katherine, before nodding and walking out the door.

"Are you *mad*?" Katherine asked.

"I need to go. You said it yourself. I can't just mope around."

"But—"

"I'm involved in this thing just as much as anyone else, and I'm not going to be any good to anyone here."

"You think Bailino might show, don't you?"

Phillip buttoned his jacket. "I don't know, but if he does, I might just be the only one who can save him from getting killed."

"Phillip . . ." Katherine grabbed the lapels of his jacket and flattened them, tightening the creases. "Let's be honest. Would that really be such a bad thing? Something happening to that man?"

Phillip bristled, and he wasn't sure why. He had wondered the very same thing over the years, how many lives could have been saved if Bailino were not around. The man was certainly no friend of his—at least not anymore. Their days as army buddies were long behind them, and the time between had been filled with separate lives on opposite sides of the law. There was no real reason he should disagree with Katherine. Yet, he did.

"And don't tell me again about the army and how he saved your life." Katherine waved a dismissive hand. "You have to realize that was long, long ago. And that was your job—to protect one another."

"We need to find Jamie and Faith Carter," was all Phillip said. "And if he knows where they are, we need to find that out. And for that to happen, he needs to be alive."

"You'll just get in the way, Phillip," Katherine said, trying another tack.

Phillip put his hands on Katherine's shoulders. "Is that your way of telling me to be careful and that you love me?"

Katherine pressed her lips together into a nervous smile.

"Stay with Charlotte and Philly," Phillip said. "Tell Rosalia she can go home. If I know you are with them, I can go and do what I need to do."

"You know, everyone thinks that *I'm* the strong one?"

"That's because you are," Phillip said. He kissed her head and headed for the office door.

❀

The FBI field office was an eight-floor stone and steel structure about twenty minutes from downtown Albany. Although the population of the FBI ebbed and flowed based on the political leanings of whatever administration was in office, the Albany location had been thriving since the early 1900s when it was established as an antidote to the underground culture of criminals that emerged in response to Prohibition.

New York had become a hotbed of organized crime activity dating back to the middle of the twentieth century when mob boss Joseph Barbara owned a rural estate in Apalachin, New York, where some of organized crime's most notorious families held secret meetings. Wilcox once showed Phillip FBI archive photos of a young Gino and Paolo Cataldi at one of those meetings. Their fresh, unblemished teenage faces seemed so out of place in the room full of hardened criminals; how things changed with time.

It was in those early days that the FBI developed its vast system of intelligence—compiling details on the key players of various mob organizations, learning who they were, what they knew, and what they could do. When Phillip was a boy, his father would often relay with awe the capture of Al Capone in Chicago and the tenaciousness and honesty of men like Elliott Ness, who refused to give up or be bribed. Truth and justice had been as much a part of the Grand household as antique guns and ammo.

When New York State's Attorney General Robert Kennedy created the Organized Crime and Racketeering Section in the Department of Justice to coordinate activities by the FBI in 1961, the government was able to crack down on illegal activities even harder. Decades later, few New York families were left standing beyond the Cataldis, DeGrassis, and LaPazzas, and by the early twenty-first century, the old dons were pretty much washed up—they were too old, and the family trees too fractured, to do much of anything, which was why the FBI's attention to organized crime, particularly after 9/11, shifted eastward to Eastern Europe and Asia. The abduction of Phillip's daughter Charlotte two years ago—right in the Albany field office's backyard—seemed to have taken everyone, including the FBI, by surprise and revived the nation's interest in Italian organized crime. Mario Puzo's *The Godfather* even made a brief return to the top of the *New York Times* bestseller list.

Wilcox turned the car onto the field office's long driveway, bypassing the hordes of media who were camped out on the sidewalks near the front entrance. With so many news cameras, Phillip had to agree with Katherine that Bailino would stay far away from the building. If he were going to make any kind of move on Cataldi, Phillip was pretty sure it wouldn't be here.

A young reporter spotted Phillip through the window of the sedan and hurried toward the car:

"Governor, what do you expect to learn from these three men?"

His questions set off the rest of the media, who rushed toward the vehicle in a swarm:

"Governor Grand, are there any leads on Baby Bailino?"

"Governor, are you still planning your candidacy for president?"

"Governor Grand, are you concerned about the safety of your family?"

Wilcox sped past them and pulled into a parking space reserved for him across from a set of double glass doors. He nodded at the two other agents in the car, and the three of them exited simultaneously. Wilcox opened Phillip's door. "Stay close, Governor Grand," he said as the three agents formed a tight circle around him. Phillip glanced at the media outside the property gates and was reminded of the scene outside the Executive Mansion two years ago. The reporters continued jockeying for position and shouting questions, but the words became lost in the distance and breeze. The men walked toward the building entrance.

Inside, the field office was buzzing with activity. Once their group got past security, Wilcox led Phillip down a long corridor toward the back of the building.

"They're in three separate rooms," Wilcox said, pushing the button for the elevator.

"I'd like to sit in on the interviews, if that's all right," Phillip said.

"I'd advise against it, Governor."

"Advise?"

"*Strongly,*" Wilcox said. "However, you're certainly welcome to watch in one of our viewing rooms."

The elevator brought them to the second floor, and the group headed toward a series of doors in the interior of the building. "Normally, these types of interviews take place on the third floor, but we wanted to change up the routine. Bringing in three family heads is rather unprecedented." He paused, and Phillip wasn't sure whether Wilcox was saying that with pride or trepidation. "The truth is that our expectation is that Bailino won't hit here, as Mrs. Grand suggested. It will be either before or after the interviews, so we have all the routes covered, including the men's lodging, The Little Yellow Hotel, for the evening."

Phillip knew that there was no real reason to have the three men return to the FBI field office the next day, other than to force them to find local accommodations for the night. The FBI was looking to extend the time it had Cataldi, DeGrassi, and LaPazza on its turf, lengthening the hang time of that carrot they wanted to dangle in front of Bailino.

Four men, dressed in black suits and slumped on benches, came into view. They looked up when Wilcox, Phillip, and the other agents walked into the waiting area, but returned their eyes back to their magazines, as if the sight of the governor of New York was uninteresting.

"The entourage," Wilcox whispered as they passed them and soon stopped in front of a door. "You'll be able to watch from in here, Governor." Wilcox held it open for Phillip, who was escorted inside by another federal agent. "This shouldn't take long." Wilcox left, letting the door softly close and lock behind him.

The room was small and had several large flat-screen televisions on the wall. Each screen featured a view of an old man sitting at a table. Seats had been arranged in rows in front of the screens like a movie theater.

"Governor," the federal agent said, motioning toward one of the chairs. Phillip sat in the second seat of the first row, while the agent stood back by the door.

All three screens looked identical until a door opened and a pixel-y Wilcox popped into the screen at the far right. He slapped a file folder on the table and took the seat facing the old man, who leaned down and turned a knob on a breathing machine that was situated under the table.

"Mr. Cataldi," Wilcox's voice funneled into the viewing room, "thank you for making the trip up."

"Goddamn FBI escorts wouldn't even let us stop to pee," Paolo said with a grunt.

"You can pee on your own time, Mr. Cataldi."

"That's easy for you to say." The old man adjusted the tubes in his nose. "Wait until you get old."

Wilcox flipped through some paperwork. "I believe this is your first time here, Mr. Cataldi, correct?" he said.

Wilcox's tone made the comment seem like a slight toward the old man, who had always played second fiddle to his older brother. The fact that he had never been called to the FBI field office before meant he hadn't been worthy.

"I guess you saved the best for last," Paolo said with a crooked smile.

Wilcox placed a photo on the table in front of Paolo. Even though it was small, Phillip could tell that it was of Don Bailino. "I assume you're familiar with this man?" Wilcox asked.

"Too damn familiar," Paolo said, glancing at the photo. "What do you want to know?"

"Have you seen him in the past forty-eight hours?"

"Yes," Paolo said.

Wilcox appeared surprised. "You have?"

"Yes, on television."

Wilcox leaned forward. "I meant, in person, Mr. Cataldi."

"Me? No, no, I haven't seen Donny in ten, twenty years. Never liked me too much. Always kept his distance."

"Ah, yes, that's right. Don Bailino preferred the company of your brother, Gino, who seemed to keep Mr. Bailino busy."

Paolo shrugged. "I wouldn't know anything about that." He gathered a wad of saliva in the back of his mouth and spit it onto the floor of the interview room. "I'm not sure how this is helping capture the fugitive that escaped your government's protection."

Now, it was Paolo's turn to offer a slight in what was turning out to be a pissing contest between the two men.

Wilcox held up another photo as if for Phillip's benefit before putting it on the table. The image was of Jamie Carter. "Do you recognize this person?" he asked.

Paolo squinted at the photograph. "Yeah, that's Donny's girlfriend."

"His girlfriend?" Wilcox said. "I think you've been reading too many unauthorized biographies, Mr. Cataldi."

"Boy, you really have no clue, do you?" Paolo dug his pinkie fingernail into the space between his two front teeth and then admired whatever it was that he had dug out of there. "Let's stop playing this game, huh? We both know why I'm here."

"And why is that?" Wilcox said.

Paolo flicked the tooth material across the room. "You tell me," he said.

"I already have." Wilcox leaned back in his metal chair. Phillip thought it was like watching two boxers in a ring, each of them squaring up but waiting for the other to throw the first punch. "I believe you have information on the whereabouts of Don Bailino, who has worked for your family for decades," Wilcox said. "You know as well as I do that one man can't be doing all this alone."

Paolo licked his shaky forefinger and scratched at something on the table. It seemed difficult for him to sit still. "If you believe that, Agent Wilcox, you're dumber than you look." He laughed at his own joke. "Now, can we talk about the *real* reason we're here, or are you going to show me more pictures?"

Phillip leaned forward toward the screen. Paolo seemed smarter than he led on, although, physically, he was a mess. It was hard to think that he had been behind the burning of the Upackk warehouses. He was certainly too frail to physically pull off something like that, but that didn't mean he didn't have help. Phillip thought about the men in black suits sitting only a few yards away from him in the hallway, all of whom appeared young and capable.

"I would think you'd be more interested in helping us, Mr. Cataldi." Wilcox said.

"Is that so?"

"Considering Bailino's botched attempt to save your brother, Gino. And how, for years, Bailino had essentially carved a wedge between you and your brother that had never been reconciled. I would think a guy like you would want to get even."

The old man shifted in his chair and turned a knob on his breathing machine. He held the tubes in his nose with a shaky hand and took a deep, long breath, his exhale sounding to Phillip like a wind through a rickety fence. "You have no idea," Cataldi said.

Phillip's private cell phone rang, and he looked at the Caller ID. Until two years ago, he never had to check to see who was calling on that phone, knowing that only Rosalia and Katherine had the number, but since Bailino had managed to get his hands on that phone number and call Phillip directly, he had developed a habit of checking first. He swiped the screen.

"Well," Katherine said, "how's it going?"

"Not much to report," Phillip whispered. "I'm watching Wilcox interview Cataldi from a viewing room. If Cataldi knows something, he's not letting on."

"And Bailino?" she asked.

"You were right," Phillip said. "Looks like he's not coming. Chances are, wherever he is, he's far, far away from Albany."

35

Bailino pulled into the service area, one of those all-in-one rest stops, and parked at the far end of a long lot.

"Okay, this is what's going to happen . . ." He dug into his pocket and handed Jamie a warm hundred dollar bill. "I'm going to drive the car to those gas pumps and fill up. You're going to pick up something to eat for you and the kid. When you're through, I'll meet you over there." He pointed toward a small playground that was located across from a long, flat building. "Fifteen minutes, all right?"

Jamie looked at the swings and slides filled with children and adults. All of them were strangers, or so she thought. Could one of Cataldi's men be among them? Could someone have followed them? Or what if someone recognized Bailino and called the cops, a Good Samaritan who thought he was saving the day? Little would that person know that arresting Bailino would be far from it.

"You'd be surprised how much more hidden you are in a crowd of people than you are in an empty space," Bailino said as if reading Jamie's thoughts, and a chill overcame her—it had been in a crowded park in which Bailino had abducted *her*.

"Okay," she said.

"And I'll need your gun," Bailino said.

Jamie hesitated. "You have my gun," she said.

"The other one."

Jamie tried to think of something to say.

"Don't lie. Just give it to me." He held out his hand.

She didn't know how Bailino knew she was carrying or, if he did, why he let her. She reached down into her ankle holster, retrieved the piece, and reluctantly handed it over to him.

"Trust me, it's safer this way," Bailino said, sticking it into the waistband of his jeans. "You don't want to set off any metal detectors in there."

Jamie reached out for Faith, but Bailino stopped her.

"Remember, the baby is safer with me," he said.

"But it might look more believable if—"

"She's safer if she's with me," Bailino said. "You both are."

Bailino reached into the glove compartment once again, handed Jamie a black knit cap—the kind worn by longshoremen—and plucked Faith from Jamie's arms. The little girl started to cry when Jamie got out of the car.

"Wanna go for a swing, cupcake? Look." Bailino pointed to the playground. "You like to swing?"

The sudden softening of Bailino's voice flashed Jamie back to the log cabin and how he had manipulated little Charlotte Grand that day by the river, how he had managed to get her to climb into his arms simply by asking her to do what he knew she already wanted to do, a little lesson in loyalty he had given Jamie that day. Faith peered out the car window and nodded. She stopped crying.

"Good girl," Bailino said and buckled her into the passenger seat. The little girl looked so tiny sitting there without a harness or booster seat. "She'll be all right," he said to Jamie. "I've got her. Now, hurry back, Mommy."

With Faith waving good-bye, Bailino drove away before Jamie could close the door, and it swung shut with a *whoosh*. She watched the car circle around the parking lot and pull up to one of the gasoline pumps. Bailino emerged from the car and started pumping gas, the gas nozzle in one hand and little Faith, who was looking toward the playground, in the other. The sight of her daughter out in the open made Jamie's chest heave, but Bailino was right: Even with all the

Amber Alerts and news stories about an escaped prisoner on the loose
and an abducted little girl, no one seemed to notice anything peculiar
about a man in a baseball cap pumping gas with a baby in his hands.

Jamie pulled the cap onto her head and walked toward the rest-
stop facility. She glided inside unobserved, past the sunglasses huts
and churro stands, to a long line of patrons snaked toward a series
of fast food restaurants. She got on the back of the line, which was
long but moving quickly—seven cashiers were whipping through
orders like an assembly line. When it was her turn, she ordered a ten-
piece chicken nugget meal and two cheeseburgers. The kid behind
the counter punched a different button for every item on her list, his
fingers working from muscle memory, his eyes carefully looking over
her out-of-season hat.

"I'm in a rush," she said in a faux-deep voice, handing him the
hundred-dollar bill.

"Aren't we all?" the kid said. He held the large bill up toward the
fluorescent ceiling light, giving it a perfunctory examination.

When she got her food, she hurried next door to a convenience
store whose large floor-to-ceiling windows faced the playground.
Outside, Bailino had finished getting gas and was pushing Faith in
one of the swings. He had put on a pair of sunglasses, but she felt as
if his eyes were watching her. She hurried away from the window
and toward the back of the store, where the refrigerated goods were
located. She pulled open one of the sealed doors, a puff of chilled air
rushing past her, and took out a half gallon of two-percent milk.

"Excuse me, ma'am," a teenage boy with braces said, startling her.
His face was hidden partially by a baseball cap whose brim was tilted
to the side.

Jamie instinctively held the milk in front of her as a buffer. "Can I
help you?" she asked.

The teenager looked suspiciously around the store, as if looking
for someone, and took a step closer. "*Shhhh . . .*" he said and reached
behind him.

Instantly, Jamie dropped the half-gallon onto the floor; milk spilled out of a long crack in the plastic container and pooled onto the linoleum.

"Jesus, lady, what gives?" The teen hopped out of the way of the puddle, and that's when Jamie noticed the six-pack of beer he was carrying in his hand.

"Sorry," she said, wiping her hands, wet either from sweat or the container's condensation, on her shirt. "I didn't—"

"You could have just said no," the teen huffed and headed toward the coffee aisle.

Jamie opened the door to the refrigerated section again and pulled another half-gallon off the shelf. She stepped over the widening puddle as a young couple with toddlers was coming her way and ducked into a nearby snack aisle.

Keep it together, Jamie told herself and quickly picked up a package of fruit snacks, a small box of Cheerios, a container of donuts, and a box of animal crackers—whatever she saw that contained calories. She headed toward the registers.

Like the fast food line, the checkout line snaked toward the front of the store. She got on the end of the line near the windows, which allowed Jamie to watch Bailino, who was still pushing Faith in the swing. The little girl was smiling and kicking her feet, and that sharp pang of fear returned. She looked so small and exposed to the highway traffic as well as the travelers lingering around the rest area. If someone really had been watching them or wanted to hurt them, would Bailino be able to protect her?

"We need a clean up in aisle six," said a tinny voice over a nearby loudspeaker as Jamie stepped forward a few feet in line, trying to juggle all the items in her arms. She should have gotten a basket.

The people in front of her were all looking down at their cell phones and didn't seem to notice anything happening inside or outside the store. Tiny lit screens were everywhere. A television, located high on a wall above an end cap of potato chips and tuned to a daytime talk show, was ignored. Up ahead in line, the young man who had been trying to ask her to buy him beer was standing beside a middle-aged woman in knee-high boots, sporting a tattoo that read *Ain't No Sunshine When She's Gone*. Jamie hid behind the person in front of her.

A police officer entered the store, and Jamie's eyes darted back out the window. Bailino was still at the playground. He was holding the swing close to him, Faith's little legs kicking with anticipation, and when she gave the okay, he pushed her as far as he could—*too far*, Jamie thought with a pang of fear. Jamie wondered if Bailino had seen the officer come in.

The officer waved to the young woman behind the cash register, picked up one of the last newspapers for sale, and got on the back of the checkout line. Jamie pulled her black cap down over her ears.

"Need help with those things, ma'am?" the officer asked her. "You sure have a handful."

"No, I'm fine," she said in a deep, guttural voice without turning around.

"Nice day today, isn't it?" he asked.

She nodded, feeling the officer's curious eyes on her knit cap, and stared up at the television screen as if captivated by its programming.

The talk show host was pretending she didn't know how to boil water for laughs, and within minutes the guest pulled a cooked plate of what looked like lasagna out of a fake oven. The host was digging her fork into a plateful when the officer tapped on Jamie's shoulder.

"Where y'all from?" he asked.

She panicked. "Pennsylvania," she said, without turning around.

"Oh, yeah, what part? A good buddy of mine lives in Pittsburgh."

"Hey, buddy, can you turn that up?" asked one of the customers, a tall guy with bushy hair and glasses, near the front of the line. He was pointing to the television, and his voice caused all the patrons on line to look away from their phones and toward the set.

The talk show had been interrupted by a special news report. A blond news anchor, looking serious, was saying something evidently important. The sound on the set was off, and Jamie read the closed captioning: *We have a breaking news story . . . Authorities believe they have . . . tracked notorious mobster Don Bailino, who . . .*

Jamie's heart hammered her chest.

. . . . recently escaped from Stanton prison, to . . . western New York, not far from the Pennsylvania border . . .

"Hey, are you deaf or what?" the tall guy asked the cashier.

"Give her a minute, pal," said the officer behind Jamie.

The girl behind the register, whose cheeks had turned a bright red, held up a remote control and pushed down on a button until the news anchor's over-modulated voice filled the store: ". . . News 14's own Rita Crenshaw spoke to an eyewitness. We are going live to her now. Rita?"

Jamie's breathing hitched when the eyewitness came onto the screen. It was the woman whom they had left behind at the scene of the car accident and who had tried to speak with Bailino less than forty-five minutes before.

"I saw the whole thing," the woman, identified as Faye Green from Wilkes-Barre, Pennsylvania, said into a News 14 microphone. "I was going to see my sister Kitty, whose daughter, my niece, is getting married this weekend. I was taking the back roads, because I don't like to drive on the main highways. I get nervous with all the trucks," she told Rita, who nodded understandingly, "and I saw the hit and run. A man with a baseball cap left that poor old man to die."

Rita Crenshaw, with a *tsk-tsk* shake of her head, looked into the camera and said, "This fast-acting witness took this photo of the man who left the scene of this despicable crime . . ."

Jamie held her breath. The screen showed a photo of Bailino from the side as he was walking toward Joey's gray Toyota. His face was covered by the brim of his cap, but some of his profile was visible. Jamie's eyes moved to the window, making sure to keep her head straight so that the officer behind her would think she was still staring at the television. Outside, standing in the middle of the playground, right there for the taking, was the man on the screen.

"Police are looking for this man," Rita continued. "He is driving

a gray car and has a woman and child with him. He is believed to be
Don Bailino and, again, is believed to be armed and dangerous. If you
see this man or this vehicle, do not approach. Call the Federal Bureau
of Investigation immediately at the following telephone number,"
which was shown on the screen.

Jamie quickly searched the parking lot for Joey's gray Toyota and
found it parked a few feet from the playground, partially hidden by an
eighteen wheeler that had pulled beside it; all that was visible from the
convenience store were the car's taillights.

"I just hope I find that goddamn son of a bitch first," the police
officer muttered behind Jamie. "If I do, there won't be any phone-a-
friend for that murderer."

Jamie took a step forward in line. She was next, but the guy in
front of her seemed to be requesting every combination of lottery
numbers there was. After a few minutes, the cashier, whose cheeks
were still flushed, finally said, "Next," and Jamie plopped her items
onto the counter.

"Anything else?" asked the young cashier. Jamie shook her head.

"No lottery numbers for you, huh?" the police officer said with
a smile. "Not the gambling type? I think the jackpot is up to five
million."

Jamie smiled and shook her head. She handed twenty dollars
to the cashier, who gave her a snide look, as if annoyed that she had
garnered so much of the officer's attention, and quickly carried the
bag of groceries out the door and toward the playground. Bailino had
already pulled Faith out of the swing and was carrying her toward the
Toyota. Jamie tried not to draw attention to herself, but vigorously
shook her head, hoping Bailino would get the hint.

He did. He stopped walking for a moment before starting again,
passing Joey's car and heading further into the parking lot. Jamie
followed, and the two of them walked parallel to one another, about
a car length apart, for some twenty feet, until they were away from
the building.

"Mama!" Faith called, spotting Jamie, but Bailino whispered

something to her and Faith's attention went in another direction. Bailino ducked in between several lines of cars, looking into the driver's side windows, until he stopped in front of a wine-colored minivan. He checked the dashboard, pulled the side door handle, waiting a beat to see if there would be an alarm, and plopped Faith into a car seat in the middle row as the side door electronically slid open.

"Get in," he said when Jamie approached, and she hurried to the other side and got into the passenger seat.

Bailino turned the keys that were already in the ignition, starting the car. Slowly, he pulled out of the parking spot and drove onto the highway.

"Mama!" Faith called, and Jamie reached into one of the bags on her lap and handed her daughter a chicken nugget. The little girl grabbed at it and stuffed the whole thing into her mouth.

"What happened?" Bailino asked.

"That man who was sideswiped when we first got into New York, he died," Jamie said. The words were flying out of her mouth in a heated rush. "And that woman who stopped, she told the police that you hit the guy's car and left him there. They think you killed him. She took a photo of you when you were walking toward Joey's car, and they showed it on the news."

"Do they know it's me?" he asked.

Jamie nodded. "Yes," she said. "They have a feeling it is."

Bailino absorbed the information. "Why didn't you tell the police officer standing behind you on line who you were?" he asked.

He *had* been watching.

"Mo, peas," Faith said, reaching her hand out. Jamie handed her another chicken nugget.

"But," Jamie said, "the news anchor—"

"I asked why you didn't tell the officer who you were."

"But . . . I . . . I don't know. I want to do what will keep—"

"Did you think I would do something to her"—he motioned to Faith in the backseat—"if you alerted him?"

"I told you, I didn't—"

"Answer me, please."

"I'm trying to." Jamie took a breath. "No, I didn't think you would hurt her." She looked back at her daughter, who was chewing contentedly. "Maybe I'm crazy, but I believe you. I think you're the one person who can get me out of this, get Faith out of this. What you said back at the house was right. You never lied to me. You did a lot of . . ." She paused and looked at the window—the sky was darkening, the red sun sinking below the line of trees and hills. "But you never lied to me. And I'm praying to God you're not lying now, that you are trying, like me, to save this little girl. My daughter." She swallowed hard. "*Your* daughter, who didn't ask for this and who deserves to have some kind of life where she's not afraid all the time and running. She deserves better."

Bailino didn't say anything. He put on his blinker and changed lanes. "We can't stay in this car for long," he said finally after several minutes.

Jamie reached into one of the fast food bags and took out a cheeseburger. She unwrapped it and held it out for him.

"What's this?" Bailino asked.

"A cheeseburger," Jamie said. "For you. I thought you might be hungry."

"You eat it, honey. I'm fine."

"I got one for me, too," she said.

Bailino glanced at her and reached for the burger. "Thank you," he said and took a bite.

"Mo, peas," Faith said, reaching her hand toward the front seat.

After a few more exits, Bailino got off the highway and turned onto a side road. He seemed more familiar with the area, and Jamie assumed they were getting closer to Albany. He made a series of turns, using back roads, some of them barely wide enough for a vehicle, and soon Jamie recognized the route names and numbers. She had grown familiar with Albany when Edward was recuperating at Albany Memorial and tried to piece together what part of town they were in. After a few more blocks, she realized where they were.

"I don't understand," she said, confused. "Why are we here?"

"Because we need a place to ditch this car," Bailino said, "and because more than anyplace else I think you'll be safe here."

He made one last hard right turn, and the minivan bounced onto the sidewalk and into the parking lot of Reynaldo's garage.

36

The beams of the headlights scanned the perimeter of Reynaldo's office as he gathered the last of the paperwork into clearly labeled folders titled *Morning, Afternoon,* and *Evening.* This would be the last of the hand-holding he would do for his brothers for a long while, if forever. He peered through the blinds of the front window just in time to see the back end of a minivan enter one of the garage bays. Reynaldo sighed.

"We're closed!" he called, shoving the folders into the top drawer of the front desk. Although he was grateful for the boost in business the garage had received in the last two years, he was amazed at how brazen many of his new customers could be, showing up just before closing, asking for special pricing. He looked at his watch. He told his cousins he would be in Queens after 10 p.m.—if he left now, he could be downstate by just before midnight. He heard the minivan's motor, rumbling through the wall, go quiet.

"*Ay, Dios mio,*" he said, locking the drawer and hanging the key on a nail next to a clipboard. He straightened a few magazines that were lying on the coffee table, opened the side door, and stepped inside the garage. The minivan was parked on the far side.

"We're closed," he said again, his voice echoing across the quiet space. "Hello?"

The garage was dark, the beams of the minivan shooting across it like lasers. The driver's side door hung open and a beeping sound echoed across the room. Reynaldo walked toward the minivan and looked in the driver's side window. No one was there. He softly closed the door, and the beeping silenced.

"Are you alone?"

Reynaldo spun around. "Who's there? Pedro, is that you?" he asked. "Ricardo, I don't have time for this nonsense. Whose minivan is this?"

Reynaldo moved toward the back of the minivan and checked the other side, but no one was there. He pulled open the sliding door, which started up the beeping again, but all that was inside was an empty car seat and a faint chicken smell. He eyed the fast food paper bags littering the floor and closed the door.

"I asked if you were alone."

Reynaldo flinched. Through the dark, a silhouetted figure walked toward him. The hair rose on the back of Reynaldo's neck, and he thrust his arm out, grabbing a wrench that was hanging from the wall particleboard. He stood stock-still as the figure, as it grew closer to the beam of the headlights, morphed into the dark, imposing outline of Don Bailino.

"Don't do anything stupid," Bailino said, eyeing the wrench.

The movies that had played in Reynaldo's mind returned with a vengeance—the sight of Jamie and tiny Charlotte Grand wet and shaking in his office, Reynaldo's near fall from the edge of Albany County Bridge. His leg ached as if it, too, were remembering.

"I asked if you were alone," Bailino said, holding a gun up toward Reynaldo's chest.

This was the closest he had ever been to Don Bailino, his face only familiar to Reynaldo from the years of television coverage. He had never really gotten a good look at him that night, and over the years his mind's eye had filled in all the details of his features. As Reynaldo stood here, now, a fury pulsed through him. "Where is she?" Reynaldo asked, his hand tightening around the wrench.

"Just one answer. That's all I need," Bailino said.

Reynaldo raised the wrench.

"Easy now, put it down, Rodriguez," Bailino said.

Reynaldo wondered how quickly he could charge Bailino before he got off a shot when another figure stirred behind Bailino and a soft voice spoke out.

"Rey . . ."

His grip around the wrench loosened, even before Reynaldo could place the voice, and into the hazy light of the garage walked Jamie with a little girl—*her* little girl—in her arms. "Rey, it's okay."

"Jamie . . ." Reynaldo's voice was strained. "What are—?"

"Rey, please, are you alone?" she asked.

All he could do was nod. The little girl's eyes were blinking as if trying to adjust to the new surroundings. "Are you all right?" Reynaldo said.

"We're okay," she said, coming forward. "We—"

Reynaldo reached out quickly and pulled Jamie and Faith behind him. "Let them go," Reynaldo said.

"Let's just stay calm here, *amigo*," Bailino said, the pistol steady in his hand. "If you do anything stupid, I'll fucking shoot you."

"Reynaldo, it's all right," Jamie said. She came out from behind his protective arms and stood between him and Bailino. When she did, Bailino aimed the gun toward the floor. Faith rested her head on her mother's shoulder, her eyes red and droopy, a half-eaten chicken nugget in her hand.

"I don't understand." Reynaldo said.

"Please, Reynaldo," Jamie said. "It's okay. You need to promise you won't yell or do anything right now. Can you do that? For me?"

Reynaldo's eyes met Bailino's.

"You heard the lady. Wipe that look off your face, friend," Bailino said. His hand wiggled the pistol.

"I'm not your friend," Reynaldo huffed.

"I'm not fucking around with you," Bailino said.

"Neither am I."

"Reynaldo," Jamie said, "please."

"Don't make me think this was a mistake," Bailino said, stepping aside and lifting the pistol back up toward Reynaldo's chest.

"No." Jamie moved closer to Reynaldo and put her hand on his chest. "Please, Rey. You need to trust me."

Reynaldo's gaze lowered to meet Jamie's face. "What's happening?" he whispered. "I don't understand."

"I'm sorry to just come here like this," Jamie said. "I didn't know that—"

"What happened to your neck?" Reynaldo said, tilting her chin up. A string of bruises, blood red splotches filled with broken capillaries and tiny pits of deep purple, sliced across the skin.

"Oh, I—" Jamie touched her neck. "It's okay, I'm fine."

She looked back at Bailino, and that was all the information Reynaldo needed. He lunged at Bailino, catching him off-guard, and landed a punch onto his jaw, causing him to drop the gun.

"No!" Jamie called as Faith let out a loud scream.

"You son of a bitch, I'll kill you," Reynaldo said and scrambled for the gun, but Jamie managed to grab it first.

"No," she said. "Wait!"

"Jamie, what are you doing? Are you crazy?" Reynaldo asked when Bailino grabbed him from behind into a chokehold, and the two men landed on the garage floor, rolling and punching at one another until they slammed into the vehicle lift in the next bay, shaking the white Hyundai that hovered above them.

"Stop it!" Jamie screamed. "Stop it, both of you!"

The men tore at one another. Reynaldo landed punches on Bailino's already bruised face, and Bailino tightened his grip on Reynaldo' neck.

"Rey!" Jamie screamed, the gun shaking in her hands. "It wasn't him. He saved me, Rey!"

Reynaldo watched Jamie's mouth, but he couldn't convert her yells into words. Her eyes were pleading with him, and he was stunned at their request. He stopped punching, he stopped struggling, and Bailino released his grip on his neck.

"Are you going to be a good boy, now?" Bailino asked, standing up and wiping dirt from his pants. He stepped toward the garage office, and Reynaldo could see him check behind the counter. He closed the front blinds of the office and put on the overhead light.

"I don't understand," Reynaldo said to Jamie. He stood up and rubbed his neck. "Do you know how many people are looking for you?"

"Yes," Jamie said. "I do."

The little girl leaned her head on her mother's shoulder again, but her eyes were following Bailino's every movement in the office until he returned into the garage.

"Why don't you take her inside, hon?" Bailino said to Jamie. "Lay her down. Maybe she can get some sleep."

Jamie nodded. "I can explain everything," she said to Reynaldo. "I promise." She kissed his cheek, placed the gun she was holding in his hands, and took Faith into the office. Bailino closed the door.

Reynaldo immediately lifted the gun and pointed it toward Bailino.

"Seriously?" Bailino said. The bruises on his face had reddened, and even in the relative dark of the garage, Reynaldo could tell Bailino's nose was bleeding, the blood pooling just above his lip.

"It doesn't feel too good, does it?" Reynaldo asked. The skin of his neck stung, and his throat burned as he swallowed.

"You don't think I've been on the opposite end of a gun before?"

Reynaldo eyed Bailino carefully. "You saved her?" he asked.

"She's in danger," Bailino said. "They both are."

"I know they are."

"Not from me, pal."

"Oh, yeah, then, well, from who?"

"It doesn't matter right now. What matters is that no one can know they are here. *No one.* For their own safety. If I can do what I have to do, you won't have to ever see me again. Do you have a place you can go with them? A safe place?"

"This isn't safe?"

"Not safe enough. You need to find a place where nobody would ever think of finding you. Can you do that?"

Reynaldo thought of the places he could go. "I'll find someplace," he said.

"The sooner, the better. Tomorrow, you need to wait to hear from me. I will call Jamie, and then you can go to the police. I'll tell her if it's safe. Understand?"

"Why can't I just go to the *policía* now?"

"Because the *policía* cannot protect them. Not right now. Only you can."

Reynaldo lowered the gun. "You're being serious."

Bailino wiped the bottom of his bloody nose with his hand. "*Sí.*"

"And what if she doesn't hear from you?" Reynaldo asked.

"Then she'll know what to do."

Reynaldo reached into his back pocket, and Bailino flinched. He pulled out a white handkerchief. "For your nose." Reynaldo held it out.

"I'm fine," Bailino said.

"It's bleeding."

"I said I'm fine." Bailino wiped his hand on his pants. "I need to go."

Reynaldo placed the handkerchief and gun on the counter and peered through the small window of the office door. Jamie was sitting on the couch next to Faith, who was lying down, her head on her mother's lap. Jamie was caressing her face.

"Do you know how to shoot that thing?" Bailino asked, motioning to the gun.

Reynaldo nodded. "*Sí,*" he said.

"Good."

"Who am I looking for?" Reynaldo asked.

"Anyone who is not me," Bailino said. He picked up the white handkerchief and placed it into his pocket. The two men watched Jamie and Faith through the office window.

"Do you love her?" Bailino asked.

Reynaldo was quiet. He searched Bailino's dark eyes.

"It doesn't matter what you say," Bailino said, "because I know you do."

"Do you?" Reynaldo asked.

"That doesn't matter either," Bailino said. "The only thing that matters to me is that they're safe."

"What are you—?"

"Take care of them," Bailino said, taking off toward the garage bays. "And get rid of the minivan, they'll be looking for it."

Before Reynaldo could answer, Bailino had ducked under the open garage door and disappeared into the night.

❀

Reynaldo put the milk and the few remaining chicken nuggets from the minivan into the refrigerator under the office counter. On the couch, Faith was sleeping peacefully on Jamie's lap, a coloring book in one hand, a crayon in the other. Jamie was absently rubbing the little girl's belly and staring out the window, even though the view was blocked by the closed blinds.

"Can I get you anything?" Reynaldo asked.

She shook her head. "Were you going someplace?" she asked, motioning toward the packed bag on the floor. "I don't want to stop you from—"

"No, no," Reynaldo waved off her concern, "I was going to look for you."

"Oh." She gave a tired smile, and her eyes crinkled with sadness. "I'm sorry to drag you into this again."

"You're not dragging me anyplace." He sat down next to her, and his knee brushed hers. He knew that he had missed her, but he hadn't realized how badly until now. "I feel like this is my fault."

"*Your* fault? Why?"

"I should have been with you." He gently moved some of Faith's hair away from her face. "I should have never left. If I had been with you . . ."

"You don't know that. I could have given you the slip, too." She gave a small smile. "You're always so hard on yourself, Reynaldo. All this"—she motioned toward Faith—"was a lot for me to ask. I know that. I'm not mad at you, and I don't blame you for not knowing how to feel about my having this baby, but I don't regret having her. Not for one single day." She took his hand in hers. "You're here now, Reynaldo, and that means something."

He closed his hand over hers. He could feel her trembling. "But I don't trust him, Jamie," Reynaldo said. "How can we? What's stopping us from taking the baby and going to the *policía*?"

"I believe him, Rey."

Faith started to stir, and Reynaldo lowered his voice. "But, but, why? Can we really believe anything this man says?"

Jamie stared again at the closed blinds. "But what he said to me is true," she whispered. "He has never lied to me."

"No, but he has done far worse," Reynaldo said and immediately wished he hadn't.

Jamie ran her finger along Faith's dark brown eyebrows. "Maybe so, but I can't think about that now. I can only think about her."

Reynaldo brought his hand to the back of Jamie's head and caressed it. He thought of them lying together once upon a time, enjoying one another. It seemed like ages ago. "Jamie, please, let's think rationally for a minute."

"You don't think I've been doing that?" she asked, her voice slightly louder. "It's all—"

"Wait, what is this?" He rubbed his finger along the curved outline of a bump on the back of her head. "How did you get this?"

She shook her head. "He said it wasn't supposed to happen, and then there was a man—"

"*¡Dios mío!*" Reynaldo popped up off the couch. His sudden movement startled Faith, whose eyes fluttered, but the caress of her mother's hand brought her back to sleep. "What has he done to you?" he whispered.

"Nothing," Jamie said, almost defensively. "He's done nothing to me. I'm making my own decisions."

Reynaldo ran his hand through his black and gray locks. "But how can this end well? How can you be loyal to someone who—"

"Reynaldo, he could have hurt us at any time. We were alone. In the woods. He said the man who did this to me"—she pointed to her neck—"was after Faith."

"And you believe him?"

"Yes, I do. They want to hurt her in order to hurt him."

Reynaldo wanted desperately to believe Jamie, but everything inside of him told him that this was not a good idea.

"I can't think about what happened *then*, which is crazy because it's all I've thought of for two years." She looked into Reynaldo's eyes. "We are where we are *right now*, and if I don't face that fact, I will put my daughter in even more danger. I need to keep her safe." She took a deep, slow breath. "I understand if you don't want to be a part of—"

"I am," Reynaldo said, sitting back down. He pulled her hand back into his and squeezed it. "I will. You both stay with me."

"Thank you." Her shoulders relaxed a bit. "But we need to go. I'm not sure it's safe here."

"What if we don't hear from him? He said you know what to do."

Jamie nodded. "He told me about a place out west that nobody knows about. If we don't hear from him by tomorrow, he said I should take Faith there."

"How will he reach you?"

She pointed to her boot. "In my ankle holster, I have a cell phone in there—a burner, he calls it. He'll call that phone when it's safe."

Reynaldo bristled at the thought of Jamie having to wear an ankle holster. "What about Edward? Have you been in touch with him?"

"I can't risk calling him. It could put him in danger, too. He'll have to understand."

"But what if—?"

"Reynaldo, please." Tears gathered in the corners of Jamie's red eyes. "I barely know what I'm doing. I'm trying to trust my instincts, but I'm afraid that they won't make any sense if I try to explain them."

"*Lo siento.* I'm sorry," he said. He thought again about where he could bring them that was safe and where no one could find them. The woods were a possibility—deep into the Adirondacks. He knew the bike and hiking trails inside and out, but it was too cold for the baby and too isolated if they got into any trouble. He could drive to New Jersey or Connecticut and check into a hotel room and pay cash, but there were cameras all over those places, and they could be seen coming and going by other guests.

"I know a place, I think," he finally said. "My father is up here on vacation with his . . . girlfriend. They have a place in Florida. It has a small, private entrance. I helped him pick it out when he first moved down there. We can drive down right away."

"Do you have a key?"

"Not on me. It's at the house, but I can ask Pedro to get it." He jumped up and crossed the office toward the wall phone.

"Wait, he can't know that we're here. He'll be put into danger."

"I won't tell him." Reynaldo grabbed the handle of the wall phone and dialed. Pedro picked up on the second ring.

"*Hermano*," Pedro chirped, "you miss us already?"

"Pedro, I need a favor?"

"What is it?"

"You can't ask me any questions, and you can't tell anybody."

"*What is it?*" he asked again, suddenly interested.

"I mean it, *hermano*. *Nobody*."

"*Sí, sí*, I get it. What's the favor?"

"I need you to bring to me the key to Papa's house in Florida."

"*¿Por qué?*"

"Pedro!" He hadn't meant to raise his voice, and he glanced at the couch to make sure he hadn't startled little Faith, but Jamie had her hand over the girl's ear, and she was still asleep. "No questions, remember?" he said. "Can you bring it?"

"Sure, as long as it's not in Papa's room. He and Pearl are louder than—"

"Pedro, focus. Can you come down to the garage and drop it off?"

"*Now?*"

"It's important, Pedro. Please."

Pedro let out a loud, inconvenienced huff. "Okay," he said, "I'll be there in ten minutes—twenty, if the key is in Papa's room—but, since I'm being such a good *hermano* and doing this, I need a favor, too."

"What else is new?" Reynaldo said. "I'll be waiting."

Rey hung up the receiver and sat on the couch. "He'll be here soon."

"Okay," Jamie said, her eyes looking for the gun Bailino had given them. Reynaldo had placed it on the small coffee table; it was less than an arm's length from her.

Reynaldo sat on the couch again and reached for Jamie's hand. She let him. The two of them looked down at the sleeping child.

"She is so beautiful," Reynaldo said. "She looks just like you."

He wiped away a tear that slid down her cheek.

"Hey," he gently grasped the tip of her chin. "It's going to be all right. You'll get through this." He tucked several strands of hair behind her ear, and she leaned her head against his hand.

They sat there like that in silence until an engine roared outside, surprising them, followed by intermittent lights through the closed blinds and the muffled song lyrics of "Aguanile" by Mark Anthony. Reynaldo peered through the blinds and saw Pedro park in one of the spots in front of the garage and get out of his car.

"Is it him?" Jamie asked, nervously.

Reynaldo closed the blinds. "Yes. Pedro may be a lot of things, but he is reliable. Usually."

"He can't see us, Rey. For his own safety as well as ours."

"I know. I'll go out." Reynaldo crossed the small office and turned the deadbolt on the front door. "I'll be right back," he whispered with a smile and opened the door as a gunshot shattered the silence.

37

The Little Yellow Hotel, a family-owned bed and breakfast in Saratoga Springs, had been a favorite of the Cataldi family over the years, mostly because of its proximity to the racetrack, which is where Gino Cataldi used to drag Bailino every summer. Even as hotel chains began upping their amenities with free breakfasts and WiFi, and Airbnb dug its claws into the hospitality arena, the Little Yellow Hotel had been able to stay in the game by making a name for itself with its expansive, private views of the Hudson River at affordable prices. The proprietors, Cole and Jean Caldwell, had roots in the area that went as far back as the first English settlers and had developed a reputation for spare, but clean accommodations, as well as what numerous magazines lauded as the best Western omelets this side of the Mississippi.

Gino Cataldi, Bailino remembered, hadn't been much of an egg-man, but he did like the privacy the hotel afforded him. It was located on the precipice of a hill, with each of its six country-styled bedrooms overlooking the river, making it nearly impossible for anyone, namely the Feds, to watch any goings-on too closely. And considering the Caldwells also made it a habit of never staying on the premises when there were guests, instead choosing to stay at a nearby relative's—the Caldwell family owned quite a bit of property in the area—the Cataldis had the run of the hotel when they were there.

Bailino parked the small hybrid he swiped from the front of

Reynaldo's garage on the street and began walking west toward the river. He walked through the woods until he reached a two-story abandoned building that, five years ago, had been a mom-and-pop gift shop owned by Rick and Molly Jansen, longtime customers of Upackk. The floundering economy had hit many of Bailino's small business customers pretty hard, and the Jansens had lasted longer than most, but they finally threw in the towel and moved south to North Carolina to be near Molly's parents. Bailino still received a Christmas card from them every year—or, at least, he had until he had been hospitalized. The windows had dirty circular streak marks, as if washed in a hurry, and the grass was knee high, a rickety For Sale sign staked into the ground beside an old bird bath.

He walked across the street and onto the grounds of St. Bernadette's, a Catholic high school that had recently closed due to low enrollment. In the dark, under the glow of the sporadic streetlights, the stone building reminded Bailino of Stanton prison with the exception of a big cross that was carved into the stonework at the top of the front doors under a quote from Saint Bernard of Clairvaux: *Learn the lesson that, if you are to do the work of a prophet, what you need is not a scepter but a hoe.* If Bailino remembered correctly, St. Bernadette's had a developed quite a reputation for heroin dealing and teen prostitution in its latter years; perhaps the students mistook the word *hoe* for *whore*.

He slipped through an opening in the front fence and walked around the perimeter of the building toward the school yard, dodging panes of broken glass that littered the ground. In the back of the building, Bailino surveyed the large expanse of land that once had been divided into a broad array of sporting subsections—tennis and basketball courts on the left, which were now swimming pools of rainwater, and a grass football field on the right. For a couple of years, in the late 1990s, the St. Bernadette's football team had been New York State champs—an accolade the school continued to promote till the end—but the field's glory days were long behind it. Weeds as tall as corn stalks swayed in the gentle night breeze.

Bailino crept up the bleachers, the boards of wood bowing beneath his weight, until he reached the top level and gazed east through his binoculars. Through an opening of trees, he spotted the front entrance of the Little Yellow Hotel about a mile out. He lowered the binoculars and could see three black limousines parked in front of the hotel, but no sign of Paolo Cataldi or any of the other family heads. He moved the binoculars left and right, finding a white nondescript van, probably carrying two or three federal agents, parked down the block of a dead-end road, and a feeling of déjà vu swept over him. Bailino had stood on this spot many times over the years in service to Gino Cataldi, checking for Feds and supervising transfers. He didn't expect to be back.

He crept down the bleachers, through another broken metal fence, and made his way toward the middle of the football field, the weeds—the tops of some of them still colored with the white yardage markings—opening a path for him with every step.

When he got to the forty yard line, he bent down and searched through the tall grass until he found a circular sewer grate. He reached into his pocket for his screwdriver, dug it into the groove of the grate's edge, and pushed down on it with all his weight until the cover gave a little and he could grip it with both hands. He heaved the cover up and over, and it fell with a dull thud as the smell of sewage and mold filled the air. He leaned back on the ground—a tightness tugged at his chest, and he took a few deep breaths. Reynaldo Rodriguez's strength had taken him by surprise. He ran his finger under his nose to check for blood, but it was dry.

Bailino shined a flashlight he found in the hybrid inside the dank, clammy space below him before jumping down and landing in a shallow puddle of water. He stood still, listening, but other than the occasional drip, creak, and echo, he heard nothing. It had been two years since he had been down there, and he wasn't sure the passage was still viable. He walked east, keeping his flashlight beam steady before him, even though he didn't need any light at all. He had the sewer grid memorized.

The sewers in this part of the area were a bit different from those under the Executive Mansion and easier to navigate. At a fork in the tunnel, Bailino turned his flashlight up until the yellow light revealed a small hole, about a foot wide, in the muddy wall. Using the back of his flashlight, he began chipping away at its hardened perimeter when he heard a shrill scream, and the face of an angry black rat poked out its head.

Bailino sighed. "You picked the wrong hole, momma," he said and jabbed the end of his flashlight at the creature, which backed into the hole, its squeals joined by a chorus of high-pitched others. He continued stabbing until the noise stopped.

He looked onto the muddy floor and found a long metal stick that resembled a car antenna. He dug its edge along the bottom of the hole, dragging out the bloody carcasses of the momma rat and six tiny babies and flicking them to the ground. He continued chipping away at the hole with the back of the flashlight until the hole's sides gave and he was able to pull out a few large chunks. He reached his hand in and felt around until he touched something cold. He grabbed at it and pulled out a large metal safe-deposit-type box covered in mud and rat feces. He placed it on the floor and rubbed off as much muck as he could until he could see the combination lock dangling on the front. With his flashlight, he tried reading its numbers, but his aging eyes wouldn't permit it, and he had left his glasses in the car. Instead, he placed his hands gently on the lock, carefully listening for each click until he set the five notches to 5-2-3-2-8—the birthday of Rosemary Clooney, for whom Gino had had a decades-long hard-on.

The lock opened, and Bailino ripped it off and pulled open the top of the box. Inside, clean and dry, as if it had been placed in yesterday and not two years before, was a gun, a box of bullets, two phony passports featuring Gino Cataldi's photo beside the name Robert Ford, a fake driver's license, also in Ford's name, four packages of Twinkies, a bottle of water, and three thousand dollars in hundreds.

The Twinkies had been Gino's idea—something with a long shelf life to tide him over while he laid low in the sewer after Bailino got him out of Stanton prison and before he fled the country. However, thanks in part to Jamie Carter, Gino never made it off the lethal injection table. In the end, the Twinkies had lasted longer than he had.

He pocketed the money and the identification, put bullets in the gun, which he stuck in the back waistband of his pants, and dropped more bullets into his pockets. He left the Twinkies and water in the box and placed it back into the sewer wall.

He continued east until he reached another fork and began counting his steps. This was the part of the sewer grid that became tricky—several tunnels emptied into a main section before fracturing off again in various directions. Bailino, the flashlight beam steady before him, kept counting and when he reached fifty, turned immediately to his left and stepped onto a slight incline before turning left again. Up ahead, the glare of a streetlight reflected down into the tunnel. He walked quickly to the checkerboard square of light on the floor and stood on it as if it were a scale.

Above him loomed the Little Yellow Hotel marquee, its curlicue lettering trailing out of sight. He kept walking east, but this time with a slower pace, listening for the slightest movement, the tiniest splash of water. Gino and Paolo Cataldi had a tenuous relationship over the years, ranging from tepid to loathsome, and Gino had kept this little passageway a secret from everyone, including Paolo, so Bailino didn't expect any company, but, still, he couldn't be sure. He turned off his flashlight.

Up ahead was another series of tunnels. He took the smaller one on the right. As he walked, the air turned drier, fresher, and for a moment Bailino thought it smelled like baked bread. He entered a small vestibule that contained a ladder and climbed toward another sewer grate. Many of the oldest buildings in the Albany area, particularly those located near the river, contained large storm drains on the property not only to drain water should there be a flood, but because there were often issues with the old sewer systems requiring routine maintenance.

He pushed on it and was surprised when it budged easily, but he felt another strain in his chest. He took several deep breaths and another step up the ladder until his back was flat against the cool metal and, as hard as he could, pushed until the sewer grate budged just enough for him to angle it so that he could slide it across the ground. He pushed it further with his hands and stepped up and onto a small patio.

Bailino slid the sewer grate back into place and headed toward a nearby door which he knew led to the hotel's boiler room. Inside, the furnace was on full blast, even though the evening was balmy, and Bailino imagined the trio of old Italian geezers shivering in their bedrooms under a stack of blankets to warm their thin skin and fragile bones. He headed toward the only door in the room and poked his head through.

The basement of the Little Yellow Hotel housed no guest rooms, only the boiler room and laundry area. The Caldwells had talked for years about adding a game room for the kids or an indoor pool, but it looked as if nothing ever materialized. Nor had they installed a security camera system, from what Bailino could tell. He walked slowly toward the laundry room, which, he remembered, was located next to a stairwell. The room was empty—no clothing in the dryer, whose open door hung lopsidedly. Bailino pushed the stairwell door open slowly and pulled the gun out of his back waistband. The faint smell of a wood-burning stove somewhere in the hotel greeted him, but nothing else. He crept up two sets of stairs to the first floor, which was where the lobby and kitchen were located, and put his ear to the door. Also quiet. He pushed it open and stared into the room.

On the salmon pink floral carpeting of the long hallway leading to the lobby lay the bodies of three men. Bailino knew they were dead simply by their body positions, the way their heads tilted unnaturally to the side. He listened, but heard nothing except the tick of an old cuckoo clock hanging nearby.

Keeping his gun pointed, he stepped into the room. The bodies were too big and bulky to be any of the old coots, and the two closest to him were dressed in black suits. Bailino hadn't seen Paolo in a suit in about twenty years. With his foot, he flipped over the first body, which had been lying on its side, and recognized the man with the bullet hole in his forehead immediately.

Aurelio Fritoni had worked for Sal DeGrassi for more than twenty-five years. Aurelio was a wise-aleck kid who grew into a wise-aleck man, and Bailino was surprised he had lasted as long as he had. The body next to him, a heavyset man also with a bullet hole through his forehead, belonged to Bonevento "Benny" Benditti, who worked for Vincent LaPazza.

It was unusual to see Aurelio and Benny away from their bosses. Back when Gino was still a free man, Bailino had spent much time in the company of the two men, all three of them watching each other carefully as the family heads conducted business. The only person Aurelio hated more than Bailino was probably Benny, and Aurelio told them more than once that if it weren't for old Sally, he would never be caught dead in the same room with either of them. Little did he know that, in the end, he would be caught dead in the same room with both of them.

The killings appeared to be the handiwork of Paolo Cataldi, who was never one to waste a bullet—one and done, he used to say—and always aimed for just above the nose. However, Bailino imagined it had been quite some time since Paolo held a gun, particularly as his Parkinson's had progressed, and assumed the shots had been fired by someone else, probably one of Paolo's underlings, whom he was grooming. The wounds were fresh, and it looked as though the men hadn't seen the shot coming—or if they had, they hadn't expected it. Neither was holding a pistol or weapon of any kind.

The third body was further down the hall from the other two, closer to the lobby, and was dressed in jeans and a hoodie that read *Oneonta*. As Bailino stepped closer, he realized it was just a kid. The body had two bullet holes—one in the left eye, the other in the middle of the chest. Bailino surmised that the kid *had* seen the bullet coming, which had caused him to move just enough to make the shooter miss the forehead and have to fire again. Loose change lay on the rug and in the kid's palm, and Bailino thought he might have been a hotel worker or delivery guy who got caught in the crossfire. Whoever it was, he would soon be missed, so Bailino had to act fast.

Bailino peeked into the lobby, which was dark and quiet. The three limos were still outside, so Paolo had left another way unless he was still in the hotel. He thought of the sewers. Perhaps Gino had squealed or Paolo knew more than he let on.

He returned to the stairwell, climbed the next two flights of steps, and creaked open the door to the second floor of the hotel. Warm, dry air flooded the stairwell, and Bailino could see a fire burning brightly in a wood-burning stove at the far end of a large living room, decorated in a colonial motif. Two small men sat hunched over in rockers before the stove—predictably, they were wearing flannel shirts and were covered in blankets. The men stopped their conversation when they spotted him.

"Donny," Sal said as Bailino stood before them. "Right on time." He leaned back in his rocker, his slippered feet poking out from under the blanket.

"Well, look who it is," Bailino said with a smirk. "Tweedle-decrepit and Tweedle-dummy."

"I'm surprised at you, Donny," Vincent said, pushing up the glasses that were low on the bridge of his nose. "I bet Sally you'd be too smart for this."

"Told you he'd fall for it," Sal said, motioning to Bailino's gun. "Did you really think you'd be able to just waltz in here and shoot us?"

"I was hoping," Bailino said. "And, to be honest, judging by what I just saw, I'm not quite sure who fell for what."

"Speak up, Donny." Vincent wiggled his right earlobe. "The old ears aren't as good as they used to be."

"I said go fuck yourself," Bailino said.

Sal brought the blanket up to his shoulders. "You look good, kid," he said. "Prison is your color."

"Maybe it's fatherhood," Vincent said. "I hear you got yourself a little girl."

"Don't mention my daughter, all right?" Bailino said. It was the first time he said the word *daughter*, and he felt another tug in his chest. He took a seat on the couch across from the men. "Where's Paolo?"

"He's not here," Vincent said with a grin, his yellowed teeth bearing the marks of decades of smoking.

"I'm not fucking around, Vincent. Where the fuck is he?"

"How the fuck you get in here, Donny?" Sal asked, intrigued. "One of Gino's famous secret passageways?"

"I'm not going to ask again, Sally. Where is he?"

"You better watch your tone, son." Vincent wagged a crooked finger at Bailino. He reached into his pocket and pulled out a phone.

"Who you calling, Vincent?" Bailino asked with a smirk. "No one downstairs but a bunch of stiff corpses."

Sal's face lost some of whatever color it still had. Sally DeGrassi was as old as fuck, but he was still sharp. Two bouts of chemo had weakened his body, but not his resolve. If his bones hadn't been riddled by osteoporosis, he would have launched himself across the table at Bailino.

"Aurelio!" Sal yelled suddenly.

Bailino shook his head. "It's over, Sally. Looks like old Paolo got the jump on your men, but saved both your asses for me."

"Bullshit," Vincent said, glancing at the double doors that led to the small balcony overlooking the lobby. "You underestimate Paolo Cataldi. You always have."

"You're right, Vincent," Bailino said. "I underestimated how much Paolo hated the two of you more than he does me." He raised his gun. "And you know what? I thought *you'd* be too smart for that."

The silenced shot pierced Vincent's temple, and his body slumped forward and tumbled onto the ground. Bailino moved the gun to Sal.

"Where is he, Sal? C'mon, you must know something."

Sal was quiet. Bailino could tell the old guy was running through all sorts of scenarios in his mind, trying to think of any way to change the inevitable outcome.

"Whatever happens here, right now," Sal said finally, "this isn't going to end well for you. You know what I mean. It can't."

"I'm not asking you again, Sally," Bailino said.

Sal shrugged his hunched shoulders. "Damned if I know," he said. "The old fuck set me up." He looked around the living room. "You know, old Gino and I used to play hide and seek in this room when we were kids."

"Paolo doesn't give a shit about you or anyone. What did he tell you? That you would come here and that you'd lure me here?"

"We did, didn't we? Maybe we *both* underestimated the old coot." Sal looked at his watch. "Let's get this over with." The old man pushed himself back in the chair until he was sitting straight and the top of his bald head peeked just over the top band of the wooden rocking chair. "You know, just for the record, I really did respect your father. Patsy was a hell of a guy." He lifted the blanket higher until it reached his shoulders, tucked the corners behind him, leaned his head back, and closed his eyes. "It wasn't personal," he muttered.

"It never is," Bailino said and fired the pistol.

38

Bailino sped the hybrid down side roads until he reached the block of Santiago's Garage. He parked down the street, turned off the headlights, and silenced the engine. The street was as quiet as he had left it hours before, the right garage bay still open, but a car was parked in front of the garage, the driver's side door hanging open.

Bailino slipped out of the car and hurried toward the building. As he got closer, he realized there was a man lying on the ground next to the car. He wasn't moving. Bailino pulled the gun out from the waist of his jeans and scoped out the surroundings. The office door was closed, and the blinds were still shut, so he couldn't see inside. He hurried over to the still body whom he recognized to be Pedro Rodriguez. The back of his head was bleeding. Bailino placed his index and middle fingers on the man's neck and detected a slight pulse.

He checked the streets again for movement, but saw none, and slipped under the open garage door, his eyes adjusting to the darkness of the garage. He crossed toward the office door, which was closed, and leaned his ear to it. Nothing. He tried the knob, but it was locked from the inside. He plucked a paperclip from a clipboard that was hanging on the wall particleboard and a wad of papers fell to the floor, fanning out below him. He straightened the paperclip and dug it carefully into the doorknob until he heard a click, and then he placed the paperclip in his back pocket, slowly turned the knob, and stepped into the dark office.

It was quiet. For a moment, he thought that Reynaldo had taken Jamie and the baby someplace safe, but a low wheezing sound caught his ear. He felt along the wall for the light switch and flicked it. The overhead florescent light blinked to life, casting the room in a dazzlingly white glow and revealing a trail of blood that began near the front door and stretched across the room and toward the back of the counter where the white of a T-shirt came into view. Bailino hurried toward the counter, behind which lay the bloody body of Reynaldo Rodriguez.

Bailino leaped forward, his feet sinking into the ragged carpeting that had been soaked by blood, and put his fingers to Reynaldo's neck—barely a pulse. Carefully, he pushed Reynaldo over on his side, blood spurting from a wound just below his clavicle as he moved. Bailino moved the soaked-red clothing away from the wound; it looked like a bullet hole. He searched the immediate area and grabbed a fabric upholstery repair kit that was hanging from a display of car fresheners and ice scrapers. He ripped it open, pulled out the cloth, and pressed it into the wound, causing Reynaldo to moan. Bailino bent down.

"Where are they?" he asked.

Reynaldo's face was glazed with sweat, his heap of gray and black hair matted down and away from his face. He muttered something unintelligible.

"Rodriguez . . . Reynaldo," Bailino said. "I need to know what happened."

Reynaldo opened his eyes, his pupils wide and searching the room.

"Where are they?" Bailino asked again, pressing into the wound.

Reynaldo stared at Bailino's face as if trying to recall what had happened. He tried to move.

"Don't," Bailino said, keeping pressure on the wound. "Just tell me."

Reynaldo pressed his lips together. "Mmmmm . . ."

"Take it slow," Bailino said.

"Men," Reynaldo muttered. His right arm reached up, feeling around his chest.

"No, no, let me." Bailino gently replaced Reynaldo's arm to his side. "How many?" he asked.

Reynaldo's words were like wisps of air. He held up two fingers.

"Did you see them?" Bailino asked.

Reynaldo nodded.

"What did they look like?"

Reynaldo's lips pressed together and his brow furrowed.

"Short guy, old, hunched over?" Bailino asked.

Reynaldo's mouth opened, and his face strained, and he shook his head no.

"Was one a big, tubby guy?"

At the word *tubby*, Reynaldo's eyes grew wide.

"Do you know where they're going?"

Reynaldo tried to move his other arm.

"Don't move, Reynaldo," Bailino said, gently pushing it down. "Stay still."

Reynaldo continued to push his arm forward, and Bailino realized that Reynaldo was holding something in his left hand. He reached down and plucked it from Reynaldo's palm.

"He . . . he . . ."

"Don't talk," Bailino said.

"He said . . . this was for you." Reynaldo coughed, and a spurt of blood shot out of his wound.

Bailino reached for a paperweight on the counter, placed it on the piece of fabric upholstery on Reynaldo's chest, and grabbed Reynaldo's hand to hold it in place.

"I love her," Reynaldo whispered, drifting in and out of consciousness.

"I know," Bailino said. "Keep this on your wound, okay?"

"I love her," Reynaldo said again absently.

Bailino reached for the telephone on the wall and dialed.

As the 911 operator asked in a tinny voice what the nature of Bailino's emergency was, he placed the receiver in Reynaldo's other hand and hurried back into the garage and down the block toward the hybrid.

Bailino got into the car, started the engine, and unfolded the small piece of paper that Reynaldo had given him. Scrawled sloppily in black ink, in handwriting that he knew to belong to Paolo Cataldi, were three words: *Burn, baby, burn.*

39

"Fuck!"

Wilcox slammed down his phone on the long wooden table in the main dining room of the Executive Mansion, startling Phillip who had been watching Charlotte and Philly nap on the small television monitors he and Katherine had placed in the room—and nearly every room—since Charlotte's abduction two years ago. They had returned from the FBI field office with little to no information, as expected, and no surprise appearances, also as expected, and Wilcox seemed as unflappable as ever, so whatever news he had obtained over the phone had to be bad.

"What is it?" Phillip asked with trepidation.

"DeGrassi and LaPazza are dead."

"What?" Phillip said.

"How?" asked Katherine, who had been typing on her computer at the other end of the table.

"Mass shooting at the Little Yellow Hotel. Bodies everywhere. *Fuck.*" Wilcox slammed his hand down on the table so loudly that Phillip glanced at the TV monitor, thinking the sound might wake the children who were sleeping in another wing of the mansion.

"And Paolo Cataldi?" Phillip raked his fingers through his hair.

"Not there," Wilcox said.

"Not there?" Katherine asked. "What do you mean? Where is he?"

Wilcox took a deep breath as if to calm himself down. "We don't know."

"You mean, you *lost* him." Katherine leaned back in her chair and folded her arms. "How could this possibly happen? I thought that you—"

"We did," Wilcox said, clipping the accusation before it could be made.

"Bailino?" Phillip asked, feeling as if he already knew the answer to the question.

"We presume," Wilcox said, "but we don't know. We're dusting for prints now. *Goddamn it.*"

"Unbelievable." Katherine rubbed her eyes carefully with her long-nailed fingers.

"Mrs. Grand, we had a team on that place, the hotel, all day. My agents saw all three men enter the hotel around five-thirty, following their appearance at the field office, and no one saw any of them come out, or anyone else, go in, except for a young boy who works at the hotel."

"Could he have been involved?" Phillip asked.

Wilcox shook his head. "I doubt it. He was one of the bodies that was discovered."

"Oh, Jesus," Phillip said, feeling responsible. "And the men accompanying the old men? The ones we saw sitting on the benches at the field office?"

"Two of them are dead. Aurelio Fritoni and Benny Beneditti. However, the two men who were with Paolo Cataldi—Marco Celli and his driver, Adriano Lampelli, were not accounted for."

"Where are they?" Katherine asked.

Wilcox looked squarely at Katherine. "They're *unaccounted for.*"

"What the hell does *that* mean?" she asked. "How could you lose them? Did you have eyes on the river?"

"Of course." Wilcox straightened. "And with all due respect, Mrs. Grand, I don't appreciate you telling me how to do my job."

"Well, it looks like someone ought to," she said.

"Maybe another party?" Phillip suggested, trying to steer Wilcox's attention away from his wife.

"No one else entered the building, Governor. It could be that Paolo double-crossed LaPazza and DeGrassi, but my money is on Bailino," Wilcox said. "Somehow he must have gotten into the hotel."

Katherine drummed her fingers on the old dining table. "I hate to say it, Agent Wilcox, but what did you expect?" She closed her laptop. "You're talking about a man who broke out of Stanton prison. Is it any surprise he got inside an old, dumpy hotel?"

"I thought your theory was that Bailino wouldn't be anywhere near Albany by now?" Wilcox asked. Phillip detected a note of sarcasm in the federal agent's usually even voice.

Katherine waved him off, choosing, as she often did, to ignore any question that she didn't wish to answer. "I mean, did you really think he was just going to waltz in there waving a gun?"

"Katherine," Phillip said, "that's not—"

"No, that's fine, Governor," Wilcox said. "It's a valid question." The federal agent placed his palms on the dining table as if he were about to do a push-up and leaned in toward Katherine—a move that might appear menacing, or at least intimidating, to anyone else besides Phillip's wife. "Mrs. Grand, I assure you, we had the entire area covered for two square miles. We are very familiar with the Little Yellow Hotel, both the geography and the history. The Caldwell family has deep roots in upstate New York, and—"

"The Caldwell family is a bunch of crooks who have the FBI and law enforcement snowed," she said with a huff. "Just because a family goes as far back as the Pilgrims doesn't make them Puritans."

"Cole and Jean Caldwell have been nothing but cooperative over the years," Wilcox said. "They are kind, simple people who deliver freshly baked bread and pastries to the local missionaries. There's no reason to—"

"I am *more* than familiar with Cole and Jean Caldwell with their overalls and ponytails and golly-gees," Katherine said. "They're invited to practically every political function in New England, paraded around by both parties as if they were some kind of lucky charm. But let's rub the pixie dust out of our eyes, Agent Wilcox. The truth is that there's a reason that their overpriced, rat-infested dump is still around when practically every small business is suffering. Their omelets aren't *that* good."

Wilcox seemed both incredulous and amused. "We've examined every tax return of theirs for fifty years, Mrs. Grand—they've handed them over *willingly*. If they're getting any money from the Cataldis or any other family, tell me, where is it going?"

"Who the hell knows?" she said. "Under their mattresses? Buried inside the graves of their ancestors in the plot next to Emily Dickenson up in Amherst? They're smart. They keep their heads down and *aw, shucks* their way through accessory to organized crime."

"That's a lovely theory, Mrs. Grand," Wilcox said, "but the thinking is completely unfounded."

"Well, at least *someone* is thinking around here."

"Did the Little Yellow Hotel have any security surveillance systems that can be accessed?" Phillip asked, eager to break the sparring match, which, knowing Katherine, could last for hours.

Wilcox shook his head. "As a property on the National Register of Historic Places, the Caldwells feel strongly about keeping the hotel as close as possible to how it was when it first opened in the early 1800s. They are very old school that way."

"All the more reason to have security cameras then, no?" Katherine asked. "I'm sure *somebody* is looking to steal all those saddle shoes and nail clippers from the Mayflower."

"There were never any thefts reported, Mrs. Grand," Wilcox said. "Nothing of consequence, anyway, and other than a few renovations over the years to replace old or broken furnishings, pipes, or appliances, the Caldwells have left things virtually the same."

"How convenient," Katherine said snidely. "That hotel has its secrets. I'm willing to bet money on it."

"Katherine . . ." Phillip said.

"Jesus, Phillip. How could you let Wilcox talk you into this little cat and mouse game with Bailino?"

"I didn't let anyone talk me into anything," Phillip said, sounding, he was sure, a bit too defensive.

Katherine waved her hand again and picked up her laptop, which, in Katherine Grand parlance, meant that she had had enough. She strode toward the dining room door, stopping long enough to glare at Wilcox. "My husband trusted you—we all trusted you—to handle this," she said. "You failed."

With that, as if on cue, the sounds of Philly stirring in his crib came from the monitor speakers.

"Great," Katherine said, her glare diverted to Phillip, "and you had to have me send home Rosalia. Now, I'll never get anything done." She stepped into the lobby.

The dining room was still, and Phillip felt the familiar urge to apologize for Katherine's behavior, but the special agent had been around the Executive Mansion long enough to know that either his apology was understood or that it was unnecessary. "No thoughts on how Bailino, or anyone, got into the hotel then?" he asked instead.

Wilcox sat down on one of the dining room chairs. He looked exhausted. "I had men stationed at checkpoints throughout the hotel's vicinity—including the river. No one reported seeing anything."

"And your agents . . . Well, I presume, they are all reliable and trustworthy?" Phillip said.

Wilcox looked taken aback. "Governor?"

"Please don't take this the wrong way, Agent Wilcox, but I know first-hand what it's like to put your trust in an employee only to find out that he has been betraying you."

"I know you do, Governor, but I can assure you that my men are seasoned professionals. I've known just about all of them for many years, and those who are new have been thoroughly vetted. I truly believe the breach is not on my end."

"A secret passageway, maybe?" Phillip asked.

"Anything's possible," Wilcox said with a shrug. "My men are turning the place upside down now. If there is a secret passageway, we'll find it."

Phillip wished he shared Wilcox's confidence. He had the sinking suspicion that something else was about to go horribly wrong when there was a knock on the dining room door and Brandon appeared.

"Sir, there's been an update." The young agent stepped into the room. He seemed freshly showered, his youthful face shiny and smooth. Phillip had seen so many young men leap at the chance to serve their country or aid their government, and over time that youthful glow would fade and harden. It was like watching silk turn to rock.

"What is it, Agent Fuller?" Wilcox asked.

Brandon straightened. It was clear to Phillip that he had troubling news, and he had not yet learned how to deliver it without sentiment, how to separate the fact from the feeling—a skill he would learn too well. Phillip braced himself.

"Sir," Brandon said, forcing the words, his voice a single note, "Reynaldo Rodriguez is dead."

40

P aolo Cataldi turned up the air on his breathing machine. He was feeling quite happy with himself. Not only had he gotten rid of old Sally and Vincent, but he had managed to get Bailino to do his dirty work for him. He imagined old Sally's face when he realized that Paolo had gotten the better of him and smiled. Everything was falling into place, and it was only a matter of time until Bailino, too, was dead—what felt like the culmination of a decades-long dream. His burner phone vibrated the little wooden table next to the old sofa, and Paolo swatted at it with his shaky hand, dust rising from the table's surface. "Yeah," he growled.

"Paolo?" Mary's shrill voice reverberated throughout the old farmhouse.

"Why you shouting for? I can hear you."

"You never called me. You know how I worry."

Paolo grunted.

"How was the ride up there?" Mary asked.

"How do you think it was? Long. And they didn't let me pee."

"Oh, that's terrible," Mary said, even though Paolo knew that she didn't think it was. "What are you doing? How was the governor? Is he as tall in person as he appears on television?"

"No, he's a fucking midget. Of course, he's tall. I can tell you that without even seeing him."

"You didn't get to meet him?" Mary sounded disappointed.

"Maybe next time."

"Are you taking your medicine?" Mary asked.

"Yes, yes," he muttered.

"Paolo—"

"And I'm wearing my sweater. Is that all?"

"Fran said to make sure Marco eats. She doesn't want him to get low blood sugar."

"That's like asking me to make sure he breathes. That boy never met a bag of potato chips he didn't like." Paolo let out a huge cackle that turned into a hacking cough.

"Are you sure you're wearing your sweater?" Mary asked. "You don't sound too good."

"I'm fine, fine. Nice and toasty. I have to go, Mar."

"Okay, have a safe ride home tomorrow. What would you like me to make you for—"

"Yeah, yeah, don't wait up," Paolo said and slapped the phone until the little green circle turned red.

His hands were shaking hard. Speaking to Mary always seemed to worsen his symptoms. It took him twenty minutes to dig his Parkinson's meds out of his pockets and place them into his mouth. He had given up on taking them with water a long time ago—you needed super-human strength to be able to unscrew those plastic bottle caps. He leaned his head back on the worn sofa, his head jittery on the cold fabric. These tremors were for the birds. He hated having to let Adriano take out Aurelio Fritoni and Benny Beneditti at the Little Yellow Hotel—and with his old AMT hardballer, too. He hadn't seen that thing in about twenty years, but the Caldwells had kept the firearms like new—not even a layer of dust on them. If only that little piss-ant hotel worker hadn't surprised Adriano, he would have nailed him in the head, too. The kid was good. Cocky, but good.

Paolo pushed himself off the sofa and shuffled his breathing machine toward the old front porch that overlooked the Hudson, whose black surface made it look like a pool of tar. So much for the Feds' Day Two of questioning—can't get much from a couple of corpses and a guy who is missing. Right about now, the FBI was probably chasing its tail trying to figure out how five men were dead and a decrepit old man and his two minions had gotten out of the hotel undetected so easily.

The truth was that it had been more difficult than Paolo had expected. He had overestimated the strength of that lardass, Marco, who dropped Paolo's stretcher three times in the sewer, once into a puddle. If it hadn't been for old Cole Caldwell and his mastery of slipknots, Paolo would probably still be stuck in the mud. Cole also came in pretty handy when it came time to raise Paolo out of the storm drain and into the Caldwells' backyard—the guy still had some muscle in him. Must be that tough Mayflower stock. Paolo couldn't even remember Marco being there, the dipshit. How on earth he was supposed to leave that kid in charge of things when he was gone was beyond him. He could barely tie his shoes.

Paolo wiped some dust off the front of his button-down shirt, which still smelled like baked bread. When Paolo's group had arrived at the Caldwell residence, Jean Caldwell had been there with a tray of banana bread in hand. Apparently, she had been baking all day with some second cousin, who was about as ugly as she was. The Caldwells had been good to the Cataldis over the years, but, damn, they weren't fun to look at. However, the homemade bread had been delicious. Gotta love those Pilgrims.

His cell phone beeped, signaling a text. Marco had made the lettering on the burner so large that all Paolo had to do was swipe at the screen and he could read the damn thing practically from across the room. The text was from Marco:

We got the pakage, and were on are way.

Hopefully, Marco's directional sense was better than his spelling. Paolo had the boys lay low for the day, just in case. With any luck, Marco didn't fuck anything up. Paolo felt better knowing that Adriano was with him.

Church bells rang somewhere downriver, and Paolo eyed the pile of firewood beside the old stone fireplace. He smiled. With the precious cargo finally in transit, he knew that the culmination of his plan, the end of Don Bailino, was imminent.

41

Charlotte bounced playfully on Phillip's lap as he watched the news coverage of the murder scene down at the old Little Yellow Hotel. Law enforcement had provided very little information to the press, which meant speculation was rampant— the reporters were blaming the deaths on everyone from ISIS sympathizers to Scientologists, with whom the Caldwells apparently had had some kind of longtime feud. So far, there had been nothing on the death of Reynaldo Rodriguez, but Phillip knew it was only a matter of time before the media got wind of it.

"Daddy, Daddy, look," Charlotte was saying as she blew spit bubbles with her lips.

"Not now, pumpkin," he said.

"But, Daddy!" Charlotte grabbed the sides of his face so that his eyes met hers.

"Charlie," he took her hands from his face, "I said no."

Tears welled up in the corners of Charlotte's eyes. She stepped off her father's lap and marched across the room toward her mother, who was watching the television screen with Philly in her arms, an open pop-up book on her lap.

There was a knock on the nursery door, and Wilcox entered.

"Anything?" Phillip asked, standing up.

Wilcox nodded. "Found some partial prints on a stairwell doorknob at the Little Yellow Hotel."

"Bailino's?" Phillip asked.

"Yes. My teams have moved to the lower floors. We should know more soon."

"Jesus," Phillip dropped his head into his hands, "this is our fault. We lured him there." He thought of the young hotel worker who had been murdered.

"Governor, bringing in a few old men for questioning is not illegal, not by any stretch of the imagination, nor does it make you responsible for any of the deaths at the Little Yellow Hotel."

"I wish I could see it that way."

"If you ask me, the world is safer now than it was yesterday," Katherine called from across the room. Her cell phone rang on the bookshelf next to her, and she glanced at the Caller ID, but ignored it. "Olsen from *The New York Times* again," she said with a shake of her head.

"Governor, we didn't know how this was going to play out," Wilcox stressed. "We expected to have Bailino in custody right now."

"Are you still running under the assumption that Jamie and Faith Carter are with him?" Katherine asked.

Wilcox hesitated. "We just don't know. It's one thing for Bailino to slip into the hotel alone. I can't imagine him doing so with a baby, although he's done something like that before." He glanced at little Charlotte who had run off to play with her dolls on the other side of the room. "But I may have another theory." He reached into his coat pocket and spread out photos onto the nursery's changing table.

Phillip scanned them: the images showed a half-filled baby bottle, an open coloring book, and a yellow crayon. "What's this?" he asked.

"We found these items in the office of Reynaldo Rodriguez's garage," Wilcox said.

Katherine was next to them now, holding Philly and scrutinizing the photos. "Jamie Carter's baby was *there*?" she asked.

"Possibly," Wilcox said. "It looks like *some* child was there."

"But where is the child now?" Phillip asked.

"Again, the assumption is if the child was, indeed, little Faith

Carter that she is with Bailino," Wilcox said. "We also ran the plates on a minivan that was parked in Reynaldo's garage. It was stolen from a rest stop yesterday."

"You think Reynaldo Rodriguez stole a minivan from a rest stop?" Phillip asked.

"We are working on the chronology, governor."

"And Jamie?" Phillip asked.

Wilcox hesitated. As far as Phillip knew, the last they had heard from Jamie was her distressed voice on Wilcox's phone, and judging from Wilcox's face it didn't look like there had been any new developments. The events of the past days had taken a toll on the longtime federal agent, whose track record with the FBI prior to Charlotte's abduction, and now little Faith Carter's, had been stellar. He was a person used to getting his man. "We just don't know, unfortunately," Wilcox said.

Phillip peered closer at the photos. "This just doesn't make sense," he said. "Why go to all this trouble to break out of prison to abduct your daughter when the only chance she has at a decent life is to be with Jamie. Bailino is smart enough to know that."

"It doesn't sound like he's been acting very smart lately," Katherine said.

Phillip agreed. It seemed unlike Bailino to be acting so haphazardly, to risk his safety to abduct the little girl and hunt down a few old organized crime bosses. He remembered a time when Bailino spoke of one day being a captain of industry and having a family; that seemed like a very long time ago. "Unless he believed his daughter to be in danger," he said aloud, almost to himself.

"From Paolo Cataldi?" Katherine asked.

Wilcox nodded. "To avenge the death of his brother, Gino. Possible."

"Death by lethal injection wasn't Bailino's fault," Katherine said.

"The botched escape plan was," Wilcox said.

"But that doesn't make sense," Katherine said, moving Philly, who had fallen asleep, to her other shoulder. "Paolo Cataldi had two years to do harm to that little girl. Why wait until now?"

"Jamie Carter had been under federal protection for the past two years," Wilcox said. "Say what you want about the debacle at the Little Yellow Hotel, but there's no way he could have gotten to that little girl with us there. Nor to *them*." He motioned toward Philly and Charlotte, who had pulled her favorite doll, whom she called MaBa, from her toy crib. "But that protection ended at the Carter residence the day Bailino was transferred to Stanton."

"Because we all believed that Jamie and Faith needed protecting from Bailino, not anyone else," Phillip said.

"Correct," Wilcox said. "Frankly, Paolo Cataldi has been out of the game so long, he wasn't even a blip on our radar."

"And yet Paolo is the one body who isn't dead at the Little Yellow Hotel," Katherine said.

Phillip rubbed his eyes, which were red and swollen with exhaustion. "Where could a man who could barely walk go?" he asked.

"And why would that baby be with Reynaldo Rodriguez?" Katherine said.

"All good questions," Wilcox said. "Right now, my men are asking Reynaldo Rodriguez's brother Pedro the same ones."

"How is he?" Katherine asked.

"Nasty gash on the back of his head that required a bunch of stitches, but he should be all right," Wilcox said. "Unfortunately, at least right now, Pedro doesn't seem to know anything. Said he was hit from behind."

"Why wouldn't the person who shot Reynaldo also shoot Pedro?" Katherine asked. "Why take a chance and just knock him out?"

"We're thinking that Bailino wanted to sneak up on Reynaldo Rodriguez—if he, indeed, had been harboring little Faith Carter—and that he probably didn't want to risk alerting him that he was there," Wilcox said, "so when Pedro pulled up, Bailino just silenced him so he could get to Reynaldo and get the baby."

Phillip thought it incredulous to think Reynaldo had Faith Carter in his possession. He had been to the Executive Mansion only a few hours before he was killed, and he was alone and distraught. There had to be some sort of mistake. "How do you know it was Bailino?" Phillip asked. "Have you found prints?"

"Found a partial on the wall phone's telephone handset," Wilcox said. "And also a footprint near Pedro Rodriguez's car that matches Bailino's shoe size."

"*Really*, Phillip," Katherine said, placing Phillip Jr. in his crib. "It's beyond me how you keep defending this man."

"I not *defending* him, Katherine. I'm just asking a question."

Phillip's phone vibrated. He absently reached for it in his pocket, but when he looked at the screen it was dark. He suddenly realized his *other* phone was buzzing, his private phone, the one for which only Katherine and Rosalia had the phone number. A wave of shame overcame him.

Rosalia.

He had put off speaking to her, telling himself he needed to acquire some more information from Wilcox about Reynaldo's death, but the truth was he hadn't been able to work up the nerve to face her. How could he let her learn about the death of her beloved Reynaldo from a police officer? She should have heard it from him. Personally. After all she had done for his family over the years. She deserved more.

Phillip pulled the phone from his pocket, looked at the Caller ID, and froze: On the screen was not Rosalia's cell phone number, but a different one. A number he had committed to memory long ago. The number that had appeared on his screen two years ago during Charlotte's disappearance.

Bailino.

Phillip glanced at Wilcox and Katherine, who were again scrutinizing the photos of the items found at Santiago's Garage. He knew he should hand his phone to Wilcox, or at least alert the agent to the call. It was the legal thing to do, but instead Phillip found himself swiping the cell phone screen until the call timer began. He put the phone to his ear.

Moments later, Phillip placed the cell phone back into his pocket.

"Jesus, Phillip," said Katherine, who was now facing him. "What is it? Who was that? You look like you've seen a ghost."

Phillip's mouth felt dry, the words caught in the middle of his throat.

"Governor?" said Wilcox, looking concerned.

"That was . . ." Phillip searched for something to say. "That was Rosalia."

"Oh, dear." Katherine came toward him. "Phillip, really," she caressed his cheek, "it's not your fault."

"I need to go. I need to see her, Katherine. In person."

"You're right," she buttoned her blazer, "I'll go with you."

"No," Phillip said. "She's very upset. And, well, you know your track record with Rosalia."

"Phillip, that isn't fair," Katherine said, and Phillip could see that he had wounded her.

"I'm sorry," he said. "I just think it's best that I go alone."

"One of my men will escort you, Governor," Wilcox said. "For your safety, and to get through the media out there. It's a zoo."

Phillip was about to offer a meager protest when Wilcox's cell phone buzzed. "Wilcox," he said, putting the phone to his ear. His face darkened. "What? When? Where?"

"What is it?" Katherine asked, without waiting for Wilcox to end the call.

Wilcox placed his hand over the mouthpiece. "My men," he whispered, "just found another body."

❋

Federal agents swarmed the Executive Mansion, phones in hand, shuffling paperwork across tabletops. Wilcox was still on his cell phone, and Phillip was able to slip out of the nursery unobserved and duck into his office. He came out moments later wearing his blazer, which was buttoned. With the news of the phone call, Wilcox had forgotten about assigning Phillip an escort. He hurried past the nursery door toward the staircase and was able to get past Wilcox, but not by Katherine.

"What's going on?" Katherine called, coming into the hallway. "Why are you wearing your jacket? You're not going to see Rosalia *now*?"

"I'll be all right."

"Phillip Grand, if you think I'm going to let you out of this house when bodies are dropping like—"

He gently took her by the shoulders. "I need to go, and I need a favor."

Katherine was searching his eyes. She had been treated harshly by the press over the years for everything from being a strong-handed political wife to a stoic mother, but she had always been Phillip's biggest supporter and, as far as he could remember, had never denied him a favor.

"What is it?"

"I need you to act like a press secretary."

"A press secretary? What do you mean?"

Phillip glanced out the window at the reporters camped outside the Executive Mansion. "I think we're about to make Jim Olsen's day."

The media crowded the front fence of the mansion, cameras poised overhead, microphones shoved through the thick black iron bars as Katherine and Phillip made their way down the front steps. Katherine had her cell phone to her ear, talking to Olsen from *The New York Times*, whom Phillip could see was already standing near the gate, digital recorder in hand. The Grands parted ways once they reached the driveway; Katherine turned toward the back of the mansion as Phillip headed toward the gate.

"Governor?" One of Wilcox's federal agents emerged from the security house at the end of the driveway. Inside was Henry, his longtime driver, seated beside another agent.

"Good evening, gentlemen," Phillip said. "Sorry to bother you, but I need you to open the gate. I need to make a statement to the media."

The federal agent seemed flabbergasted. "Open the—?"

"Right now, please," Phillip said.

The FBI agent looked at his associate inside the security house who picked up his cell phone, presumably to contact Wilcox, but Phillip's eyes met Henry's. Henry hadn't been doing much driving for Phillip lately on account of his cataracts, but he had been Phillip's ears on the ground for the past two years. Phillip motioned toward the keypad on the console of the small desk. Henry nodded, entered a code, and the large wrought iron gate opened inward, the press lunging forward with every available inch of new space.

"Close the gates, goddamn it," the federal agent said, still on the phone, but by the time he punched in the code again, the gate had already opened several yards and the reporters flooded onto the driveway like water spilling through a hole in a dam.

"Governor Grand, what can you tell us about the search for Don Bailino?"

"Was Bailino responsible for the Little Yellow Hotel massacre?"

"Any word on the location of Paolo Cataldi?"

Phillip stepped into the crowd, and the reporters circled around him, the lights on their cameras blinking on, their microphones shoved forward.

"What has happened today is a tragedy," Phillip said, scanning the eager faces before him. "Reynaldo Rodriguez put himself in harm's way to protect my family, and the family of Jamie Carter, and his death is a tragic reminder that one's willingness to do the right thing can exact the highest price."

There was a confused hush as the reporters took in the governor's words.

"Wait, is Reynaldo Rodriguez *dead*?" asked Olsen with surprise.

The reporters looked at one another, and then their eyes opened wide, and they pressed forward, tightening the circle of space around the governor.

"Katherine and I," Phillip continued, "ask all New Yorkers to join us in praying for the family of Reynaldo Rodriguez, particularly Rosalia Garcia, our beloved housekeeper and nanny. Reynaldo Rodriguez was a good man—the best of men—and he will be missed dearly, and I can assure you that the person who did this horrific crime will pay."

In an instant, the curious group of reporters became a fervent mob.

"Who did it, Governor?"

"Was it Bailino?"

"Are there any suspects?"

"Is Reynaldo Rodriguez's death related to the Little Yellow murders?"

"Are you concerned about the safety of your own family, governor?"

"My office will keep you informed as to any updates," Phillip added. "Thank you for your time."

By now, Katherine had driven Phillip's old car, a 2001 Hyndai Sonata, from the back parking lot, down the driveway, and into the crowd of reporters who flowed around it like a river, lobbing their boom microphones at it like fishing poles, their fingers feverishly pushing buttons on their phones.

As Katherine vacated the driver's seat, Phillip squeezed her hand and quickly slipped inside the car.

"I hope you know what you're doing," she whispered as she became swept up in the rush of reporters.

"Governor, where did the crime take place?"

"Was it at Santiago's Garage?"

"Is it true you are still considering a run for the United States presidency?

Behind the car, federal agents were running toward the gate, and Phillip gently nudged the accelerator, carefully navigating through the reporters who followed him, their faces plastered to the driver's side glass, onto Eagle Street until he had a clear path. In his rearview mirror, he spotted Katherine, who was speaking to an irate Special Agent

Wilcox at the top of the driveway. Phillip hit the gas and sped along the asphalt until the faces around him disappeared one by one and there was nothing left but a few reporters and federal agents chasing after him.

42

J amie rocked back and forth in the backseat of the black SUV as it rumbled along a series of dirt roads. On her lap, Faith was looking up at her, her dark brown eyes wet and confused, her small body still hiccupping, as it had all day. That morning, Jamie had finally gotten her to calm down after what had happened in Reynaldo's office, but the little girl was still trembling, and so was Jamie.

All day long, the scene played over and over in Jamie's mind— Reynaldo's smiling face jutting unnaturally forward and then his body, almost instantaneously, falling backward. The *bang* of the gunshot had sounded like a sonic boom and had jolted Faith out of her slumber and sent Jamie scrambling for the gun on the coffee table, but it had been too late. She glanced at the man who was driving the SUV; he had gotten to it first. She remembered how he had stepped over Reynaldo's writhing body, as if it were not even there, and ordered Jamie through the front door and into the waiting vehicle. "Shut that kid up first," he had said and then slapped her with the back of his hand across the face.

They had spent the day in the car in some remote part of the woods. Jamie thought that, at any moment, the men would kill them, but they didn't. They just waited. For what, she didn't know. Luckily, she had the package of fruit snacks in her pocket, along with some animal crackers, or else they would have had nothing to eat. She could tell Faith was becoming dehydrated—her diaper was barely wet.

At sundown, the guy in the passenger seat, whom the driver called Marco, sent a text, and then the driver pulled out of the hiding spot and got back on the road.

Jamie looked out the window and watched the dark world pass by, and she wondered for a moment if out there, somewhere, Bailino was ready to save them, but she pushed the thought from her mind. She needed to find a way to save herself. Relying on others only weakened her and seemed to hurt them. She thought of sweet Reynaldo and hoped that, somehow, he would be okay.

They had been driving for about forty-five minutes. The men had been mostly quiet and didn't seem too enamored with one another. The only time one spoke was to give the occasional direction or lodge an insult. Marco was digging into a bag of potato chips he found under his seat, the crinkle of the bag garnering Faith's attention. She let out a small whimper.

Marco looked back at the little girl and held up a chip.

"No, thank you," Jamie said, pulling Faith toward her.

"The folded ones are the best," Marco said. He stuck the chip into his mouth and opened it wide so that Faith could see the crumbs. She began to cry again.

"Teasing a little girl?" the driver said. "Nice."

"I'm not teasing," Marco protested. "Just trying to make her laugh." He stuck two more chips into his mouth, the crunching about as loud as the hum of the engine. Marco glanced back at Jamie. "He should have known better than to leave you alone," he said, bits of chip clinging to his chapped lips. "The great Don Bailino is losing his touch."

"Shut up, dipshit," the driver said.

"Please just let my daughter go," Jamie said, as she had several times already. She had intended to sound strong, but her voice came out small and subdued. She was probably dehydrated, too. "We can drop her off somewhere, and I'll go with you, alone. I won't put up a fight." She remembered saying the same thing to Bailino only days before.

"Who says we want *you*?" Marco asked.

"I said shut up, dipshit," the driver said and looked at Jamie in the rearview mirror. "Don't worry, it's almost over, honey."

"Hey, you missed the turn," Marco said.

"I know a shortcut," the driver said.

"I think we should follow Paolo's directions."

The driver pulled over to the side of the road and stopped the car. "You wanna drive?"

"No," Marco said.

Jamie looked around to see if she recognized the area—nothing but trees and dark woods.

"I didn't think so," the driver said and got back onto the road.

"Fucking asshole," Marco mumbled under his breath.

"What did you say?" the driver asked, pulling over again and stopping on the shoulder, this time near a scenic overlook.

Jamie's eyes scanned the surroundings again, but all she could see was unadulterated blackness and a highway sign, which was too far ahead to make out.

"Nothing," Marco said.

"I didn't think so," the driver repeated and was about to get back on the road when a hearse and a caravan of several cars drove past, their hazard lights blinking. Jamie held her daughter a little higher on her lap, thinking perhaps someone in the dark sedans might see her through the tinted windows—a long shot. The driver was watching her carefully through the mirror.

"Little late for a funeral," Marco said, checking his watch.

"Never too late," the driver said and smiled at Jamie before getting back on the road as the last of the funeral procession passed.

Jamie pushed herself back against the seat, and the metal of the phone Bailino had given her brushed against her leg inside her boot. She was supposed to turn the phone on two times—once last night and once that morning—and look for a text from the number he added to the phone's contact list, signaling that she and her daughter were finally safe. If there was no message, she needed to tell Reynaldo to take her and Faith to the address he had given her in Wyoming.

Reynaldo.

She thought of turning the phone on, as she had all day long, but worried that it might actually beep or ring. What would the men do to her or Faith if it did?

Maybe Bailino would be able to track her, she thought, and then remembered what had happened at the old log cabin—the phone needed to be on to be used as a tracking device. Now that the men were distracted by the road, she was going to have to try to power it up.

Forcing her eyes to look straight ahead, she carefully reached down and pulled the phone out of her ankle holster enough so that she could reach the side button. She pressed it, and the phone came to life inside her boot, the glare lighting up the well of the backseat, and Jamie glanced at the men, but they had begun to argue again, this time about trees native to the upstate New York area.

She was about to place it back into her ankle holster when she had a thought: What if *she* made a call? She could call Bailino, using the number in her contact list, but was he even alive? She thought of Wilcox and his concerned voice when she called him from the cabin. Could he find her in time? She glanced at the men. They had gone silent again, the driver eyeing her warily through the rearview mirror.

"It's okay, Faithy," Jamie whispered into her daughter's dark hair and, within eyeshot of the driver, slowly caressed the little girl's cheek with her right hand. Below the seatback, however, and out of sight, her left hand slipped the burner phone out of her boot, tapped the *Messaging* icon, and, with trembling fingers, began to type.

43

Phillip tightened his hands on the steering wheel and pulled into the parking lot of the old, abandoned playground. The last time he had been there Jamie Carter had been recovered after having shot Don Bailino two times in the chest. He had watched the injured bodies of Bailino and Edward Carter, who had been shot in the shoulder by Bailino, being carted into the back of an ambulance. For weeks afterward, the park had seen its share of excitement again—agents picking through its gravel searching for evidence, idle reporters swinging on its swings as they waited for live feeds. Now, though, the park was back to how it had been—forgotten and neglected, its metal, unforgiving equipment considered too harsh for today's coddled children. Phillip checked his phone and his rearview mirror one more time to see if anyone was looking for him, but both were dark.

He opened the car door, and a soft breeze met him, the metal playground equipment letting out a low creak, the rough surfaces glinting erratically in the reflected light of the moon. He walked toward the still, warped merry-go-round at the center of the park and saw a dark figure seated at the bottom of an old metal slide. Phillip opened his jacket as he slowly approached, the gravel crunching beneath his steps.

"I was beginning to think you weren't going to show," Bailino said. The moonlight made his features look flat and tired, unlike the man Phillip saw on the television screen only a few days ago. Bailino motioned toward Phillip's hands. "What the hell is that thing?"

Phillip held the antique pistol steady in front of him. It felt heavy and awkward in his hands, but it was the only firearm he had access to. And it was loaded. "Where are they?" he said.

"I wasn't sure if you'd bring the Feds." Bailino dug his shoe into the gravel until the dirt beneath the stones formed a footprint.

"I almost did," Phillip said. "I'm here, alone, so where are they? You said you knew where Jamie and Faith Carter were."

"I do. Can you put that thing down before you shoot someone's eye out?" Bailino said. "I promise, you can shoot me later, if you want to."

Phillip kept the pistol steady. "Reynaldo Rodriguez is dead," he said, watching Bailino's expression.

Bailino nodded. "I wasn't sure if he'd make it. He lost a lot of blood."

"So you were there?" Phillip asked.

"Yes."

"Did you kill him?"

"No," Bailino said. "I did not."

"Why should I believe you?"

"Because I just said that I didn't."

The traces of Bailino's trademark smirk were gone, and Phillip eyed him warily. The man he used to know as a young soldier never lied, but that was a very long time ago.

"It was Paolo Cataldi," Bailino continued. "Or one of his minions, more likely, who also shot those men, and that kid, on the first floor of the Little Yellow. I'd know that old bastard's handiwork anywhere."

"And DeGrassi and LaPazza?"

"That was me," Bailino said flatly.

There was no flicker of remorse in Bailino's eyes, and if Phillip remembered correctly, there never had been. "And what about Joey Santelli?" he asked.

The name caught Bailino by surprise. "Joey?"

"Yes. The FBI just fished his body out of the Charles River."

For the first time Phillip could recall, Bailino seemed wounded. His head tilted downward, his eyes hidden by his thick eyebrows, the moonlight highlighting the gray along his hairline. He was quiet for a few moments. "Paolo," he said finally.

"Why would Paolo Cataldi murder his own grandnephew?"

"To hurt me." Bailino raised his head again, and his eyes were once again clear and focused.

"I don't understand, how does that hurt you?"

"Phil, we don't have time—"

"Don . . ."

"Joey was my son," Bailino said.

Phillip lowered the pistol and let it hang by his side. "Your *son*?"

"Yes," Bailino said. "How was he killed? Do the Feds know? Did he drown?"

Phillip hesitated. "Don, I don't want to—"

"Just tell me."

The words got stuck in Phillip's mouth. "His body had been . . . incinerated. I'm so sorry, Don. I didn't know."

Bailino stood up, his face impassive. "I know you didn't. I didn't think Paolo did either."

"Did Gino?"

"I didn't think so, but now I'm not so sure."

"Why am I here, Don?" Phillip asked. "Where are Jamie and Faith Carter?"

"With Paolo Cataldi."

"Where?"

"I have some ideas, but there's not enough time to check them all out. I need to track them. I need you to trace the burner phone I gave Jamie. I can't risk burning one of my contacts."

"She was with you?"

Bailino nodded. "Yes, the baby, too. I left them with Rodriguez to take care of LaPazza and DeGrassi and Paolo, or so I thought. He got to them before I got back."

"How do you know they're still alive?"

"They're alive. At least for now. He won't kill them unless he has to, which is why we can't let the Feds anywhere near them."

Phillip sat down on the edge of the merry-go-round and put his head in his hands. "This has got to end, Don," he said.

Bailino came forward and stood before Phillip. Up close, the healing bruises that lined the side of his face appeared leathery and gray. "I'm trying to end it, Phil."

"Let me get Wilcox. He's a good guy, he could—"

"No," Bailino said, "I need to do this my way. He wants me there. He wants to show me how powerful he is and how Gino picked the wrong lieutenant. He has something quite spectacular, I'm sure, planned, a spectacle. I need to make him think he has the upper hand."

"Let him *think* he has the upper hand?" Phillip asked. "Doesn't he?"

"Can you trace the number?"

"This is crazy, Don. Do you know what you're asking me to do? I'd be an accessory. You realize the position you're putting me in just by being—?"

A low-pitched *ping* sounded. Bailino dug into his pants pocket, took out his phone, and looked at the screen. "It's Jamie," he said.

"Jamie?" Phillip looked at the screen of Bailino's phone as he clicked on the text:

5

"Five?" Phillip asked. "What does it mean?"

"I don't know." Bailino looked out into the dark playground as if searching for an answer.

"Are you sure that's the right number?"

"That's the number." Bailino stared at the phone. Another text popped up:

9

"Nine?" Phillip said.

Bailino brought the phone closer to his eyes. "C'mon, sweetheart, one more. What are you trying to tell me?"

"Don, please," Phillip said. "Why don't—?"

The phone pinged again:

146

"I know where they're going," Bailino said. He reached under the merry-go-round and pulled out a burlap sack. He placed it on the metal surface and opened the flaps, revealing two M4 carbine assault rifles.

"Jesus Christ, Don!" Phillip took a step back.

"You don't expect to kill anybody with *that* thing, do you?" Bailino motioned toward the antique pistol. Phillip had forgotten it was still in his hand. "Are you coming or not?" Bailino asked.

"Coming? I don't understand what—"

"They're roads, route numbers, the numbers that Jamie texted. He's taking them to the old Barbara farmhouse. We can be there in twenty minutes if we hurry." Bailino reached into his pocket and handed Phillip the piece of paper that Reynaldo had handed to him.

"What's this?" Phillip read the writing on the paper. "Burn, baby, burn? What does—?"

"Paolo's going to hurt them, Phil. Just like he hurt Joey. I need you to come with me. I can't do this one alone. If you don't come, Jamie and that little girl are as good as dead."

"Don't fucking put that on me," Phillip said. "This isn't my doing."

"Listen," Bailino said, "you can arrest me afterward. I'll come quietly. You have my word. Once Cataldi is dead, that's the last of them. I'll do my time. No one will be in danger."

"What do you expect us to do? Go marching in like soldiers?" Phillip said. "This isn't the army, Don."

"It is for me." Bailino slung the rifle over his shoulder. "Let's be honest, Phil. We both believe in killing people. Only when you do it in a small sterile room with a bunch of witnesses, it's considered legal."

"Wait, let's think about this." Phillip knew he had to try and reason with Bailino. "Did you really expect me to—I mean, this—really, this is out of my league."

"Bullshit, I've seen you do some sick shit."

"That was another lifetime ago."

Bailino picked up the other rifle and held it out. "Phil, I'm going, with or without you. We don't have time. What's it going to be? Are you with me or against me?"

Phillip hesitated. His whole life seemed to flash before his eyes.

"You always did think too much about things, Phil." Bailino wrapped the other rifle back into the burlap and took it into his arms. "Whatever happens, you're right. It's not on you. It's on me. I know you took a risk coming down here, and I appreciate it." Bailino charged toward the slide and the crumbling stone building that once housed restrooms and a concession stand, and disappeared into the dark forest.

Phillip watched him go, the pistol hanging limply by his side. The merry-go-round had begun to spin slightly when Bailino lifted the burlap bag, and it slowly shifted back to a rest. Phillip placed the gun into the waistband of his pants and buttoned his jacket. He took one last look where Bailino had gone and walked back to his car in the opposite direction.

44

Bailino inched the car along the perimeter of the old Barbara property, which consisted of about sixty acres of unoccupied land atop a small hill. The property, whose agricultural value was essentially zero due to grassland degradation, had been sold to one of Gino Cataldi's shell companies years ago, and Gino had restored much of the old farmhouse at the center of it, intending to use the place as a summer country house. However, once he was incarcerated, the estate was neglected, used only for the occasional meeting or as a storage facility by Bailino or others in the Cataldi organization.

It was dark, the moonlight hidden behind a patch of tall trees, and Bailino sat still, listening. He pulled a set of binoculars out from the glove compartment. At the top of the hill, almost at a forty-five degree angle, a small light flickered like the ash of a cigarette, and Bailino suspected that Paolo was keeping Jamie and Faith somewhere in the farmhouse.

"Out of the car," a man said, a pistol appearing beside Bailino's window.

Bailino lifted his hands into the air.

"Drop the eyes," the man said.

Bailino tossed the binoculars into the backseat and glanced at the two assault rifles wrapped in burlap that were lying on the floor of the passenger seat. "Where are they?" he asked.

"I said, out of the car."

Bailino popped the door open and stepped outside, keeping his hands in the air. He recognized the man holding the gun as Adriano Lampelli, Paolo's driver and key lackey. Adriano had a reputation for being capable and loyal, but he was arrogant, which, in this business, could be much more dangerous than incompetent.

"Shall we?" Bailino asked and started walking up the hill.

"Not so fast, friend," Adriano said. He dug a set of handcuffs out of his pocket. "Turn around, and put your hands behind your back."

"You're the boss. *Friend.*"

"Try anything, and I'll shoot you in the head—just like I did to your two friends at the Little Yellow." He smirked. "And on the off-chance that I miss—and I stress *off-chance*—the shot, alone, will alert the others, and then your girlfriend is dead. And so is your kid."

Bailino hated to play along, particularly because Adriano was enjoying this, but that was exactly what he was counting on. Arrogance begets mistakes. Bailino did as he was told.

Adriano tightened the handcuffs around Bailino's wrists. Keeping the gun steady on Bailino, he crossed to the other side of the car, opened the passenger's side door, and removed the burlap sack from the floor. "Now, we can walk," he said.

"Whatever you say, chief," Bailino said, and the two men made their way toward the light at the top of the hill.

❀

Jamie pulled at the restraints that tore at the skin around her wrists and ankles. Below her, on the hard, dirty wooden floor, Faith grabbed at Jamie's knees, screaming "Mama! Mama!" and trying desperately to climb onto her lap.

The men had brought them to an abandoned farmhouse at the crest of a wide hill. Jamie wished she still had the burner phone with her, but before she could send Bailino a fourth text, Adriano had pulled the car over and ripped it out of her boot, giving Jamie another slap across the face. The men presented her and Faith like gifts to an old man whom Jamie assumed to be Paolo Cataldi. Paolo appeared feeble, but had a sinister gleam in his eye.

Across the room, Paolo was stoking a fire that was already roaring, sending sheets of heat throughout the large living and dining area. Although Adriano had disappeared, Marco was played a game of checkers alone at the table, a two-liter bottle of soda between his legs.

"Mama, mama, up!" Faith was shouting, her dark brown eyes imploring her.

"Jesus, how do you take that shit?" Paolo said, covering his ears with his shaky hands. He returned the poker into a long metal tray and admired a series of mounted animal heads on the far wall. "That kid has some mouth on her. Marco, get the duct tape."

"No, no, please." Jamie said. "I'll get her to calm down. Just wait a minute." She folded her torso toward the little girl who began clawing at her hair. "Baby, *shhh*, it's all right. It's going to be all right." She tugged on the restraints around her wrists. She remembered writing a freelance article once about how a young woman had escaped a home invasion by breaking the duct-tape handcuffs the intruders had placed on her—the method had been a simple downward strike—but under Paolo and Marco's watchful gaze, she wouldn't be able to try.

"Mama, mama, up!" Faith screamed louder, her words turning into high-pitched cries.

"What's with parents these days?" Paolo asked with a shrug. "All this sweet talk. Just rap the kid in the mouth. She'll shut up then."

Upon hearing Paolo's voice, Faith cried even louder.

"Wait, Faithy. *Shhh*. Baby, listen to me. Faithy, listen, listen . . ." Jamie began to sing:

"Mid pleasures and palaces though we may roam . . .

The little girl's screams softened as the familiar lyrics got her attention. Jamie continued in a whisper, her eyes glancing at Paolo, who was watching her:

"Be it ever so humble, there's no place like home . . .
"A charm from the skies seems to hallow us there . . .

"Which seek thro' the world, is ne'er met elsewhere . . .
"Home. Home. Sweet, sweet home."

The crying stopped, and the little girl let out a big sigh in its place, her eyes searching for safety inside Jamie's face and leaking two long tears.

"Now, *there's* music," Paolo said. "Not like that shit they listen to today."

Faith attempted once again to climb up onto Jamie's lap, and Jamie tried to shape her legs into a ramp, but Marco had duct-taped her ankles to the legs of her chair, making it difficult to move.

"Can you untie me so I can hold her?" she asked. "Just for a minute."

"If you don't shut up, we're going to duct tape *your* mouth," Paolo said. "The kid's fine now. Relax."

A door opened, shifting the intense heat of the room, and Bailino walked in with his hands tucked behind him followed by Adriano, the driver of the car, who was carrying a package that he placed near the front wall.

"Well, well, the gang's all here," Paolo said. He sat in a worn armchair that was near the fireplace. "Marco, go get the thing."

Lazily, Marco jumped a red checker with a black checker on the checkerboard, nodded, and left the room.

"If I knew you wanted to see me so badly, Paolo," Bailino said, "I would have visited more."

Faith's head turned at the sound of Bailino's voice. She took her hands away from Jamie's calves and toddled toward him, lifting her arms to be picked up.

"Awww, isn't that sweet," Paolo said. "She wants her daddy."

Marco came back into the room dragging a wooden furnishing, and before Faith could reach Bailino he scooped the little girl up like a hook catching a fish. The little girl reached as far as she could toward Bailino, who looked as if he were about to make a move toward her, but Adriano pushed the gun into his back, and he remained still. Marco dragged the furnishing and stood it next to Paolo, and Jamie realized what it was: an old wooden high chair. He plopped Faith into it—much too close, she thought, to the fireplace. Faith tried to twist her body out of it.

"Doesn't this goddamn thing have a seatbelt?" Paolo asked, rolling his eyes.

Marco pushed Faith roughly back into the chair and held her there while he reached behind her. "I can't find the strappy things," he said.

"For cryin' out loud." Paolo's shaky hands moved toward the little girl, who screamed, "No," and swatted Paolo in the face.

"Faith!" Jamie yelled. "No!"

"I don't think she likes you," Bailino said with a smirk.

"Is that so?" Paolo said and slapped the little girl's face with the back of his hand, her little head twisting to the right, and Jamie let out a sorrowful howl. Faith's screaming became a low whimper as Marco found the straps and clasped them closed.

Paolo placed a shaky hand on the table next to the armchair and lifted the burner phone Bailino had given Jamie into the air. "Looks like your girlfriend did our work for us and got you here," Paolo said.

"You all right, sweetheart?" Bailino asked Jamie.

Jamie could hardly breathe. She felt as if she could still feel the sting of Paolo's slap across Faith's face. She nodded slightly, her eyes unable to leave her daughter.

"Awww, true love. Ain't it sweet?" Paolo said.

Faith had begun to cry again and was thrashing about in the high chair.

"Jesus Christ, shut that kid up," Paolo said, and Marco reached for the duct tape when Bailino spoke.

"It's okay, honey," Bailino said. He was looking directly at Faith, but the little girl was too upset to hear him. "Hey, hey . . . Faithy . . ." he called until the thrashing slowed down, and the little girl looked at him, her dark brown eyes barely visible, the skin around her eyes puffy and red. "You want to go on the swing later?" Bailino asked gently.

Upon hearing the word *swing*, the little girl's crying softened, and she continued to listen, her breaths coming in short heaves.

"Mama will take you to the park and you can swing really high, just the way you like it, okay?"

Faith stopped crying, but her body continued to hiccup. She lifted her hands expectantly, as if waiting to be taken to the park.

"In a little while, okay? Be a good girl, and you'll go in a little while," Bailino said, and Jamie was almost stunned when the little girl nodded.

"You shouldn't lie to the kid, Donny," Paolo said. He reached down to turn a knob on his breathing machine, sucking in the manufactured air. "Can you believe this place?" He motioned to the room. "It really held up, no? Hurricanes, snowstorms, and the building's still standing. Tough, old thing. If Gino hadn't gotten himself arrested, this house would have been a regular Buckingham Palace. I mean, it's no fancy, shmancy log cabin, I guess, but those things tend to burn down if you're not careful." He smiled. "Know what I mean, Donny?"

"Let the kid go," Bailino said. "Gino made me more money than I can ever spend in a lifetime. It's yours."

"You would give me all your money for this little girl and your whore?" Paolo asked. He leaned back in the armchair as if amused. "You know it's not money that I want, Donny." He fingered the tubes in his nose thoughtfully. "Terrible thing about my grand-nephew Joey, wasn't it?"

Jamie's eyes left Faith, and she watched Bailino, who remained still. Had something happened to Joey?

"I knew the kid wasn't the college type. Even if he *was* part Bailino." Paolo shimmied himself forward on his seat and placed his hands on the armrests, trying to push himself forward.

"I'll help you, Uncle Paolo," Marco said. He reached for Paolo's arm, but the old man swatted his hand away.

"I got it, I got it, I'm not an invalid, you know." He finally teetered to a standing position and shuffled toward the fireplace, reaching up onto the mantel and bringing down a long sword by its handle. He returned to his armchair, already out of breath, and turned the sword in his hand, admiring it. "This look familiar, Donny?"

If Bailino recognized the sword, Jamie couldn't tell.

"Ah, I'm sure it does," Paolo said. He lifted it high with his shaky hand, the blade quivering in the dry, heated air. "My brother gave it to me when we were boys. He knew how much I liked the Three Musketeers. Gino was good to me that way." Paolo gazed at the smooth steel, the light of the fire making it appear to glow. "He told me it was from the Middle Ages." He shrugged. "Who knows if it's true? First thing I did with this sword was slice the head off my neighbor's goddamn dog. I never liked that mutt. It sliced through his neck like it was paper. Took maybe five seconds to make it all the way through to the other side." Paolo smiled at the memory. "Makes me wonder . . . How long do you think it will take to slice through a little girl's finger?"

Jamie's heart threw itself at her chest. "No," she screamed, and the men in the room looked at her. Faith began to cry again.

"Jesus, shut up," Paolo said.

"What's with the drama, Paolo?" Bailino said. He appeared cool and calm. "Let the kid go. It's me you want."

"Please . . ." Jamie begged, but Paolo seemed to hear neither of them.

"What a sweet little face." Paolo ran his crooked fingers through Faith's hair, and the little girl pulled away from him. When she swatted at him again, Paolo grabbed hold of her hand and pulled out her pinky finger.

This final gesture seemed to rattle Bailino who made the tiniest move toward Paolo, but Adriano whispered something that Jamie couldn't hear, and he stopped. "I knew you were a fucking lowlife, Paolo, who never picked on someone his own size," Bailino said, "but a fucking kid?"

"Not just any kid." Paolo said. "*Your* kid. Your *kids*."

Faith squirmed, trying to get her finger out of Paolo's grip and glaring at him.

"Look at her," Paolo said. "Goddamn eyes look like they belong on a wolf. After all the fingers, they'll be the next to go."

Paolo pulled on the little girl's pinky until her chubby arm straightened, and he raised the sword high into the air with a shaky arm when a loud pop shattered the glass of the front window, knocking Paolo to the ground and pulling Faith's high chair along with him.

Instantly, Bailino roundhouse-kicked Adriano to the face and then swung around and kicked the gun out of his hands, sending it to the back of the room, about ten yards away from Jamie's chair. She dug at her restraints as Bailino repeatedly stomped like a machine on Adriano, who was writhing on the floor, while his hands worked at the handcuffs using an uncoiled paperclip he had pulled from his back pocket.

Across the room, Paolo was yelling. One of his eyes was missing, a bloody pulp in its place, and Marco was trying to lift him from the ground.

"Not me, asswipe," Paolo hissed. "Take care of *him*." Paolo began clawing his way toward the back wall, dragging Faith's high chair with him, and Jamie realized that he was still holding onto her finger, her arm bent unnaturally. The little girl's cries had turned into heaving sobs, and Jamie could tell she was hurt, and, even worse, the high chair had fallen too close to the fireplace. The flames were licking its legs.

She twisted her hands, trying to loosen the duct tape, fearful that Paolo would reach for the sword, which was lying only a few feet away from him, but instead he was crawling away from it and heading toward a large canister that stood near the wall.

Marco grabbed the duct tape and, just as Bailino freed himself from the handcuffs, charged toward him, wrapping a thin line of tape around Bailino's neck and forcing him off Adriano, who was lying limply on the ground. Jamie took a deep breath, hoisted her hands into the air, and slammed them down hard with all her might, and the duct tape handcuffs broke apart at once just as one of the wooden legs of Faith's high chair caught fire.

Jamie tore desperately at the duct tape around her ankles, but couldn't get her feet out—the tape was wrapped too tightly. She

rocked her chair back and forth until it fell over and began to claw her
way toward her daughter when a dark figure ran through the front
door and into the room.

"Help my daughter! Please, help my daughter!" Jamie screamed.

When the figure drew closer, she was shocked to see the tall,
lanky body of Governor Grand run toward the fireplace holding a
large, awkward pistol in his hand.

❋

Phillip rushed toward the little girl, the flames making their way along
the bottom of the high chair. Paolo Cataldi still held her, although
Phillip's shot had landed in his eye, and he was dragging her toward
the back of the room. Phillip slammed the butt of the antique pistol
onto Paolo's arm, forcing him to release Faith's hand, and he pulled
the little girl from the high chair just as Paolo reached up and knocked
over a large canister that stood near the wall. The smell of gasoline
permeated the room, and in a *whoosh* the fireplace burst into a plume
of flames, engulfing the high chair and stretching toward the roof. The
fire quickly ignited the brittle drapes that hung on the windows and
spread across the walls, eating away at the old, dry wood.

Phillip backed away from the wall with Faith, who felt flaccid in
his hands, her arm hanging limply by her side, when a gunshot sounded
from the other side of the room, and a man crumpled to his knees, his
arms loosening from the neck of Bailino. About twenty feet away, Jamie
Carter sat on the floor, her ankles tied to the legs of a wooden chair,
a pistol raised in her hands. Without hesitation, Jamie shot again, and
the man went down, this time the bullet piercing his head, and Bailino
ripped the duct tape from his neck and came rushing toward Phillip.

"Get them out of here," Bailino yelled, a bloody ring dividing his
neck in two. He grabbed the sword that was lying on the floor.

Phillip hurried with the little girl toward her mother as Bailino
charged in the direction of Paolo Cataldi who was crawling toward a
back door.

"I can't untie them," Jamie screamed when Phillip got to her side. He placed the little girl on the floor. "What's wrong with her?" Jamie said. "Is she all right? Faith, Faith!"

"Let's get you both out of here first," Phillip said, fumbling with her restraints.

"I think my ankle is broken," Jamie said as Phillip ripped apart the duct tape and a blood-curdling scream came from the other side of the room. An object sailed toward them, and Phillip covered Jamie and Faith with his body as a disembodied arm landed a few feet away from them with a thud, blood splattering across the walls and floor.

Phillip got the last of the duct tape off as Bailino raised the sword into the air and slammed it down onto the body of Paolo Cataldi, eliciting another scream. Phillip pulled Jamie up, but she couldn't stand on her right ankle. She clutched at Faith who was lying still on the floor.

"I got her," Phillip said. He picked up the little girl and laid her head on his shoulder.

Across the room, Bailino strode toward them holding Paolo's severed head in his hands by a few strands of white hair, blood spilling from the open neck. There was a loud crack from above, and the air in the room changed direction. The ceiling, now laced with flames, was beginning to buckle.

"Get them out of here, Phil," Bailino said.

"You're coming with us," Phillip said. "You gave me your word." He wrapped Jamie's arm around his neck.

"Not yet," Bailino said.

"Don," Phillip said.

"I need to finish something first," Bailino said. "Take them." He tenderly touched Faith's face with his bloody hand and looked at Jamie. "Remember," he said, "never hesitate," and then, sword in hand, started for Adriano, who was also crawling toward the back door.

Jamie hobbled next to Phillip as he walked toward the front entrance, but the ceiling buckled again. He crouched beneath her and threw her over his shoulder, carrying her and Faith across the room and past the old deer and moose animal mounts, which had caught fire, the flames eating away at their antlers. He darted over the threshold and into the cool outside air as another scream came from somewhere inside the house.

Phillip ran down the hill that led toward the front entrance of the property and lay Jamie on the ground about a hundred yards from the farmhouse.

"Is she okay?" Jamie was screaming, clutching the little girl from Phillip's arms. Faith's eyes were closed, and Phillip bent down and placed his ear on the middle of her chest.

"She's alive," he said.

"But she looks—"

"Hold her tight. I'll be right back."

"No, Governor," she said, "look, the roof!"

Fire stretched high above the old farmhouse now, the flames reaching like long fingers toward the sky. Phillip thought he heard sirens in the distance, but the front entrance still seemed clear enough to get inside. He stepped toward the building, but Jamie grabbed his arm.

"I have to," Phillip said, releasing Jamie's hold and making a mad dash toward the house when there was another *whoosh* and rush of air, the flames soaring from the roof suddenly disappearing as the farmhouse's ceiling caved. He ran back and threw his body in front of Jamie and Faith as shooting debris and black smoke filled the already dark woods, and the old Barbara farmhouse toppled onto itself, bursting into flames.

45

"Tell me again what happened, please," Wilcox said.

"Haven't we been over this?" Katherine asked.

The two were standing over Phillip's hospital bed and had been bickering off and on for what seemed like hours. Phillip had arrived at Albany Memorial just after midnight, and Wilcox had gotten there not long afterward. As Phillip had anticipated, the federal agent had lots of questions and hadn't been too happy.

"It's all right, Katherine," Phillip said. He fingered the oxygen mask in his hand that his doctor had requested he wear, but Phillip was feeling all right and didn't think he needed it. "I was driving to Rosalia Garcia's house to check on her . . ."

"Without the escort that I suggested you bring," Wilcox said.

"Yes," Phillip said, carefully making sure he repeated the same information he had given to Wilcox earlier. "I wanted to be alone with Rosalia."

"And that little stunt you pulled with the news media?" Wilcox asked.

"I thought I owed it to Reynaldo Rodriguez to make a statement and that the media needed to hear the news from me and not the damn Internet. I was sure you would have thought it was a terrible idea."

"It was." Wilcox appeared skeptical, as he had all morning, but he let Phillip continue.

"As I was driving, I saw flames coming from the old Barbara property."

"What time was this?" Wilcox asked.

"As I said before, I don't know. I didn't look at my watch," Phillip said.

"Are we done?" Katherine asked.

"And the fact that the old Barbara property is not quite on the way to the Garcia residence?" Wilcox asked warily, ignoring Katherine. "It's about fifteen minutes out of the way."

"I took a wrong turn." Phillip knew he was a terrible liar, and this was the part that he couldn't get himself to believe even though he had rehearsed the line in his mind many times in the last few hours. He hoped that it sounded credible, but from the look on Wilcox's face, he didn't think so.

"Phillip can memorize a deck of playing cards, but gets turned around all the time driving up here, especially at night," Katherine said, coming to his aid. "It's not so surprising to me. You spend all your time being carted around in a backseat, you forget what to do in the front seat."

Phillip could tell that Wilcox still wasn't buying it, and he wondered whether his wife was.

"Why didn't you call the fire department when you saw that it was a fire?" Wilcox asked.

"I didn't know what it was," Phillip said. "Thought maybe it was some kids building a bonfire or something. That property is notorious for all kinds of teenage mischief. When I got to the farmhouse, I saw someone struggling inside the entrance and ran to help. I realized it was Jamie Carter and her little girl, and I went to them and carried them away from harm. I tried to go back to see if there was anyone else, but by then the house had been destroyed, and I already heard the sirens."

Wilcox crossed his arms and studied Phillip's face the way he had seen him study Paolo Cataldi's. Phillip tried to look impassive and innocent, while his hands gripped the mattress underneath his bed sheet for dear life.

"Well," Wilcox said finally, "Governor Grand, I've listened to your statement several times, and each time you have been consistent and calm and more than cooperative. I appreciate that, considering all that has happened."

"Thank you," Phillip said, releasing his grip on the mattress. "So you believe me."

"Not in the slightest," Wilcox said.

"What?" Katherine exclaimed, visibly offended. "Surely, Agent Wilcox, you're not—"

"Please let me continue, Mrs. Grand." Wilcox spoke firmly, but respectfully. "I've been doing this for many years, as you know, Governor, and in my line of work—as in yours—sneaking around, side-stepping law enforcement, those kinds of actions are generally not something law-abiding citizens do."

Phillip swallowed hard. He wondered if this were some sort of FBI technique to get him to confess. If it was, it was working.

Wilcox continued, "We've known each other personally for quite some time now, working side by side, and it is unlike you to behave in the manner in which you have in the past twenty-four hours. I've seen you perform under some of the harshest and most trying of conditions imaginable over the past two years, both as a governor and as a father and friend, and you've always executed your duties thoughtfully, rather than impulsively, and with an openness and trust that is commendable and part of the reason, I'm sure, you are beloved as governor of New York." Wilcox glanced at Katherine and then back at Phillip. "Therefore, even though I am inclined to disbelieve your account of events, I am also inclined to believe that your intentions were honorable and that you acted in a manner that you thought to be right. Considering the outcome— the rescue of Jamie and Faith Carter—it's hard for a person to argue with that."

Phillip wondered if the FBI agent would feel the same if he knew of Phillip's meeting with Bailino. Would Wilcox still believe Phillip to be honorable? With luck, Phillip would never find out.

"Finally, and perhaps more importantly," Wilcox added, "the evidence seems to support your story, Governor."

"His *story*?" Katherine said.

"What evidence?" Phillip asked.

A young nurse opened the door to Phillip's room, the commotion of the nurse's station filling the space until the door softly closed. "How are we doing, Governor Grand?" she asked chirpily.

"Fine, thank you," Phillip said, happy for the distraction.

The nurse pushed some buttons on a machine behind Phillip, stuck a thermometer under his tongue, and took his blood pressure. "That was very brave, what you did, sir," she said with a smile. "I was proud to have you as my governor before, but now even more so. You looked so heroic." She examined the blood pressure monitor and pulled the thermometer out when it beeped. "Well," she said, taking the band from Phillip's arm, "everything looks normal. I'll be back. Just buzz if you need me." She nodded happily at Katherine and Wilcox and left the room.

"How strange," Katherine said. "What did she mean by Phillip looking heroic?"

"Apparently, some kids were messing around on the Barbara property not far from the old farmhouse. As you said, Governor Grand, it is a teenage hangout." Wilcox dug his phone out of his pocket, typed something, and showed Phillip the screen. "They saw the fire, and, well, do what kids do nowadays—they took video and sold it for what was probably a pretty penny." A grainy video, presented exclusively by TMZ.com, showed Phillip carrying Jamie and Faith Carter away from the burning farmhouse. The headline read: *Grand Hero*.

The color drained from Phillip's face. How much had the teens seen? Had they seen Phillip go into the farmhouse? Had they seen him shoot the antique pistol? The video began when he was already outside, but was there more?

"You do look heroic, Phillip," Katherine said with a smile. She caressed his cheek.

"I'm far from a hero," Phillip said.

"Well, Jamie Carter seems to think you are," Wilcox said.

"Was she able to tell you what happened in there?" Katherine asked.

Phillip knew that Jamie had told Wilcox a similar story to his and that she made no mention of Phillip ever being inside the farmhouse.

"Ms. Carter said the fire had been started when there was some sort of a struggle between Don Bailino and Paolo Cataldi," Wilcox said.

"Bailino was *there*?" Katherine asked. She looked to Phillip for confirmation, and he forced himself to shrug. He hated lying to Katherine, but he didn't want her involved. The less she knew, the better.

Wilcox nodded. "That's one ID we *did* make." He swiped his phone screen a few more times and then turned it again toward Phillip. He and Katherine stared at it.

Among the burnt rubble, beams of wood, and old metal of the collapsed farmhouse lay a distinct disembodied hand.

"Dear God," Katherine said. "That's all you found? His hand?"

"There are body parts strewn all over the property," Wilcox said. "Some are barely body parts at all anymore. Prior to the fire, it looks as though it had been a veritable blood bath. Jamie Carter told us as much. It's going to take some time to go through the scene to try to piece the bodies back together. The use of the gasoline makes it more difficult. Whoever set the fire intended for nothing to ever be recovered." Wilcox slipped his phone back into his pocket.

Bailino had once told Phillip that he wanted to go out in a blaze of glory. It looked as though he may have gotten his wish.

"Ms. Carter claims that Bailino saved her and her little girl from Paolo Cataldi, who intended to do the two of them harm, just as we had surmised," Wilcox said. "We found a bit of blood on young Faith's face—blood that, if the hand weren't enough, was also a match for Bailino. He was there."

"And all this is happening under the watchful eye of the FBI, I see," Katherine said with a touch of sarcasm.

"I believe *under* is the operative word, Mrs. Grand," Wilcox said.

"What do you mean?" Phillip asked.

"Well, we already knew Bailino had been at the Little Yellow Hotel," Wilcox said, "but further investigation indicated that Bailino's fingerprints were also found on the top of a sewer grate in a patio, along with some others. We now believe that's how he got into the hotel undetected."

"And the others got out," Phillip said.

"Through the sewers?" Katherine asked.

"It's difficult to tell definitively," Wilcox said. "The climate down there is wet and not conducive to crime scene investigation, meaning we're not likely to find any real evidence, but that's my belief."

Katherine's eyes opened wide. "Phillip?" she asked. Do you think . . . ?"

"That's how Bailino must have gotten into the Executive Mansion two years ago," Phillip said with a nod, "and abducted Charlotte. That was why none of the security cameras had caught anything."

"That's our thought as well, Governor," Wilcox said. "Those old properties near the river all have those oversize storm drains. We also believe that's how Bailino may have gotten into the old Barbara farmhouse. I'm having my men contact the New York State Department of Environmental Conservation to find a way to lock, seal off, or monitor the sewer systems in the areas surrounding the mansion, and those properties near the Hudson."

Phillip imagined bands of criminals running around underfoot. Even if Wilcox succeeded in restricting access to the sewer system, he knew that a *bad man*, as Charlotte had described Bailino, wound find other routes. Crime always found a way.

"How's the baby?" Katherine asked. "Little Faith Carter."

"Alive," Wilcox said. "And she's very lucky to be so. She has a severe burn on her left leg, which has been treated, and her arm is broken. Her breathing had been very weak when she first arrived last night, but she has been treated for smoke inhalation and seems to be responding well. She's definitely a fighter."

"Some good news," Phillip said with a smile.

"That little girl is going to be quite wealthy," Wilcox added.

"As Don Bailino's last remaining heir, she gets everything—all of his legal assets, including properties, bank accounts. Bailino had his will changed the morning he was transported to Stanton prison, leaving everything to Joseph Santelli and Faith Carter."

Phillip thought of Don Bailino, bloody and bruised, and of how tenderly he looked at Jamie and Faith back at the farmhouse. Bailino had tried for so many years to disconnect himself from the life he was born into. Perhaps there was some solace in the fact that maybe his little girl could do what he couldn't.

Wilcox looked at his watch. "I need to make one more stop before I head back down to the Barbara property, but there *is* one other matter, Governor, that I'd like to discuss, and I'm not sure what to make of it."

"What is it?" Phillip asked.

Wilcox hesitated. "Your antique pistol, the one I was admiring in your office. It appears to be gone."

"Gone?" Katherine said. "You mean, *stolen*?"

"I'm not quite sure I would say stolen, ma'am."

"Well, what else could have happened?" she said. "The only people who have been in the building have been your agents, Agent Wilcox."

"I'm aware of that, Mrs. Grand, but I can assure you—"

"I told you that you should have installed a camera in your private office, Phillip," she said with a huff. "Jesus, that pistol was a goddamn eyesore, but it was worth thousands. And what is your father going to say, Phillip? We'll never hear the end of it."

Phillip was barely listening. He prayed that the pistol was lost forever somewhere among the rubble of the old Barbara farmhouse and that Katherine would drop the subject, although he was pretty sure she wouldn't. "That's the least of our problems, Agent Wilcox," he said finally. "I wouldn't worry about it."

"But—" Katherine protested.

Phillip reached for her hand. "My father will have to understand," he said.

"Well then," Wilcox said, "my men will be with you as long as you need them, Governor." He stood for a moment, and Phillip was about to offer his thanks for all the agent had done for his family over the past two years, but Wilcox, as was his way, simply nodded and left the room before he had the chance.

"We should sue the FBI, you know," Katherine said, "for negligence and—"

"Katherine." Phillip squeezed her hand.

She sighed and cupped Phillip's face in her hands. "You *are* a hero, my dear. At least to me." She clicked down the metal guard rail of Phillip's hospital bed and crawled next to him, her pantyhose getting stuck on the IV. She plucked it free and leaned her head on his shoulder. "It's finally over."

Phillip thought again about Don Bailino. The two men had been on opposite sides of the law for so long and had traveled in such different circles that they barely knew one another anymore. Yet, in some way Bailino had always been with Phillip—first as a comrade, then as a friend, and then as an adversary, and then just as someone he used to know. What would Phillip's world look like without him?

"Daddy!" Charlotte screeched.

Her blond curls bounced as she jumped up and down with delight at the entrance to his hospital room. Charlotte let go of Phillip's mother's hand and ran toward him waving a homemade card, her brother stumbling behind her, and Phillip's thoughts of Don Bailino evaporated the moment his little girl jumped into his arms.

46

Faith was fiddling with the oxygen mask covering her nose and mouth.

"You have to leave that on, sweetie," Edward said, boosting the little girl in his arms.

"Good luck with that," Jamie said. The cast on her ankle felt heavy, and she adjusted herself on the hospital bed.

Faith reached for her mother, the cast on the little girl's right arm making it look like an ironing board, and Jamie sat her daughter on her lap.

"Look," Jamie said, pointing to her own cast. "We're the same. You have one like mama."

Faith smiled. "Same." She reached down to touch Jamie's cast and crept back up onto Jamie's lap, pointing to her oxygen mask. "Off?" Faith said.

"In a little while," Jamie said.

The little girl narrowed her dark brown eyes at her mother.

"I mean it," Jamie said. "We'll take it off in a little while."

There was a knock at the door, and a cheery nurse walked into the room carrying a large bouquet of tulips, roses, lilies, and other spring flowers. "This came for you," the nurse said. "Aren't they lovely?" She placed the bouquet next to Jamie's bed, handing her a card, and ran her hand along Faith's dark brown hair. "How are we feeling today, little one?" the nurse asked.

Faith pointed to her mask. "Off?" she said.

"She really doesn't give up, does she?" Edward said.

"Pretty soon," the nurse said. "Just a little while more." She smiled and scurried back out of the room as Jamie unfolded the card:

Dearest Jamie, I hope that you and the baby are okay. I am writing to tell you that Reynaldo told me that he felt most alive with you than he ever had in his whole life. That is what you should remember and hold onto. He was such a good man, and I will always miss him, as I know you will. But please know that he loved you, and that he would want you to be happy and to take care of that beautiful baby. You will always be a part of my family, and I hope that you will come visit someday. I know my Rey would have liked that. Sincerely, Rosalia Garcia

The tears spilled from Jamie's eyes, and Faith reached up to wipe them away.

"Boo boo?" the little girl asked with concern.

"What is it?" Edward asked.

She handed him the card. "From Rey's aunt Rosalia." She wiped her eyes.

"Oh," Edward said and placed the card near the bouquet without reading it.

The door opened, and the nurse poked her head back in. "Are you up for a visitor?" she asked.

"Who is it?" Jamie said.

"A Mr. Robert Scott?"

"Don't let him in," Edward and Jamie said simultaneously and then looked at one another. They both let out a loud laugh, and, watching them, Faith joined in, too. It was the first time the three of them had laughed that way—freely and completely. It felt good.

"Did I miss something?" the nurse asked.

"Ex-husband," Jamie whispered.

"Alrighty then, I'll take that as a no," the nurse said. "I'll tell him you're indisposed."

"For the rest of her life," Edward said with a smile.

Faith tugged on Jamie's shirt. She was saying something into the oxygen mask. Jamie sighed and pulled it down.

"Yes, baby?" she said.

"Swing?" Faith asked in a tiny voice.

Jamie thought instantly of Bailino, the way he had gotten Faith to calm down at the farmhouse with that one word. She had seen him do the same with Charlotte Grand and had spent two years trying to reconcile how a person could be capable of so much violence yet so much tenderness, how someone could show no value in one man's life but guard another with his own. Faith had been asking to go to the park ever since they arrived at the hospital. Would the child who seemed to remember everything remember the man who was her father?

Jamie squeezed Faith's chin. "Yes, we will go soon," she said and meant it, intending to fulfill the promise of the man who had been her abductor and who had become her daughter's savior. She slid Faith's mask back into place, the little girl's dark brown eyes looking up at her, and for the first time Faith's resemblance to her father no longer seemed like a curse.

There was a knock at the door, and Special Agent Wilcox stuck in his head. "How are we doing?" he asked.

"Come in, Agent Wilcox," Jamie said.

The agent shook Edward's hand. "It's nice to see the Carter family smiling," he said.

"It's nice to smile," Jamie said.

Edward's phone rang, and he looked at the screen. "It's Trish. I should give her an update. I'll be right outside, James. Excuse me, Agent Wilcox," he said and stepped into the hospital corridor.

"What can I do for you, Agent Wilcox?" Jamie asked.

"I just wanted to check on you one more time and also say good-bye. I bet you're happy to finally get rid of me and my men."

"Thank you for everything," Jamie said and held out her hand. Wilcox shook it, and then shook little Faith's hand when she stuck hers out to emulate her mother.

"I wish I could have done more," he said, admiring the flowers next to Jamie's bed. He rubbed his fingers on one of the rose petals.

"I'm starting to realize that we all do the best we can."

Wilcox nodded. "One last thing." He dug into his pocket. "This is for Faith." He handed Jamie a small, bulky envelope.

"Faith?" Jamie opened the flap of the envelope and poured out its contents: Bailino's large gold cross attached to its familiar thick rope chain appeared in the center of her palm.

"It was in Joey Santelli's dorm room, inside that envelope," Wilcox said, "along with this note, which was rubber-banded around it." He handed the note to Jamie. "Do you know that necklace?"

Jamie unfolded the small piece of paper, which said simply:

Property of Joseph Cataldi and/or Faith Carter.

"Yes," Jamie said. "I do."

"Well, then, I guess it's found its rightful owner." Wilcox gave a small smile. "Good-bye, Ms. Carter. Be well," he said with a slight bow and left the room.

The gold cross was tarnished and seemed smaller than Jamie had remembered when it was hanging around Bailino's neck. Faith pulled Jamie's hand down and gazed at the necklace with awe.

"Me put," the little girl said, fogging up the oxygen mask with her breath, and motioned to her neck.

"You want to wear this?" Jamie asked.

The little girl nodded.

Jamie unclasped the necklace and wrapped it around her daughter's neck, parting her dark hair in the back in order to clasp the chain. She adjusted the cross so that it hung straight down the front of Faith's hospital gown. It looked a bit ridiculous hanging on such a small body, but the little girl gazed upon it with fascination.

"Pretty," Faith said with a wide smile.

Jamie stroked the top of her daughter's head and thought about the inheritance Wilcox had told her about earlier in the day. Her daughter would be able to buy a lot of pretty things with that money, which, despite most of it having been credited to Bailino's successful and legitimate business ventures, was probably blood money. The thought occurred to Jamie to donate all of it to a worthy cause of some kind, but Bailino had wanted his daughter to have it. Perhaps when Faith was old enough she could decide what to do with it.

The little girl leaned against Jamie's chest, twirling the cross in her hands as the sun peaked out from behind a cloud and showered the sterile hospital room with light.

"Mama, sun!" Faith said, pointing the cross toward the window.

"That's right, sweetie."

After two years of uncertainty, Jamie finally felt safe, and although her injuries would likely always be there, apart from whether or not her body healed, she was hopeful that there was a bright future somewhere out there for her and her daughter—one that was filled with love, rather than fear. And she was determined to do all she could to find it. She would never hesitate. Of that, she was sure.

EPILOGUE

The log cabin was cold, as were the ashes lining the bottom of the wood-burning stove. The man returned from the front porch with two large logs, stamped the snow off his boots, and carried them to the kitchen. He shoved them into the stove and lit a match.

Ice caked along the edges of the window panes. He could tell it was going to be a cold one. In two years' time, he had learned how to read the temperature of the day simply by how long it took for the sun to melt the early morning frost from his windows.

He crossed the living room, running his fingers down the black and white keys of the baby grand piano he had restored, and flicked on the television with the remote control. CNN was showing last night's footage of New York State Governor Phillip Grand, the presumptive Republican presidential nominee, who had won the New York primary in a landslide, as he had the large majority of the Republican primaries to date. In the corner of the screen was the live feed of an unattended podium where the governor was expected to give an address from the grounds of his Executive Mansion in Albany. As the newscasters speculated about what Grand's address would entail, the live feed went full screen, meaning the governor was about to arrive. The man could see the familiar towering sugar maple tree behind the empty podium that marked the grounds of the historic six rolling acres of land above the Hudson River. It stood beside the landscape's newest addition, a scarlet oak tree, planted nearly two years ago and dedicated in a formal ceremony to Reynaldo Rodriguez.

The man sat down on the large sofa facing the television and took a sip of coffee from the mug that was set on the coffee table as Phillip Grand arrived at the podium followed by staff and family members, including his two children Charlotte and Phillip Jr. who held each of their mother's hands. The man turned up the television volume.

"Good morning," the governor said. "I am honored to have been chosen by the people of New York, my home state, as their choice for the Republican nominee for president of the United States. It has been an honor to have been your governor for nearly ten years. I was born in New York, raised here by proud New Yorkers." He motioned back to his mother and father who stood behind him and smiled. "I have made my home here, my family." He paused thoughtfully. "Those who know me know that I don't take the responsibilities of governing lightly and that I believe in a government of inclusion, not exclusion. I believe in loyalty and in doing what's right, and will bring those beliefs with me not only throughout this candidacy, as we move to Connecticut and then to Delaware and Maryland and the rest of the great states in this great nation, but also as your president. I hope you do me the great honor of believing in me and my abilities as president of this country."

The camera panned left slightly as the staff and family members clapped, and the man lifted his remote to pause the image. To the governor's left, at the far end of the screen, stood a petite brunette in an elegant blue dress, her hair tied up in a neat ponytail. She held a clipboard and a cell phone, and her hands were paused together in mid-clap as she looked toward the governor with a smile. She appeared professional and focused, but, mostly, the man thought, she appeared unafraid, and that made him happy. He unfroze the frame, and the woman disappeared off the screen as the camera panned back to the governor.

The doorbell rang, and the man turned off the television and opened the front door.

"Good morning, Mr. Carter," the boy said.

"Has it been two weeks already?" the man said with a smirk. "Are you sure you're not trying to put one over on me?"

The boy grinned as if used to the routine. "Nah." He looked at his shoes. "That'll be fifteen dollars, sir."

"Sounds good," the man said, patting his pants pockets. "C'mon in for a second."

The man crossed the living room toward the dining area, where a pair of jeans was lying neatly across the top of a chair. He reached his right hand into one of the front pockets and dug out his wallet. He knew the boy was staring again at the end of his left arm, where his left hand used to be. The awkward stump protruded past his jacket sleeve; ragged scars were all that remained where the man had sliced the steel of the rapier across the flesh of his own wrist. One day, the boy would work up the courage to ask him about his hand. The man found that most people were too polite, but he knew it was only a matter of time until curiosity got the best of his paperboy. He seemed like a smart kid.

"You have a lovely home, sir," the boy said courteously, standing in the middle of the living room.

"Thank you," the man said and handed him twenty dollars. "Keep the change."

"Great, thanks, Mr. Carter," the boy said and backtracked toward the door. "Whoa," he said, stopping on the welcome mat. "That's something." He pointed to the antique flintlock pistol that hung over the fireplace on the far wall.

"Isn't it?" the man said with admiration.

"My dad goes hunting every year with my uncle, but they don't have guns that look like *that*. Where'd you get it?" the boy asked.

"An old friend," the man said.

"Wow, he must be a really good friend. Does it work?"

"I've only seen it fired once, and it seemed to do the trick."

"For real?" the boy asked.

"Yep, I don't lie . . . well, except for once," the man said with a smirk.

"Wow, cool." The boy started again for the front door. "I'll have the paper here tomorrow just after dawn the way you like it, Mr. Carter. Have a nice day." The boy put the money the man had given him into his pocket and hurried down the wooden porch steps.

"You too, and drive safely," the man called, watching the boy get onto his bike. He gave a final wave and rode up the gravel path.

A hawk flew overhead, its shadow passing over the man, who lifted his only hand to cover his eyes and watch the bird hover over a nearby field and dive toward the ground below. In the distance, the bright morning sun gleamed along the tops of the high snow-crested mountains, the tallest in Wyoming, which rose majestically over the plains and dense forests below.

The man stared contentedly at the now-familiar view and took a deep breath. For two years, he had woken up to sunshine and a view of the mountains. His father had been right: that was enough.

At least for now.

ACKNOWLEDGMENTS

Writing and publishing this book was like reuniting with old friends in more ways than one. Thank you, as always, to Tommy, whose belief in me is one of the things that I can always count on. *Somos uno*. To Griffin, Helena, and Jack, my babies, whom I feel privileged to have watched grow into teenagers even though I am now the shortest in the family. To my Mom, whom I miss every day, and my Dad, whom I'm lucky enough to see every day. To Viki, my person and my morning call. To Rikki, who pulls me away from my computer and reminds me that writers need to take time to snuggle. To Ma'am and Sir, for their rainbow cookies and continuous support of Oh D'Dear, and Susan and Margaret, whose delighted faces I can still remember at the New York City Hot Sauce Festival in Brooklyn when I told them this series would become a trilogy (or maybe it was just the after-effects of all that reaper sauce). To Ellen Scordato, Judy Linden, and the rest of the Stonesong team whom I always feel honored to have in my corner, and, finally, to all the *Baby Grand* fans who waited patiently for the continuation of this story. Thank you for embracing these characters—although they will always be real to me, it is only with you that they truly come alive.

ABOUT THE AUTHOR

Voted one of the best Long Island authors for two consecutive years, Dina Santorelli is the author of the award-winning debut novel, *Baby Grand*, a top-rated mystery/thriller and best-selling organized crime thriller on Amazon Kindle. She has been a freelance writer for nearly 20 years and currently serves as the executive editor of *Salute* and *Family* magazines for which she has interviewed many celebrities, including Norman Reedus, Vince Vaughn, James Gandolfini, Dave Coulier, Tim McGraw, Carrie Underwood, Angela Bassett, and Kevin Bacon, among others. She has collaborated on a variety of nonfiction titles, and her book *Daft Punk: A Trip Inside the Pyramid* has been published in several languages. Dina also lectures for Hofstra University's Continuing Education Department and is a SELF-e Ambassador for the *Library Journal*. For more information about Dina, visit her website at http://dinasantorelli.com.

Follow Dina on social media:

 Facebook.com/dinasantorelliwriter

 @dinasantorelli

 @dinasantorelli

The story continues…

Look for the final book in the Baby Grand series:

BABY
CARTER

Coming soon!